The Semi-Detached Women

Alex Quaid

First published in 2023 by Bloodhound Books.

www.bloodhoundbooks.com

Print ISBN: 978-1-916978-08-9

The best memory is that which forgets nothing but injuries. Write kindness in marble and write injuries in the dust

— Persian Proverb

Part One

Chapter One

JANINE

The last days of summer have slipped away. There is a chill in the late September air and intervals of blue skies and brilliant sunshine alternate with short, sharp showers.

The single-decker bus speeds its sole passenger through winding country lanes, leaving scurrying eddies of orange and gold leaves in its wake. The ancient vehicle, certainly dating from the 1930s if not before, was full when it rattled out of the bus station into the Sheffield traffic but, in the hour since then, one by one the other passengers have been disgorged in suburbs, villages and towns across the High Peaks of Derbyshire. The women – it was mainly older women, stepping carefully down the steep steps at the front of the vehicle with their shopping trolleys – departed and were not replaced. Only the strange woman remains, having moved by stages to the back of the bus as seats became available. She now occupies the far corner of the wide bench seat by the emergency door, her small suitcase on her lap. The views over the dry-stone walls lining the roads are spectacular, wide vistas of boulder-strewn hills and valleys polka-dotted with sheep against a sky full of fast-moving clouds. The young woman sees none of it.

Stupid, stupid, stupid! Her lips move slightly as she curses herself. *They'll ask for proof of deposit!*

Yes, they will, and how can she show them a building society passbook in the name of Janine Taylor when, on impulse, she gave her name as Nadine Tyler?

The bus flies over a stone humpbacked bridge and the woman feels her stomach being left behind. She gasps and looks up, only to meet the driver's gaze as he examines her in his rear-view mirror. She looks away.

Janine Taylor is not the sort of person who is usually noticed, despite her dark skin. People's eyes seem to skim over her, as if she were a placeholder for a real person. She sometimes wonders if she was born unmemorable or if it was just life with Mother that taught her the trick of invisibility. No one noticed her in the queue of passengers waiting to board at Sheffield; no one looked up at her as she paid for her ticket and was given change; no one paid her any attention as she squeezed down the narrow aisle looking for somewhere to sit alone. The driver wouldn't have noticed her at all had she not begun changing seats as gaps appeared, moving like a chequers piece diagonally back and forth across the aisle until she was as far away from him as possible.

Even then it was not the woman herself who sparked his interest but the child's suitcase, to which she clung as if it contained the family jewels, and the strange clothes. She resembles a Second World War evacuee, an extra in shades of grey plucked from a black-and-white movie and set down incongruously in a Technicolor world. She wears a coat that the bus driver's mother might have worn before the war, its sleeves obviously too short for her; a baggy green cardigan; a faded floral print dress that is neither long nor short enough to be fashionable; a grey beret, which might once have been (and indeed was) part of a school uniform; and round wire-rimmed glasses. She lacks only a luggage label pinned to her grey serge lapel.

The road starts a long steep descent, fields to both sides. These are not the flat postage stamps of orderly green to be found in the mild south of the country, but areas of rough moorland enclosed in dry-stone walls, great outposts of craggy rock erupting here and there. The sheep are widely dispersed, many grazing on impossibly narrow ledges as if they were mountain goats.

The road flattens off and bends to the right, running parallel to an exuberant river that flashes over rocks and boulders, before entering a wood, a cathedral of orange, yellow and green foliage. After a few minutes the bus emerges from under the trees, crosses the river via a stone bridge and turns immediately left. It slows suddenly to abide by the new speed limit of thirty miles per hour, and Janine realises they are entering a village. She turns to look behind her, seeking a sign, but has evidently missed it. The bus is now crawling uphill again, through a narrow street of small cottages roofed with stone tiles. It pulls into a stop, its engine shuddering.

'Chapelhill,' calls the driver.

Janine starts from her seat and scurries down the aisle, head lowered. She walks past the driver, turning her back to avoid his gaze, and negotiates the steep steps. The man waits until she is clear of the door and the old bus rattles off in a cloud of diesel fumes, leaving the street silent.

Janine looks up and down the row of cottages with neat front gardens and cars parked by the kerb. She frowns.

She reaches into her coat pocket and pulls out a scrap of paper. She reads it and turns in a slow circle. Whatever she is looking for, she cannot see it. Her shoulders slump in defeat. Then she spots a shop sign a hundred yards away. She heads towards it.

She arrives outside a shop with tiny windows. A flaking green sign above the door says 'Dodds' Corner Store'. It looks as if it was once someone's home, the last in a terrace of houses with the date 1826 carved in the headstone above the door. A single dusty window protected by a steel grille gives little clue as to the interior, but a blue circular plaque on the front wall proclaims that Chapelhill was recorded as a settlement in the Domesday Book. She sees, just beyond the shop at a crossroads of two narrow lanes, an old-fashioned road sign. One arm points up the hill and says, 'Chapel Hill – 1 mile'; another points towards 'Glossop – 12 miles'. She frowns again. Chapelhill (one word) or Chapel Hill (two)? She pushes open the shop door.

A bell rings above her head, a lonely dull clank like a cow bell. The door closes behind her and she looks around.

She's travelled back in time. The shop looks like a museum exhibit, sagging under the weight of its own decrepitude. Dust hangs heavily in the air and the shelves are only half full. What merchandise there is looks grubby and unappetising, and two flies are engaged in a dogfight over a greasy meat counter. Janine's nose wrinkles as she smells envelope glue and cat food and, overlaying these old smells, fresh toast, which makes her stomach rumble. She has been travelling for hours, and ate no breakfast.

No one comes to serve her but she waits patiently without moving, uncomfortable to break the heavy silence. As the seconds lengthen into a minute, she realises that she has to do something or else depart.

'Hello?' she says tentatively, her voice sounding loud and alien in the stuffy space.

She waits as the gloomy shop resumes its sleepy torpidity. She turns around. Her eyes light on a hitherto unnoticed cage from which stamps, pensions and television licences are evidently dispensed. She realises with a shock that there's a hawk-faced middle-aged woman in the cage staring at her with hostility.

'Oh!' she says, her face flushing. 'I didn't see you in there.'

'We're closed,' replies the woman.

'I'm sorry. I didn't... there was no sign on the door,' replies Janine hurriedly, the words tumbling out of her like shopping from a split bag.

'Everyone knows we're shut between one and two,' snaps the shopkeeper unpleasantly, as if Janine had somehow deliberately timed her arrival to cause maximum disruption.

She is used to hostility like this. Even Mother used to call her 'Darkie' sometimes when drunk, oblivious to her own hypocrisy, for she must have left a gap in her prejudice sufficient for Janine's father to insert himself.

The woman is evidently waiting for her to depart, and Janine does make a half move towards the door when a small voice inside her rebels.

No. That's not what Nadine would do.

She halts... hesitates.

Can I be Nadine? Well... can I?

She takes a deep breath.

'I don't want to buy anything,' she hazards in a small voice, her heart thumping, and realising as the words leave her mouth that this confession will probably make her even less welcome. 'But, er – please, could you – am I in the village of Chapelhill? There was supposed to be a phone box outside, by the bus stop.'

'Tractor knocked it down.'

The woman's accent is unfamiliar. Yorkshire? Derbyshire?

I suppose they all speak like that. I'll be the one with the funny accent.

'Oh,' she says. 'Right. So – sorry – is there any other public telephone – in the village?'

'No.'

'Oh. Perhaps you could give me some directions then? I need to go to' – she looks at the paper in her hand – 'Windyridge?'

For the first time the older woman's interest is aroused.

She cocks her head to one side, her dark eyes shining like buttons, and Janine is suddenly reminded of the mangy and vicious parrot in the Hulme pet shop. The bird was a well-known character in that part of Manchester. No one seemed to want it, or perhaps the owner was fond of it, but in either case the bird sulked in the window throughout all of Janine's primary school years. She would pass it every day on her way to and from school, enjoying the spectacle of unsuspecting customers jumping when it suddenly flapped its wings or squawked loudly at them.

'You have business at the Hall, then?' asks the shopkeeper.

This conversation is already becoming uncomfortably prolonged, but Janine manages to answer. 'I was supposed to telephone. When I arrived... off the bus.'

'Telephone who?'

Janine uncurls a piece of paper, an advert with neat handwriting along the margins. 'Lady Margaret Wiscombe,' she reads.

'You a guest up there then?' sneers the woman sarcastically, eyeing Janine's clothes. There is also something else, something unpleasant, in the woman's tone that Janine cannot identify.

'Well... I don't really... sorry,' she mumbles hurriedly, as the last of Nadine's courage evaporates. 'I've got to go now.'

She spins and reaches quickly for the door handle, and safety.

Oh, Janine, you're a cowrin, tim'rous beastie! she berates herself.

'It's two miles up steep lanes,' intervenes the shopkeeper. 'You can use the phone here. If you want.'

The sudden change of attitude stops Janine in her tracks. She turns. 'Really?'

'You'll have to come round here.'

The shopkeeper steps out of her cage, opens a flap in the counter and pushes a telephone a few inches closer from underneath her dusty shelves, a pre-war Bakelite telephone with a rotary dial. Janine sees the woman is older than she imagined, very thin, and her hair is dyed an unlikely black. She has a faint moustache on her top lip.

The woman retreats into her cage but makes no move to leave. Janine lowers her suitcase to the grubby floorboards and steps behind the counter. She glances behind her and drags the suitcase closer to her ankles with her foot. With her back to the woman she scans the scrap of paper, memorises a number, replaces the paper in her pocket, and dials. The *click-click-click* of the dial as it returns to its resting place between each number seems to get slower and louder with each rotation, filling both the shop and Janine's head.

The phone at the other end rings for so long that Janine's chest begins to tighten and she feels herself holding her breath.

Finally the receiver is picked up.

'Erm... sorry... is that... er... Windyridge?'

Attempting to prevent the beady-eyed post mistress from eavesdropping, she lowers her voice close to inaudibility.

'Is Lady Margaret Wiscombe there? I'm so sorry to... please would you tell her that Nadine Tyler is at the shop... post office. In Chapelhill, yes. Okay. Thank you.'

Janine replaces the receiver.

'Thank you,' she says to the shopkeeper.

The other nods, a crumb of toast dropping from her hairy top lip onto the counter.

'That's tuppence.'

Janine digs into her coat pocket, coming up with a handful

of small change. She gives two pennies to the woman, mutters her thanks, picks up her suitcase and, acutely conscious of the stare boring into her back, hurries back to the safety of the street and 1963.

It takes ten minutes for a car to arrive, a charcoal-grey Bentley in need of cleaning, driven by a fat old woman wearing a woolly hat. Another woman of similar age but less than half the girth of the first sits in the passenger seat. Janine scurries to the driver's door, aware that the shopkeeper is standing at the window, half hidden by her unwanted wares, a mug of tea in her hand. The driver's window rolls down slowly.

'Miss Tyler?' asks the driver.

'Yes.'

'I'm Margaret Wiscombe. Hop in.'

The passenger twists round and opens the door behind her with some difficulty. Janine climbs in and closes the door, balancing her suitcase on her knees. The Bentley moves off.

'Sorry about the smell in here, but we had to transport a ewe to the vet this morning. This is my companion, Miss Chivers,' says Lady Margaret, eyeing Janine in the rear-view mirror. The companion gives the barest hint of turning her head and nodding. Had the gesture not been preceded by the introduction, Janine would have thought it an involuntary twitch.

She examines Lady Margaret from behind. She guesses the woman is in her late seventies. She wears heavy powder on her face and neck, and her eyelids are covered in startlingly bright blue eyeshadow. Her hair is white and tied up somehow under the hat, but wisps of it straggle down her wrinkled neck to her shoulders. She has a strong jaw and a large, almost masculine, nose, which is slightly red. The hands gripping the steering wheel are gnarled and arthritic with swollen finger joints, but the nails are incongruously beautiful and long, painted a striking red.

'I'm sorry for all the cloak and dagger, Miss Tyler,' says Lady Margaret, interrupting Janine's scrutiny. 'The last time I allowed someone to view the properties unaccompanied, they moved in that day and claimed squatter's rights. It took me six months and a fortune in legal costs to evict them.'

She laughs, a long, drawn-out croak that tails off into coughing. The companion, Miss Chivers, continues to stare fixedly through the windscreen but tuts loudly.

'Miss Chivers thinks I'm too trusting and I should use an agent,' explains Lady Margaret. 'But I like to see what I'm getting, personally. It's just up here.'

She turns the wheel, taking a left-hand corner at forty and throwing all three of them around in the car. The Bentley continues climbing.

'It's two semi-detached cottages, and you can have either. I'm afraid they've been empty for quite some time but, as I said on the phone, I'm happy to get them redecorated. Or you could do it, and we'll come to some arrangement on the rent. I hope you like solitude. Your nearest neighbour will be down in the village.'

Lady Margaret glances over her shoulder, apparently expecting a response.

'I like solitude,' replies Janine.

'Are you working?' asks the old lady.

'Well, not... not at present. But I've been saving for years. I should have enough money for maybe... a year's rent? And I'll find a job well before then.'

Janine watches Lady Margaret frown in the mirror and wishes she'd followed her first instinct, and lied. Miss Chivers tuts more loudly. That seems to irritate her employer, as Lady Margaret's tone changes.

'As long as you can pay the deposit and the rent comes in regularly, I'll be happy.'

The car turns right into a road called The Rise and continues to climb. To both sides are sloping fields bounded by collapsing stone walls, round bales of hay dotted about them, as if a giant had scattered spools of yellow thread across the landscape.

The tarmac of the road ends abruptly and the Bentley is now travelling on compacted mud, but Lady Margaret continues at the same speed. The ancient car bumps and rattles along, splashing through deep puddles and sending gritty sprays to either side. It comes to a sudden halt.

'Here we are,' says Lady Margaret, and the two women in front climb out.

Janine opens her door and looks to her left. Set back eighty feet from the road, standing in the middle of what seems to be an untended orchard, is a large rectangular dwelling, reached by a path of irregularly-spaced slabs between tall grasses. It is constructed of large blocks of stone, and looks as if it might once have been stables or some other agricultural building. It's the only building in sight.

The three women are facing its gable end. As Janine follows the older women around to the face of the building, she sees that the front windows have spectacular views straight down the valley. Turning in a circle, she regards the house in its setting.

Beautiful.

Isolated and a little run-down, but beautiful. Perfect.

She sees that there is a stream meandering past the building. She shades her eyes from the sun and follows its course downhill. At the foot of the valley there is a small, still lake surrounded by trees. A rope swing hangs from a willow tree growing almost horizontally over the water.

I will live here, she thinks with complete certainty.

'We used to swim in that, years ago,' says Lady Margaret, pointing to the lake. 'There might still be fish in it, for all I know. I spent most of my childhood on Chapel Hill,' she says, indicating the hill rising from the back of the house.

Janine follows the line of the woman's arm. Behind the building is what might once have been a garden. It is bordered by dry-stone walls and, at the back, a hawthorn hedge, a suggestion of a half-collapsed fence and a stile leading into open countryside. The garden is completely overgrown and little different to the wilderness above and to its sides. Beyond the stile the land continues to rise steeply and becomes a rounded hill grazed by sheep, with a stand of trees at the summit. Above and behind the building, Janine can see a footpath leading from the stile, winding its way around the hill and out of sight.

'Let me show you the inside,' says Lady Margaret, taking keys out of her coat pocket and leading the way.

There are two wooden front doors next to one another. The peeling paint on one is a faded green and, on the other, a faded blue.

'It was a farm building until the end of the last century when it was divided to make two labourer's cottages. This one,' says Lady Margaret, pointing to the blue door on the right, 'I call Magnolia Cottage. It has three bedrooms, a bathroom and a separate loo. This one,' she points to the green door on the left, 'I named Apple Tree Cottage. It has one large bedroom, a box room, and an upstairs bathroom. It's much smaller, which is why it's cheaper. You can have either. Both have telephone lines installed.'

'Which do you like best?' asks Janine.

'Me?' replies Lady Margaret, surprised.

She points at the green door. 'I suppose this one, Apple Tree Cottage. It is a bit tatty, but it keeps the sun longer in the afternoons. And… I had friends who lived here once,' she adds wistfully.

'Apple Tree Cottage, then.'

Lady Margaret frowns. 'Don't you want to look at both?'

Janine shakes her head. She is suddenly very tired.

Lady Margaret and Chivers glance at one another. Lady Margaret selects a key from a large bunch and inserts it into the lock in the green door. Her hands shake slightly. She leads the way into the smaller cottage, describing each room as she shows Janine around.

The narrow corridor opens into a single room that runs the length of the cottage, lounge at the front facing down the hill and kitchen at the back, facing up. There is a couch, an armchair and a small table with mismatched dining chairs, all covered in dustsheets. Lady Margaret steps into the kitchen area and opens the cabinets briefly, revealing crockery and saucepans.

Janine follows the old lady upstairs, leaving the companion by the front door. There is a single, very large bedroom looking downhill towards the stream and the lake. It is filled by an enormous metal bedstead. The only other furniture is an old oak wardrobe and a bedside table.

'The mattress is almost new,' says Lady Margaret, and she sits on it herself, apparently to prove how comfortable it is.

At the end of the corridor, next to the main bedroom and positioned over the front door, is a box room, and to the back of the property, a bathroom with toilet.

It takes only five minutes to inspect the whole cottage and Lady Margaret is still chattering away as they descend to the ground floor, but Janine has already decided and listens with only half her attention. Its position is perfect; otherwise, it will do. It has to; she's too tired to look any further.

They are now back in the kitchen that looks onto the rear

garden and the hill behind it. It is separated from the garden of the adjoining semi by a wall that runs only a short way back from the house. Thereafter the plots merge. Immediately beyond the windows is a tangle of shrubs, grass and weeds run riot, although close to the kitchen window Janine spots the protruding tops of fennel and mint, both gone to seed.

Was there a herb garden?

'It does smell a bit,' Lady Margaret is saying, 'but I promise that's only because it's been unoccupied so long. But' – and she runs a finger along the edge of the kitchen counter and wrinkles her nose – 'it *is* grubbier than I remember. I'll let you off the first week's rent if you clean up.'

Chivers scowls at her employer but Janine shrugs.

'Well, what do you think, my dear?' asks the old woman.

'Yes. It's fine. I'll take it. Please.'

'Sure you don't want to look at the other one?'

'No, thank you. I like this one. Also I don't need all those rooms.'

'Very well. Now, I shall need some references and a month's rent as a deposit.'

'I can't give you a reference,' Janine replies simply, too tired now to even contemplate the complexities of falsehood. 'But I'll give you two months' rent for a deposit instead.'

Miss Chivers's snort says 'I told you so' and she stalks out into the hallway and back to the car.

For the first time Lady Margaret examines the strange girl closely. Janine has pulled off her beret to reveal surprisingly beautiful hair, thick and blonde and slightly waved, and a clear strong forehead. Her skin colour is unusual, warm caramel, and contrasts with striking green eyes, which flash from behind the thick lenses of National Health Service spectacles. She wears no make-up and her clothes are unflattering and peculiar, but... she's a beauty.

Lady Margaret's gaze returns to the girl's eyes; soft, tired and anxious, but honest eyes.

'Why can't you provide a reference? Surely you know someone who can vouch for you?'

'No. No one.'

'Are you in trouble?'

Janine's eyes open wide with shock. 'You mean with the police? No, not at all!'

'A man then?' Janine's eyes meet those of the old lady for a split second before spinning off towards the garden.

Her dark skin colours and she stares at the floor. 'I don't know what you mean,' she mumbles.

'When would you want to move in?' asks Lady Margaret.

'Immediately.'

The old lady nods as if she expected the answer. 'There's no linen. I'm not even sure the electricity's connected.'

Janine shrugs again. 'All the same...'

'Where have you come from today? To get here?'

Janine smiles wanly. 'Sheffield.'

Lady Margaret regards her thoughtfully. 'But that's not where you're from, is it?'

Janine resents this interrogation but has no choice but to endure it. If the old lady says no, she'll be sleeping rough.

'No. Manchester, originally.'

Lady Margaret nods slowly, evaluates Janine for a while longer, and reaches a decision.

'Very well. And of course, you don't have the cash with you now, do you?' Janine shakes her head. 'Thought not. Bring it to me at the Hall tomorrow, in the afternoon. I'll have sorted out the services by then. Ask in the village. They'll give you directions.'

'Who? That lady in the shop?'

'You spoke to Mrs Dodds, did you? Don't worry. She is not

as fierce as she looks, but I'll pop in there on the way back. Here are the keys.'

Janine does not register anything further the fat lady says as she takes her leave. She manages to smile as Lady Margaret says goodbye but misses the concerned look she is given. She waves from the door as the two women drive off and retraces her steps to the kitchen and her meagre belongings. She collects the suitcase and goes to the lounge where she sinks gratefully into the old armchair without bothering to remove the dust sheet. She is asleep within minutes.

Lady Margaret and her companion reach the bottom of the lane.

'Strange child,' says the old woman. 'The usual bother, almost certainly, but not a usual girl.'

'She'll be trouble,' says Miss Chivers with satisfaction.

Chapter Two

LAURA

Laura Flint opens the bedroom door and looks down on the sleeping face of her eight-year-old son. The sweat that for three days plastered Luke's dark curls to his forehead is, at last, absent, and his cheeks are no longer unnaturally pink. He sleeps soundly, curled up and lying on his side. Laura offers a silent prayer of thanks.

She steps swiftly into the bedroom, careful to prevent the rectangle of hall light spilling across the pillow. She tiptoes around the bed, reaches for the teddy bear about to slip from Luke's grip and places it more securely beside him. Then, pressing her back flat against the cool wall, she sinks slowly down onto her haunches to study her son's peaceful face, absorbing every soft creamy feature.

In the months after Luke's birth she would often sit on the floor of his bedroom in the dark, like this, and watch him sleep, tears of an unanticipated and painfully acute joy sliding silently down her face. She had never felt an emotion as powerful as that love and she found it disorientating.

Notwithstanding her career, which she loved and for which she had fought so hard, Laura and her husband, Roger, both entered the marriage knowing they wanted children. The discovery, within a year, that Laura was pregnant was cause for celebration by them and by both families, for whom this would be a first grandchild.

Laura's joy dissipated swiftly in the awful months that followed. She piled on weight; her ankles swelled; she was constantly either too hot or too cold; her breasts were unbelievably sore; and she felt nauseous every waking minute of the nine months. She couldn't concentrate at work, kept making silly mistakes, and received no sympathy or support from her male supervisor, who took her performance as proof that women were unsuitable for employment by the Civil Service and, eventually, demoted her. Her mother viewed the demotion as further evidence that Laura was destined for failure in her career ('You just don't have the stamina of your sister, darling'), and began a campaign for her to 'give up this nonsense and devote yourself to being a proper wife and mother'. Laura spent the last fortnight of the pregnancy in bed following a frightening but, mercifully, innocuous bleed.

By the end of this misery, she would have done anything to bring the pregnancy to an end. She so resented the way this alien in her belly had destroyed her life she began to doubt she could love it once it was out of her.

Then, to top it all, she endured a lonely and terrifying labour. Roger was uncontactable, or so alleged his bitch of a PA – in Bristol giving a presentation to over a hundred other lawyers and several of his senior partners – and so, no, he couldn't be interrupted. By the time he eventually turned up at the hospital the midwife had already handed to Laura her son wrapped in a blanket, his tuft of black hair still slick and sticky.

And that was the moment, right then, as she looked down into Luke's peaceful face. A switch was pulled – she imagined one of those huge electrical levers operated by mad professors in their laboratories – and, as if she too had been charged by a lightning bolt, all the electrons that made up Laura Flint aligned themselves for the first time and this inexplicably powerful love flowed through her like a current. She felt as if she must have lived wrapped in gauze, so evanescent, so muted were all her previous emotions by comparison. Nothing could have prepared her to feel so wonderfully, painfully alive; no success at school, university or in her career had even hinted that she could experience happiness like this.

Eight years later it continues to perplex her that Roger doesn't appear to feel even remotely the same way towards his son. Even allowing for the fact that her husband's relationship with his parents had always been cool, formal even, she'd never have imagined he could fail to fall in love with this beautiful baby. In fact, he became, if anything, even more inaccessible after Luke's birth. She wondered if he found her and Luke's intimacy threatening, so she went out of her way to include him, yet he was always too busy to be home for bath or story time. Even at weekends he had no time to play in the park or feed the ducks. Something about Laura and Luke's relationship seemed to make him angry in some unfathomable way which, of course, when challenged, he denied.

Laura was also aware of the need to devote time to him and made it plain that she was available for sex when, in truth, she was usually too tired. Even that somehow made him irritable so, with some relief, she stopped offering herself and, if it bothered him, he made no comment. She confided to one of her closest friends that she was, essentially, Roger's employee; a combined housekeeper, nanny and hostess. Great benefits of course – you couldn't fault the holidays or the health plan – but still an employee.

She continues to hope that, one day, Roger will open his eyes and see what a wonderful son he has. To that end she keeps the kitchen calendar full of Luke's arrangements, his dental appointments, football matches and planned sleepovers, just in case. And also so she can't be criticised for not keeping Roger informed.

Her thoughts turn to her husband in Singapore, already halfway through his day. For a moment Laura hates him for not being there for their only child's first serious illness. Then she hears the gentle rattle of her mother-in-law's snoring in the adjoining room, and hates her even more.

Dorothy Redmond has been useless; indeed less than useless. Far from being the helping hand that Roger had assured Laura – on an infuriatingly delayed line – she would be, she proved a querulous, demanding house guest who didn't lift a finger to assist. At least she didn't bring her latest husband, her third, with her. Two hours of Stanley Redmond's golfing stories are all Laura can bear at one time.

It was Brigitta who saved the day. The German nanny arrived, four days ago, when Luke's temperature touched 104 for the first time and Laura was seriously considering ordering a taxi to take them to hospital. Laura knew nothing about a nanny until Brigitta presented herself at the front door. She hadn't even known that Roger had decided they *needed* a nanny, although for him to have done so, from the far side of the world and without speaking to her, was typical. For years she and Roger argued over this issue, Laura begging that they get some childcare so she could return to work, even part-time, he adamantly refusing.

'No son of mine is going to be brought up by an employee,' he would insist, entirely missing the irony that he had already demoted his wife to that very position.

Now, years later, and at a time in his life when Luke really didn't need a nanny, Roger had just swept all that aside and engaged someone without discussion. It was his way of implying that, even with the dubious assistance of his mother, Laura wasn't coping.

Had she been less frazzled and exhausted she would have slammed the door in the young woman's face. As it was, Laura simply left her on the threshold and ran back upstairs to where she last saw Mrs Redmond, leaning on the bathroom door jamb, gin and tonic in hand, holding forth about how to treat a listless child with a raging fever.

Brigitta was amazing. She left her bags in the hall, followed Laura up the stairs, introduced herself to Roger's mother, sensed immediately the simmering fury within Laura which was about to boil over into unretractable words, took Mrs Redmond downstairs to top up her drink, and started to put together a meal with what she found in the fridge. Having persuaded Laura to eat a little, she sent her to bed and took over the task of bathing Luke in cool water.

It was a true baptism of fire and the nanny confirmed her place in the Flint household. In retrospect Laura is able to give Roger credit for having heard the anxiety in her voice over the overlapping phrases and having taken action. It would have been nicer had he dropped everything to return to London, but that isn't the Flint way.

Roger is like his parents: they don't do emotional support ('coddling', Dorothy Redmond terms it) but there is always money available to be thrown at a problem. One of his favourite lines at dinner parties is that he sees himself as having two parental functions: for the moment he writes the cheques; later he will give the 'Man to Man' sex talk. It would be funny, were it a joke.

Laura stands and tiptoes from the bedroom, leaving the door slightly ajar. She hesitates on the landing, wondering if it's worth trying to grab another hour or two's sleep, but decides not. Her body clock has been completely disrupted over the last few days and she is wide awake. She wraps her nightgown round herself more tightly and descends to the kitchen, her footfalls silent on the thick carpet.

Leaving the kitchen lights off, she switches on the kettle. She wonders if she should contact Roger, but rejects that idea too. Even if she were able to track him down to his particular meeting, he'd be furious at being interrupted merely to be given good news. He'll telephone, as usual, when his corporate clients find it convenient.

He warned her. Indeed, he warned her the very day they met, although not directly, because he'd been showing off to another woman at the time.

It was their last term at Oxford and Laura had been persuaded by her flatmates to go to a party. She had little time for student parties. She took her studies seriously – her parents' incessant pressure made sure of that – and worked considerably harder than most of her peers. When she had time available, she preferred to run. She had devised a perfect five-mile route through Christ Church Meadow, along Cornmarket Street as far as the Ashmolean, north past the Bodleian as far as the half-constructed St Catherine's, then Trinity, and home via Angel and Greyhound. Forty-eight minutes on average, with a PB of two and a half minutes less than that. On this occasion, though, with her dissertation all but complete and the rain blowing hard against her sash windows, she felt she could permit herself a little downtime.

However, as soon as they arrived at the party the other girls disappeared, leaving Laura holding a glass of warm white wine in a room full of strangers. Relieved she could now slip away without being noticed, her attention was caught by a tall man with dark eyes and an intense expression. He was leaning against a marble fireplace, a full champagne glass in one hand and a bottle of Moët & Chandon dangling negligently from the other. He was speaking animatedly to another student.

'Being a partner in a city firm of solicitors brings huge financial rewards,' he was saying.

Laura could tell that he was slightly drunk, and she instantly categorised him as a complete tosser, but something about his shining eyes, floppy dark hair and gangling frame kept her in the room. She continued to eavesdrop.

'But the firm owns you, body and soul,' he was saying. 'If they say "Singapore, tomorrow" you go to Singapore, tomorrow. You won't believe this, but at the interview I was told that it's a contractual requirement to keep a current passport and an overnight bag at the office!'

When the other woman was finally able to make an excuse and slip away, Roger's eyes landed on Laura and, evidently still full of himself and his success at interview, he approached her.

Which is why I'm here now. And he's in Singapore.

Laura switches off the kettle again, bored with waiting for it to boil. She wanders from room to room looking for something to occupy her silently until daybreak.

Moonlight streams through the windows at the back of the house and she glides gracefully, a silk-gowned ghost passing silently in and out of the silver light. In the front sitting room she pauses on the balls of her feet, poised like a dancer and undecided, as she sees her current novel open on the coffee table. No, she's too distracted to read, and anyway it too bores her. She gets through two a week now; they all merge into one other.

She returns to the hall and passes Roger's study on her way back to the kitchen. Maybe the kettle will boil more quickly this time. Then she checks and retraces her steps. The study door opens silently. She loves the smell of this room, lined with the leather-bound books he never reads and containing the comfortable armchair he is never at home to sit in. The books were his father's before he died; the chair was her gift to him, to celebrate his attaining partnership. That was when she was working and had money of her own, not an allowance and a clutch of his credit cards which she reconciles every month.

She illuminates the desk lamp and lowers herself into his chair. On the desk a silver frame contains two photographs, one of her, one of Luke. Mother and son stare across unseeingly at one another. She moves the frame into the pool of light, gathers her voluminous hair behind her head with one hand, and bends to study the images. The photograph of Luke she remembers well: his first school photo, his uniform bright and clean. She spends longer on the other one, a portrait of a stranger, a skinny dark-eyed waif with windblown red hair and a hard athlete's body, smiling at something just outside shot. It was taken years ago, on a holiday in France, before they married.

I never look that happy anymore.

If this is the photograph Roger treasures, she thinks grimly; *if this is how he likes to think of me, perhaps it's no surprise that* – but she breaks that train of thought before it carries her into territory she hasn't the energy to explore.

Again, like a fly buzzing against a windowpane, the thought of her late period disturbs her. She is never usually late but then, as she reminds herself, the last few days have been unusually stressful. For the first time she drags the possibility into the light of the lamp, and studies it.

What if I am *pregnant?*

The timing is tight, but not impossible: that last and rather drunken night of Roger's short visit from New York in the summer.

After years of trying and failing to have a second child, part of her still yearns for it. To be back in that place of soft murmurs, newborn skin and tiny fingers wrapped round hers. It would be wonderful to experience that deep contentment again. On the other hand, could she face doing it now, just when a return to work might be possible, courtesy of Brigitta? And how will Roger react? After a decade of marriage, after trying and failing for so long, she has no idea how her husband would respond to being told that he is, after all, to be a father for a second time.

There is a noise on the stairs, and Laura switches off the light and rises. Brigitta appears in the doorway. She wears a thin cotton nightshirt, and the moonlight behind her reveals the curve of her breasts and the line of her hips. *Gosh, she's sexy*, thinks Laura, dragging her eyes away. *I'll bet Roger saw a photograph before signing* your *contract!*

'I could not sleep,' says the German girl. 'May I make coffee?'

'Of course. I'll come with you.'

The two young women enter the kitchen.

'I'll do it,' offers Brigitta, waving Laura to sit down.

Laura watches her empty and refill the kettle, switch it on, and locate mugs, coffee and milk. She marvels at how easily the girl has settled in, how she and the family seem to be in harmony.

'Luke's temperature is still down,' says Laura.

'Yes, I looked in before I came down. The doctor will come again?'

'He said he would.'

Deciding the newly-installed spotlights are too bright, Laura loads a tray and leads Brigitta into the lounge.

They drink in silence, sitting next to one another on a couch, facing the French windows and the dark gardens beyond. There is a faint glow in the sky and the occasional car passes outside. On the wall above their heads, lost in shadow, is Laura's latest acquisition, Jongkind's *Barges*.

They hear Luke's cry simultaneously, and both rise.

'It's all right,' said Laura, placing a hand on Brigitta's arm. 'I'll go.'

She swiftly climbs the stairs, noticing as she passes her mother-in-law's room that although Luke's cry was clearly audible from downstairs, the rhythm of the snoring from within the adjoining bedroom remains unchanged.

Thank God she's leaving today.

She opens Luke's door. The eight-year-old is sitting up in bed, his dark hair tousled.

'Are you all right, darling?' asks Laura as she sits on his bed.

Luke doesn't answer but puts his arms around her waist and snuggles his head into her chest. 'Is Daddy home yet?' he asks, his voice muffled.

'No. He's still away.'

'When will he be home?'

'I told you, in a few days.'

'And Grandma Dorothy?' He pulls back to look up at her as he asks, his face full of concern. 'She's still here, isn't she?'

'She's still here,' replies Laura, her tone deliberately bland.

She is constantly torn between satisfaction that Luke derives such pleasure from his relationship with Roger's mother, and irritation that Dorothy Redmond commands affection from her grandson without doing the slightest thing to earn it. She knows it would be selfish, but she yearns to explain to Luke what a mean-spirited, manipulative witch she is, and how she tried everything she could think of to persuade her precious son to break off his engagement with her. Dorothy Redmond fought against the marriage with almost as much fervour as Laura's parents deployed in coercing her into it.

'Can I have some more medicine?' asks Luke.

Laura looks at her wrist and remembers that her watch is by

her bedside. 'I expect so, just one spoonful. Then back to sleep, all right?'

He nods, sitting up in anticipation. Laura pours the sweet banana-flavoured medicine into a teaspoon and Luke opens his mouth very wide. Afterwards he licks the spoon. He accepts some water to rinse his mouth, and then settles back down. He is asleep again before Laura has reached the foot of the stairs. She returns to the lounge to finish her drink and get to know her new ally.

Chapter Three

JANINE

Janine stands at the open back door of her new home, gazing from the kitchen out onto the moonlit garden. The night air is cold but refreshing, banishing the last of her sleepiness. She slept in the armchair in the lounge for over twelve hours. It is now just before five in the morning.

She dreamt of Edward. She can remember little of it except his soft cow's eyes, unable to meet hers, and his arms folded resolutely across his chest, shutting her out. The thought of him causes a quickening deep in her belly, and she wonders if it's her imagination. Is it too early to feel a kick? Probably. She needs to find a library and get a book that tells her what's going to happen to her.

She has explored the house, paying more attention this time. The large bedroom with aspects to front and back is lovely. She particularly likes the faded floral wallpaper. The bathroom is smaller than Mother's in Hulme and smells slightly of mould, but it will do. She makes a mental note to acquire some bleach. She spent a long time considering the box room at the end of the landing. It's difficult to tell – it's so full of spare furniture that the door would barely open – but she thinks it will be large enough for a nursery. She will need to speak to the landlady about it.

An owl hoots from somewhere farther up the hill, and Janine looks up from her consideration of the garden. She is already formulating plans for what she might plant, subject to the soil type. She will need to explore that further too, but in daylight.

The sky is clear and distant and Janine hugs herself against the chill, but she remains where she is. Her mind turns again to Mother and wonders how she's managing. She pushes the thought away. Mother is no longer her problem; she'll have to cope as best she can.

Why do I feel so guilty?

Mother threw her out, but Janine still feels guilty. It's her fault. Everything is her fault.

She rouses herself and returns to her suitcase in the lounge from which she takes out her remaining food, an apple and half a Fry's Chocolate Cream, bruised and squashed. She eats them quickly and drinks a handful of water from the kitchen tap. The water is cold and tastes nicer than that at home.

By the light of the moon, she rummages through her few possessions until she finds what she is looking for, a building society passbook. Then she dons her overcoat, closes the back kitchen door and leaves the dark house through the front. She calculates it will take four hours to walk to Glossop, assuming it's not up and down hills all the way. Assuming, too, that she doesn't get lost.

She descends the hill towards the village of Chapelhill, the cold air chilling her lungs and tightening the skin on her cheeks. There is no street lighting, but the moon is full enough to illuminate her way, the blue light flattening the fields. She is the only moving thing in a still landscape leached of colour and noise.

She fantasises that everyone else in the world has died, and she is the last person alive on earth. It's a familiar daydream, one she has enjoyed since she was small. Until Edward, she used to think she would welcome it, being left to herself without anyone to shout at her. Or to hit her.

Then she remembers that she will never be alone again, and her hand slides across her belly as she walks, testing its shape. Still flat; no ripening curves.

'I promise you,' she says out loud, 'this will be different.'

It just after two in the afternoon. Janine's new tricycle coasts past Dodds' corner store and leans over slightly as it rounds the corner. She starts pedalling again as she enters The Rise. The incline soon forces her to slow and she realises that, even in first gear, she'll need to get off and walk. The basket is full of basic provisions, floor cloths, bleach, Ajax, milk, eggs and margarine, but even were it empty, the hill is too steep for her. She is quite strong from her physical work at the nursery – she can carry a bag of compost easily – but cycling requires different muscles, muscles that she hasn't used in the past. She will need to build up to it.

She is pleased with her purchases. The walk into Glossop took longer than expected but she was at the counter of the building society by ten. It seemed a nice little town, surrounded by hills, a pretty town hall and gardens, and a bustling market with friendly locals. But she was in a hurry and didn't stop to explore. She has promised herself that she will return at the first opportunity.

Her first stop after withdrawing some cash was a small café in a side street where she treated herself to a cooked breakfast, extra toast and two cups of tea. Sated for the first time in almost two days, she walked back to the main street and stumbled across Percival's Cycle Shop, where she saw the trike. It was part of a display in the shop window, polished and oiled regularly (she was told) ever since the shopkeeper's late father, Mr Reginald Percival, bought the business. Mr Percival junior was surprised to be asked its price. The machine was reckoned to date from well before the First World War, and no one had enquired about it in the eighteen years since he took over responsibility for the shop. The market for tricycles, formerly larger than that for bikes, he said, had disappeared.

Nonetheless, he was happy to let Janine ride it away for seven pounds two shillings and sixpence, to include, after a little haggling, a new chain and a second-hand bell.

Ten minutes spent in the Co-op, limiting herself to essential items so as not to overload the trike's basket, and Janine set off on the return journey to Chapelhill, which took an hour and a half.

Back home – the very thought that she has somewhere to call 'home' fills her with a tingle of excitement and apprehension – she unloads her provisions into the smelly refrigerator, reminding herself to clean it out on her return. Having dropped off her acquisitions, Janine heads out again, coasts back down Chapel Hill into the village, glances left and right before cycling across the High Street (although there is no traffic whatsoever) and begins to climb the sister hill, Burnham Hill.

The directions from the village shop had been simple: 'Go up the other hill.' She now understands why the parish is named Twinhills. The village of Chapelhill is not on a hill at all, but in a narrow valley between two hills, one confusingly called

Chapel Hill, on which is her new home, and another, its twin, named Burnham Hill. Lady Margaret Wiscombe apparently lives at the top of Burnham Hill.

She passes a small church in a well-tended churchyard and a field. Then the pavements end abruptly and she is back in open countryside, trees crowding in on both sides forming a green and gold arch above her head. The weak autumn sun shines through the gaps in the foliage at intervals, creating shifting spotlights on the road surface. The road becomes narrower and more potholed and, as no traffic has passed her since she started climbing, she dismounts to push the trike, following the faded centre line.

The carriageway becomes little more than a winding track with a stripe of grass spared by vehicle wheels in its centre. Janine imagines she is following a secret path to some magical destination; Little Red Riding Hood threading her way through the trees to a hidden cottage, a wisp of smoke rising from its chimney. She grins at the prospect of a wolf disguised in her landlady's enormous skirts.

She is happy, free at last and, despite her 'condition', exhilarated at what the future holds. This is how freedom tastes! Pushing her trike through beautiful rugged countryside, the wind blowing her hair behind her, she is now Tess Durbeyfield and Bathsheba Everdene combined; wronged by a man but a fiercely independent woman, determined to prove to the world she can succeed.

She continues her climb, leaning at almost forty-five degrees to the road, miniature whirlwinds of crisp leaves eddying about her feet, and hears the first drops of rain striking the canopy above her. She finds herself breathing a nursery rhyme in rhythm with her stride: 'One, two buckle my shoe, three, four knock on the door.'

She looks forward to turning and seeing the vista below her, but she disciplines herself to walk another hundred paces first. She counts the steps off aloud and then, for good measure, tells herself that she cannot turn until she has passed the old chestnut at the next bend. At one hundred and forty-one paces she stops, breathing hard, and turns.

Below her, like a toy town nestling between two green sheep-studded hills, is the village of Chapelhill. The church spire, far below, resembles a child's questioning finger raised to its teacher. Now she sees it from above, she realises there is almost no flat land within the village's curtilage. Every street is at a different height, connected by multiple stone staircases, alleyways and cobbled lanes, as the roads wind their way in tight bends and switchbacks up the lower parts of the hills. The only piece of flat land, on the other side of the valley, is a sports pitch and a white clubhouse with paling around it. The pitch, surrounded on two sides by stone cliffs, seems to have been carved from the hillside.

This is so beautiful! I can't wait to tell Edward!

Then she remembers that she can't.

Her mind is still affronted by the realisation that the shy man, whose pale skin was softer than hers and who had sworn so often that he loved her, deceived her so completely. Bizarre, impossible excuses for his behaviour still suggest themselves to her at odd moments. Maybe he'd been ill; he'd suffered a head injury and was amnesic. Or perhaps she was herself ill, in a delirium, like Marianne in *Sense and Sensibility*. So this hill, the countryside around her, the rain on her face, Lady Margaret and her companion – all are figments of her fevered imagination. Edward is probably at the nursery at this very moment, waiting for the telephone to ring, desperate with worry for her.

Stop it!

That's Nadine, bringing her sharply back to reality.

Janine looks beyond Chapel Hill into the far distance. The land rolls gently before her for miles and miles, a patchwork of fields, woods and rivers, towards an indistinct blur punctuated by a few tall glistening buildings. Manchester, she supposes. Mother is there somewhere.

The rain is heavier now and making her face wet. Her golden hair is turning into beige rat's tails clinging to the back of her neck, and her hands are getting cold. She moves on.

The lane bends suddenly to the left, and levels off. Across it is a barred gate and a cattle grid. The thoroughfare continues beyond the gate and is a good deal better made up than the public highway that Janine has just climbed. A wooden board announces it leads to Windyridge and that it is private. Janine opens the gate, pushes the tricycle through and closes the gate after her. She rides the rest of the way. Two hundred yards later the road turns a final corner around a stand of conifers, and she sees the house for the first time.

It looks more like a castle than a private dwelling. The walls are millstone grit, moss-covered blocks of yellowish grey, punctured by arched stone windows like those of a church. The house is covered in ivy that in places climbs almost to the roof. The building seems to have been constructed originally in the shape of an 'E', but parts have clearly been added to it over the years; it now sprawls in all directions in high stone walls, conservatories and gardens. The roof is stone-tiled and Janine counts four pairs of chimneys along the ridge. Scaffolding has been erected at one end of the building and workmen are struggling in the strengthening wind to get a covering over that end of the roof and to tie ropes down. Janine is reminded of pirates on a galleon, fighting a gale.

She dismounts and walks her trike through a line of contractors' vehicles parked on the gravel before the front door, looking for a sign to a tradesman's entrance. She hears a shout.

'Miss Tyler!'

For a split second, Janine doesn't recognise her new name. Then she turns to see who called. Lady Margaret is halfway up a ladder, beneath the workmen. She wears wellington boots, a brown waxed jacket with its hood up, and gardening gloves. Her face is wet and her nose red.

'Over here!' she calls again.

Janine makes her way over. Lady Margaret resumes shouting upwards and waving her hands, directing the men above her. Then she climbs down to meet Janine.

'Perfect timing,' she says, smiling, taking off a glove and holding out her hand.

Janine shakes it. It's an awkward gesture for her, but she orders herself to do it.

Nadine wouldn't hesitate.

'I've got your money,' she says.

'New bike?' asks Lady Margaret, pointing.

'Yes.'

'A three-wheeler. Not seen one of those in years. You could make a little trailer for that, couldn't you? Leave it there and come in.'

The old lady stomps off, away from the front door, talking as she goes. Janine hurries after her.

'I was doing some gardening when this rain started,' explains Lady Margaret in her croaky voice. 'Those bloody idiots just carried on drinking tea. If I hadn't been in, the whole of the east wing would have been flooded. As if things aren't bad enough already.'

Janine follows her through an arch in the wall. She gasps and comes to a halt. In front of her and to her right is a huge garden of astonishing variety. Far to the right there is a formal garden with lawns on three levels and a large pond with a statue spouting water in the centre, all surrounded by complex patterns of hedges and borders. In front of her, screened from the formal garden by a tall hawthorne and holly hedge, are tidy beds of vegetables. Most of the produce has been lifted but Janine can still identify a few leeks, fennel, carrots, cauliflowers and green beans. To her left is a herb garden.

Lady Margaret turns to see if Janine is following her.

'What's the matter?' she asks.

'N-nothing. It's just your garden.'

'What about it?' Janine looks away, embarrassed. 'Come on, girl, spit it out,' demands Lady Margaret.

'It's just... wonderful. And the herbs!' She points. 'You've more types of sage than I've ever seen – out of books, that is – and the thymes! Plus, you've got dill, marjoram, basil...' She points to each in turn.

'Do you know what they are?' asks Lady Margaret, pointing at something.

'The lavender or the tropaeolum?'

'That one.'

'Tropaeolum... nasturtiums in English.'

'Well done. What do you know about them?'

'They're edible, both the leaves and the flower. They're easy enough to grow, although not many people cultivate them for the table. I'm surprised they're still blooming. It's quite late.'

Lady Margaret regards her with some surprise. 'You know about gardening?' she asks.

'A little,' replies Janine cautiously.

'Where did you learn? Are your parents gardeners?'

'I used to work in a nursery.'

Lady Margaret regards Janine intently with her watery blue eyes, and nods.

'Come into the house before we both drown,' she says briskly, and she walks off again.

Janine follows her through open doors and copies Lady

Margaret in taking off her shoes at the threshold. They are in a sitting room with oak panelled walls and varnished floorboards covered in rugs. The room is full of heavy furniture in floral prints. Its centrepiece is a large inglenook fireplace with bench seats on either side of the fire. Janine has never before been in such an imposing room. It makes her even more nervous. Lady Margaret leads the way through the room to a hall and from there to a kitchen.

'This is the only room I keep heated at this time of year,' she says as she enters. 'I try to hang on as late as possible into October. Here.' She reaches into a drawer and pulls out a towel. 'Dry your hair or you'll catch cold. Tea? I was going to make some anyway, and a sandwich perhaps.'

Janine accepts the towel. 'No. Thanks.'

She reaches inside her jacket and holds out a bundle of slightly damp notes. 'Here,' she offers.

Lady Margaret takes the money, which disappears uncounted into the folds of her dress. 'Thank you.'

She fills a kettle, places it on the Aga and trundles slowly round the kitchen collecting cups and saucers, milk, tea and sugar, and loading them on a tray. Janine watches, puzzled. Did the old lady not hear her refusal?

'What's the matter?' asks Lady Margaret, seeing her expression.

Janine is about to repeat that she doesn't want tea, but wonders if it will sound rude. The old lady's behaviour is not what she expected, but perhaps this is normal. She mumbles something about servants.

'What was that?'

'I said, I... just thought you'd have servants, a maid or something, to do that.'

Lady Margaret laughs, her voice breaking into coughs.

'I do have Chivers. But she's not much, I grant you. Fifteen years younger than me, and still less use.'

There's no irritation in her voice, notices Janine; more triumph at having lasted the course better.

'But she's out today, visiting the Stick Insect.'

'Stick insect?' queries Janine, her surprise at the remark stinging her into speech again.

'Her brother. He lives outside Bollington. He's even skinnier than she is and has huge bug eyes that never seem to blink. They stare at one with such dispassionate concentration. As if he's just digested his spouse and is considering you for dessert. Although perhaps it's the female that eats the male? Or is that spiders? Whatever. He looks like a stick insect, even if he doesn't feed like one. I often think people look like animals. Their characters are usually just the same too. So, what do you suppose I look like?'

Janine shrugs, desperate now for some means of making her escape.

'Come on, what do you think? Just have a look at me and tell me the first animal that comes into your head.'

She poses, one hand holding aloft the kettle and the other resting on her hip, and Janine smiles despite herself.

'An elephant, right? Thick stumpy legs, a big nose and wrinkled skin as thick as hide. That's me, an elephant. I never forget, either.'

Janine almost laughs. If pressed she was going to say a toad, and is thankful she didn't.

The old woman's mad.

'Do sit down,' says Lady Margaret, indicating a scrubbed pine kitchen table.

She brings the tray over and sits opposite Janine, waiting for the kettle to boil. There's an uncomfortable silence in which

Janine hides by burying her head in the towel and rubbing vigorously.

'What attracted you to Twinhills?' asks the old woman. 'Do you have relatives in the area? Friends?'

Janine shakes her head under the towel. 'No.'

'I daresay it's none of my business–'

Janine emerges. 'Please. I know you're trying to be kind, but I'm just your tenant. I've given you the rent, and I want to go now.'

The old woman stands and goes to the Aga where the kettle is boiling.

'As you please. But there's one question I insist you do answer. You say you worked in a nursery?'

Her hair dry but tangled, Janine carefully folds the towel in two, then in four. She finally answers without looking up. 'Yes.'

'Doing what exactly?'

'What do you mean?'

'Well, you might have been working with the plants, or you might have been on the tills. The latter wouldn't make you an expert on anything except giving change.'

'The nursery.'

'Have you experience of growing vegetables and fruit?'

'Yes.'

'Which ones?'

'Most soft fruit, and the usual garden vegetables.'

'Good. Now listen. I'm not terribly keen on young people, especially those round here. I'm forever chasing them off.'

'I don't understand,' says Janine, and she really doesn't. This conversation makes no sense to her at all.

Maybe she's got dementia?

'If they're not scrumping apples in the orchard, they're fornicating in the barn. And all that sarcastic forelock-touching, "Yes, m'lady... no, m'lady" they go in for. But I think you know your plants. You see, I had to retire Pertwee, my old gardener.'

She makes little circular motions with her forefinger at her temple to indicate his mind.

'Totally batty by the end. Caught him wandering round in his drawers. Anyway, Chivers and I have done the best we can but we're no experts, and it's too much for two old women. So, here's the point: I was going to put an advert in Dodds' but, as I say, the villagers don't like me and I don't trust them. And I think you could probably do it. Can you?'

'No, I can't,' says Janine, standing. 'Really, I can't. I'm sorry, but I have to go.'

'Stop a minute, Miss Tyler,' commands the old woman. 'I'm taking a considerable risk with you. You telephone out of the blue, you've no history, no references, no job, and no one to vouch for you. Yet you expect me to hand over my cottage to you like a lamb. Why should I do that?'

'Then don't! Give me my money back, and I'll leave. I'll be out within the hour.'

She holds out her hand.

The old lady peers intently at Janine's face, frowning. 'Is that what you want?' she asks.

'I'll find somewhere else.'

'Perhaps, but I doubt it. Everyone expects references nowadays, and for someone like you – very young, no job – they'll probably want a guarantor for the rent too.'

'I can pay rent,' insists Janine, her voice rising, and she thrusts her building society passbook at the old woman, belatedly realising what a foolish gesture it is as it's in the name of Janine Taylor. Fortunately the old lady ignores it.

'For how long? Three months? Six? Then what?' she demands.

'I'll get a job.'

'There are no jobs in Chapelhill, not that you could have anyway. You're a stranger, and they're very close round here. And you have no car, so you can't look further afield. And what about when you start to show?'

Janine stares, wide-eyed, at the old lady's red nose and watery eyes.

'You *are* pregnant, aren't you?' asks Lady Margaret.

Janine's mouth opens to deny it but her eyes fall and her face flushes. She feels the heat travelling down to her chest, her abdomen and her legs. Even her toes are shamed.

'Don't worry,' continues Lady Margaret in a softer tone, 'it doesn't bother me a bit. I'm far too old to care about the morals of it, if ever I did. The point is, I doubt any other employer will be interested, will they? If they can't tell now, they soon will, and then you'll be out on your ear, whereas it doesn't bother me at all, and we can agree flexible hours to suit us both, which is much better than nine to five, don't you think?'

'Why would you offer me a job?' demands Janine. 'You know nothing about me.'

Lady Margaret's heavy features break into a smile. 'Maybe because Chivers says I should throw you out now. But let's say I want the cottage tenanted. If you don't get yourself a job, you can't pay the rent, and if you can't pay the rent, you'll have to leave.'

Janine is now desperate to do exactly that. She wants nothing more than to retrieve her money, climb on her wet trike and get away from all the questions.

'You don't understand. I have to be on my own! I don't want anyone interfering!' she says, the words bursting out of her.

'"*I vant to be alone*",' says Lady Margaret in a bizarre husky voice that Janine doesn't understand.

'Don't tease me!' shouts Janine.

The old woman recoils at the attack, puzzled. 'Garbo? No? You're not that young, you must have seen her films.'

'I don't know what you're talking about. I've never watched films,' replies Janine.

'Television?'

Janine shakes her head.

'Oh, well, never mind. I promise I shall leave you alone and you won't be obliged to me. I will pay you like any normal employer. Come on, girl, what's the alternative? Except, perhaps, to go back home.'

'You've no right to tell me what to do!' retorts Janine.

'Foolish girl! I'm not telling you what to do! I can't make you do anything. But face facts: you're alone, you're what, nineteen, twenty? You're pregnant, and you have no job. How much do you have, a hundred? Two? How long do you suppose that'll last?'

In fact, Janine has just under forty pounds remaining in her building society account.

'And do you know how much you'll get for maternity benefits? No? Because I do. It's a paltry four pounds plus an attendance allowance for four weeks. And it's payable on your national insurance record.'

'What's that mean?' asks Janine.

'Well, do you have a national insurance record, Miss Tyler?'

Janine doesn't answer. She certainly has no national insurance record in the name of Nadine Tyler.

'So, I go back to my original point. Could you do the job?' asks Lady Margaret again.

'Why should you help me?'

'I gave you a reason. If I have others, they're my business.'

She stands and returns to the Aga, where the kettle has been boiling for a while.

'Can you do it?' she repeats.

Janine nods. ‘I *could* do it, but...’

‘Very well. Three shillings an hour, plus the extra vegetables. Pertwee always managed to grow far more than we can eat. Actually, you can take some with you now. The only things enjoying the cauliflowers at present are the slugs. And we’ll start at... say... thirty hours a week, yes? There’s a fair bit of tidying up to do before winter. And, I promise, no complications. Your private life is your own. I’ll leave you completely alone.’

Lady Margaret brings the kettle over and pours hot water into the teapot.

Janine shakes her head slowly to herself.

No.

Whatever the old woman says, it *will* be a complication. Everything is going too fast! She can’t possibly handle all this with an interfering old woman looking over her shoulder. She’ll work her way in and complicate everything, when what Janine needs is simplicity.

And how on earth does she know I’m pregnant?

That’s Janine speaking, she reminds herself. What would her tentative new self, Nadine, say?

She’d say it’s a perfect job. It’s very convenient and you may not be offered anything else. And you think you might like this funny old troll who seems to say the first thing that enters her head. Finally, she’d point out, aren’t you doing exactly what Mother did – hiding from everyone? If there’s one thing you want to do differently, it’s that. You might make mistakes with the tiny life growing inside you, but shouldn’t they be your own, and not Mother’s?

‘I’m prepared to try it for a month,’ decides Janine. ‘With no obligation on either side.’

‘Let’s say six weeks, shall we?’

Janine calculates what the date will be in six weeks' time, and nods. 'Okay.'

'Excellent,' replies Lady Margaret with a broad smile. 'That'll get us through autumn, and after that there won't be so much to do. We can discuss later arrangements in the New Year. Now, sit down again and let's have some tea. And for future reference, as eventually you're going to have to call me *something*, the proper manner in which to address me is Lady Margaret. I also answer to Lady M. All right?'

Chapter Four

LAURA

The festive sign hanging above the directors' suite invites guests to have a 'Merry Christmas', and as she looks around the room Laura estimates that most of the guests have complied. Some of the younger male staff in particular sped past 'merry' some time ago and are now fully established in 'rowdy' and 'obnoxious'.

She watches with detached distaste as Roger smooth-talks his way round the party, bottle in hand, contributing a top-up here, a joke there, always at the appropriate elbow. He has no need to act as waiter – there are plenty of uniformed young women weaving their way between guests with trays of finger food and champagne flutes – but Roger knows that it gives him an air of humility, being 'part of the team'. It also enables him to break off conversations at will and move on if he spots someone more important.

He is good at it, she acknowledges. These parties, to which the firm's clients are always invited, are her only opportunity to study him in his work environment, and each year she is left impressed and cynical by his easy, handsome hypocrisy. This, she supposes, is how he shinned up the greasy corporate pole to his partnership. He has just the right touch of unctuousness for those whose help he still needs and contempt for those who need him; his blarney charms and his put-downs cut, but both are executed with finesse. She has difficulty reconciling this consummate corporate shark with the man with whom she fell in love. Then she was always able to find the shy and tentative young man whose over-confidence and rudeness hid someone who was hopelessly ill at ease in company. Now she wonders if that person is still there at all. If she were to meet Roger now, like this, he would repel her.

He continues to circulate, ignoring her, moving from one prosperous developer to another, working the room. He has his work cut out. He frets constantly that his billing, in common with all the others in the commercial conveyancing department, is well down on the previous year. The economy has still not recovered completely from the recession of the last two years, and interest rates are persistently high, so the big commercial building projects which form the bulk of Roger's work are still struggling to raise finance. There are murmurs of redundancies, even in the big firms, unless the first two quarters of 1964 improve significantly.

Laura stands alone, a full glass in her hand. She turns to the black window overlooking the lights of the city and examines her slim reflection. She approves. The black silk dress Roger brought back from Singapore is sexy, so sheer that she can't wear anything underneath it, and it sets off her pale skin and long red hair perfectly. Over the last year she has increased her training regime and is now as trim as she was when they first met. Every now and then she catches a huddle of men flicking glances at her. One or two have sidled up with silly grins, watched surreptitiously by their colleagues, to assay a few remarks, but she shuts them down with monosyllabic answers and each has sauntered off, trying to look unconcerned.

She wasn't pregnant after all. Part of her is sorry but the greater part is relieved. It would have brought everything to a head, and she is not ready for that yet. She very nearly refused to come this year, but she knows Roger has recently embarked on a new affair, and she wants to see if she can identify the putative co-respondent.

It's not his first. She doubts it's even his second, although she only has proof of one, with the bitch assistant who left without explanation shortly after Luke was born. In fact, she doesn't have proof positive even of that as Roger, outraged, denied it. Nonetheless, the woman was gone within a week of that row and Laura knows how highly Roger valued her. She rose with him through the firm and he was forever singing her praises. He developed 'mentionitis'; her name kept popping into his conversation – always in innocuous contexts – but a little too often. For her to have been sacked so peremptorily was all the evidence Laura needed.

As to this one, there have been few signs. Indeed, had she been asked for hard evidence of infidelity, she'd have struggled to answer. She just knows. It started with something in his eyes, an evasiveness, which at first she put down to worry. Roger's mother was never allowed to bother her little head about family finances, and Roger's attitude is the same as his father's, notwithstanding Laura's master's degree in statistics. So at first she assumed it was due to his uninspiring billing figures and concern over the eye-watering mortgage. But then there were a couple of inconsequential, unnecessary lies and, finally, there had been a supposed 'work-through-the-night' session to ready a file for completion before the markets in Hong Kong opened the next morning. Laura heard on the radio, completely by chance, that there was a public holiday there. So she did what she had never done before, rang the private number reserved for only the direst emergency and asked security to search the building for him. He couldn't be found.

She turns back to the room with a sigh and threads her way to the board table and the food. She helps herself to some grapes, feeling eyes on her. She wonders how many people know of the affair and decides that, probably, most do. It's usually impossible to keep that sort of thing quiet in an office, especially one used to working long hours, home and abroad, in a tight-knit team. Everyone knows, and everyone will keep quiet. Wives command no loyalty here; they count for nothing.

She has yet to challenge Roger about this infidelity, although she did, once, call him a liar, in front of both Luke and Brigitta, which left him puzzled and worried. Her knowledge gives her power over him, but she has yet to decide how to use it. She is still playing out the line, letting him dip and flash in and out of the water, when all the time she has him hooked and is waiting, biding her time before reeling him in.

'You look thoughtful,' says a male voice behind her.

She turns, and sees Martin Rush, the senior partner.

'Hello, Martin. Merry Christmas.'

'And to you. How's Luke?'

She likes Martin. Perhaps, more accurately, she dislikes him less than the others. He is fifty-five, a millionaire since forty-seven, and now works part-time. He can afford to slip onto the hard shoulder of the rat race and watch the others stream past, and he seems to have rediscovered how to be a human being. Unlike the other males in the room, he doesn't wear a suit and he has an easy, gentle air about him. He always remembers her name and that of her son, he listens when she speaks, and the unconscious condescension in which the voices of the other male partners are dipped is absent. Perhaps he treats her with respect because he knows she was, once, a professional woman in her own right. Or perhaps he's just a nicer type of man than is usually to be found in this environment.

'He's fine, thank you. And Hilary?'

'Very well. With her mother for Christmas.'

'Do you see much of her?'

'Only when she runs out of money, or when they row. Then she spends a few days with me, they kiss and make up, and she goes back home. They're too alike.'

They stare in silence at the people milling around, each disliking the party for their own private reasons.

'How old is Luke now?' he asks.

'Eight.'

A tall woman slips through the crowd, looks about her, and walks purposefully towards Martin. She has a sheaf of papers in her hand, and she raises an eyebrow and nods slightly to one side.

Martin touches Laura lightly on the forearm. 'You'll have to excuse me, Laura, but it looks as if something's blown up. Have a happy Christmas.'

'Thanks.'

Chapter Five

JANINE

Janine sits at the dining table, two Christmas cards left in the packet on the table before her, her fountain pen in her hand. By her side is a wastepaper basket containing her two rejected first attempts. Behind her, the pink, white and blue lights of her Christmas tree reflect back at her off the windowpanes. None of the windows in the dwelling has curtains. She can't afford them or the curtain poles they require and, in any case, the cottage is so isolated that no one ever walks past to see inside.

My first Christmas without Mother!

Despite the discomfort and broken nights, Janine is happy. This is now, truly, 'home' in a way that Hulme never was.

Her fears about being lonely, living alone for the first time in her life, proved groundless. She now realises that, despite being Mother's sole companion for nineteen years, she has always been alone. At school she was 'the Darkie', or 'that strange girl', the one not permitted to join the choir, the hockey team or even the reading club. She was a ghost in a bustling, noisy building. If, occasionally, a classmate saw beyond her strange appearance and shyness, she could never go to their homes nor bring them to hers. Early flickers of friendship suffocated through lack of oxygen.

Life with Mother was chaotic imprisonment, whereas life here is peaceful solitude. Janine relishes the difference. And, in any case, she won't be alone much longer.

Books line newly erected shelves on both sides of the chimney breast, each representing a treasured afternoon spent delving through dusty boxes at the second-hand bookshop in Buxton, found during a Sunday afternoon bike ride. A special shelf contains the handful of new books she has been able to acquire on her meagre wages, and a particular prize, her first book of poetry. That was a birthday present from Lady Margaret. It had been Nadine, not Janine, who let slip, with shy excitement, that it would be her birthday two days before Christmas. Every new acquisition, every new experience, takes her further away from Janine and breathes greater life into Nadine. She has made the transition, changed her life, made a new home, found a job. She is becoming the person she thought she could be and is shedding the person she was.

On the mantelpiece is a single Christmas card, from Lady Margaret and Chivers, and under the tree there lies a package, not to be opened until Christmas morning. It is also from Windyridge, further proof that Lady Margaret is very taken with her.

'She's a find,' Janine heard her employer and landlady say, as she worked beneath Windyridge's kitchen window one afternoon.

'Early days,' grunted the caustic Chivers.

Janine feels a kick and places a hand softly on her bump. Not that early; only seven weeks to go.

We're ready for you.

She puts the pen down and goes upstairs again. Climbing

the narrow staircase has become increasingly difficult, but she can't resist having another look.

She has converted the box room into a nursery, and she cannot quite believe the transformation. Some of the old furniture formerly piled in the room was loaded by Chivers into the boot of the Bentley, but most was taken away by the dustmen. Mother did no decorating in the house at Hulme – like Miss Havisham, she and the property grew dusty and grey together – and Janine wasn't sure she'd know what to do. But a couple of books borrowed from the library and the loan of some basic equipment from Windyridge later, and even Chivers nodded her approval when she came to recover the folding pasting table and freshly-cleaned brushes.

Janine's eyes scan the room, remembering every detail of the work she did so lovingly, the sanding, filling, hanging wallpaper and the painting. She did it all without assistance: the colourful wallpaper, shiny gloss skirtings, the old cot which she painstakingly sanded and repainted, and the charity shop bedside lamp with its new shade. All now waiting for the little person shortly to arrive and for whom this will become the safest place in the universe.

A picture of Mother forms in her head and a surge of pity fills her breast. Mother couldn't have felt this joy, this terrifying excitement, before her baby was born. Janine's grandparents were staunch Catholics, and Janine might easily have been handed to the nuns for adoption. Instead, Grandfather Watts, leader of the fishing fleet and a fierce tight-lipped man, simply dragged his pregnant daughter by her hair to the front door, and slammed the door on her without a word.

Mother only ever saw him once after that, and Janine was never left in doubt whose fault that was. Even before she was old enough to read, she knew she was a shameful thing, something to be hidden, lied about and punished; and then, nineteen years later, thrown from the door just as Mother herself had been.

What will Mother be doing now, she wonders? She's definitely still alive, because Janine telephoned Mr Patel at the Co-op. She asked him, in a matter-of-fact way, if the milk account was paid up, but in truth it was an excuse to ascertain if bottles were still being delivered and empties collected from the doorstep. They were. So, whatever Mother's condition, she is still making tea. She'd not been found at the foot of the stairs with her neck broken, or slumped at the kitchen table having aspirated her own vomit, either of which quietus Janine would have predicted, and might still occur. Janine had been clearing up Mother's sick since she was five.

She looks at her watch: nine o'clock exactly. If it's been a drinking day, Mother will be asleep, head down on the kitchen table or, if steady enough to climb the stairs, on her back on her bed, snoring. If it's not been a drinking day because there's nothing left to drink – which is likely, as it's the day before she gets her disability pension – she'll be hunched over the table, browsing and ordering her stamp collection.

Stamps were the one 'normal' thing that interested Mother. She was a collector. Every week or two, tiny cellophane presentation envelopes would arrive from Stanley Gibbons or one of the other stamp merchants, containing brightly coloured, gummed squares of paper, each bearing the face of a foreign leader and markings for strange, alien currencies. They represented all those far-flung places – the Belgian Congo, Persia, New Guinea – that Mother would never visit but whose stamps represented her one thin strand of connection to a world outside the grey house.

But for an event that occurred when Janine was about five or six, Mother's enthusiasm was something she could have shared with her daughter. Janine found an old shoebox under

Mother's bed and was sitting on the wooden floorboards, cross-legged, examining its contents. It contained postcards from all over the world, each bearing one of Mother's treasured stamps, awaiting transfer to her album. Humming to herself, Janine was happily leafing through them, fascinated by the pictures of foreign mountain ranges, waterfalls and wide rivers on which there were boats piloted by dark-skinned bare-chested natives. She had never seen people with skin coloured like hers before, and she was wondering if perhaps she might be related to them.

She reached a card which looked different to the others. The front was divided into quarters, each with a black-and-white photograph of a seaside town. There was a crowded beach; a bay with sailing ships, their sails full as they skimmed across the water; a quayside crowded with fishing boats; and a grand building, like a town hall but bigger. In the middle of the card, overlaying the photographs, was an oval in which was printed one word. It took her a few tries to decipher the word; it was one she hadn't seen before.

Janine was proud of her reading. She had taken to it 'like a duck to water', in the words of Mrs Jennings, her form teacher, and she was at the top of the A stream, a few of whom had already moved on to *We Look And See*, a book ahead of the rest of the class.

This word said: 'Lowestoft'. Janine repeated it several times softly to herself until she was confident she was saying it right. She turned the card over. Unusually, there was handwriting on the other side, formed of big, rounded letters. She started to read it aloud, her little finger tracing the letters from side to side. The card was addressed to Mother (although she was called 'Joyce') and was signed 'from your loving brother, George' with two crosses for kisses. George wrote that he was shortly going on a trip to North Africa, and he would try to send Mother cards from wherever he stopped en route. Janine didn't understand the words 'en route' but she understood the sense. It was a nice, friendly card and she wondered who George might be. Mother had never mentioned a brother; she never spoke about her family at all.

She was pondering this when Mother's hand swooped down from behind her and snatched the card from her grip.

'How dare you go into my things!' she shouted, and she hit Janine twice, quickly, once with her palm and once with the back of her hand.

It was so quick, and Janine had been so engrossed, that she was taken completely by surprise.

Thwack! Thwack! went the blows, the first landing on one cheek and the second, as Janine was turning away, on her upper lip and nose, bringing the taste of blood instantly to her mouth.

'How dare you?' repeated Mother, and she bent to gather all the cards back into the box. 'Go to your room, and don't ever let me see you in here again!' she shouted.

Janine ran to her bedroom, crying, and she never again mentioned the box of postcards or George. It was another lost opportunity. She and Mother never spent a Sunday afternoon together at the kitchen table, steaming the pretty stamps off the cards and sticking them carefully into the albums; they never wondered together about the exotic places shown on the cards, or looked them up in the atlas; they never spoke about the gentlemen whose noble faces were printed on the stamps; and they never mentioned George or any of Mother's relations, if indeed there were any.

Janine sighs, extinguishes the light in the nursery and returns to her seat downstairs to wrestle further with the immediate problem.

The question is, should she send a card to Mother at all and, if so, what should she say? She'd like to repair the breach between them if possible, but at the same time she doesn't want Mother actually in her life. Most particularly, she doesn't want Mother in the baby's life. If she sends a Christmas card, where will it lead? If she omits her address, will it look pointed? Will it make things worse? *Could* it make things worse? Maybe not for Janine and the baby, but what of Mother's state of mind?

She reaches a decision, takes out the penultimate card, unscrews the top of her fountain pen and simply writes *Happy Christmas, Mother. Janine* and seals the envelope. The card will probably be thrown in the bin without being opened anyway.

The last card remains before her.

There is no part of her day when Edward isn't, in some way, in her thoughts. Working at Windyridge is the worst – she has constant conversations with him in her head about the plants, the texture of the soil, the slugs and the weather – but other times are almost as bad. Every time she passes a telephone box on the street, she has to resist the impulse to go inside and call the nursery; she aches to hear his soft, tentative voice.

More, she aches to feel his calloused, dirt-ingrained hands on her. It's not the sex she misses but his gentle touch; the hugs and caresses. No gentle hand had ever touched her before Edward's.

At night she feels him sleeping in bed with her, his broad grizzled chest rising and falling in time with her breathing. So powerful is the illusion, she has more than once sat up to check he's not actually there, on the other side of the bed. Sometimes, in a garden, hers or Lady Margaret's, especially when prompted by a particular scent, she is sure that were she to turn round quickly she would catch him, watching her from behind a tree, like early in their courtship.

She is being haunted by a live fifty-year-old gardener in trilby, gumboots and, sometimes, pyjamas.

Should she write? Janine wants to give him the opportunity

to get back in touch; to confess he'd made a terrible mistake; to beg her to let him back into her life.

To be a father to their child.

That's Janine's fantasy. Nadine on the other hand wants to throw a Christmas grenade into his smug comfortable life and see what happens; to imagine how he explains *that* to his wife of twenty-five years and his four almost-adult children.

In the end she does nothing. She sighs, rises, places the remaining Christmas card in the sideboard drawer for another year, and warms some milk to take up to bed.

Chapter Six

LAURA

Laura wakes suddenly, her heart thumping. There was a noise, a loud noise, at the front door.

A burglar?

Brigitta is away for the weekend, visiting a student friend in Edinburgh. Laura and Luke are alone in the house.

She slips out of bed, pulls on a dressing gown, and creeps down the first flight of stairs in her bare feet. She is peering into the darkness when the hall is flooded with light. A second later there is a crash as a piece of furniture is knocked over.

'Shit!' swears Roger.

Laura turns the corner in the staircase and sees her husband bent over by the front door. He has knocked over his suitcase, and that in turn has overturned the table in the lobby.

'What's happening? Why aren't you at the airport?' asks Laura.

'I'm not going.'

Laura walks down the final steps and approaches him. 'Why not?'

'I don't fucking know!'

'But it's been organised for months. What about all the work you've done?'

'I don't fucking know!' he repeats.

He is still bent over, trying at the same time to pick up the table and the keys and gloves that were on it, and is getting into a tangle and a fury. He gives up, throwing the lot back on the floor with a crash.

'Shhh!' remonstrates Laura. 'You'll wake Luke! Get out of the way.'

As Laura rights the table, Roger angrily pulls off his coat, crosses the hall and throws it, jacket still inside, over the end of the banisters. He watches Laura's bent form for a moment, loosens his tie and stalks into the lounge. As Laura separates the coat and jacket and hangs them on different hangers in the hall cupboard, she hears the chink of the Scotch decanter against a glass. She follows Roger into the lounge. He sits on a couch in the dark, half a tumbler of whisky in his hand. Laura sits next to him.

He looks at his watch. 'Everyone else is now halfway over the Atlantic,' he says morosely.

'I don't understand.'

He turns to her. 'Well, neither do I,' he says aggressively.

So, this appears to be my fault too.

She is reminded of how her father addresses her mother. For thirty years, whatever misfortune ever befell Brian Smith, somehow it was always Annabel's fault.

Laura's first impulse is to give up and go back to bed, but she has never seen Roger quite as uncontrolled as this. The hand holding the glass is shaking and he is so tense, perched on the edge of the seat, she's reminded of a sprinter at the starting blocks.

She puts her arm behind him and begins stroking the back of his neck.

You don't deserve this, you bastard.

After a moment she hitches up her nightdress, climbs behind him, kneeling with a knee on each side of his hips, and uses both hands. Gradually she feels the muscles relax and his head sinks forward slightly. He breathes out slowly.

'Tell me what happened,' she says calmly.

'A message came as we were going through to the departure lounge. Someone was needed back in the City, and I'd been elected. Rush's personal order.'

'But you're supposed to be leading the team.'

'Exactly.'

'So what happened when you got back?'

'Bugger all. It was hardly a panic, and anyone in the department could've dealt with it. There's something else behind it, but no one's talking. Everyone's jumpy.'

That's no surprise, thinks Laura. She sensed it at the Christmas party.

'And this quarter's billing?' she asks.

He looks up at her sharply. If he was going to obfuscate, he evidently changes his mind.

'Still awful. That's why I don't understand why I was chosen to stay. I *need* this completion! They know I do. I did all the client work and wrote every sodding word in that bible.'

They sit in silence for some minutes, Laura still kneading Roger's shoulders.

'Why don't you come up now?' she asks. 'There's nothing to be gained by sitting here, brooding on it.'

'Hmm,' he replies, luxuriating in the calmness her hands are bringing to him. 'Would it be worth my while?' he asks.

Laura's hands stop moving, and she looks to her left at the clock on the wall. It is ten past midnight.

'Oh, charming,' he says. 'I ask my wife if, for once in a blue moon, she'd like to make love to me, and she looks at the clock. Can't you spare the time?'

'Oh, I'm sorry, Roger,' she replies, contrite, but half laughing. 'But it *is* late and I've got to be up in six hours. Don't be angry, please.'

He turns his back to her, drains the rest of his whisky and puts the empty glass on the table with a bang.

'I'd like to make love with you. All right?' she says, mollifying.

'With one eye on the clock? No thanks.'

She places a hand on his shoulder but now he is rigid and resistant.

'If you think about it, it's a compliment, really,' she says. 'If we only took two minutes, it'd be different.'

He makes no response, but she senses that he is relenting.

'I promise not to look at the clock once,' she says. 'You can take as long as you...' and she realises her mistake, but too late.

'*I* can take as long as I like? What about *we*? That about sums it up, doesn't it? You lying there wondering how much longer I'm going to be, and me getting it over with as quickly as possible so you can go to sleep!'

He stands abruptly.

'I wouldn't dream of inconveniencing you,' he says, and he walks swiftly out of the room to the hall cupboard. Laura hears him taking his jacket back off the hanger.

'Where are you going?' she demands, following him.

'Back to work. I've got plenty to do, and right now I don't feel like going to bed.'

'You're not going to the office, and we both know it,' she spits. 'You're off to see your little tart!'

Her hand flies involuntarily to her mouth to keep the thought in, but it's too late. It's out, in the open, the words lying there like bright spilled blood on the beautifully impractical carpet. The careful, considered phrases she's been trying out in her head for weeks are now useless, and she curses her indiscretion.

She's thought of nothing but his affair for months, in particular since the firm's Christmas party. She went to show the woman, whoever she was, that Laura Flint was no dowdy housewife to be cuckolded with impunity, and that she threatened their marriage at her peril. The sort of dramatic action of which Jennifer would have approved. Had Laura been able to identify the woman, she intended something dramatic, at the very least leaving her dripping, an empty bowl of punch on her head. But she departed disappointed. She'd discerned no secret glances, no furtive kisses in the stationery cupboard, no one who seemed a likely candidate for a punch bath.

That was the high point of her mood. The defiance that got her dressed to kill gave way over the days that followed to depression. She found herself crying on the floor of the bathroom. She had to get away from Roger, take Luke, her passport and disappear. Her desperation even caused her to reach several times for the telephone to call her parents.

Each time better sense prevailed.

Laura's parents, especially her mother, believe that their handsome solicitor son-in-law, he with a new luxury car every year and a large house in St John's Wood, is perfect. Nothing Laura says will persuade her otherwise; Annabel will hear nothing against him. An earlier tiff which prompted Laura to ring her mother produced half an hour of 'Are you sure you're not overreacting?' and 'You were so selfish as a child'.

Annabel has for decades suffered her husband's bullying and his repeated, flagrant infidelities in silence. She has invested too heavily in self-deception to acknowledge that her son-in-law is cast in the same mould.

The Smiths' disappointment in their younger daughter

found new expression when she married. Her deficiencies could now be shared with a willing new participant, her husband, who brought to the pastime of criticising her a whole new matrimonial dimension. Even her cookery skills came in for jocular condemnation by the three conspirators, her parents and her husband, and she was supposed to smile, blush guiltily, and confess falsely to a total inability even to boil an egg when, among their friends, she was considered the best cook in the group.

No, Laura can seek no support there, and she has nowhere else to go, no job, and little money. Roger will prevent her withdrawing their savings, and she'll have to crawl back.

She even started blaming herself. If, superficially, Roger had everything – an ostentatious house, five weeks of holiday a year in exotic destinations, an elegant wife/hostess who gave up her own career to look after the home, and a beautiful son – why then would he need an affair? Maybe it *was* her fault, at least in part. Maybe he worked such long hours because he was unhappy when he did come home; maybe she, a non-lawyer, never understood the pressures he was under.

Maybe she was, as he frequently complained, frigid?

She decided that if she was at all responsible for the mess they were in, she'd abjure the knee-jerk reaction of many cheated wives by screaming, throwing things and demanding a divorce. She was more grown-up than that. Even if there was only a one in ten chance of getting the marriage back on the rails, she reasoned, surely she owed it to Luke to try? Yes, she decided, they needed to talk about it calmly, perhaps with some help; try to re-dedicate themselves to each other. She just needed to find a way to broach the subject.

And now, having spent weeks trying to find the right words to open discussions, she'd ripped the plaster off with one tired, exasperated comment.

She watches Roger's face contort as he tries out and rejects the varied responses of denial, outrage, dismissive humour and non-comprehension. In the end he settles on confusion and plays for time.

'What do you mean?'

Laura sighs. 'You know what I mean. I'm not a fool. I've known for ages.'

'Known?'

'Please, Roger! I'm too tired for games. If you want to discuss it sensibly, let's go into the kitchen and sit down. There'll be no screaming and no tears, I promise. But if you're just going to deny it, I'm going to bed and you can go to her.'

He intended to deny it, she can see from his expression, but he suddenly caves in and nods. Laura leads the way into the kitchen and fills the kettle. Roger slumps onto a stool at the breakfast bar, rubbing his eyes. She turns to face him. He cannot meet her stare.

'I want to know how long you've been having an affair,' she says, her back against the counter, her arms folded.

'A year, a bit more maybe.'

'Oh.' She had thought much less, a few months at most. How had she missed the signs before then? 'And are you in love with her?'

'No. I don't actually like her very much. She's in litigation support–'

'Stop!' commands Laura, her hand up. Roger looks up. 'I don't want to know anything about her, not her name, her job, not anything. All I want to know is what you think is going to happen to us. You, me and Luke.'

Her eyes fix on his face, unwavering. She is in charge for the first time since she discovered his infidelity, perhaps for the first time in their relationship, and they both know it. He nods again and she releases his gaze. She makes two mugs of tea, brings them to the table and sits opposite him.

'Do you want a divorce?' she asks.

'Me?' he replies, astonished. 'I thought I'd be asking *you* that. Of course I don't. I love you.'

'Really? You've a strange way of showing it.'

'I...' he shakes his head. 'I know.'

'Why, Roger?'

'I don't know, really I don't. I've asked myself thousands of times how I got myself into this mess. I didn't seek it. I knew she was interested for some time, and then when we were in Leeds last year it just happened. I was away so much, and even when I was here, you seemed... distant. I felt lonely.'

'Lonely? How the hell do you think I've felt? I've barely seen you during daylight hours for the last year. At weekends you're working or playing sport with your clients. Golf, squash, cricket–' She begins to list them on her fingers.

'Have you asked yourself why?' he says, his voice rising slightly but not yet shouting. 'You're like a stranger to me. In the month leading up to our anniversary last year, we went ten complete days without any physical contact at all. I counted them. And I don't mean sex. I mean a simple kiss on the cheek, a touch on the arm, a hug. Nothing. You go to sleep with your back to me–'

'Only since–'

'No! Not only since then! This has nothing to do with you... us... not getting pregnant. For years! You go to sleep without a word, with your back to me, you don't kiss me goodbye in the mornings or hello when I get in, you don't even do those things like straighten my hair or tie anymore. I've felt like I've got the plague! When I reach out to touch you, you recoil.'

'I don't.' She reconsiders. 'Do I?'

'Yes. You're not even aware of it.'

She stops in mid-gesture and thinks back. He's right. She can see herself weaving patterns round him when he's in the house to avoid getting too close.

'We had sex...' she begins, and then falters.

'When? It was over two months ago; it was bloody awful and you know it. Remember now?'

'Can you blame me? Knowing she's been all over you? I've been lonely too, but *I* haven't resorted to screwing around!'

Her shout echoes around the kitchen.

'Sorry,' she says quietly after a moment. 'I promised myself we wouldn't row. I just need to know what happens now.'

'That's pretty much in your hands, isn't it? I mean, do *you* want a divorce?'

'I don't think so.'

'What then?'

'Well, firstly, I want a promise you'll never see her again.'

He smiles. 'You have it.'

Oh, too easy, thinks Laura, seeing the confidence seeping into his posture. 'And I insist you tell her in front of me.'

His mouth falls open and he half laughs. 'You can't do that. It's not fair.'

'To whom?'

'To her!'

'What are you worried about, hurting her feelings?'

'Yes. It'll be bad enough without humiliating her completely.'

'You weren't bothered about humiliating *me*. How humiliated do you think I was at your bloody Christmas party with everyone knowing, and looking at me?'

'I can't do it with you standing there, listening,' he replies, and Laura notes that he doesn't deny that everyone in the office knew of the affair.

'Those are my terms.'

He holds his head in his hands and she notes the increasing number of grey hairs round his temple protruding through his fingers. He is only thirty-five, but she has a picture of him twenty years hence, and knows that he'll still be infuriatingly handsome. It's so unfair.

'Okay,' he concedes wearily, 'but not at the office. At least allow her the dignity of being told somewhere away from everyone.'

'All right. You decide when and where, and tell me.'

'Anything else?' he asks, not expecting anything.

'I want us to go to marriage guidance.'

'Oh, Laura, really? I'm not telling some stranger all about... everything, even our most intimate stuff! It's not for people like us.'

'It's entirely confidential.'

'Yeah, sure,' he says dismissively, 'just like everything I do is confidential.'

'What does that mean? This isn't some business deal! They'd be our own private counsellor who'd hear what we each have to say, that's all.'

'We don't need a referee. We can talk between the two of us, without paying some social worker to listen.'

'No, we can't. That's half the problem. You never let me speak, you never listen to me. Every time I–'

'That's rubbish, Laura–'

'QED! Listen to yourself! You're always cutting me short, preventing me from finishing. That's what the counsellor's for, to make sure we each get a say.'

'How do you know so much about it?' he challenges.

'I've made enquiries. We've been on the waiting list for almost six months.'

'What?'

'You heard.'

'You had no right to do that without consulting me first.'

'Consulting you? I barely speak to you from one weekend to the next! I've even thought of ringing your secretary and making an appointment under a false name. At least as a client, I'd have had your undivided attention for an hour. Maybe that's what's wrong: we don't communicate any longer. And that's where marriage guidance could help.'

'I really don't think there's any point.'

'But you will come?'

'If you insist. But I make no further assurances.'

'Ever the lawyer! What's that supposed to mean, you shit? "*I make no further assurances*"!'

'Just that I don't expect it to do any good.'

'Well, if that's what you mean, bloody well say so! Is it any wonder I don't trust you? And you'd better realise that I'm going to watch you like a hawk from now on. I'm going to telephone you and check up on you all the time, and if I catch you out once, that'll be it. Understood?'

'Fine.'

'And I've changed my mind about something. I want to know her name and her department. And her phone number.'

'Why? So you can cause trouble for her?'

'I don't see why I shouldn't. She knows you're married; she should've known better. But no, I'm not going to make trouble. I just want to know whose name and number to look out for while I'm trawling through the phone records.'

He looks up at her, expecting her to be joking, but she is resolute.

'Her name's Jennifer Smith.'

Laura is unable to speak for a moment. 'Is this your idea of a joke?' she finally asks, stunned.

'No, that's really her name. It's just a coincidence.'

'A coincidence that you're sleeping with someone who has the same name as my dead sister?'

'Do you really think I went round London looking specifically for a Jennifer Smith to shag? I'm telling you, it's a coincidence. She's just a secretary, in litigation support.'

Laura considers this explanation. The logical part of her realises that he must be telling the truth, but... this can't be a coincidence, surely? Jenny has haunted her for years; will it never end?

Roger is talking. 'Please don't cause her any trouble. She's only a kid, and she's got a bastard of a husband who hits her. She's pretty screwed up already.'

Now there is sincerity in his voice, a tenderness that chills Laura and makes her wonder afresh about their future. She is surprised too; she imagined a predatory thirty-something singleton or divorcee, not a young married woman.

Is he to be believed?

'Does she have children?'

'Yes, one.'

Another reason to try to make this work, then, thinks Laura: two innocent children to protect from this mess. She wrestles with the problem for a few seconds, but then gives up. She's too tired to work it out and she wants to think carefully when she's rested.

'I'm going to bed,' she says. 'I can't think straight anymore.'

She picks up the two mugs of tea, both untouched, and tips their contents into the sink. Without a further word she leaves the room, leaving Roger staring after her. She's pleased to note that he looks anxious, even a little frightened.

Laura stands by the side of the bed looking down at the sleeping form of her husband. It is five thirty in the morning, and she has not slept despite overwhelming fatigue. Roger on the other hand sleeps soundly, his face young and sensitive in repose. In the crystal clarity that exhaustion sometimes brings, she suddenly knows that this will never work. Before this moment she has never truly imagined a time without him, even when she discovered his infidelity, but now she knows. Maybe, if he agrees to go to marriage guidance; if he really *listens* and then does his best to change; *maybe* they can postpone the inevitable. But she has no illusions; the best they can hope for is a postponement. The truth is she doesn't trust him, and doubts she ever will, and she won't spend the rest of her life either being made to look stupid by trusting him while he continues cheating, or going through his jacket pockets.

Mixed in with all her feelings of anger and betrayal she detects some sympathy for the 'other' Jennifer Smith, the allegedly unhappy, bullied woman, and her own innocent child. But they are not her problem. There is only one imperative from now on, she decides, and that is Luke.

I have to protect him from this as much as I possibly can. I will not let him be damaged.

She studies Roger's sleeping face, trying to identify the feeling he now generates in her and, like pieces of clothing, she tries on in succession hate, love, anger and bitterness, but none feel right.

I am blank, she decides.

She leaves the room silently and goes next door to Luke's room. She pushes the door open, slips in, stepping carefully over the toys on the floor, and sits on the edge of the bed. Luke sleeps on his back, one arm thrown across his current favourite soft toy, a kangaroo. Laura smooths the dark curls out of his eyes, and lies on the narrow bed, moulding herself to her son's sleeping form.

She breathes in the smell of baby shampoo and little boy, and closes her eyes.

Laura's eyes open wide and she is suddenly awake. It takes her a moment to recognise the tingling 'big' feeling she remembers from breast feeding, for whereas the reality was painful and difficult, with both mother and baby distressed, this feeling is full of satisfaction and success. She looks down at Luke, his position unchanged.

Was I dreaming of you? she thinks.

As she watches, his eyes open.

'Why are you smiling?' he asks sleepily.

'Am I?' she whispers.

'Like that cat in the cartoon,' he says, referring to *Alice in Wonderland*.

'Go back to sleep,' says Laura, and he does, closing his eyes immediately. He is asleep in the space of two breaths.

Chapter Seven

JANINE

Roberta Anne Tyler, to be known familiarly as Bobby, is born three weeks premature in the early hours of 14th January 1964 at Stepping Hill Hospital, Stockport, Cheshire. She weighs seven pounds one ounce.

It was not a straightforward birth. Janine, as ever putting her faith in books, had relied exclusively on her library research to inform her what was going to happen, and attended no antenatal classes. Fourteen hours into her labour she was informed by the experienced midwife that the baby was in breech position and was becoming distressed. The young obstetrician in attendance suggested calling Mr Martindale, the consultant, but the midwife, a no-nonsense Lancastrian, persuaded him that, given the prematurity and size of the baby, it was worth trying to turn it before calling in 'a knife-happy consultant' for Caesarean section. Perhaps because Janine was unaware of the risks presented by a baby in breech position, she surprised the staff by remaining remarkably calm throughout, despite her pain and the fact she had no one to support her.

The midwife was proved right and, between them, she and the obstetrician managed safely to turn Bobby, who was born two hours later without surgical intervention except an episiotomy.

'Well done, love,' said the midwife to Janine as she handed Bobby to her for the first time. 'You've got some grit, young lady.'

'Where's the father?' asked the thoughtless young doctor.

The midwife prodded him into silence with a swift elbow. Janine pretended not to have heard.

Janine and Bobby have now been on the ward for six days. Their notes record that they receive neither visitors nor telephone enquiries. After a couple of days Janine starts to notice other mothers throwing glances in her direction. Most stop speaking to her. On one occasion, while in a toilet cubicle, she hears one older mother commenting that the woman in the end bed is 'no better than she ought to be'. She knows they are referring to her.

However, the staff remain professional and record that mother and baby have bonded well; there are no problems with breastfeeding; mother has learned how to top and tail baby, and she is managing her episiotomy stitches well. The notes state that she should be ready for discharge at the end of the week, the eighth day after confinement, slightly earlier than average for a *primipara* mother.

The day before the planned discharge, a woman arrives at Janine's bedside. Janine is sitting in an armchair beside the bed, gazing out of the window at the roofs of Stockport as she feeds Bobby.

'Miss Tyler?' says the woman.

Janine looks up. The speaker is tall and angular with greying hair tied in a bun, and she peers at Janine over half-moon spectacles.

'Yes?'

'Good afternoon. My name's Helena Brathwaite, and I'm the Registrar of Births at the hospital,' she says in a clipped, businesslike manner. 'Do you mind if I sit down?' She indicates the bed.

Janine shakes her head. The woman walks around the foot of the bed to sit next to, and above, Janine. She looks down at Bobby, cradled in Janine's arms. The baby's eyes are closed and she sucks noisily. The skin of her eyelids is almost translucent, a delicate mauve, as if she were wearing light make-up.

'She's adorable,' says Brathwaite, but the comment seems devoid of emotion and Janine suspects it's the woman's stock response to seeing a newborn. She smiles but does not reply. Brathwaite takes out a pen and tears a sheet of paper off her pad, clipping it to the top of her clipboard.

'Right,' she says, pen poised. 'This shouldn't take more than a few minutes. I just need some details from you.'

'What details?'

'Well, the baby's name, the names, addresses and occupations of the parents, things like that. Nothing difficult.'

Alarm suddenly flashes across Janine's face.

'Do we have to do it now?' she asks. 'I don't want to disturb Bobby while she's feeding.'

'Will talking quietly disturb her?' asks Brathwaite, surprised.

'Yes, it does, sometimes. It takes a while to get her settled.'

'I suppose I can come back,' says Brathwaite a little reluctantly. 'You've forty-two days to register the birth. After that you can be fined. So, best to do it while you're still here, yes? And it'll save you a special trip to the registry.'

'Of course, but can we leave it for today, if that's okay?' says Janine softly, indicating Bobby.

'Very well. I'll pop back tomorrow morning.'

The woman walks away, pausing to have a word with the staff nurse at the desk. Janine sees from their glances that she is the subject of their conversation.

That evening, after everyone has finished their tea and the trolley has been round to collect the plates, Janine settles Bobby in her cot by the side of the bed and closes the curtains. She is not alone in that; several young mothers have done the same and are already asleep. She quietly empties the contents of the bedside cupboard into her bag and gets dressed. She was wearing dungarees when her waters broke but is now grateful she packed a skirt. She is still very tender from her episiotomy and her bulky dressing would have made wearing trousers uncomfortable.

She waits for the ward to become quieter. It is usually around this time that the night staff take it in turns to have a tea break. She peers out from behind the curtains. There is only one nurse, not one of the formidable staff nurses, at the desk. Janine hasn't seen her before, which is lucky.

She picks up Bobby, who stirs but does not wake, tucks the baby inside her overcoat, grabs her bag with her free hand and walks towards the desk. The nurse looks up.

'Where are you off to?'

'I'm going home,' says Janine, evidencing surprise. 'Weren't you told?'

'No.'

'My mother-in-law's waiting downstairs in the car. She spoke to staff nurse this afternoon to arrange it.'

The young nurse stands. 'Which staff nurse?'

Janine shrugs. 'I don't know. I was just told to be ready to leave at eight o'clock.'

'I'm sorry, but you can't just walk out like this. We've got to discharge you properly.'

'But it's all arranged. I've got a long journey, and I can't do it by public transport,' says Janine, injecting a note of desperation into her voice. 'I can't ask her to come back again.'

The nurse looks around her anxiously. 'Just wait there, yes?'

'Of course,' says Janine, putting down her bag.

The nurse scurries off. The moment she has rounded the corner, Janine picks up the bag and trots out of the ward.

It is her unfamiliarity with the hospital that enables her escape. Becoming confused, she walks away from the exit and gets lost on the floor below. By the time she has found her way out via the entrance to the X-ray department twenty minutes later, the route to the main entrance has been searched by staff without success, and Janine is able simply to step into the cool night air.

Her luck persists. She is waiting at a bus stop a couple of hundred yards from the hospital, not completely confident that the bus to take her home actually stops there, when a taxi is forced by traffic lights to a halt next to her. She steps into the carriageway and asks the cabbie if he is available for hire. Half an hour later she is unlocking the door to Apple Tree Cottage.

Having slept for the whole journey home, Bobby is now awake and crying. Feed time. Janine drops her bag in the hall and climbs the steep staircase directly up to the cold nursery, her stitches pulling uncomfortably.

Some weeks earlier, before she became too big, she managed to manoeuvre one of the lounge armchairs up there so she could feed Bobby at night without taking her out of the room. She read in one of the library books that it was advisable to resist having baby sleep in bed with mother. It was recommended that baby should sleep in its own room from day one for mother to avoid the anxiety caused by every cough, snuffle or pause in the baby's breathing.

She lies Bobby down in the cot while she takes off her coat and undoes her blouse and nursing bra. Then she picks her up, settles into the armchair, places her glasses on the bedside table and puts Bobby's face close to her breast. The baby stops grizzling immediately. She arches her neck, her mouth open, making soft squeaky noises. Janine takes her swollen breast and strokes her nipple, now enlarged from a tiny button to a pink raspberry, up and down across the bumps of the baby's lips, and within a moment Bobby fastens on and has begun to suck.

Janine can't actually feel the milk coming out of her – Bobby's mouth is too hot and sucky for that – but she feels a warm tingling spreading across her chest. She shuts her eyes and lets the sensations wash over her. The velvet closeness of the baby; the smell of sweet skin and sweet milk; the gentle contractions of her womb; they combine into such contentment. This is so much better than in the hospital. This is where they belong, where they are safe.

Chapter Eight

LAURA

'What do you mean, he's not coming?' demands Annabel Smith.

She stands in the open front doorway of The Old Rectory, Laura's childhood home.

'Just that. He's not coming,' replies Laura.

'Work again, I suppose,' says Annabel. 'Well, are you coming in?'

She claimed to have been taken by surprise at Laura's early arrival on the doorstep ('I must look like a scarecrow!'), but she looks as well coiffed and elegantly dressed as if she were on her way to church. Flatterers often used to say, when speaking of her and her daughters, that she looked like the oldest of three sisters. Such comments aren't usually supposed to be taken seriously but in her case, until quite recently, people meant it. Laura wonders if her mother's outrageous flirting with Roger was something about which she should have been more concerned.

A bit late for that.

'No, thank you,' replies Laura. 'Luke and I are going to look at the property anyway.'

'Without Roger?'

'Yes, without Roger. Here.'

She hands her overnight bag to Annabel, who takes it without thought.

'Brian!' calls Annabel over her shoulder.

Laura's father appears in the doorway. He wears slacks and an open-necked shirt under a golf jumper, and has a cup of tea in his hand.

'Hello, darling,' he says to Laura. 'Where are Luke and Roger?'

'She says they're not coming in,' explains Annabel.

Laura points behind her. 'Luke's asleep in the car. Roger isn't here.'

'Work again?' asks her father sympathetically.

Laura takes a deep breath. 'No, actually. We've... well, we've decided to separate.'

'Don't be so silly,' says Annabel after a moment of shocked silence.

'I'm not being silly, Mum. We've been having counselling for months... at least I have; he hasn't turned up for most of the sessions. But I've known for a while the marriage is over.'

'Come inside and talk about it, darling,' says her father kindly. 'You can't deliver news like that on the doorstep.'

'There's nothing to talk about, Dad. Oh, and you might as well know, as well as having an affair, your precious son-in-law's lost his job too.'

'What?' exclaims Brian.

Laura calls over her shoulder as she walks back to her car. 'Made redundant, along with half his department.'

Annabel and Brian look at one another.

'I don't believe it,' says Annabel.

She pushes past her husband and disappears inside.

'Where are you going?' he calls after her.

'To call Roger,' she shouts back. 'I don't believe any of this.'

Brian calls to Laura. 'Laura, please come in for a moment. I'm worried about you.'

He does sound genuinely concerned, but Laura opens the car door.

'I can't, Dad. We've an appointment with the estate agent in an hour,' she replies. 'But I'll be back this evening. Luke and I would still like to stay overnight, if we may.'

She gets into the car without waiting for an answer, pulls out of the gravelled drive and heads back to the A6.

She's not sure what she's doing. Her life is in freefall, so she's sticking to the last plan she had because at least it's a direction of travel and seems no better or worse than any other. She has relinquished control to the whims of the Fates.

Martin Rush delivered the bombshell some weeks earlier. Roger was devastated but not altogether surprised, and bounced back with impressive speed. He swore Laura to complete secrecy and started making discreet enquiries of his connections about 'openings which might present new challenges'. By then she was clinging to the marriage by her fingernails and had a plan on how she was going to move out.

However, within a week Roger informed her that he'd had a good offer from a firm in Manchester. He was reluctant to leave London but it was tempting because it worked so well financially. The equity in the St John's Wood house should buy them a bigger house in Manchester, with a much more manageable mortgage, and the firm making the offer, although not in the same league as the big City firms, was respected and respectable. As long as he brought a few of his clients, they were offering partnership within a year.

'We'll need somewhere to rent while this sells,' he said, referring to the London house, 'so I can start work up there. Can I leave you to line up some viewings?'

Laura was taken by surprise. She hadn't imagined for a moment that Roger would consider leaving London. It meant abandoning his international clients, the newspaper-worthy deals and all the prestige that went with it. Maybe the Roger she once knew and loved was still inside there, somewhere, after all? All sorts of new possibilities began to occur to her, and for a while she was no longer sure of her course. Maybe a fresh start could make all the difference? Her parents still lived in Bakewell, Derbyshire, about an hour's drive from Manchester, and although she didn't want to live close by them, at that distance they could be properly involved in Luke's life, which they'd never been before.

Perhaps it's a sign? she thought.

She found herself being more affectionate with Roger and he commented on how her mood had lifted. The more she thought about it, the more she convinced herself that moving away, a fresh start, was all they needed to get the marriage back on track. London felt jaded, spoiled by the demands of Roger's work, the grinding need to service a mortgage with monthly interest rate hikes, and his affairs. Moving north would also release her from membership of the group she'd secretly named the 'Lunching Ladies', a clique of Roger's partners' wives whom she was expected to see at least once a week and who bored her to tears. Finally, it should also ensure that the affair with Jennifer Smith was definitely over.

She would need to speak to Brigitta, persuade her to move with them, but she was reasonably confident she could manage that. The two women were more than employer and employee now; they were friends. If she could be persuaded to leave London with them, Laura could start looking for work at the same time. Like Roger, she was probably a little over-qualified for the provinces, but there must surely be a job for an ex-Civil Service statistician somewhere in Manchester?

Her tentative optimism lasted a fortnight. Then, while Roger was in the shower one evening, she saw his open briefcase at the foot of the bed. She'd never really carried through her threat to monitor his contact with Jennifer Smith. In essence, she was too trusting. Roger seemed more engaged with her and Luke so, after a while, she'd stopped looking for clues. But poking out of a sheaf of documents was the corner of a lavender-coloured envelope; a pretty envelope; an envelope which, she knew instantly, had come from neither a client nor another lawyer. It had already been opened.

As Roger hummed in the shower, she took it out of his briefcase.

Inside was a week-old letter from Jennifer Smith declaring her undying love for him, referring to a recent meeting between them and begging him not to leave London. The letter ended with an ill-defined threat that if he left her she 'couldn't see any way of carrying on.' Although she knew it was completely illogical, she studied the handwriting, comparing it to her memory of her dead sister's hand. Jenny's elegant writing was always being praised by her teachers, but this Jennifer Smith wrote in big rounded letters, as if she were a child. So, it was, after all, just a coincidence. Nonetheless Laura couldn't completely banish the suspicion that there *must* have been more to it than that. Did Roger choose this woman with whom to have an affair out of some subconscious desire to hurt Laura?

Laura couldn't tell from the letter's contents if the affair was continuing or not, but one thing was clear: Roger had lied when insisting he'd had no further contact with her. They'd met, at least once, and very recently.

She folded the letter carefully, replaced it in the envelope, slid it back into the briefcase between the work documents and carried on as before. She needed time to think.

She knew now that the marriage was over – she would never

trust him again – but if she immediately demanded a divorce she doubted he'd move out of London, and she was certain of one thing only: she wanted to get out of the capital. Roger would want to stay where he had friends and contacts, and that would make sharing care of Luke almost impossible. A poor excuse for a father even when living in the same household as his son, at two hundred miles distant Roger would, she was sure, disappear from Luke's life altogether. For her son's sake Laura would do everything possible to avoid that.

She was also clear-sighted enough to think about the money. Selling the St John's Wood house should release enough for them each to have their own home if they looked outside London, where property was much cheaper. On the other hand, if he stayed in the capital, she'd have to fight for enough to get her own accommodation.

So she resolved to say nothing until he accepted the Manchester job and the St John's Wood house was sold, or at least under offer.

This sort of calculation was not in Laura's nature, and she was uncomfortable with the realisation that she could be as devious as her husband, but she had to focus on Luke, and he needed a secure home. She also wanted to leave Roger with enough to pay maintenance, at least until she found work; if he bought in Manchester and was reasonably sensible, the figures would work. They'd not enjoy the sort of lifestyle they were used to, but it would work.

The day before their planned weekend of house hunting, a week after Roger accepted the new job, he announced they had an offer for their house at the asking price.

That was Laura's moment.

She told him she had seen the letter from Jennifer Smith and that she would be seeking a divorce. She refused to discuss it further, spent the night in the spare room and left early with

Luke the following morning. She called the estate agents from a service station to tell them to thin out the viewings; she was now only interested in the smaller properties, at the cheap end of the range.

'Where are we?' asks Luke, waking and rubbing the sleep from his eyes.

The road atlas is still clutched in his hands. He loves maps and understood them intuitively from the first time he was shown one. Now whenever he is taken out in the car, he insists he has a map – the *London A–Z* for local trips and a large road atlas for longer journeys.

'Just left Buxton.'

'Did I miss Grandma and Grandpa?'

'Yes. I'm sorry, but we had no time to stop. You'll see them later. Now, can you see where we are?'

He looks out of his window, notes a road sign and scans the atlas, turning the page. Laura watches in the rear-view mirror as his chubby finger carefully follows a line on the map.

'Yes. We stay on the A6 for... ten miles.'

'Copy that, navigator.'

'Over and out, captain,' he replies, yawning.

Laura snatches a further glance at Luke. He is reading signposts and following their progress on the map. He seems perfectly normal but, with Luke, appearances are often deceptive.

They had the 'talk' on the long drive up. Laura hadn't wanted the discussion about the divorce while she was driving and Luke was in the rear seat. She wanted to be available to hold his hand, to cuddle and reassure him. But he raised the topic, and she shouldn't have been surprised. If Laura ever wanted to know what was going on in Luke's life, or in his head, she only needed to take him on a good long car journey. He always talked most freely in the car. It was like therapy on a psychiatrist's couch, she thought; one could speak more candidly to a disembodied voice, when not looking into the listener's face.

They had been driving for over an hour when, out of the blue, Luke piped up.

'Dad's not going to live with us, is he?'

'What makes you say that?' she answered, trying to keep her voice light.

'You've not been friends for ages. And I heard you crying last night.'

'Was I crying?'

'Yes. Dad was shouting at you because you couldn't forgive him and you were moving out with me. Then you went to the spare room.'

She paused. 'I'm going to turn off so we can talk properly,' she said, scanning the road ahead for somewhere convenient.

'No. It's okay. I think it'll be better.'

Laura felt as if someone had punched a fist into her chest and squeezed her heart. How much had Luke overheard? They had been careless, thoughtless! And how much hurt must he be carrying, all alone, to think it would be better if his parents didn't live together?

'But will Dad come up here too?' he asked.

'I'm going to pull off...' she repeated.

'No!' shouted Luke. 'I don't want to talk about it! I just want to know if Dad's coming, even if he doesn't live with us.'

'Yes, he's coming. I promise.'

'Good.'

'You know none if this is your fault, don't you, Luke? Daddy and I both love you very, very much. We always will. It's just that...'

'You don't love each other.'

'No. Not the way we did, anyway. Daddy'll always be my friend.'

'Really?' said Luke, disbelieving. 'You didn't sound like friends.'

'Of course we are. We share the most important thing in the entire world.'

'What's that?'

'You!'

And there the conversation ended. Laura tried to reopen it, but Luke wouldn't respond. They did eventually stop for petrol and wees and she was able to give him a long hug then, but he had withdrawn into himself.

Luke is an unusually sensitive and thoughtful boy. Laura knows that he will process it in his own time. What he needs is for her to continue to reassure him and to be especially affectionate, while remaining vigilant and available when he does want to talk.

They are now driving through Chapelhill. They come to the crossroads and Laura pulls into the side of the road. She leafs through the estate agent's particulars on the passenger seat.

'Here it is. "Turn left at the village store",' she reads. 'Very useful. It depends which way you're coming.' She looks about her. 'All right,' she says, setting off again, 'let's try this one.'

The road winds its way up the hill and the further Laura proceeds, the more sure she is they've taken a wrong turn. The carriageway gets narrower and more potholed. They suddenly find themselves at the entrance to a large estate with a sign saying 'Windyridge'. Laura pulls over and turns off the ignition.

'Can I have the map for a moment?' she asks, turning to Luke.

Under the trees it is difficult to see any landmarks. She gets out with the atlas and the property details, walks to a barred gate in a dry-stone wall and looks down.

Before her is a breathtaking view. Three-quarters of the compass are spread out below, an undulating patchwork plain in shades of greens and blues, from which the hill she stands on rises abruptly. To the north is another hill, a twin of the one they have just driven up. To the west is a suggestion of more high ground, but the hazy blue merges imperceptibly with the sky and Laura is not sure if she imagines it. In the valley below is a river, a glinting thread of silver far beneath them, and the sides of the hills are grazed by sheep, flecks of white on a lush green carpet. The village of Chapelhill lies across the river at the foot of the valley.

Luke joins her and climbs the lowest bar of the gate.

'I see what we did,' says Laura. 'There are two hills, and we went up the wrong one. But look at that!' she says, pointing to the hill on the opposite side of the valley. 'Got to be a first in the history of estate agency.'

'What?'

'The truth. Here, the estate agent's details,' she explains, pointing to the top of a page. 'We really are looking at a village that "nestles in a fold in the hills".'

A hawk circles below them and they watch it until it stoops out of sight. An updraft of air, smelling faintly of grass and slurry, causes Laura to shiver despite the heat.

'Come on,' she says. 'Now we *are* late. We have to go back down the hill and up the other one.'

A new Austin is parked in front of the property at the end of The Rise when they arrive. Laura and Luke get out of the car and walk round to the front of the building.

'Gosh, isn't this pretty?' says Laura, looking down towards the lake.

She sees a young man wearing a suit and holding a clipboard standing beside two adjacent front doors, one green and one blue. He has Brylcreemed hair plastered to an oddly small head and dark shining eyes that seem slightly too close together.

Laura and Luke approach him.

'Mrs Stone?'

'Mrs Flint,' corrects Laura.

The young man looks at his clipboard. 'Oh, quite right,' he acknowledges.

'I know I am,' says Laura, smiling.

The estate agent tries again. 'Apologies. I'm Simon Cartwright,' he says.

'Sorry we're late, Mr Cartwright. We got a little lost.'

'Not to worry,' replies the estate agent.

He turns to the two front doors.

'It's the blue one, Magnolia Cottage,' he says as he fiddles with a set of keys.

'Have the previous tenants already moved out?' asks Laura, seeing through the windows into empty rooms.

'It's been empty for quite a while actually, but the owner's local and has continued to maintain it.'

He manages to get the door open and leads the way into the house.

'Is there a magnolia tree?' asks Laura.

Cartwright looks around. 'Why? Oh, "Magnolia". Doesn't look like it.'

He gives a very quick tour round the house, looking at his watch twice while doing so. He explains that the room with the range and Butler sink is a kitchen and the one with a bath is a bathroom, but Laura doesn't heed his pointless patter.

From the moment she crossed the threshold, she knew. She walks round the house in a state of tension, waiting for the awful room, the frightful aspect, the unacceptable smell – any one of the logical or illogical things that would tell her the house is unsuitable – but it doesn't happen. Each room is perfect, as if the cottage was waiting for *them*. The very first house they've viewed! It has to be Fate, she tells herself.

'Do you like it?' she whispers to Luke.

He nods enthusiastically. 'Yes. But Dad won't.'

'Why's that?'

Luke avoids her gaze. 'Can I go outside?' he says.

Laura's first instinct is to press for an answer but instead she replies, 'Yes. Stay close to the house.'

He runs downstairs and out of the front door.

'It's thirty-nine pounds, eleven and six per month,' Cartwright is saying. 'Would you want any of the furniture?'

'No, thank you. Will that be a problem?'

'Not at all,' answers the young man. 'The landlord will arrange for it to be removed if you prefer.'

'Thank you. We have our own furniture. By the way, I looked at the map. Am I right: the school's about a mile away?'

'The infant school, yes. After age eleven they go to Glossop. The bus goes from outside Dodds'.'

'Isn't eleven a bit young to go on the bus?'

Cartwright shrugs. 'All the kids use it. It's a public bus, but very safe, not like London. The Catholic school in Glossop is the best in t'borough. Everyone goes there. They actually take kids from age five.'

'Is it only for Catholics?' asks Laura.

'Oh no. There are a lot of Catholic families in the Chapelhill area, but we're not, and me kid brothers all went there. That's where most youngsters go after the village school.'

Laura looks down from the bedroom window into the back garden. It seems as if it might once have been an orchard, as it's dotted with apple trees, but they are now gnarled islands in a sea of tall grasses, weeds and overgrown shrubs. The space stands in complete contrast to the adjoining garden, the other half of the semi, which has been tamed. It is clearly a work in progress, but some of the trees have been felled and others pruned back and there are new flowerbeds. The beds are half empty; small shrubs, many with their labels still attached, alternate with patches of freshly-tilled soil, but there are areas already bright with daffodils, purple crocuses and white hyacinths.

Somebody knows what they're doing.

Only then does she see that the adjoining garden is occupied. Sitting at a wooden table with her back to her is a young woman in a heavy knitted jumper reading a book.

'Can you tell me anything about the neighbours?' she asks.

The greasy-haired estate agent looks down and grins. 'That one? Only village gossip.'

'Gossip?'

'She lives wi' 'er baby, but no husband. There never was, if you take my meaning.'

Laura looks again at the woman but she remains still, her back to the onlookers. Laura only knows one woman with a child born out of wedlock, a friend of a friend, who lived a rather bohemian life in Camden Town. Her parents would be scandalised, she knows, but the issue of illegitimacy is so far removed from Laura's conventional, middle-class existence, she's never addressed much thought to it.

'I'm sure she's very nice,' she says, instinctively coming to the defence of the woman reading. 'Attitudes are changing, you know.'

'I 'spect they are, down south,' says Cartwright in his Yorkshire accent, 'but not up 'ere. Seen enough? We need to get cracking if I'm to show you t'other one.'

He taps the other property particulars clipped to his board.

'Can you give me a moment?' says Laura, and she goes downstairs and out through the open front door.

Luke is running towards her through knee-length grass.

'It's got a river!' he shouts breathlessly. 'And a little lake at the bottom with a swing over it!'

She bends to his level. 'You like it then?'

'And apple trees – look!' He takes out several wormy apples from his pockets and shows her. 'And conker trees! It's brilliant! Can we take it?'

'There's another one to see after this, and somewhere tomorrow.'

'They'll never be better than this one,' he replies confidently.

Laura silently agrees with him.

'Sure?' she asks.

She's not sure how much to trust this enthusiasm. The excitement of an eight-year-old boy when presented with a stream, a lake and a tyre swing will eclipse most things for a while, even divorcing parents.

'Sure!' he says, and he scampers off towards the back of the house.

Cartwright is locking the front door. He turns.

'Well?'

'We'll take it.'

'Won't Mr Flint want to see it before you agree?'

'No. We'll follow you to the office, and I'll write you a cheque for a holding deposit.'

Cartwright frowns, doubtful, and then shrugs.

'If you say so.'

Chapter Nine

JANINE

March unfolds with gentle rains and warmer than average temperatures. The buds on the surrounding trees burst into delicate fresh-minted leaves; the flowers and shrubs that Janine planted in the back garden sprout new growth; and daffodils paint a blaze of yellow along the path leading to the front door. Inside Apple Tree Cottage, Bobby thrives and gains weight as Janine heals and recovers her strength. Today she plans to cycle with Bobby to Windyridge for the first time since her maternity leave began.

For weeks she wrestled with the problem of how she was going to return to work. Bobby was an easy, good-natured baby who slept a lot, so Janine, in an optimism born of inexperience, was confident she could still get quite a lot done in Lady Margaret's gardens even if she had to stop every now and then. The pressing problem, as Janine saw it, was transport. She couldn't take Bobby on the trike and she had neither a driving licence nor means to pay for either a vehicle or lessons.

Matters came to a head when Bobby was about four weeks old. Lady Margaret asked to visit the cottage to make the acquaintance of its new occupant. Janine put her off several times but, in the end, had no choice but to acquiesce.

She made a pot of tea while Lady Margaret cooed over Bobby, and all seemed to go well. As the old lady and her companion were about to depart, Janine spotted Miss Chivers giving her employer pointed glances. After some embarrassed hesitation, Lady Margaret wondered out loud if it was, after all, going to be possible for Janine to continue working. How would she manage? Perhaps, confessed Lady Margaret, they had been a little over-optimistic about how it would all work. She left the comment hanging.

That evening Janine remembered her employer's suggestion that she might be able to connect a trailer to the tricycle. She spent until midnight at the kitchen table with a pencil and a pad of paper. After a number of sketched attempts, she came up with the design for a four-wheeled trailer and a method of connecting it to the rear axle of the tricycle. The next day she took it to the garage in the village and timidly showed it to the mechanic. She knew he had a sideline in repairing farm machinery; could he make something like this? The man wasn't sure but his father, who'd recently retired, said he thought it might be an interesting challenge. He'd see what he could come up with.

Three weeks later father and son delivered the trailer, complete with a sprung box with a cushioned seat, securely fixed in a semi-reclining position to the trailer base. They were very proud of it. They had even thought of restraints for its tiny occupant: webbing belts cut from a parachute harness.

Janine wraps Bobby up in so many layers of clothing that she resembles a miniature Michelin Man, pulls her woollen hat over her head and straps her into the harness. The seat is angled so Bobby can see the back of Janine's shoulders and head but also has a view of the sky. Once settled, she doesn't complain.

Janine sets off. She has deliberately not warned Lady Margaret of the visit. She needs to try the journey first.

She cycles through the gates into the rear gardens at Windyridge, out of breath, but delighted. Lady Margaret is in the garden, kneeling in front of a flowerbed with a trowel in her hand. When she hears the trike approaching, she turns.

'Hello, hello, hello!' she booms happily.

She struggles off her arthritic knees and hurries across.

'Amazing!' she exclaims, walking around the trike and trailer. 'How ingenious!'

'It was your idea, Lady Margaret, remember?' says Janine, shyly. 'The first day I came here.'

'I do indeed remember. And how was it, the journey up?'

'I had to get off and push for the last bit of the hill,' replies Janine, unfastening Bobby's harness, 'but I'll get used to it. And Bobby seemed to enjoy it.'

Chivers emerges from the house and comes over. As usual the woman says nothing, but she is smiling.

'May I?' asks Lady Margaret, holding out her hands to Bobby.

'Of course.'

The old lady lifts Bobby out and hugs her close.

'Don't you smell wonderful!' she says softly. 'Baby and fresh air. They should bottle it.' She closes her eyes and spends a second inhaling Bobby's scent, and then moves off towards the house, Bobby still in her arms. Chivers scurries after her.

'You will stop for a cup of tea, won't you?' she calls to Janine over her shoulder. 'You know,' she adds, addressing Chivers, 'I think there may be some boxes of toys still up in the loft. We should have a look.'

Thus was set the pattern. From that day on, whenever Bobby arrives at Windyridge, the two old ladies compete to look after her. They squabble over who is to heat her milk; how one spends longer playing with her on the lounge floor than the other; even whose turn it is to change her nappy. After the first week Lady Margaret gets down an old cot that has been gathering dust in the attic for a generation, and toys and clothing start to appear in the household. It seems to Janine that almost every other day Lady Margaret finds something in one of the local shops for Bobby that she 'simply couldn't resist'.

Janine finds that she is able to work almost uninterrupted. Lady Margaret and Chivers are energised by having a baby to coddle and fight over her when she wakes, and Bobby soon grows accustomed to being passed from one old lady to the other. She has acquired two grandmothers.

'We forgot what it was like to have young people in our lives,' confides Chivers to Janine one day. It is the first time Janine can remember the sour companion ever speaking to her directly and she interprets it as an apology.

Lady Margaret has given Janine the afternoon off. Bobby has a rash on her face. Janine was not much concerned by it but Lady Margaret insisted that it be looked at by the village doctor.

The doctor was reassuring. As Janine guessed, Bobby has a teething rash which, the doctor confirmed, could come on weeks or even months before teeth actually erupt. Nothing to worry about, he said, and it explained why Bobby, normally a very placid child, had been a bit grizzly for the last couple of days.

Janine cycles home and puts the child down for her afternoon sleep, unexpectedly finding herself with the rest of the afternoon free. She returns to the task that has occupied her for the last two weekends.

On clearing the knee-length weeds and grass in the garden behind Apple Tree Cottage some weeks earlier, she discovered that there must indeed have been a herb garden situated under the kitchen window. However, the position was wrong. A self-seeded rowan tree was growing out of the garden wall, and she saw that, once fully in leaf, it would cast too much shadow on that area. Herbs require six to eight hours of direct sunshine in the growing season. She considered but rejected the idea of cutting the young tree down – it was beautiful and healthy – and decided instead to move the herb garden. She created a new bed in an area that was not overshadowed and then, one by one, carried stones from the orchard's collapsed walls into the back garden to form a low wall around it.

It is this task on which she is still engaged, and it is proving much more difficult than she imagined. She only wants three courses in height, but constructing the wall requires an enormous amount of trial and error. She has to try multiple blocks in each position to find stones that fit together and are stable. Frustratingly, more than once an entire section of wall collapses. The job is taking many hours, and Janine's nails are broken and her knuckles grazed. She has developed a new respect for the skills of dry-stone wallers, for whom it seems so easy.

She has been working for almost an hour when she hears a knock on her front door. She sits back on her haunches.

No one knocks on her door.

She stands and walks quietly through the cottage to the front. In the hallway she stops, ears straining. When the visitor knocks again, louder this time and from only a few inches away, she jumps. She opens the door.

'Yes?' she asks nervously.

A woman in sensible shoes, a severe skirt and a white blouse stands before her. Behind her, parked at the top of The Rise, is a small car. The woman has thin features, a hawkish nose and a mass of auburn hair, coiled tightly in a bun at the back of her head. She wears a lanyard round her neck and carries a leather satchel in her hand and a manila file under one arm.

'Miss Tyler?' she asks. 'Nadine Tyler?'

'Yes?'

'My name's Mary O'Reilly. I'm a social worker,' she says in an Irish accent.

She smiles and holds out her hand. Janine makes to shake it but then remembers that her hands are dirty.

'Sorry,' she says, holding them up to demonstrate. 'How can I help you?'

'Ah, bless you,' says the woman, 'it's how I can help you, sweetheart. May I come in?'

Janine hesitates. 'Well, I am right in the middle of something.'

'I'll be very quick, I promise you that,' says O'Reilly and she takes a step over the threshold.

Janine doesn't want to let this stranger in, but she is crowded into taking a step backwards as O'Reilly comes surging into the hallway. Janine retreats to the kitchen, O'Reilly following her.

'So,' says the social worker, keeping her voice low, 'where is the little one?'

Alarm bells start ringing in Janine's head.

'She's sleeping. What's this about?'

'We just need a wee chat about the baby. You discharged yourself from hospital, and there are forms to complete. Can I sit here?'

Without waiting for a reply, she sits at the kitchen table and starts taking documents out of her satchel.

'I don't suppose I could beg a cup of tea, could I? You're my last call of the day and I've not stopped for a moment. Sure, and I'm parched.'

O'Reilly smiles, her eyes friendly and crinkly, but Janine's sixth sense is telling her not to trust her.

'No, I'm sorry, Mrs...'

'Miss.'

'Miss O'Reilly. Why are you here?'

'Why, there's no reason to be unfriendly. I'm here to help you. The registrar informs me that you didn't register the baby's birth before you discharged yourself. Is that right?'

'I had to go. I was being picked up. It was arranged with the staff nurse.'

'Is that so? Which staff nurse?'

'I don't remember. But I went into Stockport to the registry and registered Bobby there.'

O'Reilly takes out another document from her satchel. 'That's true, you did.'

'Well then? If you know I registered the birth, what's the problem?'

'You didn't include the name of the father.'

'The registrar said it wasn't obligatory.'

'And she was right, but it is normal. So, can you give me his name?' she asks, pen poised.

Janine's heart is now beating like a sledgehammer. She tells herself to remain calm, but she's sure O'Reilly can detect her anxiety. She tries to smile, but her features won't obey and form into a lopsided grimace.

'If the registrar said I didn't have to register the father's name, I don't see why you insist on knowing it.'

'What are you trying to hide, my dear?'

'Nothing at all.'

'Then what's the father's name?'

'William.'

She is about to add 'Tyler' but stops herself.

Janine wishes now that she hadn't given the false name to Lady Margaret – she did it on the spur of the moment, trying to erase her past and evade any pursuit – but it was foolish and a mistake. Then, faced with having to give an official name for Bobby at the hospital, she felt obliged to use Tyler again. The lie is still growing, and seems to have a life of its own.

'So, that's William Tyler?' asks O'Reilly, her pen poised.

'Yes.'

'See, that wasn't hard, was it? Is Mr Tyler in employment?'

Oh, God, do I have to make up an employment history?

'Yes. He's a soldier,' she says, the first occupation that pops into her head. 'In Germany,' she adds, hoping that that additional detail might be sufficient to explain the fictional William's absence.

She watches O'Reilly's fountain pen scratching across the form she is completing, recording faithfully the lies that are surely going to lead to more trouble.

'And what shall I put for the child's religion?' asks O'Reilly, looking up.

The question surprises Janine. 'Why do you need to know that?' she asks.

O'Reilly indicates a section of the document before her. 'It's on the form. It's a standard question.'

Janine frowns. 'I don't know. My mother's Catholic but... I'm not really sure...' She stumbles to a halt, and then an idea occurs to her. 'William's C of E, and we haven't discussed what we're going to do about Bobby's religion.'

'I see.'

O'Reilly stares up at her with watery blue eyes. Time seems to expand like elastic. O'Reilly's scrutiny continues, her gaze unwavering. Janine wills herself to remain still and relaxed.

Finally O'Reilly screws the top back on her pen and stands.

'That's grand. Now, may I see Roberta.'

'Why? She's asleep right now.'

'I need to weigh her and make sure she is reaching her milestones. It's quite normal, dear.'

'No, I'm very sorry, Miss O'Reilly, but it's not convenient. I don't want to wake her. She's not been sleeping well. The doctor said she has a teething rash.'

'She's seen the doctor, has she?'

'Yes, this afternoon. And he weighed her,' lies Janine.

O'Reilly hesitates. Then: 'Very well. I think we can probably leave it, this time.'

She tidies away her papers and reaches into her pocket. She hands a card to Janine.

'That's got my name on it and a phone number where you can contact me.'

'What's Cedars Moral Welfare?' asks Janine, reading.

'I work with them. We help girls.'

Janine frowns. 'Help girls? How?'

'Girls who are struggling to bring up a baby alone.'

'Well, I'm not struggling. And I'm not alone.'

O'Reilly turns her gaze to Janine again. 'If you say so,' she says, but she doesn't sound convinced. 'I'll pop in again, soon.'

'That really won't be necessary. We're managing very well here.' Another thought occurs to her. 'And when William comes home, we'll probably be moving. To wherever he's based then, you understand.'

O'Reilly doesn't reply, but bustles towards the front door. She opens it herself.

'Bye-bye, dear,' she says, without turning round.

Chapter Ten

LAURA

'How am I supposed to drive up from London with the removal men, take Luke to his first day at school, get to the estate agents to collect the keys and be at the cottage ahead of the lorry, all at the same time?' demands Laura.

'I don't see how any of this is my problem, Laura,' replies Roger. 'This is all your doing.'

'No, it's not. The school would like him there for the start of term, and so would I. It's going to be hard enough for him anyway as the new boy. But even if it *was* all my fault, he's still your son, and he's starting a new school where he knows no one. Don't you want to be there to support him?'

'Of course I do, but I've just started a new job and I can't take a day off. At least you have a home to move into, which is more than I do!'

Roger has started work at his new firm in Manchester but has yet to find anywhere to live. In Laura's opinion, it's his own fault for not taking enough time off work to look, but she keeps that to herself. Whatever the cause, Roger has spent the last three weeks in a small hotel in south Manchester during the week, looking at properties in the early evenings and commuting back to London at weekends. He hates it.

'You've got removal men. Just tell them what to do,' he says, and slams the phone down.

Laura replaces the receiver. She remains where she is for a few seconds, calming herself, consciously putting Roger's irritation out of her head.

She wanders through the rooms, taking stock. The house is strange and echoey. All of Roger's stuff is still in place but almost everything that Laura is taking north is boxed up and labelled. She will finish the few remaining items in the morning. The walls look strangely bare without her paintings and prints – the cause of the most bitter row they have had to date.

The large house gives rise to mixed feelings. Formerly a little run-down, the haunt of poets and artists, St John's Wood's gentrification began soon after they moved in. She has to give Roger some credit, she thinks. When it comes to property deals, he has an unerring ability to make money, and the house is selling for much more than they paid for it.

She has grown to love the area; its wide tree-lined streets, handsome properties, good local shops and easy access to the West End's theatres, art galleries and restaurants. She used to love the house itself, too. This was where she and Roger spent their first two or three untroubled years; where she really learned to cook; where they held pretentious but nonetheless hilarious dinner parties and she played hostess every weekend; it was where she learned about sex, and wondered what all the fuss was about. It was where Luke was conceived.

But it is also the place where everything went sour; where she couldn't seem to conceive again; where they rowed constantly; where she was often lonely even before she discovered Roger's faithlessness; where she cried for days; where she felt useless.

Both she and Roger have spoken to Luke, together and separately, and those discussions have gone as well as could be expected. As always, Luke is processing the events in his own quiet, deliberative manner. Laura is proud of his maturity but at the same time finds herself wishing sometimes that he were a more conventional eight-year-old. A few tears and tantrums would at least reveal how he *really* felt and would open a path to communication. As it is, she cannot judge how well he is facing the imminent changes. Her greatest worry is that he is putting on a brave face to prevent *her* further tears. Since learning that he had overheard the last major row between her and Roger and the tears that followed, she has been very careful to be cheerful and upbeat whenever Luke is around, but there have been moments of sadness and short-lived flare-ups of tension between her and Roger – like that last telephone call – which he must have witnessed.

Laura spends her last night at St John's Wood tossing and turning, watching the clock tick away the hours, and fretting about the coming day. Roger was right: it was bonkers to try to move home and have Luke start school the same day, but she was desperate for him to be there for the start of term. Having signed the lease and got him on the roll, she only then realised that the Easter holidays were the most popular time of year to move home. She couldn't find an available removal company. All the established firms were booked up. Eventually she found a company, a small one-lorry outfit, but there was something about the man who came round to estimate that made her uneasy.

She gives up trying to sleep when daylight starts coming through her bedroom windows – her Liberty *Eustacia* print curtains are carefully folded in tissue paper and packed in a box downstairs – and she descends to the kitchen to make sandwiches for the day.

Three uncommunicative removal men arrive at 6:30 am. Before she can open her mouth, they complain that they expected everything to be packed and tell her they have another delivery to do at the Derbyshire end after hers. Flustered, she gives directions as far as she is able while persuading Luke, half asleep, to eat his breakfast, making sure his new school bag is packed and ensuring he has all he needs for a four-hour car journey. Then, with enormous trepidation, she bundles him and two suitcases of essentials into her car and leaves the men to their task. She would have preferred to see them out of the property, but she has to go via the estate agents to collect the keys before the lorry arrives at The Rise.

As she pulls out of the drive, she offers a silent prayer that they will identify the last few marked items correctly and break nothing important. She has informed the school that Luke won't be there in time for registration and they were understanding but, looking at the time, she realises she'll be lucky to arrive much before mid-morning.

Sullen clouds gather like an omen as Laura heads north, and within half an hour it is raining heavily. Driving conditions are poor and traffic is slow. By the time Laura reaches Glossop it has gone eleven and she begins to worry that the removal men will arrive at Magnolia Cottage before her.

She runs into the estate agent's office and collects the keys. Back in the car, lightning rages over black skies and rain drives horizontally at the windscreen. She drives as fast as the conditions will allow over the winding hills to Chapelhill. Visibility is dreadful and she misses the turn to the village school. It takes a further ten minutes of driving around and doubling back on herself before she stumbles on it by accident.

She hurries Luke inside and they wait at reception, water dripping off them, Laura tapping her foot with exasperation. Finally, ten minutes after they arrive, the deputy headmistress approaches to greet them. Luke hasn't met the woman and so Laura makes hasty introductions and rushes off, knowing that she is a terrible mother.

Oh, what a mess! Why did I allow myself to be persuaded that he had to start today?

She arrives at the end of The Rise to find the lorry waiting for her. The unmade road is a quagmire. Laura unlocks the front door to Magnolia Cottage and takes up a position at the foot of the stairs, attempting to direct three delayed, dripping and, by now, discourteous removal men who ignore her and stack chests in ever-widening puddles on the hall floor. By the time one of them slips on the wet threshold, tipping half the contents of a tea chest over the floor and blaming her for not sealing the lid properly, it is all Laura can do to hold back tears of furious frustration. She mumbles something and retreats to the kitchen.

She stares at the rain dripping off the apple trees, breathing deeply to regain her composure. The idea that a removal man, roll-up hanging from his lips and half a hairy backside exposed, could reduce her to tears would once have been laughable.

She blows her nose and gazes at the garden. The tangled patch of waist-length grass has been matted and flattened by the downpour, and the thought of trying to tame it is depressing. She has turned her back on the days of landscape gardeners, decorators and interior designers. It will be back to basics, at least for a while, and that means rolling up sleeves, donning wellingtons, and doing personal battle with the grass. Somewhere at the back of that thicket – or so the slimy Mr Cartwright said – is a stile leading into the field behind, and Laura has a sudden urge to leave the removal men to get on with it, put on her boots, locate the stile and climb the hill. Then she realises that she has no chance of finding her wellington boots in the pile of boxes growing in the hallway. But what about the kettle? That was one of the last things to be packed, and isn't a nice cup of tea the sort of thing that might mollify surly removal men?

She returns to the hallway.

'Would anyone like a cup of tea?' she asks brightly.

Receiving enthusiastic assent, Laura drags a likely box into the kitchen.

Wrong box.

She tries another. Again, the wrong box.

JANINE

On the other side of the hall wall in Apple Tree Cottage, Janine hears the front door banging repeatedly against the wall and tea chests crashing to the floor as the removal men traipse in and out. She is in a state of near-panic.

Neighbours! I've got new neighbours! This is going to be impossible! Why didn't Lady M warn me?

The volume of noise, especially in her hallway, astonishes her. It's as if the walls were made of cardboard. She lived with such sounds for almost twenty years in Hulme, both resenting and envying the lives being lived on the far side of the thin skin of brick. All the things she was denied; laughter, play, arguments, even television programmes. She can't go back to that. She won't. She and Bobby will have to find somewhere else to live.

But where?

There is little or no housing in the area that she could afford.

Stockport, maybe?

She has cycled into and out of Stockport on many occasions. There are some nice bits, but she wouldn't be looking there. She might be able to afford a room, perhaps two, in some of the rougher areas, where redevelopment is still some way off. Not quite as bad as the slums of Hulme, but not far removed: narrow terraced streets with everyone living on top of one another. No, she can't go back to that. There are some new tower blocks being built in the town centre, and maybe she could afford to rent somewhere there, but that would mean no garden, not to mention an hour's journey each way to Windyridge in heavy traffic. In any case they are still shrouded in contractors' sheeting and scaffolding, unfinished.

While Laura empties boxes, Janine loads Bobby into the trailer and cycles up Burnham Hill, fuming and desperate.

'But have you spoken to Mrs Flint?' asks Lady Margaret after Janine barges into her kitchen, Bobby in her arms and rain streaming down her face.

'No. Why would I want to speak to her? That's the last thing I want to do! I need to be on my own. I don't want someone living on top of me, listening to everything I do, watching me coming and going!'

'But she may be lovely! She's on her own too, I gather, with a little boy. You might become friends.'

'I don't want a friend,' replies Janine childishly. 'I don't have friends!'

Janine hears herself utter the sentence, and it stops her in her tracks.

What's happened to Nadine?

Where, when she needs her, is the strong, independent woman she was determined to become? The Nadine who was going to avoid the mistakes made by Mother? In that moment Janine feels all her gains of the last months slipping from her grasp. She searches inside herself for the inner belief, the determination that got her to Chapel Hill and then through childbirth all on her own. She can't locate it.

She shakes her head as if to throw out the fear and confusion raging within.

Lady Margaret is still talking. 'I'm really sorry, my dear. I should have warned you. But we have no choice. The roof cost thousands, and now we have those awful mushroom things growing on the beams in the cellar. The estate agents have been on at me for years to let both properties, and I can't afford to leave the other one empty. I know you value your privacy, but there's no reason to assume that Mrs Flint is going to disturb you.'

'But I can hear everything through the walls!' shouts Janine.

'Well, I'm sure it's at its worst today, while she's moving in. I can't help thinking you're panicking unnecessarily,' says Lady Margaret, her tone softening, 'but then I don't know what may have happened to you before you came here' – she sees Janine's expression – 'and I'm not asking.'

But Janine is too upset to listen. She rushes out of the house and cycles back to Chapel Hill.

LAURA

Laura has cleaned inside the grubby kitchen cabinets and unloaded the contents of four boxes into them, but she has still found no method of boiling water. She is halfway through the next, which turns out to contain mostly Luke's toys, when she hears a cough behind her. She turns to find the removal men in the kitchen doorway looking pleased and unprecedentedly deferential.

'All done,' says one, his sodden cap in his hands dripping onto the floor.

Laura frowns. Has this one been with them throughout?

She doesn't recognise him. It's the first time he's smiled, she concludes. That's it. She looks at the others.

How ghastly. They're all smiling.

'Good. All the boxes stacked in the hall, yes?'

'Yup.'

There is a moment's pause.

'Thank you. Well, I'm really sorry I couldn't find the kettle. I'm sorry too that I kept you waiting. But I shan't hold you up any further,' says Laura with a brisk smile.

The leader's grin slips somewhat. 'We could unpack a few, if you like, before we go.'

Laura has actually paid for a full unpacking service, but having seen their performance so far there is no way she is going to let these men loose on her tablecloths and bedlinen.

'No, that's fine. Don't you worry about it. I paid in advance, so… cheerio.'

Their faces resume their more familiar sourness. There is an uncomfortable silence. The men look at one another and file out.

That's better, thinks Laura. *They must have been so uncomfortable with all that smiling; it really didn't suit them.*

Only then does it occur to her that perhaps they were waiting for the customary 'Here's something to get yourselves a drink'. She realises she hasn't heard the front door close.

Are they still there, in the hall, muttering to one another?

She steps around the boxes, feeling in her jacket pocket for her purse, but they have gone, leaving the door swinging in the wind. The lorry is pulling away, disappearing down the hill. She closes the door.

She surveys the jumble in front of her and looks at her watch. Luke has to be collected in twenty-five minutes. Then she sees that the box directly before her, its lid scattered elsewhere, has a kettle on top.

'Tea,' she announces to herself. 'Tea first.'

Her stomach grumbles loudly and she remembers that she'd better eat something too. She rummages around for a mug. She thinks for a moment that the tea must be in a different box, but after some further digging she finds it and a packet of water biscuits. She looks inside to discover only one left. She laughs at her idiocy in bringing a single biscuit all the way from London, fills the kettle, plugs it in and switches it on, the stale water biscuit held between her lips. Jumper next, she promises herself, because she is freezing.

As she passes it, she reaches over to feel the kettle from which no sound is coming. Still stone-cold. The little red light is not illuminated. She flicks the switch on and off a few times. She unplugs the kettle and tries another socket. Still nothing.

'Oh, God. Really?'

She pauses, wondering if she was ever told the position of the fuse box. Probably not. Anyway, if she packed any fuses from home, she'll never find them. Then another thought occurs to her. She tries the light switch. Nothing. No lights in the kitchen nor the hall. So it's not just the ring main; there's no power in the house. No wonder it's so cold.

She is interrupted by the abrupt hiss of air brakes from outside, followed immediately by a clatter and a crash. Laura looks through the lounge window to see that the removal lorry has returned. It has backed to the end of The Rise and from its open doors at the rear, two of the men are in the process of lifting a wooden chest. They each have hold of a rope handle and are swinging the box back and forth, back and forth, gathering momentum, until with one last effort they let go. It flies up into the rain and describes a parabola before crashing heavily on the road surface, sending a muddy splash high in the air.

'Hey! You bastards!' cries Laura, running into the hall.

By the time she has the front door open the lorry is already disappearing again down the hill. One of the men waves mockingly at her as the lorry drops out of sight. Laura runs towards the chest, her expensively unsuitable shoes splashing mud and water up her legs.

She reaches the chest, and groans. It's the wooden linen box that contains all her most valuable personal possessions, greetings cards that hold sentimental value, family photographs, her wedding dress; years of accumulated and irreplaceable memories. The box was the first item loaded onto the lorry and was evidently missed when the men departed.

She attempts to lift one end, but it's useless. Even intact it would be too heavy for her to lift on her own, and she now notices that one of the rope handles is lying in a puddle some feet away, still attached to the end panel, and the planks making up the floor of the box have separated.

Laura collapses to her knees and starts to cry, not genteel weeping, but howls of released anxiety and despair, as she tries desperately to repack the box.

JANINE

Janine watches from the front window as her unwelcome neighbour kneels in the mud, crying, lifting sodden and ruined treasures out of the puddles. She knows that, whether she wants a neighbour or not, she has to help.

'I won't be a sec,' she calls to Bobby, and she opens the door and runs out into the storm.

The woman doesn't appear to hear her approach. She looks up sharply as Janine crouches next her, fright on her face. Janine realises how she must look with her duffel coat hood pulled low over her face and her eyes obscured by rain-spattered glasses. She shakes her hood back and smiles.

'Let me help you,' she says.

'Who are you? Where have you come from?' sobs the crying woman.

'Next door. I'm Janine, your neighbour. Come on, if you take one end, we should be able to carry it inside.'

'Thanks. It's very nice of you to help. I'm Laura,' she says, sniffing.

They each take an end of the box and manage to get it into their arms and off the ground, but they have barely travelled three paces when the base hinges away from them, completely detaching from two of the three remaining sides.

'Oh no!' cries Laura.

She lowers her end, trying to get it to the ground before everything falls out, but it's hopeless. The box is disintegrating in their hands. They each manage to grab a few items as they fall, but most land in the water.

'Leave the chest, just collect the things,' instructs Janine. 'It'll only take a few trips.'

With that she collects an armful of items and runs towards Laura's open door. Laura follows suit, still crying.

They run back and forth four times each. On her last trip, Laura leaves Janine still crouched in the mud, her hand wiping across the surface of the road, feeling for something. Laura dumps her last load on the hall floor.

'Yes!' exclaims Janine, lifting her hand in triumph. She runs back and meets Laura at the door. 'Here,' she says, and places in Laura's open palm two muddy pearl earrings. 'I caught one as that box of jewellery fell, and I thought I saw another in the water. I've found it.'

'Oh, thank you so much! They're not valuable, but they

were my grandmother's. I'd have hated to lose them. Is there anything else still out there?'

'I don't think so, but there may be one or two small items underwater. Also, my glasses are so wet, it's impossible to see clearly.'

They are interrupted by the sound of crying from the open doorway of Apple Tree Cottage.

'You have a baby,' says Laura. It is half question, half statement.

'Yes, hang on,' replies Janine, turning back to her door. She reappears in Laura's hall a moment later, a chubby blonde baby in her arms. 'I'll let you get on,' she says. 'Have you got candles?'

'Candles?' asks Laura, puzzled.

'Yes. We're having a power cut,' says Janine.

'Of course we are. Why wouldn't we? Silly me. Just when I thought the day couldn't get any worse.'

'Well? Do you have any?'

'Candles? Yes. I mean no. Well, probably, but I'm not sure I could find–' begins Laura. She slaps her forehead, and scrabbles under her sleeve for her watch. 'Oh my! Luke! My son! I have to collect him from school!'

'In the village? The road's like a river all the way down.'

'But it's gone half past! He'll be waiting in the rain. His first day, and no one to pick him up.'

'Is that your car?' asks Janine, pointing towards the road.

'Yes, but I'm not sure I can find the school. I got lost on the way there.'

'It's simple. Listen,' says Janine, and she starts giving directions but she can see that Laura is too distressed to take them in. 'Come on,' she says, reaching a decision. 'I'll show you.'

'Really? Thank you!'

Laura pats her pockets to make sure she has both house and car keys and pulls the door shut. Janine reaches to the adjoining door and, with Bobby still in her arms, closes it. She follows Laura to a small car parked amid the puddles.

'You know your lights are on, don't you?' she says. Laura whirls round, looking back at the house. 'No,' clarifies Janine, 'the car lights.'

Laura looks and sees that the headlights of the car are indeed still on, but they look ominously pale.

'I had them on when driving through the rain. I must have forgotten to turn them off. God, it's been hours!'

She opens the driver's door, sits in the seat, inserts the ignition key, closes her eyes and turns her wrist. There is a click followed by an exhausted cough as the remaining power in the battery fails to turn the engine over. She tries again with no better result. She looks up at Janine.

'What am I going to do?' she asks despairingly. She appears completely defeated.

'How old is your son?' asks Janine, leaning into the car.

'Eight, why?'

'And can you ride a bike?'

'I used to, years ago.'

'Well, it's a trike, actually, and you're welcome to use it. It's downhill all the way, so you'll be there in five minutes, and your son can stand on the bar at the back and hold on to your shoulders.'

'A trike?'

'Look,' says Janine and points back to the trike in the garden, just visible under a tarpaulin.

'I don't think I could ride it for the first time in this weather, on roads I don't know at all. And I'm still not sure where the school is.'

'It'll take you twenty minutes to walk it, especially in this downpour.'

LAURA

Laura wants to scream.

It's just too much! This is so unfair! How can everything go so wrong?

'Do you want me to get him?' asks Janine.

What? She's offering to collect Luke, on her own?

Laura shakes her head doubtfully. 'You? He doesn't know you. He'll be frightened.'

And I don't know you either.

Laura finds herself suddenly the object of intense scrutiny by the bedraggled young woman. There is a long pause as the rain lashes the car roof.

'Okay,' says Janine, evidently coming to a decision. 'You take Bobby,' she says. 'It's the logical solution. While I ride down, ring the school and warn them I'm on my way.'

Laura opens her mouth to protest.

How can this complete stranger expect me to let her fetch Luke? And what sort of mother offers her baby to a stranger in exchange?

But then she thinks again.

But how can I not trust her? When she's prepared to leave her baby with me.

'Okay then,' says Laura, uncertainly. 'I'll have to use your phone, though, as ours won't be connected 'til tomorrow.'

'It's in the kitchen, at the back. Here's the key. The number will be under Greenfield in the book beneath the telephone.'

Janine hands Bobby to Laura and strides back to the garden. She disconnects the trailer, pulls the tarpaulin back over it, and climbs onto the wet trike seat.

'Won't be long,' she says. 'What's his name... your son?'

'Luke!'

'Oh, yes, you said,' says Janine, and she pedals quickly out of the garden and away down the hill.

Bobby in her arms, Laura opens her neighbour's front door, flips the latch so it will open when Janine returns, and walks along the corridor towards the rear of the house. Initially the child seems completely at ease but, as she realises that she can't see her mother, she starts craning her neck, seeking her. She begins to whimper.

'Just a second... just a second,' says Laura distractedly as she locates the telephone book and looks up the number.

As she waits for the phone at the other end to be picked up, Laura pulls faces and plays peekaboo with the child. Bobby, distracted, relaxes.

The deputy headmistress answers. Laura has already forgotten her name, but she apologises profusely, explains that there have been problems with the removal men, promises that she is, in fact, extremely reliable despite all evidence to the contrary and says Janine is on her way. The teacher is definitely huffy. She makes it plain that they expect children to be picked up promptly; teachers are not paid overtime to babysit beyond school hours, are they? She explains brusquely that all the other children have already been collected, and that Laura has no idea of the manifold duties required of staff after the school bell rings. She actually says 'manifold', and a corner of Laura's mind is pleased that one of her son's teachers is both strict and has such a good vocabulary.

Laura apologises whenever she is able to interrupt the teacher's flow, expecting Luke to be expelled or, at the very least, for her to be given lines.

I shall not keep staff waiting. I shall not keep staff waiting.

Finally, the woman decides Laura has been sufficiently scolded and agrees to wait for Janine to arrive.

Laura hangs up. Her ears are burning, but she is extremely relieved.

She looks at the placid child in her arms. Bobby regards her gravely with wide-open eyes. Laura is mildly surprised that the child seems so comfortable with a total stranger but then, she reminds herself, Luke was similar; he just trusted people.

'Well, Bobby, we should be introduced,' says Laura, sighing, and feeling calmer than she has in several hours. 'How do you do? I'm Laura.'

By way of reply, Bobby smiles at her, a great wide gummy smile.

'Oh! That's the nicest thing anyone has said to me all day!' says Laura, and she hugs her neighbour's baby to her, feeling a lot better.

She looks up and out of the kitchen window at the back garden. The rain seems to have stopped as suddenly as it started, and there are patches of blue in the sky.

'Your garden is so lovely,' she murmurs. 'Did Mummy do all that by herself?'

Laura pulls out a kitchen chair. She starts rocking Bobby gently in her arms and playing This Little Piggy with her chubby little fingers.

A few minutes later the front door bursts open and Luke runs through it, followed by Janine. He bounds up to Laura, a half-eaten biscuit in his hand.

'That was brilliant! What a great bike! We went really fast, and I stood on the bar at the back.'

He gives Laura a hug.

'I'm so sorry I wasn't there,' says Laura. 'The removal men forgot a box and just threw it into the road. The lady...'

Laura stalls, having forgotten her neighbour's name.

'Nadine,' says Luke.

'Yes, she helped me pick everything up.'

Janine enters the kitchen. She too is eating a biscuit, and Laura can see the packet protruding from her duffel coat pocket. Janine catches her line of sight and takes out the packet, putting it on the table. Fig rolls, favourites from Laura's childhood.

'Help yourself,' says Janine, slipping out of her wet coat. 'I carry a packet around with me the whole time. Ever since I fell pregnant.'

She holds her arms out and Laura hands Bobby over.

'Oh, the hunger! Yes, I remember that,' agrees Laura. 'It comes on so quickly–'

'And if you let it go on even a tiny bit too long, you feel sick.'

'Exactly.'

'Please, help yourself. Have a couple,' offers Janine.

'Thank you,' says Laura, taking two biscuits.

She now has an opportunity to examine her neighbour properly for the first time. She is in her early twenties, much younger than Laura imagined from the way she took charge so confidently. And she's a beauty. She has luxuriously thick honey blonde hair, an oval face with full lips, a strong nose and green eyes. But it is her skin tone which is truly amazing. She is golden brown, like cinnamon toast. Laura has never seen anyone with this astonishing combination of features.

Why does she hide all that under awful NHS glasses and shapeless, washed-out clothing?

'He looks just like you,' says Janine, pointing to Luke.

Luke has just helped himself to another biscuit without asking. Laura has eaten hers quickly and wants a third but doesn't like to ask.

'People say so,' says Laura, 'although the dark hair's more like his father. Look... I'm so sorry for the histrionics.'

Janine starts to wave away the apology but Laura, embarrassed, ploughs on.

'The last few weeks have been very stressful and today's

series of disasters… well, the final straws, I suppose. I can't thank you enough for your kindness.'

'It's nothing, really,' says Janine. A flush spreads across her cheeks. She looks at the floor and pulls her baggy cardigan round her, as if trying to lose herself in it. 'Will it be just you and Luke next door?' she asks.

'Oh, yes,' replies Laura, with emphatic certainty.

The lights in the hall come on.

'Ah!' exclaims Janine. 'The power's back.'

'Thank God.'

'You'll get used to it. I've had three power cuts since I moved in.'

'Why?'

Janine shrugs. 'Don't know. Living in the country, I suppose. Well, bye then.'

Laura smiles at being dismissed so peremptorily, but she senses that Janine is not being rude, just awkward. She stands.

Then, moved by an unexpected affection, she leans forward and kisses Janine on the cheek. Laura is as surprised as Janine. She is usually so guarded with new people and she has just kissed a total stranger.

This has been a very stressful, and very odd, day, she thinks, her cheeks reddening. 'You really have been a lifesaver,' she says, standing back.

'N-not at all,' stammers Janine, looking at the floor afresh.

Laura leads Luke swiftly out of the green door and opens the adjoining blue one. They hear Janine's door closing gently after them.

'She's nice,' says Luke.

'Yes,' says Laura thoughtfully. 'What did you say her name was?'

'Nadine.'

'Really? I thought she told me something else... Janine, maybe.'

'She could have two names. I have.'

'Yes,' says Laura doubtfully.

She frowns as she thinks back to the moment they were crouched together in the rain and mud, but then shakes the query out of her head in favour of more important matters.

'Right. I want to hear all about it. How was school?'

'Horrible,' says Luke, pulling a face.

'Come in the kitchen and tell me everything. I'll make some toast.'

Part Two

Chapter Eleven

LAURA

Laura's eyes open to the unfamiliar ceiling of her new bedroom. The clock on her bedside table informs her that it is still early, not yet 7 am, but the windows have no curtains and sunlight floods the room. She swings her legs out of bed and skirts around the unpacked boxes in bare feet and T-shirt to the window. The sky is Alice blue and cloudless. Yesterday's last spiteful swipe of winter, apparently timed to cause her maximum distress, has been replaced by a calm, benevolent spring.

The view down the hill is breath-taking, a water-colour landscape in washed-out greens and blues. The tall grasses and the trees, those in the orchard beneath her and those following the line of the river to her left, are utterly still. Mist rises from the bottom of the valley, veiling the lake in light gauze. There isn't a single building in sight.

She has to push the swollen timbers hard, but Laura manages to open the bedroom window. She leans out on the sill. For perhaps the first time in her life on awakening, she cannot hear any sound of human activity. No cars, no planes, no voices; merely birds and the occasional bleating of sheep.

Never has she felt so *right* in a new place.

'Mum?' comes Luke's voice from the adjoining bedroom.

Laura rouses herself. 'Coming!' she calls.

They eat breakfast and get ready to go out. Luke leads the way on foot to his new school. In the balmy weather everything looks fresh, new and more friendly than it did the day before. After dropping Luke off, Laura returns to Magnolia Cottage to start getting their new home straight.

Thus is set the pattern for the next few days. Slowly the boxes are emptied, stacked or flattened, and the house starts to feel as if it's theirs. Laura is surprised to note that it is beginning to take shape quite differently to her home with Roger. Had she been asked, she would have said their tastes were similar, and that the St John's Wood house looked pretty much how she wanted it. Now she is living without Roger, she sees that the home she is creating is in fact quite different. Without his influence, the cottage has more colour and softer edges. It's not as tidy perhaps, but it's more comfortable. Once, on coming home from shopping and dropping into an armchair, she found the right way to express it: it was like being hugged.

She has asked Luke how he feels about their new home, only to discover with some disappointment that, despite all her efforts, the interior of the cottage is of little interest to him. He is in love with the countryside. She had worried that, as a 'town boy', Luke would feel lost here, especially somewhere so isolated and at a new school where he knew nobody.

She could not have been more wrong. Luke is relishing every moment of his new life. It's as if he's been set free. Exploring the garden in the days after the move, he discovered an old bird feeder hanging from a branch of one of the apple trees. The next time they went to Stockport, he insisted on going into a pet shop to enquire about birdseed. He entered into a detailed conversation with the shopkeeper about what seeds were appropriate for the local birds, paid for a small sack out of his own pocket money and, on returning home, refilled the feeder. Within a few days it became a magnet for local birdlife, and when Luke realised that Laura couldn't identify all the birds, he demanded that they locate the local library so he could borrow *The Children's Guide to Birdwatching*.

Now they and the local birdlife enjoy breakfast together, and Luke keeps a notebook in which he records the visits of robins, goldfinches, bullfinches, blue tits and coal tits and, his favourites, the mask-eyed nuthatches, which flash towards the feeder at twice the speed of the others and land on it upside down.

On school evenings Laura can barely get him to focus on his homework, so keen is he to get outside and continue his exploration. At weekends, were she to let him, he would run off after breakfast and not appear again until called in for tea. He climbs over rocks, splashes through the stream, and hunts around the lake and surrounding fields. He returns, shorts muddy and legs scratched, and pockets bulging with leaves and berries, interesting stones, unidentified seeds and, once, a dead field mouse. On another occasion he had a tiny bright green frog cradled in his hands and would have kept it had Laura not insisted that it couldn't survive in the house. Laura's one rule is that he cannot climb the round hill behind the house without her. He would be out of sight and she is uncertain about the woods at the top.

In only one respect is Laura concerned about her son. Luke's teachers report that, although he is doing well with his lessons and seems to get on with everyone, he has made no particular friends. She looks forward keenly to his first invitation to play after school.

As for Luke himself, the sole cloud on *his* horizon is the

absence of his father. He asks, almost daily, when he is going to see Roger.

Laura has had no contact with her ex-husband for weeks. Although he didn't, in the end, dispute the divorce, there was a lot of wrangling between their respective lawyers over the money, and although Laura tried hard to keep the temperature down – and she sensed that Roger did too – with the solicitors locked in battle and sending tendentious letters to one another, it was impossible to prevent it spilling over. She and Roger had several blazing stand-up rows and, by the time a settlement was finally reached, couldn't bear to be in the same room.

Their eventual agreement gave Roger the right to see Luke every second weekend, but he hasn't been in touch to make arrangements. Laura received a cheque from her solicitor representing her share of the equity in the St John's Wood house, so she knows it's been sold, but she doesn't know if Roger has bought anywhere to replace it. She assumes not; mutual London friends let slip on the telephone that Roger is still in his shoddy little hotel in south Manchester during the week and sleeping on their couch at weekends. That, concludes Laura, presumably explains his reluctance to have Luke with him.

She decides to leave matters as they are for a while. She will take the initiative and contact Roger at his new office, but not yet. Perhaps, given more time, he will find somewhere to live. In the meantime, although the small amount of capital she has received means she is under no immediate pressure, she starts scanning the local newspaper for part-time employment.

The only time she sees her next-door neighbour is when the young woman cycles off in the mornings, to work she supposes, with Bobby strapped to the trailer. The two households have interacted only once, when Janine knocked on the door just as they were preparing to leave for school. Luke opened the door and was handed a small object and asked to give it to his mum.

Luke left Janine at the front door and took the object to Laura in the kitchen.

'Oh!' she gasped.

Luke placed in her hand a folding comb with a mother-of-pearl handle, a honeymoon gift from Roger, bought from a beautiful antique shop in Perugia. Despite the pain of more recent years, Laura still treasures the object; it represents one of her happiest memories. She hadn't realised it was missing.

She turned it over in her hand. It was very clean and she realised that her neighbour must have washed the mud and grit off it. She ran back to the front door to thank her, but the young woman's bike and trailer were gone and her front door closed.

One Saturday morning at the end of the first month, and with Magnolia Cottage largely ordered, Laura decides to start work hanging the paintings and prints. She fought harder over these than over any other household items.

Laura spent years building her collection of artwork. Many she bought cheaply from local artists or markets like Portobello Road, but on some, like an early Mondrian, she spent serious money, her own money, saved from the days when she worked in the Civil Service. She was damned if she would trade off the art she loved against the vacuum cleaner or the freezer. On the other hand, Roger considered artwork merely part of the decor; if it matched the carpet, he was happy and paid it no further attention. However, that didn't prevent him from fighting over it, presumably because he appreciated its financial value.

So Laura offered to give up all the furniture, including the new David Hicks rugs and the Castiglioni lamps given to her by her godfather (which she adored) for her choice of paintings. In the end it hadn't come to that, and Roger had relented, allowing her to take most of the artwork as well as enough of the furniture to get started.

She carefully unwraps each canvas and framed print, spending time trying out different locations where each might be displayed to best advantage, gauging the light, leaving them propped against the chosen walls once a decision is reached.

She fetches a hammer and some nails from her rudimentary collection of tools but, just as she is about to start putting them up, considers the neighbours. She doesn't know if the sound will travel through the walls but she's anxious not to wake Bobby if she might be asleep.

'I'm just popping next door!' she shouts to Luke, who is in what has now become a playroom, the room adjoining the kitchen.

'Okay!' he calls back.

Laura opens her front door and knocks on the one adjacent to hers. There is a short pause before Janine appears. Her blonde hair is tied in a bun and held together with what looks like a pencil, and she is wearing a red and white check gingham blouse that has been washed so often that Laura can see the individual threads of the material around the collar.

'Yes?'

Janine speaks abruptly, almost rudely. She's squinting at Laura and for a moment Laura can't see why she looks different, but then she realises that the young woman is not wearing her glasses.

'It's me, Laura. From next door?'

'Oh, yes. Sorry,' she says. 'I take my glasses off while feeding Bobby. She grabs them.'

'Is she asleep?'

'No. Why?'

Laura lifts the hammer and smiles. 'I'm about to start hammering and I didn't want to disturb you if it's a bad time.'

'No, now's fine.'

The door starts to close again but Laura speaks quickly.

'I'm really sorry, but I'm a bit confused. I thought you told me your name was Janine, but Luke's convinced you said "Nadine", and I don't know what to call you.'

'Oh,' replies Janine. 'It doesn't matter.'

'Well, I'd like to call you something,' says Laura with a smile. 'It'll be awkward otherwise.'

Laura waits for an answer to what should be a very simple question, but the interval lengthens.

'My name's Nadine,' answers the young woman eventually. 'Some people... some people used to call me Janine.'

'Okay. Nadine it is,' says Laura, smiling again and backing away.

Janine steps back and starts to close the door again but then stops. 'Could I just say...' she says, and points to the hammer in Laura's hand.

'Yes?'

'That's not going to work.'

'What, the hammer? Why not?'

'It's the walls. Most of them are solid stone, except a section where the two properties were divided. I've tried, and the only way you can fix anything is by using a drill.'

Laura looks at the small hammer in her hand and laughs. 'Really? I've no experience in this sort of thing. I just thought a hammer and a nail...'

She sees Janine shaking her head.

'I've got a drill,' offers Janine. 'Would you like to borrow it?'

'I wouldn't know where to start,' says Laura, laughing.

The other woman hesitates. Laura has the impression that she is witnessing an internal debate being resolved as, a moment later, her neighbour's face brightens and her expression alters.

'Would you like me to do it?' she offers. 'I don't mind.'

The unexpected offer of help from the taciturn neighbour takes Laura by surprise.

'Well, if you've got the time. But there's a lot of them. Maybe I could watch you once or twice and learn?'

Janine doesn't answer but disappears into the cottage, leaving Laura at the door. A few moments later she returns with Bobby in one arm and a toolbox held in her free hand. She is now wearing her spectacles again, and Laura catches an odd thought passing through her head.

I wish she'd take them off again.

This isn't the first time she has responded to another woman like this, but it is the first in many years. She has no time to consider it further because, without a word, Janine thrusts Bobby into her arms.

Laura is again surprised at the ease with which Janine hands over her baby. She's sure she'd hesitate before doing the same were their positions reversed. She studies the young woman's face as she pulls her front door half-shut behind her.

Her new neighbour is an odd mix. There's the reticence, almost rudeness, and the lack of social graces; but every now and then kindness and a disarming openness burst through. And she is utterly beautiful, but hides it under hideous clothes. She's all contrasts.

Laura leads the way back into her semi, Janine following.

'It's a lot bigger,' says Janine, looking around. 'You've a dining room, and that room next to the kitchen.'

'I suppose it would be,' says Laura, 'as we've got two sash windows at the front and back and you've only one. So two extra rooms down here and two more upstairs, I guess.'

'I've never really thought about it before.'

'That slimy estate agent said it was originally one building. They divided it to make one small home and one larger.'

'Estate agent?' asks Janine. 'The one from Glossop with the round head that looks too small?'

'Yes. And the shiny suit.'

Janine laughs in recognition, and Laura watches her face change; as if a light bulb has suddenly illuminated her from inside.

'I know the one! I call him The Weasel,' she replies, with more animation than Laura has seen before.

'Yes, he *is* like a weasel, isn't he? That little head and those dark, darting eyes that linger on you.' Laura screws up her face, imitating a weasel. 'Creepy.'

'How old are you?' asks Janine suddenly.

'Thirty-two,' replies Laura, smiling at the abrupt change of direction and Janine's unabashed curiosity. 'And you?'

'Twenty.'

There is a long pause. Janine appears to have nothing further to say, and Laura watches as the light inside her fades again.

'So,' says Laura, pointing at a bare wall above a sofa, 'that's where I'd like this one.'

Propped on the sofa is a large painting of a woman sitting alone in a garden looking out over a Scottish loch. A bicycle is propped against a moss-covered wall.

'It's an Eardley, one of her early ones,' explains Laura, with some pride.

Janine pays no attention to the actual painting but leans it forward to look at its back. 'The picture wire is fine, and strong enough, but I think you'll need two fixings,' she says. 'It's a bit big and heavy for one, and it won't stay level.'

'Okay. You're the expert.'

'Not really. But I've done mine. Not like this of course, just things from the jumble.'

'Show me what's necessary so I'll know for next time. Luke!'

Luke enters in his pyjamas, a toy train carriage in his hand.

'Hello, Nadine,' he says cheerfully. 'Can I play with Bobby?'

'I was going to ask you to sit with her while Nadine shows me how to do this,' replies Laura. 'Is that all right with you?' she asks Janine.

'Yes. Watch her carefully, Luke,' instructs Janine. 'She can sit up alone now but she does still flop backwards unpredictably. And don't let her put things in her mouth.'

Laura puts Bobby down on the rug and Luke sits in front of her with her in the 'V' of his open legs, and takes one of her hands. He starts playing Round and Round the Garden on her palm, and Bobby grins her toothless grin and squeals with enjoyment.

The two women move the sofa from the wall to allow easy access, and Laura watches as Janine measures the print and the distance between the back of the sofa and the ceiling. She takes a spirit level from her toolbox and marks two pencil crosses on the wall.

'That's where I'd put the fixings,' she says. 'If you're happy with that.'

'Yes, fine. Thank you.'

'If you get a brush and pan, we can sweep up as we go,' advises Janine. 'It gets quite dusty.'

Within ten minutes the painting is hanging on the wall and Janine is repacking her toolbox.

'I'll leave the toolbox with you,' she says. 'There are about thirty Rawlplugs; use as many as you need.'

'That's so kind of you. Can you stay for a cup of coffee?' asks Laura. 'I understand if you're busy, but I've not thanked you for helping me on the day we moved in. Nor for finding my beautiful comb.'

Janine looks at Bobby and Luke playing on the floor. 'I

suppose so. But I don't drink coffee. Well, I don't know if I drink it. I never have.'

'I've got tea if you prefer?'

'No, I'll try it.'

Laura makes a pot of coffee and brings it in on a tray. She puts it down on the table and sits next to Janine on the couch. As she leans forward to pour, the back of her hand accidentally brushes the warm skin of Janine's forearm. She feels a tingle of electricity and, for the first time in years, she is reminded of Li Xiu.

LI XIU

Laura is fifteen, and this is her first morning at Weybridge Hall, an all-girls boarding school in Surrey. The entrance hall, where she and her mother stand at present, feels like a museum, with wood-panelled walls covered in boring portraits of boring people, mostly grey-haired men.

Laura has argued, wheedled, shouted, slammed doors and even tried a short-lived hunger strike, but she lost the battle and here she is. Three whole years, maybe more if Dad's posting is extended. She still can't believe how rigid, how adamant, how *selfish* her parents are!

She tried to recruit Jennifer to the cause and her older sister was sympathetic, but Laura sensed that she wasn't keen to be responsible for a fifteen-year-old while in her second year at Oxford.

'It's only three years, Lols,' she said. 'And you've got your exams. You're probably best off there.'

'I don't understand why Mum has to go as well,' complained Laura.

'I agree,' said Jenny sympathetically. 'I think she should've stayed, but you know how much she loves cocktail parties and servants. And if there's one thing British expats in Hong Kong have in spades, it's cocktail parties and servants.'

'It's so selfish!'

'But on the bright side, I'm sure you'll make friends for life there. You know Alison, don't you? The tall girl I live with? She's from a service family, and she's still bosom buddies with at least half a dozen mates from her boarding school. There's always one of them up at weekends.'

Laura had been dragged to Weybridge Hall before the final decision was made, and she did not share her sister's optimism. The school catered to the children of service personnel, expatriates and foreigners, and there was a constant churn of girls coming and going, but much less so in the older classes where important exams were about to be taken and friendship groups had formed over a couple of years. She knew what the cliques were like at her own school; it would be more or less impossible to break in, especially in the run-up to the School Certificates when everyone would be working hard.

Before she knows what's happening, her mother has bade her a swift and unemotional farewell and Laura is taken to what will be her room, shared with three others. They are all elsewhere. Her unpacking is interrupted by a disinterested sixth former barging in without knocking, with instructions to give her a guided tour of the school. After the tour, Laura is told to finish unpacking and then go down to the common room where the senior girls have an hour of leisure before Study.

She takes her book and descends the wide staircase. She's forgotten where the common room is but locates it by following the noise. She looks through the glazed doors. Beyond them is a large room with a view of the school playing fields, comfortably furnished with sofas, chairs and a couple of large tables for those able to study in such noisy surroundings. A wireless is playing Glenn Miller and two of the girls are dancing. Laura enters quietly and finds a chair in the corner. She is surrounded by boisterous strangers. No one pays her any attention, so she opens her book on her lap and pretends to read.

Then she spots Li Xiu.

Looking back on it, Laura has never been sure what caused the instant attraction between them. Part of it was probably the coincidence that Li Xiu came from Hong Kong, the very place to which Laura's parents were going. Li Xiu had, only a few months before, been released from Stanley Internment Camp. Another part was probably the fact that Li Xiu was herself new to the school, having arrived only a day before Laura, and had yet to find entry into House social life. However, in truth, Laura has always suspected it was simply a physical, and mutual, attraction. Although the same age as Laura, Li Xiu was taller, more poised and, so it seemed to Laura, incredibly elegant. Make-up was banned at the school and yet somehow Li Xiu was getting away with it, and although she was wearing the same uniform as everyone else, on her it looked good.

Li Xiu, stationary just inside the door, sees Laura looking at her, smiles, and walks straight over. She holds out a hand.

'I'm Li Xiu,' she says. 'You have such beautiful hair.'

'Oh,' says Laura, blushing, and putting her hand up self-consciously to smooth it.

Laura's hair is wavy and almost waist-length, an untameable mane of coppery red. She used to hate it but from that moment and for the rest of her life she was proud of it.

'Thank you. So do you. I mean... I'm not just saying that... honest... it really is lovely!'

The two girls become inseparable. They partner up for chemistry experiments, do all their study together and during their free time walk around the Quad or the running track, arm in arm. Some of the girls whisper they are 'lezzers', but no more than might be expected in a school full of raging female hormones and crushes.

In fact, their relationship is never overtly sexual, although it comes close. On one occasion, a geography field trip, they have to share a bed – there was a mix-up with the youth hostel and most of the girls have to pair up – but nothing happens. Laura spends the night in a torment of unspecified longing, her thighs and belly in contact with Lu Xiu's backside as they spoon, but she doesn't know what to do. Anyway, Li Xiu seems to be asleep and Laura can't bring herself to wake her. She is pretty sure that Li Xiu won't reject her, but 'pretty sure' isn't enough. What if Laura has misread all the signals? What if she launches herself at Li Xiu and is rebuffed? The thought horrifies her. She loves Li Xiu too much to risk losing her friendship. Anyway, she doesn't know how to achieve it, practically. How is one supposed to segue from friendship, even a very tactile, physical friendship, into sexual intimacy; how does one cross that line?

So nothing happens. Nothing is said either, although Li Xiu looks at her penetratingly the following morning as they eat breakfast. In the years that follow, after they leave school and Li Xiu returns to Hong Kong, Laura has one or two boyfriends. Nonetheless, when she is alone in bed, it is often that night, the curve of Li Xiu's buttocks and the smell of the soft skin at the back of her neck, which she holds in her mind as she makes little circles with her fingers and strokes herself to sleep.

Chapter Twelve

JANINE

Bobby has just finished her feed. She only wakes once in the night now, at around midnight, but otherwise she sleeps from seven to seven. Janine stays awake, reading or sketching plans for her gardens, until she hears Bobby's cry; then she feeds and changes her and is able to sleep for an uninterrupted seven hours. She knows from the books how lucky she is.

Janine sighs. Just as she is fastening the safety pin on a clean nappy, Bobby's face assumes that familiar expression of calm contentment and Janine knows instantly what it signifies. She removes the filled nappy, and starts again.

'Did I mention what a busy day we have tomorrow?' she chides quietly. 'Madam?'

She does indeed have a very full day. As she was feeding Bobby her tea, she received a telephone call from a posh lady who needed help in her garden. She said she was an acquaintance of Lady Margaret who had, apparently, recommended Janine. Including Windyridge, Janine now has three clients, four if she accepts this new offer. This property is a bit further away than the others, but Janine is confident she can manage it on the trike as long as she plans her week carefully. So, on top of all the work at Windyridge and a short visit to Mrs Reid, an elderly client who just requires a little weeding, she has to find time to look at a new garden.

Janine usually tries not to engage Bobby at the midnight feed. Given any encouragement the baby will wake fully and start babbling. She believes herself to be talking and there are, it is true, some sounds that are close to recognisable words. So it is better to lift her gently, feed and change her in the dark while she is still half asleep, and settle her back down as soon as possible.

However, tonight Bobby is wide awake. She reaches up and yanks the glasses off Janine's nose while Janine's hands are too occupied to stop her. The plastic arm goes straight into her wet mouth. She's still teething, and constantly wants something to chew.

'So, shall we be friends with our new neighbours?' asks Janine as she wipes Bobby's bottom again. 'Or shall we go?'

Her anxiety about them has receded. She rarely hears anything through the walls from Magnolia Cottage and the woman has been respectful of her privacy. Janine now thinks it might be all right after all. Also, there is something about the weather, the feeling of summer round the corner, that suggests she should stay. She did look at other possible accommodation but it was all horrible and reminded her too much of Hulme, so she stopped. She continues cycling to Windyridge as before.

'She's a bit scary though, isn't she?' says Janine softly to Bobby as she pins the clean nappy.

Bobby gurgles in reply.

Janine's face flushes as she recalls the encounter that morning. She opened the door to find Laura standing on her doorstep, shading her eyes from the sun. The light striking her hair turned it copper, bronze and chestnut in different places, and Janine was mesmerised by it. She had never seen hair look so wild or so beautiful. And her clothes! Laura wore faded blue shorts with little turn-ups, open-toed sandals and what Janine guessed must have been a man's shirt, its tail tied in a knot around her waist and its sleeves rolled up to her elbows, revealing creamy white forearms. She should have looked messy, but instead she was dazzling. She reminded Janine of the billboard models in Manchester, twelve-foot-high posters of modern, independent women advertising some new perfume or hair product. The sort of woman of whom Janine is in awe; the sort of woman she will never be.

After she returned to Apple Tree Cottage, for the first time in her adult life Janine went up to her bedroom and stood in front of the full-length mirror, taking a long, critical look at herself and her clothes.

How does Laura wear such scruffy mismatched things and still look so stylish? she wondered. *Mine are old and mismatched too but, while Laura looks like a model, I look... just odd.*

Lumpy.

Clownish.

It isn't just Laura's clothes, she realises; it's her confidence. She makes fun of herself, like she did with that silly hammer. In her place, Janine would have curled up with embarrassment at looking so foolish, but Laura just laughed at her own stupidity, as if no one would care. And the laugh itself, so natural, bubbling up from deep inside her chest and emerging with such ease; exactly the sort of laugh that goes with a woman who looks and dresses like that, thinks Janine.

Is it because she's rich?

She lies Bobby down in the cot again. The child's eyelids are fluttering, almost closed.

'Good night, sweetheart,' she whispers.

She closes the door behind her, goes to her bedroom and slips into bed.

She usually falls asleep within minutes, but tonight sleep won't come. She is restless, imagining all sorts of 'friendship scenarios'. They will be like Elizabeth Bennett and Charlotte Lucas from *Pride and Prejudice*. They'll take long walks in the hills; they'll go shopping together, giggling and sharing secrets (she can't imagine any secrets that someone like Laura would have, but still); they'll take the children together for happy, sunlit picnics. Pictures whirl around in her head like a carousel: Laura; her and Laura; the two of them with the children.

She realises that she no longer wants to leave; she is fantasising about becoming Laura's best friend.

But how? How do such things happen?

Therein lies another charge in the indictment against Mother. Janine has no idea how to go about making friends.

School was bad enough, but at home it was intolerable. The cobbled streets of Hulme teamed with children playing football, hide and seek, hopscotch and skipping, but Janine could never find entry to the shifting alliances and cliques. She watched from the fringes, wearing the awful, ill-fitting second-hand clothes Mother bought from the Samaritans. One of the kids, a little Scottish urchin, once called her 'jakey', a beggar, and it caught on. Until her tormentors became aware of her skin colour and it was replaced by 'Darkie', 'Jakey' was Janine's childhood nickname, thrown at her whenever she passed the tribes of footballers or skippers. And it was ironically apt, because Janine was indeed forever begging Mother for new clothes. 'Can't afford it', was the routine answer, although there always seemed to be enough for gin and stamps.

Janine's only childhood friends were the fictional characters she encountered in books. Elizabeth Bennett, Nancy Drew, Anne Shirley and Jo March; her friends and her role models.

From the second she arrived home from school, she longed to be able to lose herself in whatever book she was reading, and the minute Mother was asleep in the lounge, her glass dangling limply from her hand, she would return to it. She read constantly. She had been putting herself to bed since the age of six and didn't even relinquish her book when sitting on the toilet or brushing her teeth. The last explained *Mother's* nickname for her – 'Dribbler' – earned because she so often had toothpaste dribbles down the front of her pyjamas.

'You are the most careless, dribbly brusher of teeth I've ever known,' Mother would say, seeing the pyjamas the following morning, and the next time Janine asked for a new blouse or a school cardigan that fitted her, Mother would just point to the toothpaste stains without a word.

Janine tosses and turns, trying to get comfortable, but her mind will not settle. Finally she slaps the mattress in frustration.

'Stop it!' she rebukes herself out loud.

Who do you think you're kidding? Why would a woman like that ever want to be friends with you?

So, having argued herself round in a complete circle, she finally falls asleep, exhausted, still uncertain whether she should stay in her semi or renew her search for somewhere else.

Chapter Thirteen

LAURA

'You won't need your wellies,' says Laura to Luke. 'Dad lives in a town.'

'Like St John's Wood?' asks Luke, putting his wellington boots back on the mat by the kitchen door.

'I don't know. Probably not quite as posh.'

Laura is packing Luke's bag for the weekend. It will be the first weekend he has spent with his father, and he is very excited. As for Laura, although she is curious to see the new property into which Roger has moved, she is nervous. This will also be the first time they have met since the decree absolute.

'Do I need anything to read on the journey?' asks Luke.

'You've got the map, haven't you?'

'Yes.'

'Probably not, then. It's less than half an hour.'

Laura opens the blue door to her semi at the very instant as Janine opens the green door to hers.

'Good morning!' says Laura enthusiastically. 'Isn't it a gorgeous day?'

'Yes,' replies Janine.

She turns with Bobby in her arms and locks up.

'I'm going to see my dad!' says Luke, bouncing with excitement.

'Are you?'

'It's Roger's first weekend – my ex – and Luke's very excited,' explains Laura as she too locks her door. 'I wonder, are you going to be in later this afternoon? I thought I might explore the hill behind the houses. Luke's convinced he's seen horses running round up there. Do you fancy coming for a walk?'

Janine busies herself with strapping Bobby into the trailer seat. After a while she straightens up.

'I don't think so, thank you. Bobby has her afternoon sleep.'

'But she's usually awake by mid-afternoon, isn't she? We can hear her in the back garden.'

Janine colours. 'I'm sorry. We didn't mean to disturb you.'

'It's not disturbing us, not at all! I love hearing happy children playing. Honestly, please don't worry about that. I just meant we could go after her sleep. In fact, I've got one of those things for carrying babies on your back, like a rucksack. I found it when emptying my last box, yesterday. If you don't have one you could borrow it.'

'No, I really–'

'Actually, you can have it, because I can't see me having any more children. You'd be very welcome to it. Come on, let's go on a little adventure.'

Laura can see that Janine is wavering and she puts her hand on Janine's as it rests on the trike's handlebar.

'Okay then,' capitulates Janine.

'Excellent! You can cheer me up,' and she leans in to whisper in Janine's ear, 'cos I might be a bit lonely. First time here without Luke,' she explains, laughing.

'Oh, of course, yes,' says Janine, looking worried.

'Don't look so alarmed! It'll be fun.'

Laura runs to catch up with Luke who is waiting impatiently by the car. She waves over its roof to Janine.

'See you later! Knock on my door as soon as Bobby's up!'

Laura and Luke get into the car. Luke opens the map on his knees and with great seriousness tells Laura to drive to the bottom of The Rise.

'I wanted to come up the hill with you too,' he complains.

'I know, but it's a big hill, and I'm sure we won't explore even a tiny part of it. This is just early reconnaissance.'

Roger's new house in Didsbury, south Manchester, is much bigger than Laura had imagined. In a wide, tree-lined suburban road, she finds a double-fronted detached house with an in-out drive behind tall privet hedges. The front door opens as she pulls onto the drive, and Roger stands in the porch. Luke leaps out and runs into his father's arms, Laura following behind with the overnight bag.

'Stained-glass windows?' she asks, pointing to the leaded lights around the front door.

'Nice, isn't it?' replies Roger over the top of Luke's head.

If he harbours any rancour over the divorce settlement, he shows no sign of it. In fact, he looks happy and relaxed in corduroys and a check shirt and is smiling at her. Laura is pleased but also slightly put out. She made an effort to look her best, wanting Roger to wonder how he let her get away, but he doesn't seem to notice.

'How many bedrooms have you got?' she demands.

'No more than you.'

'Yes, but mine's a semi, converted from stables! How much did this cost?'

'None of your business!' he says, grinning.

Luke runs into the house to explore. Laura approaches Roger and, a little to her surprise, he kisses her on the cheek.

'Please don't tell me you took out another whopping mortgage,' she says quietly. 'I know you couldn't have bought this on your share of the equity.'

He shrugs. 'I did get a mortgage, yes, and it will be a bit tight for my probation period. But after that, once I'm a partner, it won't be a problem. I'll have it paid off in ten years. Want to come in and have a look?'

'No, thank you. But why do you need something so ostentatious? There's only you here. Or is there something you're not telling me?'

Roger laughs. 'Don't be daft! I've only been here a few weeks.'

'You've been working in Manchester for months. And I know how fast you work.'

'Look, Laura, no offence, but it's none of your business how I arrange my finances or if I've found someone to cheer my lonely existence. I have Luke coming every second weekend, don't I? I want this to be his home, just as much as your place is. So why shouldn't I have the same amount of space?'

She sighs. 'Yes, sure, you're right,' she concedes. 'I just wonder who you need to impress with such a swanky property. Anyway, make sure he's back by five tomorrow, okay? He's done all his homework, but I don't want him having a late night.'

'Promise.' He turns and calls into the house. 'Luke!'

Footsteps thunder down the stairs and Luke appears at the door.

'Mum's leaving,' says Roger.

Luke pushes past his father in the doorway, and Laura crouches to hug him.

'Be good,' she whispers. 'You've got our phone number, haven't you?'

'Yes, in my notebook,' he breathes hotly in her ear.

'Good. Call me if you get lonely or you need anything.'

'I won't get lonely. I've got Dad.'

Laura's heart feels a little pang.

As she said to Janine, this is the first time she and Luke have been separated since they moved to Chapelhill. She's genuinely pleased at Luke's excitement to see his father; more pleased still that Roger has promised faithfully to do no work over the weekend. After all, this is what she wanted: to give Roger and Luke a fresh start. All the same, she's going to miss her son and she's faintly, and irrationally, jealous.

Laura stands and walks back to the car, waving cheerfully as she goes.

'Have fun!' she calls back to them both.

Chapter Fourteen

JANINE

Janine knows that walking is something people do for pleasure, such as Boy Scouts and hikers, but it's not something she has ever imagined doing herself. Who goes walking in Hulme for the scenery? There's nothing attractive about smoke-belching factories, soot-stained slums, undeveloped bomb sites and hungry children playing on cobbled streets.

Mother refused to leave the house unless it was unavoidable. Before she fled, Janine had never been on holiday or even a weekend away. School holidays were spent in her room, reading. At the start of term she would hear classmates enthusing about trips to the Pennines or the Lake District, occasionally even a week in Blackpool, but the concept of being taken on a jolly family outing, exploring lakes or the seaside, building sand castles, flying kites and eating ice creams, was more fantastical than the fictional worlds in which she took nightly refuge.

She recognises that her neighbour's invitation to explore the hill behind the house was a gesture of friendship, which is why she allowed herself to be persuaded, but now she wishes she hadn't capitulated. What's the point of walking up a hill and back again? On the other hand, she reminds herself, for years she never liked leaving her bedroom, and she now loves being outdoors, surrounded by nature. And she has often wondered about the mysterious hill that rears up behind their joint properties. To Janine's fertile imagination it is the habitation of unknown beasts, even monsters. So, she tells herself, make the best of it, and get to know Laura a little better. That's what Nadine would do.

She goes to her bedroom, wondering what walkers wear. Walking boots, she assumes, and trousers. Laura, of course, will look as stylish as ever, whatever she wears. Janine only has her work boots and dungarees, and they are muddy and clodhoppery; most definitely not stylish.

What then? The long ill-fitting dresses chosen by Mother will surely get in the way and snag on bushes. She only has one pair of proper trousers, her new ones. They were on offer at one of the Glossop shops and caught her eye as she walked past. They are called 'hipsters' – a word Janine had never heard before – and they're soft brushed cotton in pale fawn. The moment she tried them on she knew she had to have them. They are the first pair of fashion trousers she has ever owned, and they fit her perfectly, as if she had been the cutter's model. She also finds a lightweight cotton sweatshirt in off-white which seems to look okay, but with the low-cut trousers it leaves some of her midriff bare. She tries on various alternative tops but eventually reverts to the sweatshirt.

It's just a walk! she reminds herself. *No one's going to care what I look like.*

Bobby wakes at her usual time. Janine hears her calling from upstairs and runs up with a beaker of water. This is all she usually wants on waking in the afternoons. It is her best time of day; after having a drink and being changed, she is wide awake and wants to play and talk. Janine changes her and puts her into warmer clothing. It is hot in the garden and while she would normally allow Bobby to crawl around the grass in her nappy, she imagines it will be windy further up the hill.

She can hear Laura singing to herself in her garden, so she takes Bobby and leaves Apple Tree Cottage by the back door, grabbing a windcheater from the hook by the door as she goes.

'Hi there!' calls Laura as Janine emerges.

'Hello,' replies Janine, nervously.

She watches Laura's eyes land on her and widen slightly. The older woman is looking her up and down. Janine blushes.

'I... didn't know what to wear,' she confesses. 'Is this all wrong?'

'Wrong?' Laura takes a deep breath. 'No. Absolutely not. You look fabulous! I've just never seen you in... fashionable clothes before.'

For a second the older woman continues to stare, really *looking* at her. It makes Janine both uncomfortable and pleased at the same time.

Laura finally looks away.

'I've got this for you,' she says, holding up something, a cross between a rucksack and a harness. 'Have you seen one of these before?'

Janine had been anxious that Laura would be upset about being separated from Luke, and worried she wouldn't know what to say, but the older woman seems perfectly chirpy. Luke reminds Janine of a Labrador puppy, shaggy, friendly and excitable, and she sees now that he gets it from his mother. They seem so resilient; they have the knack of living in the moment, thinks Janine.

While I seem always to live in my head, plagued by... thoughts.

'No. How does it work?' she asks.

'Hold Bobby up and I'll get her legs in,' replies Laura.

Once Bobby is safely strapped in, Laura helps get the harness onto Janine's back. Janine is acutely conscious of Laura's hands on her shoulders and arms. It is the first gentle touch she has felt in months.

'That looks great,' says Laura, bending to tighten the straps under Janine's arms.

It feels very intimate. Janine can smell the other woman's perfume and would only need to bend her head slightly to bury her nose in Laura's mane of red hair. She has a sudden urge to do just that, and flushes again.

'Is Bobby happy?' she asks, deliberately looking up and away. 'I can't see her.'

'She's smiling,' says Laura, stepping back, having made final adjustments, 'and she has a great view over your shoulders. Ready?'

'Yes.'

'Don't sound so nervous!' says Laura, laughing. 'This is going to be fun!'

'I've never been walking. I mean... obviously, I walked to school and the shops but...'

'If you don't like it, we'll turn round and come back. How's that?'

'Okay.'

Laura pulls a small rucksack onto her shoulders and they set off towards the back of the garden. An arrowhead of eight or ten Canada geese flies over the house in the same direction, honking, heading uphill.

Bobby looks up, points and makes an inarticulate exclamation.

'They're pointing the way,' says Janine, who immediately wishes she hadn't said it because it sounded silly, but Laura seems just as excited.

'I love them, don't you? Do you hear them flying over us at dawn?'

'Yes. I'm usually up doing Bobby's first feed.'

'The way they soar in perfect formation over the house against a clear sky. It's magical.'

'Yes, it is.'

They find the stile at the back of the garden. It doesn't look as if it's been used in years and has more or less collapsed. The women help one another over the broken pieces of timber and protruding nails, and head uphill.

Beyond the gardens there is a wide swathe of grass that seems to encircle the hill, as it stretches out of sight to both left and right. The going is easy here as the grass is short, cropped smooth by rabbits and sheep. The path they are on, if path it is, follows the line of a brook whose clear water runs and jumps over stones and boulders on its way down the hill. Laura chatters away, with Janine contributing little.

'This must feed the stream running past the house into the lake,' comments Laura.

After they've been walking for twenty minutes or so the soil becomes more sandy and the grass gives way to tracts of heather and clumps of gorse. Here there is no discernible path, although it appears that sheep or some other animals have carved tracks through the undergrowth. Laura leads the way.

It is more colourful at this height. The heather is violet and purple and the bright yellow gorse flowers, although past their best, resemble swarms of tiny butterflies fluttering in the wind, clinging to the bushes. The land flattens off for a while, as if they have reached the hill's shoulders, before suddenly becoming much steeper as it climbs again towards the summit. They negotiate a stile set in a dry-stone wall and continue upwards through taller grass.

Both women are now breathing hard and Laura stops talking.

'Are you okay?' she asks finally between deep gulps of breath. 'Would you like me to take Bobby for a while?'

'No, I'm fine. Thank you.'

Bobby makes a noise.

'Is she all right?' asks Janine.

'She's pointing.'

'At what?'

'I don't know. Ahead. Perhaps the trees.'

About fifty yards away is the stand of trees at the summit of the hill and, not far above them, cruising in lazy circles on the updraught, are two buzzards. The women hear the birds' familiar descending shriek, and Bobby points up again.

'Maybe she's pointing at those birds,' says Laura.

'They're buzzards.'

'Let's stop for a moment,' says Laura. 'That patch of grass, over there?'

They walk to an area partly sheltered by gorse bushes. Laura goes behind Janine and lifts the harness off her shoulders. The back of Janine's windcheater is a darkened patch of sweat. They extricate Bobby and Janine places her on the grass between her open legs and hugs her to her chest, facing the way they have come. The breeze blowing up the valley and into their faces is deliciously cooling.

Laura takes a flask out of her knapsack and offers it to Janine first. 'It's just cold water.'

Janine takes it, puts her head back and drinks deeply. A small rivulet of water escapes her mouth and runs down her neck into the front of her sweatshirt, and she is conscious of Laura's eyes following it.

She wipes her mouth on her arm and hands the flask back.

Laura looks away swiftly. She delves again into her bag and comes up with a sealed beaker and offers it to Janine.

'Ribena – blackcurrant squash,' she says. 'Does Bobby like it?'

'Yes. Thank you, that's very thoughtful.'

'I'm an old hand at this,' says Laura. 'When he was a baby, I used to take Luke walking on Hampstead Heath.'

She takes the top off the beaker and hands it to Bobby. The three of them sit in silence, enjoying the view.

The Cheshire countryside is spread below them, a patchwork of subtly different greens and browns, darkening and brightening again as fast-moving fluffy clouds scud across the sky. Laura points down, towards the building where they both live, now a small grey rectangle in a sea of green and, further down still, the tiny roofs of Chapelhill. The buffeting wind is much stronger up here. It flattens and combs the grassland below them in undulating waves and both women have to hold on to their long hair to prevent it blowing in their faces.

'That's some view,' says Laura.

Before Janine can answer, the peacefulness of the scene is shattered by a sudden pounding of hooves, and they both whirl round in alarm to see half a dozen riderless horses race across the hill above them, passing from left to right across their field of vision and then disappearing behind the trees. It is so sudden, so extraordinary, and so quickly over, that Janine wonders if she imagined it.

'Did you see that?' she asks.

'Yes. Amazing!'

What if we'd been in their way? That power... and the speed!

Then, as if to prove that it really occurred, the sound returns and the horses break cover and thunder back the way they came. Five seconds later, the hill is again deserted, the grasses rolling silently in the wake of the charge.

'I wonder whose horses they are,' says Laura.

'Maybe they're wild,' offers Janine.

'Maybe, but I've never heard of wild horses in England, except New Forest ponies,' replies Laura diplomatically. 'Perhaps their owner allows them to graze up here during the summer.'

Janine stands, lifting Bobby at the same time. She looks to the top of the hill, from left to right. 'But where did they go?' she asks.

'Round the other side, perhaps? Shall we go back down? I don't want to get caught in a stampede.'

Janine has the sudden fanciful idea that the horses are in fact princes, placed under a spell by a witch, and she wants to see them again. She starts putting Bobby back into the harness. 'No, let's go up to the trees,' she says. 'We've come this far.'

Laura hesitates but acquiesces. 'Okay, but we'd better keep our ears open. We don't want to be trampled.'

They reload Bobby onto Janine's back and set off again.

They see and hear nothing unusual over the remaining distance, although they cross a track of recent hoof prints.

They are soon entering the woodland at the hill's summit. It consists principally of old oak and beech, and their passage is not interrupted by much in the way of understorey. Every here and there the remains of old buildings may be seen among the trees. Moss-covered stone foundations outline the footprints of small houses, pushed out of shape by self-seeded trees and bushes. There are also entire sections of walls, crumbling courses of stone leaning at odd angles and rotten corner posts.

'It's a ghost village,' says Janine, marvelling.

'Isn't it wonderful?' replies Laura. 'The sort of place where you expect to see fairies or elves.'

After a few minutes of walking through the trees they emerge into sunlight on the other side of the woodland. The ground drops suddenly in front of them. They have traversed the summit of the hill.

In what is evidently a parking area for a viewing point from this side of Chapel Hill, they see a campervan, hand-painted in great swirls of bright colours, with rainbows, stars and rockets. On its side, painted in large purple letters, it bears two words in a foreign language.

'Look at that!' exclaims Laura.

'Looks like part of a circus.'

'I didn't realise there was a road coming up this side of Chapel Hill, did you?' asks Laura.

'No.'

'Good afternoon,' says a deep male voice.

The two women jump, looking sharply to their right. A man crouches a few feet away beside a pile of stones. A dry-stone wall runs along the side of the car park, but some of it has fallen away and he is evidently repairing it.

'Hello,' replies Laura.

The man stands, unwinding very long legs, and reaches for a flask resting on the wall beside him. He is extremely tall and thin, and as he leans over the wall he reminds Janine of the bent matchstick men painted by Lowry. She was introduced to his paintings on a junior school trip to the Manchester Art Gallery, and has never forgotten them.

'You're the first people I've seen up here in three days,' says the man in a strange accent.

'That's surprising,' replies Laura. 'I'd have thought in the middle of the summer holidays this view would be very popular.'

'There's no sign to it from the valley,' says the man. 'The council's paying me to put one up once this wall's repaired.'

The man evidently feels emboldened by Laura's engagement to walk towards them. Janine is surprised to see that he is younger than she assumed. What she had taken for shoulder-length grey hair is in fact blond, almost as light as an albino's, although the skin on his face and forearms has been darkened by the sun and is almost the same colour as hers. She has never seen a man with hair that long, nor one wearing an earring and a necklace.

'Did you know the old village is supposed to be haunted?' asks the man, pointing back to the trees.

'No,' replies Laura, 'but it doesn't surprise me.'

'That was Chapel Hill,' he says. 'Then the Black Death came, and the survivors moved down to the river, taking most of the old stone to build new homes. There's the remains of a church somewhere over there. You can still see some gravestones, many with the same year of death, 1349.'

Laura and Janine look at one another.

'Are the horses real?' asks Janine, blushing furiously as she realises how odd the question sounded.

She would never usually address a stranger at all, but the whole afternoon has become slightly surreal, as if it were happening in a dream. *Odd things occur in dreams, don't they?* she thinks, *including conversations with odd people.*

'I can see why you'd ask,' says the man, towering over the two women, 'but they're real enough. It's pretty creepy up here at night. You hear them running, but all you can see are shadows moving through the trees.'

He takes a half-smoked roll-up from behind his ear and cups his hands around a match to light it.

'They've been put out to pasture,' he says after a pause, drawing a deep lungful of smoke. 'A couple of them were pit ponies from Northumberland. Some of the others used to pull milk floats. A local farmer takes them in, to save them going to the knackers.'

Not princes then, thinks Janine, disappointed. *Or, perhaps, just very elderly ones.*

The man takes another deep drag on the cigarette and holds the smoke in his lungs for a second or two. The smell when he exhales is odd, unlike any tobacco Janine has smelled before.

'Is that who you're working for?' asks Laura.

'The farmer? No, I've a contract with the council. I've been repairing walls for them for the last couple of years. Never here before, though.'

'That's your profession, is it? Dry-stone walling?'

The man grins. 'One of several. You can't make a living doing this alone.' He pauses. 'Listen, you don't know anywhere I could park the van overnight round here, do you? I stayed up here last night, but there's no water and even close to the trees the wind's that strong, I got no sleep. There doesn't seem to be any flat land in this village.'

'I don't think there's anything like a caravan park,' says Laura.

She looks at Janine, who is staring at the young man's extraordinary appearance.

'There's the church car park,' offers Janine, quietly.

The man turns to her. 'Really? Where's that?'

'At the crossroads in the centre of Chapelhill there's a sign to Burnham Hill. The church is a couple of hundred yards up there.'

'Thank you. I'll try that.'

The young man's eyes crinkle as he smiles. He wipes his hands on his overalls and offers one to Janine who, after an instant's hesitation, takes it.

'My name's Ifan Davies,' he says, 'but everyone calls me Ianto.'

'Ianto?' asks Janine.

'It's a nickname. I don't like it much but unfortunately I'm stuck with it.'

'I was trying to place your accent,' says Laura. 'I thought at first German but... Welsh?'

'I grew up in Wales with my father, but I've spent most of the last decade in Holland.'

'Which explains that,' says Laura, pointing at the words on the side of the van. 'What does it mean?'

'It means "Merry Pranksters".' Ianto grins at the two women but offers no further explanation. 'So, who is this?' he asks, circling behind Janine to Bobby.

'That's Bobby,' says Janine.

'Helo un bach,' says Ianto gently to Bobby. 'Onid ydych chi'n hyfryd?'

Bobby reaches for his hair. He lets her take a handful and pull for a moment, before disentangling her little fingers.

'I'd better get on,' he says. 'If the light holds, I might finish up here tonight. See you around, maybe?'

The women start walking back through the trees.

'What an extraordinary chap,' says Laura thoughtfully.

'He reminded me of Lowry's matchstick men,' says Janine.

'He reminded *me* of a pirate. But instead of *The Walrus*, he captains the good ship *Volkswagen*.'

'Robert Louis Stevenson,' says Janine.

'You know it?'

'Of course. Don't you think this afternoon's been a bit...' starts Janine, but her voice tails off and she doesn't finish the sentence.

'A bit what?' asks Laura.

Janine shakes her head. 'No, you'll think I'm strange. Forget it.'

'Oh, go on! I won't think you're strange, I promise. Anyway, I like strange. Everyone I used to know was so utterly boring and predictable. I knew exactly what they'd talk about every time we met. I think you're much more interesting.'

'Well,' says Janine hesitantly, 'don't you think this afternoon's been very... odd? Like something out of a book, or... a dream.'

'Yes! Absolutely! When I said we'd have an adventure, I didn't imagine invisible horses and pot-smoking pirates. There is something... *magical* about this hill.'

'Yes, there is. Wait; did you say "pot-smoking"?'

'Definitely. Didn't you smell it?' asks Laura with a grin.

'I smelled something unusual, but I didn't know what it was. So that's cannabis? I've heard of it, but I'd no idea what you're supposed to do with it. You smoke it?'

'Yes, you smoke it. Although some of our friends in St John's Wood used to cook with it, put it in cakes, for example.'

'I see. And you've read *Treasure Island*?'

'Of course; a childhood favourite. In fact, I loved any book I could get my hands on with pirates or princesses.'

'Me too. I used to read all the time... until this one came along,' says Janine, jerking her thumb behind her to indicate Bobby. 'Now it's an hour or two in the evenings, if I'm lucky.'

'Ooh, this is going to be fun!' says Laura.

Janine looks across at Laura's face. Her white cheeks have a pink glow to them and her eyes shine. She looks excited, like a young girl.

There is something so charmingly ingenuous about Laura's expression that on impulse Janine reaches for her hand and squeezes it lightly. It's an instinctive gesture of friendship – extraordinary enough for Janine, who is usually so reserved – but at the same time it feels dangerous, illicit. Her hand tingles, as if it had suddenly grown thousands of new touch receptors.

Janine can't quite believe that a grown woman can be like Laura. In her mind, adults – especially middle-class adults – are sorted, in control of their lives, on mapped-out journeys; safe, solid, purposeful. They think about paying the rent, career progression and schools for their children. Janine's mind, on the other hand, teems with tragic heroines on windswept moors, bewitched princes and sailors battling whales. For the first time, it occurs to Janine that she and Laura might have something in common. Laura may be rich, well-educated and much older than her, but perhaps she too has weird and fantastical thoughts whirling around her head.

Laura grips Janine's hand more firmly, and Janine's heart sings as they head back down the hill, hand in hand. It isn't what she intended, but the closeness is so lovely, so spontaneous and so genuine, she feels her heart lift.

'Right,' says Laura, as if bringing a company meeting to order. 'Favourite authors.'

So the two women chat easily about the books that shaped their childhoods as they descend towards their homes, and when they have to disengage to climb over walls or negotiate narrow parts of the track, it is the most natural thing ever for Janine to reach for Laura again afterwards.

By the time they each shut their respective doors, Janine realises that she has never spoken to anyone for as long or with such ease. She feels strangely light-headed.

This must be what it's like to be a little drunk.

We're definitely *becoming friends*, she thinks as she starts making Bobby's tea.

But there's something else, too, she realises. She can still feel the pressure of Laura's soft hand in hers.

I wanted to kiss her.

Chapter Fifteen

LAURA

'But I don't want to!' complains Luke.

They are in the kitchen, eating hurried bowls of Frosties.

'I'm sorry, sweetheart, but I've no choice.' She indicates her clothing. 'I've got to go into Manchester for an interview and you can't come with me.'

Laura is wearing an ivory A-line dress with off-centre giant brown buttons studded from one shoulder all the way to her knees. A short matching jacket with three-quarter sleeves hangs over the back of her chair. It's a very flattering style for her, and the colour sets off her mane of red hair. After some hesitation, she slipped on her killer red shoes. She is becoming desperate, and desperate times call for desperate measures. *It's probably too much*, she thinks, *but what the hell?*

'Can't I stay with Nadine?' persists Luke.

'No you can't, because she has to work.'

'I could go with her and look after Bobby,' he suggests.

'Look, I said no and I mean no. You'll only be there for a few hours, and you'll know everyone.'

She has booked a place for the day for Luke to attend a

summer holiday club held at the village hall, organised by the local branch of the farmers' union. She hadn't wanted to. It's expensive and he complains there's not enough food at lunchtime; on the two occasions he has gone in the past he has come home famished. However, her interview is at midday and she really likes the look of this job, so she has no choice.

'I don't know *anyone*. They're not from school.'

'I'm very sorry, Luke, and I'll try to make this the last time, but help me out, please. We need me to get a job, you know that.'

He scowls, staring at the floor. Laura reaches over and strokes his soft cheek.

'Thank you, darling,' she says. He shrugs her off.

Laura chivvies him through brushing his teeth while she packs a sandwich and chocolate bar for him in case he gets hungry. Twenty minutes later she locks up and deposits him at the village hall. He refuses to acknowledge her departure and makes no eye contact with her.

Laura heads across the hills towards Manchester.

She arrives in good time and finds somewhere to park close to the office building. She presents herself at reception and is directed by a middle-aged woman in spectacles to a line of chairs where two other people already wait, one a woman of about Laura's age and the other an older man.

My competition, I suppose.

The job is for a fast-expanding family-run transport business requiring logistical expertise. Laura is almost certainly overqualified for it.

The three competitors sit in silence in the stuffy reception area. Laura notices that the carpets are very dusty round the edges and the notices and other documents pinned to the noticeboard have curled and browned with age. The calendar above the female receptionist's desk features large shiny trucks with bare-breasted young women reclining on the bonnets.

I bet she loves that above her head, thinks Laura.

The clock ticks the minutes by, and her appointment time comes and goes. Laura sees the other woman looking repeatedly at her watch, and she leans forward, speaking across the man in the centre.

'What time was your interview?' she asks.

'Forty-five minutes ago,' whispers the woman.

'And yours?' Laura asks the man.

He shrugs, evidently not as concerned as the others. 'Oh, a few minutes ago.'

A telephone rings on the receptionist's desk. She speaks briefly to someone and hangs up.

'I'm very sorry,' she says. 'But Mr Vernon has just called to say he has to cancel.'

'Was Mr Vernon the man interviewing us?' asks the other woman.

'Yes,' confirms the receptionist. 'He's the finance director.'

'But I've had to leave my daughter with a friend,' says the woman.

'And I've had to pay for childcare,' adds Laura.

The receptionist looks genuinely apologetic. 'I do understand, honestly I do, but he's the boss. He says he'll rearrange in the next week or so.'

'The next week or so? The advert said you needed someone urgently,' points out Laura.

The receptionist shrugs and pulls a face. Laura gets the impression that this sort of behaviour from Mr Vernon is not uncommon. She loses her patience and stands.

'You can tell Mr Vernon not to bother calling me,' she says. She turns to the other applicants. 'Best of luck.'

Laura leaves the office and finds herself standing on

Deansgate in the heart of Manchester. She has three hours to spare before she needs to pick up Luke. She decides to spend some time exploring the city. She doesn't know Manchester well, and has only been in and out for interviews since she and Luke moved to Chapel Hill. She heads for the side streets.

Manchester proves much more interesting than she imagined. Behind the main thoroughfares there are mazes of narrow cobbled roads lined with unusual shops. After a while she stumbles across a narrow bookshop on four floors, and enters.

This is dangerous, she knows. Even when she promises herself she will only browse, she has never entered a bookshop without leaving with at least one book, and more commonly half a dozen. However, this time she has an idea, and a purpose; she wants to buy two gifts for Nadine, Virginia Woolf's *A Room of One's Own*, which had a huge impact on her when she first read it, and Mary McCarthy's *The Group*, which has just come out. She has yet to read *The Group* herself, but she loved McCarthy's first work, *The Company She Keeps*. She'll borrow the new book from Nadine when she's finished it.

Purchases made, she spots a pavement table outside what turns out to be a tiny Italian restaurant. The smell of fried food – fish, she thinks – makes her stomach grumble and, acting on impulse, she decides to treat herself to lunch. She takes one of the interior tables and, without much consideration, orders fried mozzarella, garlic bread – neither of which she has ever seen before, let alone tried – and a green salad. It's a surprisingly delicious meal and she resolves to return with Luke. Maybe even with Nadine.

I wonder if she'd try Italian food?

At half past two she heads back to the car. Despite her frustration over the interview, she has had a very enjoyable afternoon.

The lane leading to the village hall is crammed with parked vehicles by the time she arrives. She realises that Luke was right; many of the children attending the holiday club don't live in the village and have been driven in. She parks at the end of the lane and walks up. She can hear excited laughter and cheering long before she reaches the hall.

Sitting in semi-circular ranks on the grass in front of the building is a group of twenty or thirty children, their parents standing behind them in the sunshine. All are watching some entertainment, but Laura cannot see beyond the adults with their backs to her. Then, above all the heads, a large tool, perhaps a hammer, flies into the air in an arc and descends, followed by a pink hula-hoop and a plastic duck. The audience applauds as the sequence is repeated, and repeated again. Laura pushes her way through to stand at the front of the adults and behind the children.

In the centre of the group is the tall thin man she and Janine met at the summit of Chapel Hill. He is juggling with the three items she has already seen, to which he now adds a fourth, a large wooden skittle. Now he is showing off, grasping each object as it descends and throwing it up again through his legs from behind. The excitement of the crowd increases.

Laura scans the crowd and finds Luke sitting in the second row of children, his mouth a round 'O' of astonishment.

The performance ends and the man catches the last item to descend, which Laura sees is a heavy lump hammer that must weigh eight pounds. The man takes a deep bow to further applause. The crowd breaks up almost immediately with parents claiming children and walking them back to their cars. Laura picks her way across the remaining seated children towards Luke.

'Mum! Did you see that?' he says, eyes bright with excitement.

'I did.'

'That's Ianto,' he says, and standing up and grabbing Laura's hand, he drags her over to the man who is packing away his juggling equipment.

'Ianto, this is my mum,' says Luke. He turns to Laura. 'I've told him he can park his van in our garden.'

Ianto turns and smiles as he recognises Laura.

'Hello again,' he says in his deep voice. 'So Luke's yours, is he?'

'I've never seen this child before in my life,' she replies. 'I believe he's some sort of letting agent.'

'No, don't worry about that, man. Luke offered, but I didn't take it seriously. I can find somewhere else.'

'No good at the church?' asks Laura.

'The junior vicar – what do they call them, the curate, or deacon? – didn't want me parked there overnight. I got a flea in my ear this morning. Apparently I'm a beatnik.'

Laura laughs. 'How long are you going to be in the village?' she asks.

Ianto looks around the curtilage of the hall. Like everywhere in this area, the walls are dry-stone and Laura can see that several require work.

'Another month, perhaps,' replies Ianto. 'This lot haven't been done for years.'

'I suppose you could park in the area at the front of the house,' muses Laura, 'as long as Nadine doesn't mind.'

'She won't mind,' asserts Luke confidently.

'And there's an outside tap you could use,' continues Laura. 'What about emptying your toilet?'

'Are you on a septic tank or the mains?'

'Septic tank.'

'Should be fine then. I can empty into that. I wouldn't need to come into the house.'

'Okay. As long as Nadine agrees. We live in adjoining semis at the top of The Rise. There are no other buildings for miles, so I can't imagine anyone would mind. The land's pretty steep though.'

'That's great, thank you very much. I can block the wheels, no problem.'

'Okay. You can follow us up if you want. Or do you have more work to do here?'

'I've got to work until it gets dark, but I'll find you.'

'See you later, then,' says Laura, taking Luke by the hand. 'So, dry-stone waller and juggler. Anything else?'

Ianto laughs. 'Loads. Renaissance man, me.'

Chapter Sixteen

JANINE

The cottages bake in the August sunshine. There isn't a breath of air and the willow trees down by the lake are so still it's as if they have been painted on a backdrop. The south-west facing rear of the property, throughout the year a sheltered suntrap, has seen the thermometer rise by fifteen degrees Fahrenheit since the morning. East Cheshire is presently enjoying hotter weather than Spain.

The buildings are cool for much of the year but once the old blocks of stone have absorbed the heat, they radiate it round the clock. The air inside Apple Tree Cottage has warmed gradually over the week, and Janine feels like a slow-poached egg. Even stripped of all but her nappy, Bobby is fractious and sweaty, her mood not helped by the fact that her first teeth are erupting.

Next door, Laura has propped open both front and rear doors to allow any breeze there may be to blow through the cottage. Janine spots her from the back garden, wearing only her underwear, just inside the kitchen threshold, poring over a newspaper with a pencil in her hand.

Looking for jobs, I suppose, thinks Janine.

Luke, usually a mini-powerhouse of energy from dawn to

dusk, has taken refuge in the shade of a gnarled apple tree at the front of the building, lying on his back and reading a comic held at arm's length to shield him from the sun.

The sound of Ianto's regular strokes drifts up the hill as the lanky Welshman swims back and forth in the lake. Laura was walking around its perimeter the previous week when she spotted him floating, naked, on his back in the cool water. She mentioned it to Janine.

'I just thought I should tell you, in case you got an unexpected eyeful,' explained Laura, laughing. 'I don't blame him, though. It's hot enough in the cottages. It must be unbearable inside his campervan.'

'Do you think...' asked Janine hesitantly, 'well... do you think he might have been doing it deliberately?'

'Deliberately?'

'For our benefit? To see if one of us might be interested?'

The two women looked at one another for a moment, and both burst into laughter. Evidently, neither of them fancied Ianto. Laura offered to request the Welshman to stick to specific times if possible, or to acquire some trunks if not and, having spoken to him, assured Janine that there was no calculation behind his nudity. He was acutely embarrassed. He'd been timing his swims to an hour when he believed both women would be elsewhere; he swore to be more careful in future; he even offered not to use the lake at all if they preferred him not to.

In the days that followed the women didn't see much of him, although the multi-coloured van remained parked at the front of the house. In an effort to reassure him that they were not upset, they put a note under his windscreen wiper inviting him to dinner. Perhaps, Laura said to Janine, they might get to know their enigmatic hippy a little better.

Ianto brought chocolate cookies with him for dessert, and

for the first time in either of the women's lives, they got slightly stoned. After they finished eating Ianto went to the campervan to fetch his guitar, and the three of them stayed up late, sitting in the garden around a small bonfire, lit for illumination rather than warmth, singing and giggling under the stars. It was a special evening, and one that ended, at least in Janine's eyes, in a strange way.

The bonfire had settled into a heap of glowing red embers, a few lonely sparks drifting up into the night air. Janine and Laura were sitting on one side of the fire, leaning back to back, while Ianto lay on the grass on the other. He had stopped playing and had his hands under his head as he stared into the night sky. He was knowledgeable about the constellations and had been pointing them out to the women, but had been silent for a while.

'Well,' he said at last, 'I think it's time you two went to bed.'

His diction was slightly blurred but his cadence even more sing-song than usual.

Laura giggled. 'That sounds rather suggestive,' she said, and she turned to face Janine. 'What do you think? Is he inviting impropriety?'

It took a moment for Janine to understand what Laura meant, but then she snorted with laughter and embarrassment and then, even more flustered at the noise she had made, she fell sideways in another fit of giggles.

'Well, won't Luke be up in five hours?' replied Ianto. 'And Nadine's going to work, isn't it?'

But by then the two women were laughing so hard they were paying no attention.

'I might have to change my recipe,' said Ianto ruefully. 'Well, night-night, ladies. Thanks for my supper.'

He collected his guitar and loped off to the caravan.

The women continued chatting quietly for a while. Eventually they too rose and returned to their front doors. Then, as Janine turned to say goodnight, Laura leaned forward from the complete darkness and kissed her on the cheek.

It was not a sexual kiss, but Laura's soft lips lingered for a second or two longer than Janine expected. Then, without another word, Laura was gone, her front door closing softly behind her.

In the days that follow Janine thinks often about that kiss. She remembers Laura's hair touching her face; its smell of bonfire; and the tentative touch of the older woman's fingertips on her hip.

What did it mean? Did it mean anything? Was she just high, like me? Does she even remember it?

A few days later Ianto returns the dinner favour by asking if he can use one of the kitchens to cook the women a meal – no grass this time, he promises – and within little more than a fortnight he has somehow become a peripatetic member of family. Every few days Janine wakes to find the van gone, but it always returns after a day or two. She and Laura start allowing him to use their bathrooms when he returns from his dusty work, and when the two women spend the evening together in Magnolia Cottage, as they often now do, he will put his head in the back door and ask if he can join them.

He has also started doing odd jobs around the cottages, like repairing the fence posts and the stile at the back of the gardens and lifting heavy blocks of stone for Janine's use in her increasingly established garden. He cooks for the two households at least once a week. The women have come to enjoy his odd vegetarian cooking, a cuisine he learned, he said, while living in a commune in Holland.

Luke is not a fan of vegetarian food and demands that

Ianto's meals are served with at least one sausage, but otherwise the man can do no wrong in his eyes. When not working, Ianto spends time showing him guitar chords, playing with him in and around the lake and roaming the surrounding fields and woods. Ianto is teaching him to forage for food, and Luke tells them all excitedly how he is learning how to survive in the wild if he had to. He shows them his collection of edible ash seeds, elder berries, something the Welshman calls 'goutweed' which can be eaten in salads, and dog rose petals.

Every day Janine feels she is growing closer to her neighbour and new friend. When Laura presented her with the books, she was almost overwhelmed. Other than the poetry collection from Lady Margaret, Janine had never received a gift that was not second-hand clothing. To be given a present, something so thoughtful, for no other reason than she was liked, moved her intensely. And when Laura kissed her on both cheeks, she was incapable of controlling her emotions, and tears filled her eyes, which merely embarrassed her all the more. Laura seemed to understand. She laughed affectionately and hugged her.

The last couple of months have been the happiest of Janine's life. She feels warmed by Laura's friendship, more at home in her company than she has ever felt before with any human, more so even than with Edward. But there is sadness too; she missed all this while growing up. She is almost twenty-one, and Laura is her first friend. How many others might she have had, had Mother permitted it?

They often spend the evenings sitting quietly, reading at opposite ends of Laura's couch. To ensure they can hear Bobby should she cry, Janine puts her down in Laura's bed. Now the little girl can pull herself upright, Janine is worried that she'll soon be climbing out of her cot so, if anything, this feels safer.

They talk about books, the children and Janine's plans for

her clients' gardens; very little about their pasts. Janine doesn't want to pry into Laura's divorce for fear of raising a painful subject, and she assumes Laura is showing her the same sensitivity regarding her history. She hasn't yet been able to talk about life with Mother, or Edward's betrayal. She's kept that all bottled up for so long, she's not sure what will happen if she takes the cork out.

The heatwave continues.

It is late afternoon, and the sun is at last losing some of its intensity. Janine is in the back garden of Apple Tree Cottage. She can hear Laura swinging a scythe on the other side of the wall. Her neighbour has finally got round to attempting a first cut on the two-foot-high grass. Janine can't presently see Laura as they are both working close to the building where the wall separates the gardens, but every now and then she catches sight of Luke's dark head bobbing up and down towards the back, near the stile, talking excitedly to himself. The Rolling Stones are declaring that 'It's All Over Now' from Janine's new transistor radio on the kitchen windowsill.

Music has never before formed any part of her life. No television, no radio, no gramophone – those perfidious agents of the world forsaken by Mother – was permitted in the grey house in Hulme. Then Janine heard some music playing in a shop in Stockport. She slowed as she loaded her basket. It was exciting and optimistic. A few days later she heard the song again, recognised it and timidly asked the shop assistant what it was. The young woman, who was close in age to Janine herself, looked at her in astonishment.

'It's the Beatles.'

Janine frowned. 'I recognise the name, but don't think I'm familiar with their music,' she said.

'It was number one for weeks. You must have heard it!' scoffed the girl. 'It's "From Me To You".'

'I don't think so. How can I listen to it again?'

The assistant gaped at her as if she were half-witted. 'There's a record shop round the corner, on Middle Hillgate,' she replied, leaning forward and speaking very deliberately. 'Or buy yourself a transistor radio.' She pointed across the road towards an electrical retailer, shaking her head in disbelief.

So Janine bought a transistor radio and has been listening to Radio Luxembourg and Radio Caroline ever since. She's decided she likes pop music – not all of it, but most – and so, apparently, does Bobby. Whatever she is doing, when the music comes on she hauls herself upright, her head cocked like a robin's, and bobs up and down in approximate time to the beat.

Janine has finished fixing a trellis to the kitchen wall and has dug the three holes she will require for the new clematis plants. They are going in much later than she would recommend to her clients, but they were almost giving them away at a local nursery, so she thought she might as well try them and see what happened. She is in the process of lifting the first saturated root ball from its bucket when she hears Laura's voice.

'Nadine?'

Janine turns round. Laura has appeared at the end of the wall where the two gardens merge. She holds a jug and some plastic cups.

'I heard you working, and you're probably as hot as I am. I've made lemonade for Luke and me. Would you like some?'

Janine looks up and smiles. She no longer hesitates when speaking to Laura. She turns off the radio.

'Yes, thank you. I was just thinking of getting a drink.'

Laura takes a couple of steps into Janine's immaculate garden and starts pouring lemonade into one of the cups.

'Bring it over here,' offers Janine, pointing to a small circular table. It stands in the sheltered corner formed by her kitchen and the garden wall.

'Okay.' Laura turns and shouts towards Luke. 'Lemonade, Luke!'

Janine takes off her gardening gloves, lays them on the table and sits at one of the two garden chairs.

Laura comes over. There is a light sheen of sweat on her forehead, arms and upper chest. She puts the cups on the table, pours the drinks and sits next to Janine. She shuffles her chair until she is also facing the sun, and now they are so close their forearms could touch. She has sunglasses perched on her head holding back her voluminous hair and she slides them down onto the bridge of her nose.

She's like a model. Doesn't she realise how glamorous she is?

'It's a real sun trap in this corner, isn't it?' says Laura.

Luke bounds up, takes a drink and, without speaking, gulps down the entire cup. He wipes the dribbles off his chin with his forearm and races back to what he was doing, shouting 'Thanks!' over his shoulder.

'Sorry about that,' says Laura. 'He's made a den at the back and is in the middle of a battle. I should've tackled the grass long ago, but at least he's happy.'

'You should let me have a go at your garden,' says Janine.

'No, I couldn't ask that.'

'But I'd enjoy it. I've got a few ideas, too.'

They hear a war cry from Luke followed by protracted death throes. The two women laugh.

'He seems really happy here,' says Janine.

'I was a bit worried at first but, yes, he loves it. We both do.'

'Why were you worried?'

Laura laughs lightly. 'Oh, that was just me, being daft.' She pauses to drink. When she continues speaking it's with her eyes closed. 'He's a town boy, not a country boy. We used to live in a great big house in the suburbs of London and all his activities were local. He'd already started cycling to his friends. I was worried about moving somewhere so isolated, particularly as Roger's bought a house in an area pretty similar to the one we were in before.'

'Does he have another family?' asks Janine, thinking of Edward.

'Another? You mean a new wife? No. But he will.'

'How do you know?'

'Because he's rich and handsome, and very persuasive. When he turns on the charm it's hard not to be blinded by it.'

'So you were worried Luke would like his father's house better than here?'

Laura nods. 'Exactly. The poor man's still trying to impress his late father,' Laura adds, more to herself than to Janine.

'Sorry?'

'Oh, it's not important. And not my problem any longer, I'm pleased to say.' Janine frowns. 'Roger's parents,' Laura explains. 'Not nice people. Social climbers, always showing off their big parties, big cars and big holidays to their important friends. I don't think Roger got much affection when he was little. He was praised for doing well in his exams or when he landed himself an important job, and that's what passed for love in that family. So I think he has a compulsion to prove himself, especially to his father, despite the fact that the old man's been dead for years. Hence the ostentatious new house.'

'It made him what he is, though, didn't it? Pushed him to succeed,' comments Janine, thinking of Mother, who never praised her for anything.

'I guess so. But I did okay, and my parents more or less

ignored me until I was seventeen. I tried for years to get their attention.'

'So, pretty much the same thing, then.'

Laura turns to the younger woman, as if evaluating her afresh, and a slow smile illuminates her features. 'For someone who says they've no idea about "normal" people, you're pretty perceptive. I think you have something there.'

The women relax into a comfortable silence.

'So,' asks Janine after a while, 'how did you go about trying to get your parents' attention?'

'Oh, the usual. Being difficult and rebellious.'

'But that stopped when you were seventeen?'

Laura grimaces. 'Long story. In short, my sister, Saint Jennifer, committed suicide.'

Janine gasps. 'Oh, I'm so sorry! I shouldn't have asked.'

'It's fine. I've not spoken about it, not properly, for years. But it's always in the back of my mind. How can I explain this? I feel like I shouldn't still be thinking about it. I mean, it was sad, right, but not unusual. University undergrads have been committing suicide for ever. To most people, the police, the coroner, the university authorities, she was just another statistic. They dealt with it – or not, as in the case of the university – and moved on. Even my parents, in a way. Sometimes I think I'm the only person for whom it's still a big deal.'

'It must be a big deal for your parents, though? I mean, your mum...'

'You'd think so, but...' Laura shrugs '...I don't know. Maybe it's just stiff-upper-lippery, which they are very good at, but they absolutely *don't* want to talk about it. They never did, even straight afterwards. I think they're ashamed, terrified their friends and neighbours will think they were at fault.'

'Were they?'

Laura laughs joylessly. 'Oh, boy! *Were* they? Yes. They most definitely, positively were. They killed my sister.'

Janine doesn't know how to answer. She has never spoken to anyone like this, about feelings, hers or theirs, or the complicated, private things that occur behind closed doors. It feels like an honour to be allowed in, but it is daunting too, a responsibility she doesn't believe she has earned.

'Jennifer was the clever one,' continues Laura, 'top of her class throughout school, waltzed through the Oxford entrance exam, you know. But once she went up–'

'Went up?'

'It's the phrase they use for going away to university. Once she was there, I knew things were going wrong almost from the start. Mum and Dad wouldn't see it. They kept on at her, and on, and on – how proud they were, how she couldn't let them down, how she was sure to get a First. They didn't *want* to see it, their brilliant elder daughter, struggling.

'But I knew. She was different, stressed out and evasive. We'd been so close before then. I mean, I hated her sometimes for always being the centre of attention, but she was my hero too. My big sister, who'd protected me for years. And all of a sudden, she couldn't do it. She had no patience for me, no support left, like a wrung-out flannel. First year exams aren't important, so there were no alarm bells at that stage. We only found out at the inquest that she'd failed them, and most of her second year exams. She'd lied about it to us. She was supposed to do resits or something but, I don't know, I'm not sure she even turned up for them. At the beginning of the third year, she went off to Oxford as normal, but at the end of the first week we got a call saying she had died of an overdose. Sleeping pills and wine.'

'That's awful,' says Janine in little more than a whisper. 'Was it definitely suicide?'

'There was no note, and my father paid for a barrister to

persuade the coroner there wasn't enough evidence of suicide, and the coroner went along with it. So he found death by misadventure. But I knew. I knew how desperate she was, and I knew she couldn't tell our parents.'

'Why not?'

'She had to succeed. They wouldn't accept anything less. And after Jennifer died, I was supposed to take over her mantle. They came back from Hong Kong and started on me. I wanted to kill them for going off and leaving me at that school, but once they came back I realised I'd been better off as the stupid one, the one they could ignore. I was the spare.'

'Spare?'

'You know, how the royal family have an heir and a spare?'

'N-no, I don't think...'

Laura closes her eyes again, sinking lower in her seat. She speaks slowly, her former animation spent.

'Charles is the heir, Andrew's the spare, just in case anything happens to Charles. Well, I was the spare. Kept in the background... until the heir did herself in.'

There is a long silence. Laura opens her eyes. Janine is staring at her, eyes wide open.

'What?' asks Laura.

'Sorry,' replies Janine, looking away swiftly. 'I didn't mean to stare.'

'What is it?' says Laura, starting to laugh.

'It's just that... well... I don't know how you do it. You talk about such personal stuff.'

Laura grins, and shrugs. 'Too much?'

'No. I admire you for it.'

'Why?'

'I don't know how to. I grew up knowing that everything that happened to Mother and me was a secret. Her background, how she came to be living in Manchester, what happened at home, you know, between us. I always knew, even from when I was very little, that I wasn't supposed to speak about any of it. But you... you're just the opposite! Have you always been so... open?'

'I guess so,' says Laura, stretching out. 'When I trust someone.'

'You trust me, then?'

Laura closes her eyes again and doesn't answer for a moment. 'Of course I do. We're friends.'

Janine thinks about that for a long time. 'I hope so... I think.'

Laura opens one eye. 'You *think*? I'm on probation, then?'

'No, no, no, nothing like that,' says Janine hurriedly, now alarmed she's caused offence.

'I'm teasing you.'

'It's just that... I don't want to disappoint you. I'm not good at friendship.'

'What on earth makes you say that?'

'I'm not sure I know how to do it. When I was at school, I used to watch the others. Everyone else seemed to make friends, but I couldn't see how it happened. No one *said* anything. The boys joined in whatever football game was going on and the girls launched themselves into the skipping songs. I could never do it.'

'So what did *you* do?' asks Laura, looking puzzled.

'Well... nothing. I didn't have friends. I think I... I had a rather odd childhood.'

'You and me both. But don't worry on my account; in the friendship stakes, you're doing fine.'

Laura sinks even lower in the chair. There is silence between them for a few minutes. All that can be heard are the buzz of the insects, the breeze stirring the tall grasses and the distant bleating of sheep, punctuated every now and then by Luke's excited voice.

'I could go to sleep here,' says Laura quietly. 'It's so peaceful.' She starts unbuttoning her blouse. 'You don't mind, do you?' she asks. 'Ianto's away. But I'll go back behind the wall if you prefer.'

Janine is shocked, but manages to say, 'No, it's fine.'

Laura slips her blouse off her shoulders and lies back in her bra. 'I haven't the money for a holiday, so I grab the sunshine when I can.'

Janine cannot prevent herself looking at Laura's body. She has seen adverts on buses and billboards, but she has never seen another woman close up in her underwear.

Her shape's quite like mine, she thinks, *in fact, I'll bet our bra size is identical – but her skin's quite different, like ivory, several shades lighter than mine. We're like two scoops of ice cream, vanilla and coffee.*

Laura's hair hangs behind the back of the chair, a thick mane of curly red and copper. Not for the first time Janine longs to feel its texture. She also has an impulse to touch Laura's skin, still glistening from her earlier exertions. Janine's eyes linger for a while on the soft depression at the base of Laura's neck where the skin pulses. She knows she shouldn't, but she allows her eyes to travel down to the cleft between Laura's breasts and from there to the darker areas under her bra where her nipples are visible through the fabric. Janine is aware that her breathing has become shallower and her body is tense.

'Don't you just love having the sun on your bare skin?' drawls Laura slowly, her eyes still closed. 'I used to strip off completely in St John's Wood.' Her voice is low and languorous, as if she's slipping into sleep. 'There was no one overlooking our back garden. It made Roger furious.'

Janine tears her eyes away and tries to focus on the conversation.

'Sunbathing, you mean? I've never done it. Mother and I

didn't go on holidays. And there's not a lot of sun in Manchester. But since I've lived here, I love being outside.'

Pause.

'I don't know who my father is.'

The words have left Janine's mouth before she can stop them. Later she will go over the events, her ears burning, trying to locate the moment at which she decided to confide in Laura, but at that moment her motivation is simple; she feels she owes her new friend something, a confidence, to reward the trust Laura has shown in her. Laura has exposed herself to her, both physically and emotionally, and she has to reciprocate.

Laura's eyes open and she turns her head towards Janine. 'I wondered about that,' she says gently, 'but I didn't like to pry. I thought you'd tell me if you ever wanted to.'

'For years Mother told me I had no father. None at all. Until I was eleven I believed I was like baby Jesus.'

'A virgin birth?'

'Yes.' Janine sees the glint of amusement in Laura's eyes. 'Honestly, that's what she told me. Or what she led me to believe, anyway.'

'Crumbs,' says Laura, suppressing her smile. 'Were your parents not married then?'

'I don't think so.'

Laura nods. 'You could probably find out who it was, if you really wanted,' she says after a pause. 'Someone who knew your mother at the time must know who she was... going with. Unless, of course...'

'Unless she was raped? Yes, I've recently asked myself if that's what happened. But when I was little, after I realised that I must have had a father, I used to imagine going to Lowestoft and tracking him down. I'd be a detective, like Sherlock Holmes. I'd find him, and he'd be amazed. He'd hug me and cry, explain where he'd been – probably on a long sea voyage, or something like that – and he'd apologise for not having been there while I grew up. And from then on we'd live together.'

'Oh, you poor thing!' says Laura with feeling. She reaches out. The gesture startles Janine and she almost flinches. Laura's hand lands tenderly on her cheek. 'Thank you,' she says softly.

'Thank you?'

'For trusting me.'

'I've never told anyone about my father. Not a soul.'

Janine feels her heart thudding. Laura is so close to her, her blouse off, her white skin inviting and her hand still touching Janine's cheek. The girls at school were always touching one another, plaiting one another's hair, applying their friends' make-up in the toilets, even walking around holding hands. Janine used to wonder what it must be like to trust someone so completely to let them touch you, to let them inside your personal space, and this is it, this is what it feels like, and the intimacy feels wonderful and unexpectedly sexual.

Without thinking she leans forward and kisses Laura on the mouth. She sees Laura's eyes opening wide in shock, and for a split second Janine is sure she has made a terrible, terrible mistake. But then Laura's lips soften, and her other hand reaches up so she has one hand on either side of Janine's face, and she is pulling Janine gently into her. Janine sees Laura's eyes closing as she gives herself to the kiss and she too closes her eyes, acutely conscious of and aroused by Laura's breast pressing against her upper arm.

A little voice is heard from inside Janine's semi. Bobby is awake.

Janine's eyes open and Laura releases her. Their faces remain close. Janine feels Laura's jagged breath on her skin.

'Sorry,' says Janine, her eyes frightened.

'Don't be.'

Bobby's cry is getting louder and more impatient.

'I'm not sure...' starts Janine.

'Nor am I,' says Laura. 'And maybe we should talk about it. But please don't regret it. I've wanted to kiss you like that so often in the last few weeks.'

Bobby is now in full voice, demanding attention.

'Coming!' calls Janine.

Chapter Seventeen

LAURA

School term has started again, but the weather remains as glorious as it was in August. Laura steps out of the office building onto the busy pavement of St Ann's Square, central Manchester, muttering to herself. She wears a smart linen suit, a cream blouse tied with a bow at the neck, and court shoes; her other interview outfit.

It's been a waste of time. Again.

She hadn't really wanted this job anyway; it was full-time and she's not ready to have Luke cared for in the afternoons by a stranger. To cap it all, the man in the middle of the panel, the head of department, made several unpleasant comments about divorced women, and how someone who looked like Laura would have to be kept away from the males in the department. As if she was some sort of sexual predator. He thought it hilarious to joke (although he wasn't really joking) that she'd only stay long enough to snare someone else's husband, a replacement for her own.

This attitude is something that Laura hadn't foreseen prior to her divorce, and she's begun to think it explains why she's not securing jobs for which she is more than qualified. This interview, the last of several inexplicably difficult meetings, was the best example and helps make sense of the others. Men, she has concluded, are frightened of divorced women.

It's about sex. In fact, where men are concerned, it's *always* about sex, one way or another. Divorced women have had sex. They know about sex. They might even like it. Now they're not getting any, they're dangerous, hungry for it, and are prepared to steal other women's husbands to get it. Accordingly divorced women have to be controlled or their sexual urges will create societal breakdown.

Her parents' attitude is similar. Laura fully expected to be lectured that she'd let the side down by not struggling on with Roger, but she hadn't prepared herself for the moral condemnation. Apparently, Laura has brought shame on the family.

Soon after she moved into her semi, her father came over, ostensibly to bring some unused curtains that might fit the cottage windows. At the time Laura was surprised her mother didn't come too as she hadn't yet seen the property, but she accepted the pretext that Annabel was busy that afternoon. Having looked around and complimented his daughter on the cottage, in particular its location which would be wonderful for Luke while growing up, Brian took the opportunity to have a heart to heart.

Of course they still loved her, he said, and he and Annabel were delighted that she and Luke lived a bit closer now, but he didn't think she had grasped the extent to which they felt let down by her. Most of the people they knew would consider Laura a 'loose woman' or, at the very least, a failure for not being able to hang on to her husband. Not them, of course, but most people. Such attitudes towards divorced women were still very common, and he and Annabel had a position in the community and at church to uphold. Annabel had missed Sunday service for weeks because she was terrified of the gossip, and that was, if Laura thought about it, her fault.

So, he concluded, they would be grateful if she didn't just pop over, with or without Luke, without arranging it first, in case they had company. He was sure she would understand and respect their feelings. It was all about thinking about other people and, let's face it, he said with a sad smile, that was Jennifer's strong suit, not yours.

Laura understood.

She looks at her watch and increases her pace. The car park is a ten-minute walk away, she's in uncomfortably high heels for running and, unless she's very lucky, she's going to be late picking up Luke.

Back on the road home she allows herself to consider, yet again, The Kiss.

What on earth *happened*?

Laura is aware that her affection for Nadine has been growing steadily. She looks forward to seeing her every day. Days when they are too busy to get together in the evenings are flat by comparison. When Nadine and Bobby aren't there, Magnolia Cottage feels empty, despite the constant boisterousness of an almost nine-year-old boy.

But this... this was different. Their lips met and parted, and she was instantly and overwhelmingly aroused. If Bobby hadn't woken, she knows it would have gone further. She'd *wanted* it to go further.

As she drives through the busy traffic in the heart of Manchester she sees other young women, alone or with friends, sitting at café tables, going in and out of clothes shops, walking on the pavements. When the traffic forces her to stop every now and then, she takes the opportunity to study them.

Do I fancy any of these women, in their pretty summer frocks? Or is it just something about Nadine?

She acknowledges she enjoys looking at some of them, but that's not the same. Most women she knows recognise beauty, even sexiness, in another. So this is the wrong question.

Would I want to have sex with any of them?

She suddenly realises that even posing the question to herself means she *does* want to have sex with Nadine. That truth, as it unfolds in her head, shakes her. She recognises her own desire and is unnerved by it.

I want to have sex with another woman. This isn't some cool, intellectual thing. I want to have real, hot, sticky sex with Nadine.

She flushes and feels her armpits becoming clammy. *There's something wrong with me*, she thinks. *How can I be...* and she recoils at the word she has heard her father use... *a deviant? It's not possible. I've always been normal. Haven't I?*

Then she reminds herself of the rows with Roger over sex. He so often complained that she said no most of the time and, even when he could persuade her, she seemed detached, uninvolved. In fact, now she thinks about it, it hadn't been any better with Mark either, the only man with whom she'd slept before Roger.

Laura doesn't want to be someone on the outside, pointed out, the subject of gossip. Being a divorced woman is bad enough, but... a lesbian? Her parents would never speak to her again.

She has never doubted her identity as a normal woman – a married woman, at that – and these new feelings are disquieting. She backs away from them.

Perhaps what I'm feeling is protectiveness, she thinks. *Yes, that would be entirely possible; protectiveness for a naïve young woman alone in the world. I see her vulnerability and I want to look after her. Not to forget admiration; Nadine's a remarkable, strong, person. She managed to break away from an abusive alcoholic parent; she dealt alone with an unplanned pregnancy; she set up a home and a fledgling business and, with no one to guide her, has become a good mother to her baby. She's amazing.*

So, it's not sex. It's intense friendship and...

Laura stops herself.

'Liar,' she whispers to herself in the car. 'Liar, liar, pants on fire.'

For they are on fire. She is aroused, now, in the car, driving in heavy traffic through Gorton as she imagines having sex with Nadine. From the first time she laid eyes on her, she found herself looking at her in a way that in the past she associated only with men. In the same way as with Li Xiu half a lifetime ago, there was an instant attraction and some of it, if she's being honest with herself, was undoubtedly sexual.

How does Nadine feel? Is she this confused too?

Laura has tried, haltingly, to raise the topic with her neighbour – no, her *friend* – since The Kiss, but the younger woman seemed reluctant and Laura backed off. They remain close, seeing one another almost every day and, so far, without awkwardness. Laura is loath to put that at risk, but it remains a conversation she is desperate to have.

But what if she's regretting it?

Laura arrives at the school five minutes after the children have been let out. The lane is blocked by a tractor so she has to park at the end and run the rest of the way. She arrives outside the school gates, breathless and with a blister forming on her heel, to find Luke in conversation with a boy and an elegant woman who is also too well-dressed for the school pick up. She is smoking a cigarette, leaning against a Land Rover parked half on and half off a grass bank at the side of the lane.

'Hello,' says the woman, 'you must be Luke's mum.' She offers a hand. 'I'm Christine Carter, Mitch's mother.'

Christine is an elegant woman in her forties. She is slim

with light brown hair and she wears blue tailored trousers and a cream waisted jacket. Laura notices pearl earrings. She looks like one of the rich wives of Roger's former partners.

'Am I in trouble?' asks Laura. 'I got a terrible ticking off from Mrs Anderson the day we moved in.'

'No.' Christine smiles. 'You've been lucky. It appears our boys have arranged for Luke to come home with us this afternoon.'

Laura looks down at Luke.

'Can I, Mum, please?' he begs.

Laura is in two minds. Luke knows very well that he is not supposed to make arrangements without running them by her first, and they had plans to go to Glossop to buy him new shoes, a painful process that usually takes a couple of hours. On the other hand, this is the first time he's been invited back to another child's home and she's encouraged to discover he's made a friend.

Luke half-turns away from Laura, and mutters the single word 'Film!'

It takes Laura a second or two to appreciate the significance of the word. It will be Luke's birthday in a few days' time. Offered a party at The Rise or at his father's new house, he asked instead to take half a dozen of his classmates to see *A Hard Day's Night*, which was still being shown at the Plaza in Stockport. At first Laura was worried that his choice was designed to avoid disappointing either parent, but his incessant singing of Beatles songs persuaded them that it was what he genuinely wanted, and so she and Roger agreed.

She points surreptitiously to Mitch, and Luke nods vehemently. So, it appears to be very important that Mitch is among the cinema guests.

'What about your shoes?' she asks. 'You were complaining this morning that your sandals were too tight.'

'Oh, Mum, that can wait! And Mitch has a pool!'

This news makes Laura even more hesitant. Luke is not yet a confident swimmer, and she doesn't want to leave him in the care of someone else if he'll be in a pool. She's still nervous when he's playing around the lake with Ianto, who's proven he's a very strong swimmer.

Christine seems to read her mind.

'Why don't you come too?' she asks, crushing her cigarette out on the grass. 'Stop for a cup of tea for an hour or so. You'll still have time to get the shoes.'

'Are you sure?' asks Laura.

'Absolutely. I've been looking forward to meeting you.'

'You have?'

'You moved into Margaret Wiscombe's property, didn't you? At the end of The Rise?'

'That's right,' replies Laura, puzzled.

'I know Margaret quite well. She was a friend of my mother's. Come on, follow us back, and we can get to know one another over a cuppa.' She moves off around the front of the Land Rover. 'Although,' she calls back, 'they call it a "brew" up here.'

Laura feels Luke tugging at her jacket. 'Can I go with Mitch?'

'Why?'

'It's a Land Rover!' he says, as if the answer were obvious.

Laura nods. 'Okay. But be polite.'

She runs back to her car and follows the Land Rover out of Chapelhill. She is taken down winding lanes that she has not explored before, worrying distractedly if she'll be able to find her way back.

After ten minutes the car in front of her slows and turns left through tall iron gates set in imposing stone piers. To one side is a carved sign announcing 'The Lodge'. Laura follows, her car rattling slowly over a cattle grid.

To her surprise no house comes into sight. The driveway dips and winds its way through countryside for another half mile.

'This can't all be theirs, surely?' she says to herself.

The drive straightens and leads through an honour guard of poplars before taking one final dip. It reaches the crest of the next hill, and Laura sees the house below her. The purr of her tyres changes to crunching as she follows the Land Rover onto an enormous expanse of gravel with a central fountain. She has arrived at a stately home.

'Good God, it's huge!' she mutters.

An enormous double staircase flanked by a stone balustrade leads from the sea of gravel to doors twelve feet tall. The house is three storeys high, built of heavy grey blocks of stone.

'And it's got battlements!'

The Land Rover pulls into a space between a line of three other cars, another Land Rover, a Mercedes and a vintage Rolls Royce.

I'm going to look completely out of place here. I feel like the nanny!

She parks her little Triumph Herald at the end of the line of vehicles. A large oak door set in a stone wall to the right of the house opens inwards, and a man's head pops out. He lifts his hand in salute at Christine and approaches. He has barbecue tongs in his hand and wears shorts and a florid baggy T-shirt. From her distance away, Laura can't hear what he says, but he kisses Christine, looks down at Luke and offers his free hand to him. To Luke's credit and Laura's pride, Luke reaches up and shakes it without hesitation. Christine is obviously telling the man who Laura is, because he turns to her as she gets out of her car.

'Laura Flint, I gather!' he says as he walks over. 'I'm delighted to meet you. I'm Michael Carter. Call me Mike.'

Mike Carter is a short, tubby little man, with a head of thick sandy hair, and a wolfish look in his blue eyes. Laura knows the type instantly. He and Roger would get on famously.

'Pleased to meet you, Mike. I feel a bit embarrassed, barging in like this.'

'Not at all, not at all.'

'Are you entertaining?' she asks, nodding at the barbecue tongs.

'Only you and your lad, if you'd like something. I was in charge of the older kids today, but I'm a terrible parent and only got started on their lunch a while ago. But it's Friday, the weekend beckons and the weather's glorious, so I thought I'd keep them happy on crisps and other rubbish until I got the barbecue going. Come on, follow me.'

Laura follows him to the doorway in the wall.

'I saw the sign as we came in,' she says. 'So if this is The Lodge, how big is the main house?'

'Ha! It's sort of a joke, I gather. There was a porter's lodge at one time, and that was called The Manor. This' – and he waves airily at the house – 'is what we call The Lodge. Chrissie'll tell you about it during the grand tour, I expect. It's her ancestral pile. I just married into it.'

Carter leads her around to the back of the house. Christine and the two boys have disappeared.

An enormous swimming pool is situated on a terrace from which wide marble steps lead down to a lawn. The lawn sweeps three hundred yards into the distance, broken by groups of mature oaks. A river curves gracefully through the short grass, willows dipping their leaves into its water, until it broadens out into a lake surrounded by reeds. On the far bank of the lake is a pavilion with a white domed roof. A wooden boat is tied to a jetty outside the pavilion. Beyond the river to the east, reached by an ornate bridge, is a tennis court. Beyond that, faded into green-blue by the haze of the afternoon heat, is a line of tall poplars, their tops swaying in the breeze. The scents of cut grass and cooked meat waft across the terrace.

'Wow!' says Laura quietly.

'A bit corny, eh?' says Carter. 'Capability Brown, I gather.'

Two children are in the swimming pool, conducting a noisy and wet battle from two mini-dinghies. Carter calls over to them.

'Caroline, Roddy, can you stop that for a second? This is Laura Flint. Her son, Luke, is here somewhere and he's Mitch's friend from school. Please make him welcome.'

The children continue splashing one another immediately.

'Can I get you a drink?' asks Carter.

He points to a smoking barbecue by the side of which there is a plastic barrel of iced water, cans bobbing on the surface. 'I'm on beer, but we have pretty much everything.'

'Christine said something about a cup of tea, actually. I have to drive.'

'That's a shame. You and Luke should make an evening of it. We've dozens of bedrooms.'

Christine emerges from extremely tall French doors. She has changed into a sarong and flip-flops. Laura looks at her more closely. Now they are standing on level ground she realises that Christine is very tall, probably six inches taller than her husband. She has a wide mouth and brown eyes, and sports a suntan that looks as if it's never allowed to fade. For a woman pushing forty who's had three children, she has an astonishingly good figure, thinks Laura. She regards Mike Carter again, as he turns quarters of chicken on the sizzling barbecue. *That little chap's punching well above his weight*, she thinks.

'Drink?' asks Christine.

'Mike's just asked, but I think I'll go for that cup of tea, if you don't mind.'

'Yes, of course,' replies Christine and returns the way she came.

A second later Mitch runs out of the house in bathing trunks, followed almost immediately by Luke, who has obviously been lent a pair. Mitch leaps out over the water, his knees held to his chest, and bombs the two children already in the pool. Luke is a few paces behind him and running at the same speed, but Laura sees a momentary hitch in his stride as he realises that he has no choice but to follow suit or look scared. He too jumps into the water, a little less exuberantly, and splutters quickly to the surface, water having shot up his nose. He doggy-paddles to the corner of the pool, smiling blindly, his eyes still full of water.

'Take a seat,' says Carter, pointing to a line of pool-side recliners.

Laura does so. 'Quite a place you've got here,' she says.

'Not bad, is it? I don't mention it as a rule. People tend to get the wrong idea. "The Lord of the Manor" and all that.'

'Are you?'

'What?'

'The Lord of the Manor.'

'Not the title, but most of the duties, which Chrissie's family would say I neglect horribly. They've never forgiven her for marrying me, although I'm still better than the last chap. But there are only two or three tenants now. Most of the land was sold off in the twenties when Christine's father had the place.'

'Does Christine work?'

'She owns a wine bar in Hyde.'

'What, Joseys?'

'Yes, do you know it?'

'I've driven past it a couple of times. What do you mean "the last chap"?'

'Ancient history. Chrissie was married before, to a marquess. He was very suitable, except that he drank and screwed anything in a skirt.' He pauses, swigs some beer, and winks. 'But he finally went off with the land agent's wife and what was left of the family silverware, so Christine divorced him. The clan never liked me – too common for a start, and the wrong religion – but I was stable and boring and I loved the kids, so they put up with it.'

'The kids?'

'Caroline and Roddy aren't mine. But they're terrific, and I love them as if they were. Caro's even called me Dad once or twice by accident, which I love. Anyway, that's enough of the family saga, how're you getting on in Chapelhill? Settled in now?'

'The house is pretty straight, but the garden's still a jungle.'

'I should give you the name of our gardener. Assuming she's still around.'

'Sorry?'

'Well, she hasn't shown up the last couple of times. But she's amazing. I've never seen anyone with such an affinity with plants. Everything she's put in has thrived, and the colours! The head gardener left last year and the other two were taking it easy. She's only young but she really shook them up, I can tell you.'

'*Head* gardener?'

'You don't think I cut this lot myself, do you?' he says, indicating the lawn. 'Yes, we have three. Rather, we *had* three. I don't know what happened to her. We owed her money too.'

'Can't you call her?'

'No. It's odd. A friend of Christine's late mum put us onto her, and she rang us. She looked the place over, said she'd be here every week, and that was that. Turned up on her trike, bang on time every week, did her stuff and toddled off. We never had cause to telephone her. When she didn't show, Christine asked her mum's friend to get us the girl's number, but she came over all mysterious and said that she had no authority to give it out.'

Trike? thinks Laura. *Surely there can't be more than one female gardener locally that rides a trike?*

Christine returns with a tray bearing a silver teapot, cups and saucers and sugar bowl with tongs. Over her arm is a piece of material. She puts the tray down on the recliner next to Laura's.

'I brought you this,' she says.

She shakes out the material and Laura sees that it's a silk sarong or, perhaps, a kimono.

'You won't be comfortable wearing those work clothes. Do you want to try it? Get a bit of a tan while you have the chance.'

'I don't have anything to wear underneath it.'

'I can lend you a swimming costume.'

'Thank you, but you're six inches taller and at least one size slimmer than I am.'

'Well, try this then. You can leave your underwear on and put this on top. And honestly, Laura, you don't have to worry if you want to sunbathe or go in the pool. There's no one around except us, and no one'll mind. You won't mind, will you, Mike?'

He looks over at Laura and winks at her again. 'Not for a second.'

Laura hesitates. There's no way she's going to swim in her underwear in front of Mike Carter, to whom she's taken an immediate dislike, but she would like to get out of her suit, not least because she's sweating and the linen is creasing.

'Okay. Thank you. Where can I change?'

'Follow me,' says Christine.

She leads Laura into the house.

'Mike was saying you've mislaid your gardener,' says Laura. 'It wasn't Nadine Tyler, by any chance?'

Christine spins round, forcing Laura to a halt.

'Yes. Do you know her?' she demands.

'Yes. She's my friend, my neighbour in the other semi.'

'Good. Tell her from me to stop making passes at other people's husbands,' says Christine angrily.

Laura takes a half-step backwards, feeling as if she is under attack.

'Nadine?' She shakes her head. 'Impossible. I don't believe it. She's... *pathologically* shy. She'd never throw herself at a man. Never. She can barely make eye contact, even with me.'

'Well, that's what Mike said.'

'I'm sorry... I don't know Mike at all, so I can't comment. All I know is, I'd believe it of any woman I've ever met, before I'd believe it of Nadine Tyler.'

Christine examines Laura's expression for a moment, nods to herself, turns and strides off. Laura doesn't know if she is supposed still to follow, but then Christine turns and smiles, as if the short conversation had never occurred.

'Come on then,' she says, walking backwards as she speaks.

Chapter Eighteen

JANINE

'How long have you been collecting these books?' calls Laura from Janine's lounge.

'The gardening books? Since I've been here. I found a wonderful place with boxes of second-hand books for as little as sixpence each,' replies Janine through the arch from the kitchen.

She hurries in. 'Are you sure this is okay?'

'Course I am.'

'It's just that since Mrs Reid's fall she can't manage Bobby, especially now Bobby's mobile. The garden's only tiny so I'll be gone less than two hours, but I don't like to let her down. She's very sweet.'

'We'll be fine.'

Janine looks over to the couch where Luke is playing with Bobby. She frowns and chews her lip, still undecided.

Laura comes over. 'Don't fret,' she reassures. 'I know exactly how you feel. The first time I left Luke for more than a few minutes was hard. But Bobby's fed, changed and happy, and we'll stay in here, where she's at home.'

'No,' replies Janine, 'I know she'll be fine, and do take her next door if you want. There's a bottle of expressed milk in the fridge and I've left a saucepan on the ring. You fill that with water, and put the bottle – yes, of course! Sorry!'

She bends, picks up Bobby, gives her a squeeze and a kiss, and puts her back on the couch. 'I'll be back soon,' she says, and she strides to the front door.

Janine returns an hour and a half later, hot and sweaty from having cycled up the hill. The others are sitting outside in the back garden of Magnolia Cottage. Laura has spread a blanket on her patch of scruffy lawn and erected a parasol to protect Bobby from the sun.

'Hello,' calls Janine from outside.

'We're in my garden,' shouts Laura back.

Janine appears from her kitchen door. 'How was she?' she asks. 'Everything all right?'

'Absolutely fine,' replies Laura. 'Not a single tear, didn't need changing and didn't need feeding. You timed it perfectly.

Janine bends and picks up Bobby.

Laura stands. 'Nadine? Could I have a word with you in private?'

'Of course.'

'But not for little ears,' she says quietly, nodding towards Luke, who is lying on his front and reading a book. 'Maybe Luke could take Bobby inside for a moment?'

Janine frowns and starts to shake her head, not understanding.

'It's important,' insists Laura.

Janine studies Laura's expression, and then shrugs. 'Luke, would you mind taking Bobby inside for a while? I think she's getting a bit hot.'

Luke looks up. 'Okay. Shall I take her to ours? I can read her a story.'

'Yes, that's fine,' says Janine.

Luke stands and holds out his hands for the little girl. The two women watch him walk with her through Laura's back door.

'He's such a lovely boy,' says Janine.

'Shall we sit down?' asks Laura.

'What is it?' asks Janine. 'You're starting to worry me.'

'Please?'

Janine follows Laura to the blanket on the grass and they both sit.

Laura clears her throat. 'This is difficult, and I've been meaning to mention it for a few days but wasn't sure how to raise it. It's not about... what happened between us.'

Janine looks hard at Laura, her eyes narrowed. *What have I done? Have I done something wrong?*

'Have you been gardening for Christine and Mike Carter?' asks Laura.

Janine freezes. *Oh no! I know what's coming.* 'Why?' she asks cautiously.

'Turns out her youngest goes to the village school and is friends with Luke.'

'I thought their children went to boarding school,' replies Janine, avoiding her friend's eyes.

'Maybe the oldest do, I don't know, but Mitch is certainly in Luke's class.'

'Okay. And?'

'They were explaining that they had a young female gardener who rode a trike, but who suddenly stopped going. Was that you?'

Janine bridles, colouring. 'Laura, I don't want to offend you, but I don't see how that's–'

'I'm trying to look out for you,' interrupts Laura. 'Christine Carter says you made a pass at her husband.'

Janine's jaw drops. She shakes her head but no words emerge from her mouth.

'I didn't believe it,' says Laura. 'I've met that man, and I bet I know exactly what happened. But that's what he's told Christine.'

Janine finally manages to get words out past her shock. 'It's a lie!'

'I'm sure it is. He tried it on with you, didn't he?'

'I don't know what you mean by "tried it on". But he put his hands all over me. He was trying to get... inside... I had to fight him off! He called me... he called me... a whore.'

Laura's mouth opens in an 'O' of surprise. 'Jesus! Why didn't you tell me?'

Janine shrugs. 'What for? Doesn't this sort of thing happen all the time? I mean, I've never been called... *that* before, but on the buses in Manchester men were always...' She tails off, blushing.

'This is more than being "accidentally" groped on the bus, or being patted on the bottom by male colleagues. What you're describing is an assault. Have you thought of reporting it to the police?'

'Yes, I did at first, but obviously I can't. Who'll they believe? He's some sort of lord isn't he, a churchwarden and all that? And I'm an unmarried mother who's morally lax. I've got other local clients, and I need to keep them.'

'"Morally lax"?'

Janine nods. 'He said if I was morally lax enough to have sex with other men to whom I wasn't married, why not him?'

Laura gasps. 'The bastard. What did you say?'

'I slapped him.'

'Good for you!'

Janine shakes her head. 'No, I shouldn't have done it. You might get away with something like that, but I'm not you. And now I've lost a client, and they still owe me for two weeks.'

'When Christine Carter mentioned it to me, I told her I didn't believe it. I said you were the last person in the world to do something like that.'

'Did she believe you?'

'I'm not sure, but I think so. There was something about her response. That man's got a roving eye; I'd be very surprised if you were the first.'

'Maybe, but he's never going to admit it.'

Laura nods. 'That's for sure. He's married into loads of money, a prominent position in the community and a gorgeous wife. He'd say anything to hang on to all that. I'm so sorry, Janine.'

'Thank you for sticking up for me. A lot of people wouldn't have.'

'You're my friend.'

There's a knock at the front of the building.

'Yours or mine?' asks Laura.

'Mine, I think.'

Janine stands, crosses into her garden and walks through the cottage. She opens her front door. Standing before her is the social worker, Mary O'Reilly.

'Hello, my dear,' says O'Reilly with a smile. 'I was just passing and thought I'd pop in and see how you're getting on.'

'We're fine, thank you,' replies Janine, forcing a smile to her face. 'But I have company right now, so–'

'No, no, don't worry about that. I'll only come in for a moment,' says O'Reilly.

Mindful of how the social worker pushed her way in last time, Janine reacts quickly and starts to close the door. She doesn't intend it, but O'Reilly's front foot, already over the threshold, is squashed.

'Ow! That was uncalled for! You've damaged me ankle!'

Janine reopens the door, her face white.

'I'm so sorry, Miss O'Reilly! It was an accident.'

'I could have you for assault!'

'Well, it was an accident...'

'I need to come in and sit down,' says O'Reilly, now stepping into the hallway. 'I think you've broken it.'

Janine can't imagine how such an innocuous event could possibly have caused a broken ankle, but now she doesn't feel able to refuse entry. She opens the door fully and stands back, allowing O'Reilly to pass in front of her and head for the kitchen, limping theatrically. Janine closes the door and follows her. O'Reilly pulls out a kitchen chair and sits down, making a show of rubbing her ankle. Then she opens her satchel and starts taking out papers.

'Right then,' she says abruptly, now all businesslike. 'Have you received your maternity allowance?'

'I don't need it. I have a job.'

'But that's not the reason now, is it?'

'What do you mean?'

O'Reilly pauses for a moment. When she speaks again, her voice is less aggressive. 'Look, you silly girl, why don't you just tell me the truth and we can start afresh?'

'I've told you the truth.'

'No, you haven't. I've been looking for your national insurance record. There's no one of your age with the name Nadine Tyler. That's why you've not had your allowance, isn't it?'

She stares at Janine from her position at the table, shaking her head sadly. Janine doesn't answer but her face betrays her. 'And your supposed husband, William Tyler, a soldier, you say?'

'What of him?'

'What's his date of birth?'

Janine cannot think quickly enough to answer.

'You see? You don't even know your husband's birthday!' says O'Reilly triumphantly. Her tone softens even further. 'Listen, girl, I can help you. Honest to God, I can. You don't have to struggle on here, on your own. Cedars Moral Welfare has been helping girls like you for over fifty years. We can offer you a job, safe, secure housing, and a decent start in life for Bobby with a good Catholic family.'

'What do you mean, "girls like me"?'

'You want me to spell it out? Girls who've got themselves into trouble. Girls who want to do the right thing by their babies and not bring them up in a sinful house.'

'This isn't a sinful house!' protests Janine angrily. 'I think you should leave.'

'Let's call a spade a spade, shall we? Your baby girl's a bastard, and I call that sinful.'

Janine knows she should remain calm but fear gets the better of her. 'Get out!' she says, almost shouting.

O'Reilly seems stunned by the violence of Janine's response.

'I said get out!' This time she does shout.

O'Reilly's expression changes again. Now there is no pretence at kindness. 'It's a great pity you can't discuss this rationally. It only demonstrates, in my professional opinion, that you're not a fit person to bring up a child.'

She stands just as Laura appears at the back door.

'Is everything all right?' asks Laura. 'I heard shouting.'

Both Janine and O'Reilly turn towards the voice. 'And who might you be?' asks O'Reilly.

Laura smiles, and Janine is astounded by her calm confidence.

'I'm Miss Tyler's friend and neighbour. My name is Mrs Laura Flint.' She turns to Janine. 'Everything okay?'

'This is a private matter, Mrs Flint, and I'll thank you to leave me to discuss it with Miss Tyler.'

'There's no discussion to be had,' says Janine. 'I want you to go. I don't need your help, and I don't want it.'

O'Reilly looks from one woman to the other. 'Very well. But I *will* be back,' she says, tucking her documents angrily into her satchel. 'You can be sure of that.'

Laura follows the social worker out of the house and watches her get into her car and drive off. She closes the door firmly and hurries back to the kitchen. At the same moment Luke emerges through the back door with Bobby in his arms.

'What was that?' he asks.

An irrational fear grips Janine and she strides the two paces towards Luke and takes Bobby from him, hugging her tightly to her chest and rocking. She starts to weep. Perhaps her distress communicates itself to Bobby, or perhaps Janine is simply holding her too tight, but the baby inhales deeply and lets out a wail. Janine slumps in a kitchen chair with Bobby clutched tightly in her arms and gives herself up to misery.

'Oh!' cries Laura softly, and she crouches before Janine, her hands on the young woman's warm brown knees.

Janine suddenly leaps to her feet. 'I've got to pack!' she cries.

'No, you don't.'

'But they'll... they'll...' hiccups Janine, unable to speak through the sobs.

'Hush, it's okay,' soothes Laura. She turns to Luke. 'Go outside and play. I won't be long.'

Luke looks from his mother to the distraught woman and the crying child in her arms, and then back to his mother. He looks confused and frightened.

'It's okay, Luke, I promise. But go outside.'

Luke nods and complies.

'It's *not* okay! They're going to t-take Bobby away!'

Laura frowns, uncomprehending. 'What do you mean they're going to take Bobby away? Who *was* that woman?'

Janine is too distressed to answer but she points at the mantelpiece. Laura goes over and picks up O'Reilly's card.

'A social worker? But why? Social workers don't take babies away.'

'She said...s-she said...'

'What did she say?'

'Sinful... I was sinful, and I wasn't a fit mother, so she would take Bobby away!'

'Sinful?' asks Laura, still not understanding. 'Are you sure you understood her properly?' She embraces Janine and Bobby together.

Janine takes several deep breaths and manages to control her crying sufficiently to blurt out, between gulps of air: 'It's because I couldn't put Edward's name on the birth certificate' – gulp – 'because I'm not married' – gulp – 'and because I'm a Catholic.'

'No,' says Laura softly into Janine's hair, 'no. She can't do that. I promise you, she can't do that. We won't let her.'

Janine feels herself rocked gently from side to side, like a boat at anchor, and her panic starts to recede. She drops her head onto Laura's shoulder. The older woman smells of garden and fresh air.

Bobby is still whimpering.

'I need to feed her,' whispers Janine, reluctant to move from the safety of Laura's embrace.

'Then go on,' replies Laura, also in a whisper, her words hot and breathy in Janine's ear. 'Don't mind me.'

'I'll go upstairs.'

'Not on my account.'

'But... I've never done it in front of anyone else. Except the nurses in hospital.'

'It doesn't bother me. I breastfed Luke. But if you're embarrassed...'

Laura disengages and stands back. Janine regards her steadily for a few seconds, incapable of preventing her chest from juddering every second or third breath, and sits down. She undoes her blouse and nursing bra and puts Bobby to her breast. The child quietens instantly as she sucks, pausing only to gulp air through her mouth every few seconds.

Laura crouches beside them. 'Poor little sausage,' she says gently. 'Her nose is so blocked from crying, she's taking in more air than milk.'

'I know... she'll need... winding afterwards,' hiccoughs Janine, still not completely calm.

'Okay,' says Laura. 'While you do that, I'll put the kettle on, and you can tell me what that woman said.'

'I'll have to tell you about Edward, then.'

'Only if you want to.'

'I think I do want to.'

EDWARD

Janine is almost seventeen.

For the last two years Mrs Brown, her favourite teacher, has been lending books to her. Not only has Janine sped through all of the texts on the syllabus, but she has also read everything in the sparse school library. So Mrs Brown brings a new book from her home every few days, and they talk about them during break and, sometimes, at lunchtime. Mrs Brown has even mentioned the possibility of Janine going to university to study literature.

One Saturday morning Janine is mopping the kitchen floor when Mother tells her to put the mop down and run a bath. Janine knows that this presages something unusual as she normally has to clean the house from top to bottom on Saturdays and have a bath in the evening when she's finished. Mother doesn't like her bathing more than once a week because it is an old heater and it wastes the gas.

Mother simply tells Janine to forget any nonsense about going to university. They haven't the money for that. Instead, Janine is to start work. That day.

Janine is a little disappointed about university but she never really believed it was possible anyway. She is, however, excited about the thought of a job, so she does as she's told without comment. Mother hands her some money for bus fares and tells her to go to a nursery in Chorlton. Janine initially believes she is being sent somewhere to look after small children, but when she arrives she realises it's a place where they grow things, like plants, vegetables and fruit trees. It is huge.

Janine is expected. A frightening woman wearing a tight jumper, a beehive hair-do and clutching a cigarette in a holder looks her up and down like she's a specimen. She asks a few questions that Janine can't answer and picks up the phone. With Janine in front of her she speaks to someone.

'The girl's a moron. She's got no conversation, she can't make eye contact, and she looks as if her mother dresses her.'

Apparently, whoever is on the other end of the line doesn't care about any of that, and Janine is put on repotting seedlings. The woman tells Janine to her face that she doesn't expect her to last to the end of the week.

But she does. She absolutely loves the work and it's wonderful being away from Hulme and Mother. She even thinks she might make some friends – there are quite a few other young people working there, especially at weekends – although that doesn't happen. But having something of her own, something she is good at, feels like she finally has a life, a real life, outside of the books.

She enjoys everything about it: the feel of the soil between her fingers; how a tiny flat seed will, if treated right, grow into something as complex and beautiful as a plant; how every plant and seedling has to be treated differently and just right to make it grow; how they all smell different. She can't talk to the other people working there – once again she is outside the group – but she can talk to the plants, and she does, and they respond. Everything she germinates, re-pots or divides thrives. She learns all their wonderful Latin names – *tropaeolum, rosa rugosa* and *lavandula angustifolia* – a secret language that Mother has never heard and will never understand. She sucks up knowledge like a sponge. The other apprentices laugh at her, at her clothes, at the fact that she knows nothing about music or the television programmes they watch, but even they start asking her for help when they get stuck.

At the end of the first week she has to take her money home to Mother. She is given a payslip, but Mother doesn't ask to see it. She thinks, perhaps, that Janine is only paid cash in hand; or maybe she's forgotten what happens when you have a proper job. Whatever the reason, she takes the cash and returns enough for fares and lunches for the following week.

After a month, the people at the nursery start giving Janine other things to do, and her wages increase. In fact, they increase two or three times over the course of the next year. She doesn't tell Mother. Instead, she goes into a building society, opens an account and deposits the difference every Friday before going home.

After she's been at the nursery for about six months, she becomes aware of a funny little man who watches her as she bends over the seedlings or prepares pots for cuttings. She sees him out of the corner of her eye but, every time she turns around, he disappears behind a cotoneaster or *phyllostachys*. He is so quick that, for a while, she wonders if she is imagining it, or if perhaps he is an elf. She is quite prepared to believe in elves. She doesn't know anything except what she reads in books, and she reads a lot about fairies and elves. She wants what she reads to be true.

Then one day Janine spots him in conversation with the manageress, and concludes that he must be one of the farmers who supplies the nursery with compost or vegetables. They don't grow everything; some of it comes in from local farms. The man doesn't look as if he belongs in a nursery. He looks too smart to be an employee. Although he always has muddy gumboots on his feet, he wears a jacket, cardigan, shirt and tie. And a brown trilby. Janine loves that trilby.

It turns out that he is her boss; he owns the nursery.

He continues to watch her, and she isn't frightened by his attention. Indeed, she looks forward to it. He is the only person there who notices her. It reminds her of the game the other children played at school, Grandmother's Footsteps. Janine likes his caution, his circumspection. He is saying 'I won't get too close unless you want me to'. Like one of his more difficult plants, she has to be cultivated gradually, given exactly the right type of soil, water and sunlight if she is to germinate.

One afternoon he places a hand on Janine's bare arm. She feels a hot tingle spreading throughout her body. She can't remember anyone ever touching her before, except Mother of course, and that is usually to hit her. It is also the first time he speaks to her.

'I've been watching you,' he says.

Janine doesn't turn round but she says, 'I know.'

'Do you mind?' he asks.

And Janine says she doesn't; actually, she likes it. Saying it made her blush, but he smiles at her.

'That's all right then,' he says, and he disappears again.

After that he often comes up to her, and they talk about the plants, the seedlings, the changes in the seasons. He doesn't need to talk about these things – Janine knows what her duties are – but she divines instinctively that they are actually talking about something else.

Janine has read many books in which people fall in love. The conversations feel like that. His eyes and his words caress her as his hands caress the plants. He woos her with Latin plant names, propagation techniques and soil types, the soft syllables rolling off his tongue and into her heart.

One day he tells her she is beautiful, and he kisses her hand. She feels as if her legs will give way. No one has ever, *ever* told Janine that she is beautiful. She goes home that evening confused, light-headed, tremulous about what is happening and what might still happen, and twitching with impatience for it to occur.

At first nothing does occur. Sometimes he speaks to her and sometimes he doesn't. Days when Janine doesn't see him at all are empty and flat. She is constantly looking over her shoulder, looking for his hat. She is jumpy and irritable.

Mother never notices anything.

Then he plants his seed. Not the seed of his life, that comes later, after he cultivates Janine and brings her on for another year, as if she were a difficult and valuable crop, a luscious rare fruit, so that when she is ripe, he needs only to tickle her and she falls gently into his palm. No, this is the seed of their love.

He approaches her as she is taking off her leather gloves at the end of the afternoon. Most of the other employees have gone home, but Janine wants to finish some repotting. Her back aches after hours of bending. She turns to face him. He pauses, leans forward and, without speaking, kisses her on the lips. She is taller than him, so he stands on his tiptoes.

Janine has been imagining that kiss for weeks. She knows from the books, Thomas Hardy and the others, that this is what men do, and she knows from Mother that it always leads to shame, babies and disgrace. She still aches for him to do it. She knows, with utter certainty, that his kiss will set her free. Like Snow White. She has all sorts of scenarios and possibilities running through her head, but they all conclude with the same thing: she will leave Mother and Hulme forever and live with Edward.

Janine keeps her eyes open, and the kiss seems to last for ever. She notes the smell of him – aftershave and clean, friable soil – and she wonders at the softness of his lips and how they part ever so slightly when in contact with hers. When the kiss ends, he opens his eyes. They were closed throughout she noticed, not screwed up, but closed so the lashes just met lightly, as if he was asleep. He steps back and she feels bereft, as if something has been stolen from her. She moves towards him but is surprised when he puts up a hand to stop her.

He looks at her, a puzzled frown on his face. He is breathing deeply, his eyes bright and his round face flushed. Then he shakes his head and walks away.

She is left standing there, confused. She has failed some sort of test. The kiss was so marvellous, it set her heart thumping and her body yearning in ways she'd never experienced before, but she must have done it wrong.

All the way home and all night she tries to decipher his expression as he halted her. She thought the red cheeks and flashing eyes were a good sign – she's sure she looked like that herself – but perhaps he'd been angry or disappointed.

Janine doesn't see him for several weeks. He is never in, or perhaps he avoids her. He's changed his mind, she thinks; he doesn't like her after all. Her heart hurts so much she thinks she cannot possibly survive the pain. She will have to find a different job. She can't bear to be at the nursery and not see him.

Then, one day he is there and he speaks to her again. It's as if the kiss never occurred, but she is still happy. Within a few days things go back to the way they were. She knows something is going to take place between them, and she starts lying to Mother about having to work late to create an opportunity for him. It eventually happens on the floor of his office. Then in his van and, a few times, in a caravan he keeps at the back of the nursery.

Janine doesn't enjoy it. It is painful and much messier than she expected, but he is so affectionate, stroking her for ages afterwards and telling her how lovely she is, it makes her feel beautiful; worthwhile and good at something. And she knows from the books that it makes men happy, and she *so* wants him to be happy. So it doesn't seem to be asking too much to let him do it.

After they have been making love for a few months she misses her period. She doesn't realise at first – she's never bothered to keep a diary – but one night she wakes up in bed in the dark and it suddenly strikes her: *It's been six weeks!* In fact, when she checks, it is over seven weeks.

Janine knows immediately what it means. She is giddy with happiness. She can barely wait to tell him, in their own private language, that the seed he has sowed in her has germinated. Everything is going to change. They will marry; she will continue working at the nursery until the baby arrives; she will leave Mother; they will live together. It doesn't occur to her, not for a second, that he won't be as deliriously happy as she.

She realises something is wrong the minute she tells him, but she can't grasp it, or perhaps she doesn't *want* to grasp it.

She doesn't understand what he is saying. She sees his mouth moving, and she is listening, but a foreign language is coming out. All she can gather is that he is displeased with her; he isn't filled with joy like she is; he isn't hugging her excitedly and making plans. Instead, he is embarrassed and awkward. It is like being trapped in a nightmare.

And, really, it is such a simple thing to explain. How difficult is it to say that you've been married for twenty-five years, that you have four children, one of whom is in a wheelchair, and that you can't possibly leave your wife?

Janine takes the bus home in a daze. She must have forgotten to put on her coat, because she arrives in her drenched cardigan and without her handbag or keys.

Mother opens the door.

'Where are your keys?' she asks.

Then all the questions, Mother's face too close, her mouth also moving and making no sense. Finally, somehow, she asks the right question, but for the wrong reasons.

'Has someone interfered with you?' she keeps asking. 'Have you been violated?'

She examines Janine's legs for scratches, her underwear for tears and her fingernails to see if they are broken.

Janine wants to say 'Yes!' to those questions, and at the same time 'No! That's wrong, it's just the opposite! Someone has cultivated me, fed me with love, brought me to flower and now to fruit. He has given me a life, turned my world inside out, and made me happy for the first time ever!'

But she doesn't say any of those things.

Mother throws her out that night.

Chapter Nineteen

LAURA

Laura spends the next two days finding reasons to pop into Apple Tree Cottage. Ianto is working somewhere in Lancashire and is not due back until the weekend. Laura has missed him, his calm wisdom and his funny cigarettes, and wishes he was here to help her support her friend.

She doesn't think Nadine has slept since O'Reilly's visit. In the still of the night Laura can hear her pacing up and down next door, opening and closing cupboards. Packing, she supposes. When she goes into Apple Tree Cottage she finds her friend alternating between manic list-making while checking railway timetables, and curled into a ball, weeping. Laura is so worried that, if left alone, Nadine will cut and run, she even cancels a job interview. She doesn't believe that social workers have the power to take children away from their mothers merely because they are illegitimate, but nothing she says seems to reassure Nadine. In Nadine's mind, O'Reilly is an older, wiser professional; she has an identification badge and a clipboard. She must know what she's talking about.

Laura tries to soothe her; she talks to her and, when the

young woman is too upset to listen to reason, sits on the sofa with her head in her lap, stroking her honey-coloured hair.

Finally, and reluctantly, Laura concludes that there's only one solution.

'If I get some proper legal advice, will you promise not to leave?' she asks.

'How?'

'My ex-husband's a lawyer. I can ask him.'

Nadine shakes her head. 'I've made up my mind. I'm going somewhere she can't find me.'

'When?'

'I need to see Lady Margaret first, so not before Monday.'

'What if I speak to Roger now and get some advice? Will you promise to wait?'

'I promise I won't go before Monday, unless that woman comes back before then.'

'Good. I'll do it now.'

Laura returns to Magnolia Cottage, pulls the telephone down onto the kitchen table and sits before it. It is Friday, which means completion day for conveyancers. Roger is likely to be very busy, but will probably still be at his desk.

She is reminded of all the times she needed him during the course of their marriage but was too scared to call in case he shouted at her. She knows that he often left explicit instructions with his office to lie about his whereabouts, sometimes because he was genuinely too busy to take her calls; sometimes, she guessed, because he was out somewhere, conducting one of his little affairs.

Other than the fortnightly handovers, she's had no contact with Roger since she moved to Cheshire. She knows nothing of what's going on in his life. For all she knows he has a new girlfriend. Now she has to phone him, out of the blue, and ask for a big favour on behalf of somebody else.

She is grateful that Luke is at school and won't hear the conversation. On the first couple of occasions after he returned home from staying with his father, Laura tried gentle probing about what Roger was up to, but it obviously made Luke uncomfortable.

'Doesn't Dad ask questions about what we're doing?' she asked.

'Sometimes.'

'And do you tell him?'

Luke was playing studiously with his toys and at first Laura didn't think he was going to respond.

'No, I don't,' he said finally.

Since then Laura hasn't pressed. If Luke wants to keep his two homes and two parents in separate boxes, not talk about either to the other, she must respect it. His little face becomes anxious even when his father rings to make weekend arrangements. The truth, Laura conceded sadly, is that Luke overheard far too much during the divorce. They have no one to blame but themselves if he has become a nine-year-old diplomat, keeping confidences from both sides.

Laura steels herself to be shouted at and dials Roger's office number. To her surprise she is put through to him immediately.

'What's up? Is Luke okay?'

It's a very different response to those she received during the marriage, and Laura is pleasantly surprised.

'He's fine. I'm sure you're very busy, so I'll come straight to the point. My neighbour is in desperate need of some urgent advice, and she has absolutely no one to turn to. I wondered if you could spare a few minutes to help her.'

'Well?' replies Roger, after a pause. His voice is dry, not exactly angry, but clearly impatient.

'A social worker turned up unannounced at her door. Bobby, her baby, is illegitimate and she didn't give the name of the father on the birth certificate. The social worker threatened to take the baby away. I've told her I don't think that's possible, but she's terrified and I'm no lawyer. The social worker, someone called O'Reilly, apparently works for Cedars Moral Welfare. Have you ever heard of them?'

'No.'

'Do you know of any power that would permit a social worker to remove the child of a single parent?'

'Just because her parents aren't married? No. But I specialise in corporate conveyancing, so what do I know?'

'Is there anything you can do to help?' Roger doesn't answer. 'Please, Roger. I wouldn't ask if I could turn to anyone else, you must realise that.'

She hears him draw a deep breath.

'I suppose I could do a company search and see where that leads,' he answers. 'And the firm does have a family lawyer. He might know something about the state's powers regarding illegitimate children.'

'Thank you. I need it as soon as possible. My neighbour's scared out of her wits and is threatening to disappear with the child.'

'I'll see what I can do.'

'Can you get back to me before the end of the weekend?'

'I'll try.'

'Thank you. I'm very grateful.'

'Is that all? If it's okay with you I need to finish my proper job before I start pro bono work.'

'I'll see you at the weekend.'

It is now Saturday, early afternoon, and Bobby is having her afternoon sleep. Laura dropped Luke off in Didsbury earlier that morning – letting him out of the car and watching only until the front door was opening before speeding off to return to Apple Tree Cottage.

The two women have spent the morning in their respective gardens. Nadine has barely spoken but Laura has been chatting away from her side as she works, attempting, without success, to lift her spirits. Laura has spotted, but said nothing about, the bags and boxes in the hallway of Apple Tree Cottage, ready for a Monday morning getaway. She is surprised but heartened by the fact that Nadine is still working on her garden; it suggests at least that she'll keep her promise until the end of the weekend.

As for Laura's own garden, the jungle behind Magnolia Cottage, it is at last half-tamed, but the grass having been cut for the first time in years, Laura now finds that, with little rain and no new growth, she has a patch of browning, weedy stubble. She looks up again at what lies on the other side of the boundary: a verdant green lawn surrounded by multi-coloured flower beds, herbs and shrubs.

'What can I do with this?' complains an exasperated Laura. 'It's so spiky, you can't even walk on it in bare feet whereas yours...' and she steps across the divide to the lush lawn and throws herself full-length onto it, 'feels like a velvet bedspread!'

Nadine is on her knees, weeding. She speaks without turning round.

'Yours needs scarifying, spraying to get rid of the weeds and moss and probably re-turfing or seeding. Too early for either. I can leave you some instructions, if you like.'

'*If* you're going,' reminds Laura.

There is no response.

Laura rolls onto her side and props her head on her hand. She observes the girl from behind. Nadine's blouse is tight and Laura watches the muscles of her slim torso moving underneath it as she works. Laura's eyes move down. Nadine's shorts have ridden up and exposed the back of her brown thighs.

I can't let her leave.

I want her.

On impulse she stretches out her arm to stroke the firm flesh and is only inches away when she loses her nerve. Instead she rolls onto her back again and stares at the sky.

'I love what you've created here,' she says softly. 'The colours and the fragrances; it's so peaceful.' A thought occurs to her. 'You must've hated having a complete gardening novice as a neighbour, letting the side down. Maybe you should put up a fence, hide my bit.'

Nadine turns and sits back on her haunches. 'Would you want me to? If I were staying?'

'Not unless you do. Would you prefer that?'

Nadine regards her steadily. Laura becomes aware of a tension between them. She sits up.

'No,' says Nadine.

'I'm pleased,' says Laura, returning her gaze steadily. 'I did wonder. At the start I thought you didn't want anything to do with us. In fact, I thought you'd leave.'

'I almost did,' admits Nadine. 'I liked this place because it was isolated; I didn't think anyone else would want to live up here.'

'And now?'

Nadine locks eyes with her for so long, it becomes almost uncomfortable. Finally the gaze of the younger woman breaks away. She looks down, plucks a few blades of grass and fiddles with them. Her hair falls over her face, creating a blonde curtain. Laura is desperate to close the two feet of distance between them and to wrap her in her arms.

And kiss her again.

'And now?' repeats Laura softly, her heart quickening in her chest with anticipation.

Nadine lifts her head slightly, most of her face still hidden by her hair, unable to make eye contact.

'If it weren't for... that woman, O'Reilly... I'd want to stay here...' She stops, pauses and then adds, '...with you.'

With me?

Laura hears in those two last words more than merely occupying an adjoining semi-detached cottage. But she is still uncertain, fearful of leaping to the wrong conclusion. She remains very still, unwilling to break the spell, hoping Nadine will continue.

'We're friends now, aren't we?' asks Nadine tentatively.

'I think you may be the best friend I've ever had,' replies Laura.

Nadine looks up and her eyes meet Laura's again. She is about to say something further when Laura's front doorbell sounds. They both ignore it, but then it rings again, twice, in quick succession.

'Damn,' curses Laura softly. 'This is the second time we've been interrupted. Please don't move. We need to finish this conversation.'

She stands and crosses swiftly to her own garden, through the kitchen and down the hall to her front door.

'Mum!' comes Luke's voice faintly from the other side.

She opens the door to find Luke standing before her, his clean T-shirt splotched with what looks like ketchup.

'What is it? Why are you back?'

Luke pushes past her and runs up the stairs. 'Need a poo!' he shouts as he runs.

Roger is standing beside his car at the end of The Rise. Laura leaves the door open and walks through the old orchard towards him.

'What's going on?'

'Nothing. We're on our way to Chatsworth for afternoon tea and he needed the loo, that's all. You were closer.'

'Are you all right?' she says as she reaches him.

'I'm fine. Why?'

'You look dreadful.'

He has dark rings under his eyes and his face looks much thinner than she remembers.

'Charming.'

'No, seriously, Roger, you don't look very well.'

He sighs and flicks the dark hair out of his eyes. 'Just tired,' he says, looking away.

Laura glances at her open front door, willing Luke to return so she can resume the conversation in the back garden. She returns her attention to Roger.

'Is this work? You've worked stupidly long hours before and been absolutely exhausted, but you've never looked like this. What's going on?' Roger drops his head to his chest and folds his arms as if suddenly chilled. 'Is it the new firm?' she persists.

'Partly. I'm not really enjoying it as much as I did.'

'You enjoyed it in London.'

'I liked the money and the status,' he corrects her, 'but the work? Not so much for the last couple of years.'

'You didn't tell me.'

'Well, you might remember, we weren't exactly close confidantes around that time.'

She laughs grimly. 'Yes, okay, good point. But there's something else, isn't there? You look as if you've the weight of the world on your shoulders.'

'It's just... proving more difficult than I thought. Some of my biggest clients made promises, but now the existing files are completing they're not sending new work. Turns out, being two hundred miles from London is a problem after all.'

Now Roger has Laura's attention. This might have serious implications for her and Luke.

'And the partnership?' she asks.

He doesn't answer immediately. 'I've been asking to see the deed and they're stalling,' he admits finally.

'You think they're having second thoughts?' she says.

'I think so.'

'Are you looking elsewhere? You've still got a reputation, haven't you?'

'In the City, yes, and if I have clients to bring with me. But I don't want to go back there if you and Luke are up here. Anyway, that's not really the problem.'

'What is, then?'

Roger looks away again and shakes his head. 'Don't worry about it.'

They hear the toilet flush inside the house and Roger opens the driver's door.

'What have you done?' she asks, suddenly suspicious.

'Who says I've done anything?' he says over the roof of the car.

'You think I don't know you, after all this time?'

He takes another deep breath. 'Remember I said I'd taken a mortgage? That wasn't exactly accurate. It was a loan, bridging finance, to cover the first year. The bank have agreed a mortgage in principle, but it's dependent on getting the partnership.'

'And if you don't?'

He shrugs. 'They'll call in the loan.'

Luke runs out of the house and opens the car door.

'Did you wash your–' starts Laura, but Luke shows her his wet hands.

It is only then that Laura notices that Luke's eyes are red. She puts a hand on his chest, preventing him from sitting in the car.

'Are you okay?'

'Yes, fine,' he says, but without looking directly at her.

He sits in the car and starts fastening his seat belt. Laura bends into the open door.

'Have you been crying? Luke?'

'He's fine,' says Roger.

Luke gives her a bright smile and pulls the car door closed. Roger gets into the driver's seat.

'See you tomorrow,' says Roger. 'Oh, I almost forgot,' and he turns and takes a manila envelope from the back seat and hands it through the open widow. 'You might as well have this now. There's not much, but Cedars Moral Welfare is a charity that supports "fallen women". It's not overtly Catholic like the Magdalene Laundries in Ireland but it is staffed by Catholics, some salaried, some volunteers, like your social worker, O'Reilly.'

'I've never heard of the Magdalene Laundries.'

'They're the Catholic equivalent of the workhouse. For prostitutes, unmarried mothers, women with mental disabilities. Sometimes just inconvenient women from posh Catholic families. According to my colleague – there's a memo in there – Cedars Moral Welfare fulfils a similar function over here. The women and girls in there are pressurised into giving up their babies for adoption. But the point is they can't force your neighbour to do anything, and they can't take the baby away unless the mother's an actual danger to her. Just having a child out of wedlock isn't enough anymore.'

'She was putting Nadine under pressure.'

'Yes, but that's all she can do, unless there's some other reason, like neglecting the baby.'

'Nadine's a wonderful mother. And she's certainly not a prostitute. She got taken advantage of by an older married man.'

She regards Roger pointedly.

'Well, she'll be fine then,' says Roger, ignoring the implication. 'As a matter of interest, why are you so invested in this? She's just a neighbour, right?'

'No, she's more than that.' Laura choses her words carefully. 'She's a good friend, and an incredible young woman. She had a totally f...' – she flicks a glance at Luke – 'messed up upbringing from what I can tell but, at twenty, she might be the strongest woman I've ever met. She's amazing. And although she didn't finish school, she's very bright.'

'Okay,' says Roger, starting the engine, 'nothing to worry about, then. I've put details of the National Council for the Unmarried Mother and Child in the envelope. They support people in her situation, help with benefits and so on. See you.'

Laura watches him turn around and drive back to the bottom of the hill. She returns swiftly to the garden. Nadine has complied with the injunction; she hasn't moved at all since the interruption.

Laura kneels on the grass facing her. She pushes her mane of hair back and smiles.

'That was Roger. He's looked into it. There's absolutely nothing that O'Reilly can do to take Bobby away.'

Nadine's eyes open wider with tentative hopefulness. 'Really?'

'Yes, really. It's all in here,' says Laura, brandishing the envelope. 'He's done some digging into Cedars Moral Welfare. O'Reilly's an interfering Catholic busybody whose morality you've offended, that's all.'

'And if she comes back? She said she'd come back.'

'Then we tell her to mind her own business.'

Laura watches as Nadine absorbs the news. The young woman's eyes fill with tears of relief, but she is smiling too. Laura reaches out for Nadine's hand to comfort her, but the younger woman almost falls forward and wraps her arms around her. Laura drops the envelope.

They remain clasped together on their knees for several seconds. Then Laura feels Nadine's lips on her neck. The kisses travel in soft increments up towards her ear and Laura finds herself holding her breath. She shudders and lets out an involuntary gasp. Nadine leans back for a second, gripping Laura tightly by her shoulders and looking with piercing intensity into her eyes. Then she leans in again and kisses Laura on the mouth.

Confused thoughts wrestle in Laura's head but she ignores them and allows her body to take charge. It knows exactly what to do. Her lips part and her tongue touches Nadine's. She feels as if she's being carried downstream in ever-faster water, as sensations explode in her lips, her tongue and between her legs. It feels so different from kissing a man. Nadine's lips are soft and sensuous, her tongue light and playful against hers; her skin is like silk, and her breasts, pressing against hers, are soft and yielding, quite unlike the hard flat chest of a man.

Their mouths are still locked together in foreplay but their long hair is getting tangled in Nadine's glasses.

'Wait,' she breathes.

She takes the glasses off but the two women are still joined by them, strands of blonde and red wound in the bridge and hinges. They pause, both laughing. Patiently they tease out the strands.

'There!' says Nadine, and she tosses the glasses a couple of feet away onto the soft grass.

She reaches urgently for Laura again and the kissing recommences with even greater intensity. A moan escapes Laura's throat and she slides her hands down Janine's back and then back up under her shirt. Nadine reaches round to the back of Laura's thighs and Laura feels her hands going up, underneath her shorts to her bottom.

'Here?' breathes Laura, her chest heaving.

'Why not?' replies Nadine, her voice hoarse with arousal. 'We'll hear if anyone approaches. And it's so beautiful.'

Laura pauses, and frowns. The short hiatus has allowed her intellect to start working again. *This is happening too fast!*

Her reaction, her hunger for this young woman, are so removed from any version of herself she recognises, the situation feels surreal.

Nadine must have interpreted Laura's pause as rejection, because she recoils, immediately embarrassed and ashamed.

'I'm so sorry... I shouldn't have...' she starts.

Laura reaches for her. 'No, no! I'm confused about what this means about me, but not about *this*. I want this,' she says urgently.

Nadine's face is still flushed, her eyes shining, but she remains at a distance, her chest heaving, apparently unsure.

Laura pulls her blouse over her head in one movement, ignoring the buttons, and throws it to one side. She unfastens her shorts and slides them off. She doesn't mean to do it, but her panties come off with them. She doesn't care and throws both on top of the blouse, aware of a light breeze on her bare skin.

'Please,' she sighs, reaching out, 'let's not stop.'

Laura is in a daze. They spend the next couple of hours together, sometimes in the garden, sometimes wandering into one or other semi, barely speaking, circling one another, stopping to look at each other with wonder, and to kiss, embrace and fondle. It seems to Laura almost dreamlike in its unreality. After a while it becomes too hot to remain in the sun and they return to Nadine's living room. For a while they sit on the couch, holding hands but not speaking. Nadine gets up to make a drink for them both and Laura follows, for no other reason than she doesn't want to be out of the other woman's presence. As Nadine fills the kettle, she points to the fridge from which Laura takes out a pint of milk. Before she can turn around, Laura feels hands stroking her hair, her back and her backside. They start kissing again, the tea forgotten.

Towards the end of the afternoon Nadine stands and starts preparing a salad with tomatoes and leaf cut from her garden while Laura feeds Bobby puréed apple. She makes enough for two without asking if Laura is staying. While she bathes Bobby and gets her ready for bed, Laura returns next door and collects a tray on which she loads a bottle of wine, a corkscrew, two glasses and some cheese and biscuits. She goes to the bathroom and brushes her teeth and her hair. She sees that her blouse has lost a button and has grass stains on it. She decides to wash and change.

She returns with the loaded tray to Apple Tree Cottage. As she lays the table and opens the wine she can hear Nadine upstairs, singing softly to Bobby.

Nadine eventually comes down. She too has changed her clothes.

'That looks nice,' says Nadine, nodding to the table.

'So do you.'

Laura indicates the meal laid out. 'I thought we should make it a little special.'

The two of them stand facing one another in the centre of the room. It is dusk and they are in semi-darkness. Laura takes both of Nadine's hands in hers. They look at one another for a long time without speaking.

'My head is full,' says Laura eventually. 'It's like a torrent of thoughts and feelings and questions. But at the same time I have never felt so... *still* inside. Do you understand? Like a pool of cool water.'

'Have you ever...'

'No. Never. I had a crush on a girl at school once, but we didn't... do anything. Nothing like this. You?'

'I've only ever had sex with Edward, and it wasn't anything like this.'

Laura smiles. 'Both novices. Did we do it right, I wonder?'

'I've no idea, but' – and Nadine laughs in a way that Laura hasn't heard before, as if unshackled – 'it certainly felt right.'

Laura laughs with her. 'And I'm not taking advantage of you, am I? I'm really conscious of the age difference. Especially given what happened with Edward.'

Nadine reaches out to stroke Laura's face. 'No. I've been thinking about it for ages.'

'Me too. I sometimes felt we were dancing around one another. You were... *are*... amazing.'

'Yes? I had no idea what to do, so I just did what felt right. Mother would be horrified.'

'You're not sorry, are you?'

Nadine shakes her head firmly. 'No. The... intimate stuff with Edward was... different. He was kind and gentle, and of course I have Bobby as a result, but this... what we did... I've never felt anything so powerful. Like coming home. You seemed to know...' She stumbles to a halt, blushing.

'What? Don't be silly. Isn't it a bit late to be shy?'

Nadine can't look Laura in the face, but she does answer. 'You seemed to know me... my body... better than I do.'

'Me too.'

They pause and resume caressing each other with their eyes.

'So, what now?' says Nadine.

'Now we have a glass of wine, or two, and we eat that lovely salad. I don't know about you, but sex makes me hungry.'

'But afterwards, I mean. What do we do… from now on?'

'Let's think about that later,' says Laura. 'I'm hoping you're going to invite me to stay in that big bed of yours tonight.'

'Yes. I'd like that. Oh, and Laura?'

'Hmm?'

'Call me Janine. My real name's Janine Taylor, not Nadine Tyler.'

Chapter Twenty

JANINE

Janine wakes early the next morning. She feels unexpectedly rested and alert considering the time at which they finally lay down to sleep and the fact that her mind was even then still racing with excitement, relief and possibilities.

She rolls over in bed and regards the sleeping woman next to her. Laura's skin is white and perfect, like a bowl of cream, and her hair spills like fine coils of red metal across her shoulders and the white pillowcase. She reminds Janine of the fairy-tale princesses of her childhood, the heroines of her storybooks and her fantasies.

Janine was, of course, Rapunzel, locked in her tall tower, awaiting rescue by a handsome prince. To be honest, the prince, when he arrived in the shape of a fifty-year-old market gardener with mud under his fingernails, was some way from the princes as advertised. Nonetheless, he was kind and seemed to offer an escape. But this? Janine never envisaged being rescued by another princess.

Perhaps we're rescuing each other?

She slips quietly out of bed and pads next door to Bobby's

room. It's still early even for her, and she sleeps soundly on her side, her thumb in her mouth, snuffling every now and then. Janine looks up and out of the front window. Ianto's van is back in its spot in front of the house. He must have finished early and arrived overnight.

I wonder what he's going to say about this?

But then he already lives outside common convention, she thinks, so perhaps it won't bother him.

She leaves the room and goes quietly downstairs. It's a sparkling new day, the sky ice blue and cloudless, the crescent moon hovering above the horizon. It is still dark in the back garden so she goes to the lounge and looks down the hill towards the little lake surrounded by trees. Peach sunlight slants through the branches. *We should have a last picnic down there*, she thinks, *before the weather changes. Maybe we can show Bobby the fish, if the water's clear enough.*

She's still astonished that someone as educated, intelligent and beautiful as Laura would want her. *I know nothing of the world*, she frets. *All I know are books; lovelorn heroines, adventurers and silly romances. And plants, I suppose.*

She must think me such a child!

She thinks about Laura's body, and what she was doing with and to it in the night. She knows very little about sex and sexuality, and nothing about homosexuality. Mother was unable to talk about intimacy in anything more than the most general elliptical terms. She would have been unable even to articulate words such as 'homosexual' or 'lesbian'. So what Janine knows comes only from overheard playground taunts and bullying, none of which seemed to have anything to do with her.

The realisation that she is deeply, intensely attracted to Laura does not upset her or make her question her sexual identity, because that was never fixed or clear to her. Until now she was a blank page on which life had yet to write. Mother's strictures were like rules imposed on a convicted prisoner; Janine had to learn them to survive, but they weren't hers. School was a matter of survival, and while she watched from a distance as boys and girls paired off and split up again, that was a parallel universe, one to which she had no admission. Insofar as she can recall – and she is now racking her brains to recall – she experienced no identifiable sexual stirrings at that time, whether directed at males or females. Even her response to Edward was, in an odd way, passionless. Edward represented kindness and safety and she accepted his caresses as his way of expressing it. She thirsted for his gentleness and she devoured it like a starving child. But lust? No.

The intense feelings of radiance and comfort that now fill her are new, curious and exciting, but not unnatural or inconsistent with any self-image she had before. And as for Mother's concept of sin, whatever is happening to her, it feels so absolutely right, so pure, she cannot conceive that it could be wrong. She does what she has so often done when presented with a conundrum she couldn't take either to her teachers or to Mother; she resolves to see if the library has any books on female homosexuality and its history so she can inform herself. Now she appears to be a member of this particular club, she feels she ought to learn something about it.

She feels arms encircling her waist from behind.

'Missed you,' Laura mumbles, her mouth still not fully awake.

'Sorry if I woke you,' says Janine. 'I was too excited to sleep any longer.'

She turns round in Laura's arms and kisses her lightly on the lips. Laura is wearing one of her bath towels. The knowledge that with a gentle tug, Laura would again be naked in her arms excites her.

'So... *Janine...*' says Laura, smiling. 'It's going to take a while. You've always been Nadine to me.'

'Sorry.'

'No apology required. But why? Where did "Nadine" come from?'

Janine blushes and shakes her head. 'It was a spur of the moment thing. Something to do with breaking with the past. And hiding from Mother and Edward, I guess. I've always liked the name Nadine. Nadines are strong and independent, while Janines are weird and dull. Like me. Do you think that's silly?'

Laura shakes her head. 'No, of course not. I can continue using Nadine, if you prefer.'

'No. I want you to... be with... *me*... to like *me*. Not some...'

'Alter ego?'

'Yes. I don't need to be Nadine anymore. Not if you...' Her voice tails off, and she looks down.

Laura lifts her chin tenderly. 'Not if I like Janine.'

Janine nods. 'Yes,' she whispers, so softly that were they not in one another's arms, Laura wouldn't have heard her.

'Well, that's all right then. Because I do.'

'Good. So, this isn't just a one-off then? We're going to continue...?'

'I want to. If you do.'

Janine leans forward and kisses Laura deeply, feeling her desire mount again. 'I want to,' she says.

Laura grimaces.

'What?' asks Janine, suddenly worried.

'Well, to be honest, I have a thundering headache.'

'Oh. Well, you did drink quite a lot of wine.'

'Yes. Much more than I'm used to.'

'Good. Sorry! What I mean is... I'd never be able to keep up with you,' replies Janine with a wry smile. 'I'd fall asleep.'

'Which would've been a shame,' says Laura, disengaging. 'But I need some aspirin, and coffee. Lots of coffee.'

They hear a gentle cry from upstairs.

'You get the coffee and I'll get the Bobby,' says Janine, heading to the stairs. 'You know, we should leave the two back doors open from now on, at least while the weather's so good. We can use the semis as one house.'

'Yes, I agree. But...'

'But?' Janine pauses. 'Oh. Luke.'

'Yes. And Ianto, for that matter.'

'I doubt Ianto'll be a problem. But what are you going to tell Luke? *Are* you going to tell him?'

'I've been thinking about that.' Laura's face clouds. 'I don't know. The idea of sneaking around, waiting until he's asleep or with his father... it doesn't appeal much. But what can I say? Especially in a way he'll understand. People don't ever talk about... well, their intimate relationships, do they? Even when they are...'

'Normal?'

'Yes, I suppose so. Though this feels normal to me. Did your mother ever talk to you about this stuff? My parents never did, not even before my wedding.'

Janine laughs shortly. 'Mother only ever spoke about sex in code. I haven't told you about that, have I?'

'No.'

'She gave it a title, like a bedtime story.'

'What?'

'Yes. It was called All Men Are Liars.' Janine pauses. 'Look, how do you feel about a picnic by the lake this morning? This may be our last chance before the weather changes.'

'Sounds lovely.'

'Let's get organised, and then I'll tell you All Men Are Liars.'

ALL MEN ARE LIARS

Janine is nine years of age and she's standing outside the house in Hulme, school satchel over her shoulder, her ear pressed to the front door. She is listening for clues, and she's apprehensive. Most days she is able to use the half hour of breakfast to gauge Mother's mood. It's not a guaranteed system, because sometimes Mother will be jolly in the morning but shouting drunk by half past three, but usually Janine can tell if a day is going to be a 'drinking day', in which case she needs to stay out of the way, or a 'non-drinking day', in which case it may be okay.

Today, however, she has no evidence on which to base a judgement because, when she left for school, Mother was still in bed after a night of crying and drinking in the kitchen. Janine knew better than to wake her.

The door opens suddenly and Janine almost falls into the hall.

'Listening at the door?' asks Mother.

'No.'

'Daydreaming again, I suppose,' says Mother.

Janine walks past her, close enough to detect alcohol fumes, but is reassured; Mother smells only of cigarettes and shampoo. Her hair is damp, so she's had a bath. It's going to be a good afternoon.

'Did you get the shopping?' asks Mother.

'They had no tins of tuna, but I got the macaroni,' replies Janine, unpacking from her school satchel the bag of pasta, the receipt and the change.

She looks up at Mother anxiously but no explosion comes.

'Macaroni cheese, then,' says Mother. 'Did you have a bath last night?'

'No. You didn't say I should.'

'All right. You can have one after tea.'

Lying in the bath after tea, humming to herself, Janine is daydreaming about Buck as she has just finished rereading *Call of the Wild*, and she is wondering if Mother might let her have a puppy.

Mother enters unexpectedly and Janine sits upright, worried that she is in trouble for having stayed in too long. Some water sloshes over the end of the bath.

'Well, you can clear that up, for a start,' says Mother, regarding the puddle on the linoleum, but she's not actually angry.

This is the best she's been for weeks.

'Get yourself dry, and we'll do your hair,' she says.

Now they are in Mother's bedroom. Mother perches on the edge of the bed and Janine, wearing her boy's second-hand pyjamas with the gap to let them wee, sits beneath her on the floor. Mother is brushing her thick hair with long firm strokes. She breathes heavily, in rhythm with her right arm rising and falling. The pull of the brush is hard, a tug on Janine's scalp with each stroke, but it isn't unpleasant.

'Who are you playing with at school, now?' asks Mother.

'No one special.'

'No best friend?'

'Not really.'

'No boyfriend?'

'Of course not.'

This is the expected answer and Mother's hand continues its rhythmic pull.

'Good. No boys, remember? Boys are not to be trusted. The bigger the boy, the bigger the liar... and...'

'And men are the biggest of them all,' completes Janine.

It's a ritual incantation, the priest and the congregant each playing their complementary parts. Only this night Janine departs from her lines.

'Why, Mother? Why are they all liars?'

She is thinking of Ruth, who sits next to her. Actually, she is thinking of Ruth's daddy who, since her mummy lost the baby, has been collecting Ruth from school. Every afternoon Ruth runs out to meet him and he sweeps her off her feet and throws her, squealing, high into the air and catches her as she comes down. He always has a surprise for her in his pocket, a small bar of white chocolate, a gobstopper or a string of red liquorice. Then they walk hand in hand to the big blue Humber car waiting by the side of the road.

Ruth sometimes gives Janine a wave but she is usually too excited to remember. As far as Janine knows, Ruth's daddy doesn't even know her name. To him, she's probably just the strange dark-skinned girl in odd clothes who sits next to his daughter, and who observes everything from a few feet away.

But there was that single occasion when he noticed Janine's hungry eyes and tossed her a liquorice string too. She had to eat it before reaching home, eradicating all traces of it from her mouth before walking up to the front door. Mother would be waiting, eagle-eyed, behind the dirty net curtains.

Even at nine, Janine knows that Mother does not approve of tall men in big cars who throw their daughters high in the air; even at nine she knows what to tell and what not to tell. The point is, however, that Ruth's daddy doesn't seem to her like a liar.

Mother's hand doesn't falter or pause at the question, but continues in its downward sweep.

'It's in their nature,' she answers, her voice sounding sad, as if she wishes it were otherwise but, like the colour of the sky, the mendacity of the male sex is an unalterable fact. 'They may *seem* nice, on the surface, but they're all the same underneath. They tell lies so that they can do things to you.'

'What things?'

'Things I'll explain when you're older.'

'Do they beat you? Are they the things?'

'No. Much worse things than that.'

'Then what things? What do they *do*?'

Janine can't imagine anything worse than being beaten. She lives in terror of Mother's beatings.

'I'll tell you another time.'

'Even daddies? Do daddies do those things too?'

'Yes. Even daddies. Especially daddies.'

Janine pauses, considering the answers, and Mother waits. Janine is not a child to drop something until it has been turned over, looked at from all angles, understood and filed away.

'Is that why I don't have a daddy?'

The rhythm of the brush stops, a full score of strokes short of the usual complement, and Janine knows that she has asked one question too many.

'You never had a daddy. Now that's enough.'

And it is enough, at least until she is eleven. If men are so bad, then Mother is wise not to have one in the house. And anyway, Janine knows from her teachers that baby Jesus didn't have a daddy. So she is just like Jesus then, and she quite likes that idea. Janine and Jesus; both fatherless.

However, two years later, in her first year at St Cuthbert's, Janine's class receives two hours of rudimentary sex education. It is confusing at first because although it's entitled 'Birds and Bees' it's mainly to do with frogs and flowers, but one thing is clear: in common with everyone else, she *did* have a daddy.

She is transformed by the knowledge, but she has to guard it carefully. Mother is not to be trusted. Mother says different things at different times. It's a complex game; sometimes what is true when Mother is drunk is untrue when she is sober, and sometimes it's the other way round. But Janine knows, unequivocally, that Mother has lied to her.

And if she's lied about not having a father, thinks Janine, she's probably also lied about them all being liars.

The women spend the whole day by the lake. The body of water is really no more than a large pond, but it's extremely pretty. Home to a wide variety of waterfowl – geese, moorhens, ducks, and even a heron that stands, motionless as a statue, at the water's edge for hours on end – it is surrounded by a strip of grass kept short by the geese, is overhung with willows and ash trees, and has a small island at its centre. Where the stream cascades from between its narrow stone walls into the lake, it disturbs the silt, but elsewhere the water is clear. Walking along the bank, looking for a suitable place to lay out the blankets and picnic hamper, Laura and Janine can see through to the lakebed. It is strewn with smooth white, grey and green stones, like duck eggs. Shoals of tiny fish cruise in the shallows until the light above them is interrupted, and then they flash out of sight into the weeds.

The women play with Bobby; use the rope and tyre swing (now repaired by Ianto); hold hands and gaze up at the sky through the branches of the willow; dabble their feet in the water; and talk, talk, talk. They move with the sun, keeping to the shade. By early afternoon the willow no longer provides shade on the bank, so they move and re-establish camp under the leaves of a giant field maple, the largest tree in the valley, whose roots snake into the water's edge like great writhing pythons.

After eating their picnic lunch they lie on their backs in the soporific heat, side by side, catching the maple seeds that drop every so often like tiny helicopters spinning towards them. Bobby is asleep on the blanket next to Janine.

'May I ask you a question?' she asks.

'Of course,' replies Laura, her eyes closed.

'Do you think your parents will ever accept this... us?'

Laura sighs. 'I doubt it. Would that be important to you?'

'I don't think so. I was just thinking about Mother. After she fell pregnant with me, she was left to fend for herself, completely alone. She's never seen her family since, and now she's lost me too.'

'But she threw you out.'

'I know. And I'm not alone the way she was. But I feel sorry for her. I know how I'd feel if I lost Bobby, as Mother has lost me, the only relative she still has. Your parents lost Jennifer, and now, maybe, you too.'

'If so, it'll be their choice. I don't feel sorry for them. I'm tired of being their disappointment, the cross they have to carry.'

'Are they really such bad people?' asks Janine.

'Bad? No, they're not actually evil. I suppose they wanted the best for Jennifer and me. But they are utterly selfish. We were like their holiday home or Dad's pension fund. Something to display, to show off. We always had to be graceful, accomplished and brilliant, to show up their friends' children. And I was constantly letting them down. As did Jennifer, in the end.'

'How did you let them down?'

Laura laughs, and Janine is relieved that it sounds genuinely carefree.

'Oh, in countless ways! Starting with getting in trouble at school, then doing a "weird degree" in statistics – my father didn't understand it, so he couldn't boast about it – and ending with breaking up with Roger. This, our relationship, will be the final straw.'

They fall silent.

'Maybe that's what we have in common,' suggests Janine thoughtfully after a while.

'What's that?'

'The fact that we're both such a disappointment to our parents,' says Janine.

'Yes, probably.' Laura leans over and kisses her. 'And we don't care anymore,' she adds, softly. '*That's* the important bit. We've broken away.'

'Yes, we have,' says Janine. 'But I'm not sure I can say I don't care anymore.'

By early afternoon Bobby becomes grizzly and they decide to return to the cottages to let her sleep in her room. In any case, Laura has another interview the following day and wants to iron her clothes and prepare, and Janine has yet to read the contents of Roger's envelope carefully, and plans to do so while Bobby has her afternoon sleep. So they pack up their picnic things and start climbing the hill.

'Where's the interview?' asks Janine.

'Manchester city centre. And, very inconveniently, at half past two, which means I can't pick up Luke.'

'Have you asked Ianto?' asks Janine.

'Yes, but he can't help. Luke says he's fine walking up the hill on his own, and I can leave the key by the back door for him. I should be back by four, four thirty at the latest. He won't be alone long, and he's very sensible.'

'Would you like me to pick him up? He could stand on the

back of the trike like he did that first day, or I could walk down with Bobby to the school.'

'I assumed you'd be working.'

'I only have Mrs Reid tomorrow. It's an hour and a half, two at most. I could go now, which frees up tomorrow afternoon. Shall I? If you don't mind holding the fort?'

'If you're okay to work on a Sunday afternoon, that would be great.'

Janine nods. 'Okay. I'll go as soon as Bobby's settled. You can bring your clothes round and use my ironing board.'

'Thank you.'

Bobby, still tired from several hours in the open air, falls asleep the moment she's put down. Janine dons her dungarees and work boots and leaves Laura ironing her blouse in the lounge.

She cycles out of Chapelhill towards the hamlet of Rowarth where Mrs Reid has her little mill worker's cottage. It is not far as the crow flies but the hills are steep and there are many of them. It's a tough cycle ride, especially with the tools on the trailer. Nevertheless, the journey is spectacularly beautiful and since Janine moved into Apple Tree Cottage her legs have become much stronger.

It takes her twenty-five minutes to reach the cottage. Her arrangement with Mrs Reid is that she gets on with the work on whatever day of the week suits her, and every fortnight Mrs Reid will leave her money in an envelope by the back door. However, because, unusually, Janine is working at the weekend, she decides to knock on Mrs Reid's door to let her know she's there.

She can hear the Home Service on the radio inside so she knows Mrs Reid is at home. Since she fell, the old woman is almost immobile and very rarely leaves the house except for church, for which she is collected with a wheelchair.

Janine waits patiently and eventually sees her client through the glass of the back door, hobbling slowly towards her.

'Good afternoon,' says Janine once the door is opened to her. 'I didn't want you to be worried if you heard someone outside, but it's me. I can't come tomorrow so I thought I'd do your weeding this afternoon.'

The old woman, bent almost double, peers through rheumy eyes and thick spectacles.

'I was going to have a word with you tomorrow. You're a polite enough girl and a good gardener, but I'm afraid I have to let you go.'

Janine frowns. 'You don't need me to come anymore?'

'That's right. I've got your wages ready, and I've added another week.'

She hands Janine an envelope.

'Can I ask why?'

Mrs Reid pauses. 'Let's just say it's not working out.'

'But... have I done something to upset you?' Janine sees evasiveness in the old woman's refusal to look her in the eye. 'I really need the job, Mrs Reid. I helped you out when you couldn't–'

'I'm very sorry, but my mind's made up. You're not the sort of person I can have working for me.'

'What do you mean?' asks Janine. 'Has someone said something? Michael Carter, by any chance?'

'Mr Carter is a member of my church.'

'What's he told you?'

'I'm not discussing it, young lady. Take your money before I change my mind and give you nothing.'

'But what's he said?' shouts Janine. 'It's not true, you know. I did not make a pass at him.'

'A pass? That's not what they called it in my day.'

'Then... what?'

'Offering your body for money was called harlotry. Now get off my property.'

The old lady shuts the door in Janine's face without a further word.

Janine stares at the closed door for a few moments and then retraces her steps, her heart pounding and outrage colouring her cheeks. She's so upset, it takes her several attempts to turn the trike and trailer round in the narrow lane. She cycles furiously back to Chapelhill.

Bobby is still asleep when she enters Apple Tree Cottage, and Laura is sitting at the kitchen table making notes.

'That was quick,' says Laura, looking up. 'Problem?'

Janine throws herself onto the couch dejectedly. 'She's sacked me.'

'What? Why?'

'Carter's a member of her church. He told her I was a prostitute.'

Laura puts her hand to her mouth. 'Jesus,' she whispers. 'That evil bastard! I suppose Christine must have challenged him and he's upped the ante.'

'I suppose.'

'Will it make much difference without Mrs Reid, financially, I mean?'

'She only paid me a few shillings a week, but of course it makes a difference. More importantly, if Carter's going round my clients, who else has he spoken to?'

'Do any of the others go to the same church?' Janine shrugs. She doesn't know. 'Didn't you tell me that Lady Margaret had a connection with the Carters? Isn't that how you got the job?'

'Oh no! I'd forgotten that.' Janine looks completely crestfallen. 'If he tells her, I'll *have* to move. What am I going to do, Laura?'

Chapter Twenty-One

LAURA

The end of September is marked by rain and grey skies. The leaves of the ash trees bordering the lake are the first to drop, followed by the maples. Although the weather improves, the mornings now are colder and the sun dips behind the trees in the valley earlier in the afternoon. The stone cottages are noticeably chilly by nightfall.

Janine doesn't know if her two remaining clients have been approached by Mike Carter, but neither shows any sign of dispensing with her services. She reports to Laura that Lady Margaret appears to be her usual businesslike, bustling self, always delighted to see her and Bobby, and the customary surliness of her other long-standing client, a Mr Barron, seems unchanged. Laura watches Janine carefully but gradually, as the days pass, she is relieved to see her lover regaining her equilibrium, although she still peers anxiously out of the front windows whenever a vehicle approaches.

Luke has started returning home from his foraging expeditions with his pockets full of shiny new conkers, and the kitchen of Magnolia Cottage is often pungent with the vinegar used by he and Ianto to soak and harden them. The Welshman has gradually become part of the family. He still has plenty of work in the area and seems happy to remain in the garden for as long as the women will let him. When not working he spends a lot of time with the children. He is still roaming the countryside with Luke and has started to teach him some songs to play on the guitar. He is so good with Bobby, amusing her with games on the floor and changing and feeding her occasionally, that both women have wondered if somewhere in Wales or perhaps Holland there's a thin child with white-blonde hair about whom he prefers not to speak. He has avoided answering questions on that subject, and the women haven't pressed him.

He makes himself useful in other ways, too. On one occasion Laura wondered out loud if the chimney in Magnolia Cottage worked and within a day Ianto had cleaned the flue and started building a stack of cut timber, dragged from the surrounding woods, ready for winter.

The women have discussed what will happen when the weather gets colder. Ianto claims he will be perfectly comfortable in his campervan whatever the weather but, as Laura pointed out to Janine, they in fact have a spare bedroom, two if they were to share. No decision on that has yet been taken.

The households in the adjoining semis have gradually merged, and everyone has settled into a new routine. They've done as Janine suggested and whenever one of them is home during the day, the back doors are left open. There is no barrier between the gardens in any case. Luke is already running in and out of the two houses as if they were one, the children end up eating at the same table in whatever cottage a meal is presented and the women spend the evenings together.

Although Luke doesn't seem to have noticed the deepening relationship between his mother and their next-door neighbour, Ianto certainly has. He says nothing, but his smiles and unconcerned attitude at their intimacy reveal that he is not bothered. If anything he seems to approve, and so they are able to relax completely around him in the evenings.

So far as Luke is concerned, the 'sneaking around' that Laura feared has not been necessary. She waits until Bobby's last feed is completed and then slips into Janine's huge bed with her. They are invariably woken by Bobby in the morning before Luke stirs, and by the time he is up Laura is already in the kitchen setting out the breakfast things.

On the other hand, there have been moments when she has reached out to caress Janine or to recall with her some intimate moment, and has had to restrain herself because Luke was present. She has found that difficult. At Laura's centre is her belief that people are, for the most part, good. As long as she and Janine hurt no one, they should be allowed to live their lives as they please, openly and without shame. Her love for Janine, her desire for her, seem so normal, so *right*, she cannot believe there is anything wrong with them. She recognises them as part of her true self, and people should be able to accept her as she is. Most especially those who love her, like Luke.

She knows what homosexual men are forced to do to avoid prosecution and obloquy and, for the first time in her life, she really understands it. But, unlike between men, homosexuality between women is not illegal; she and Janine are in the fortunate position of not having to avoid criminal sanctions because they fell in love. Nonetheless, most people would consider their relationship unnatural and sinful. If it became common knowledge, it would surely provide Janine's enemies with further ammunition against her.

Luke, now aged nine, has expressed no curiosity about sex, and Laura is sure he knows little about it, and certainly nothing about homosexuality. He'd be unlikely to talk to Roger about it deliberately – he still maintains a strict Chinese wall between his two households – but something would be bound to slip out sooner or later. Were that to occur elsewhere, at school for example, it could be disastrous. Further, Laura feels uncomfortable placing a secret on his young shoulders. So, with some ambivalence, she has said nothing to him.

She still wonders about the label she's always applied to herself, because she really did consider herself – without any thought or doubt – heterosexual. But her response to Janine demonstrates, unequivocally, that that's not right. Or it's not as simple as that. She's either unexpectedly bisexual or she falls in love with the person regardless of their sex. For a while she wrangles with these possibilities, unsure which she prefers, but eventually concludes that it doesn't matter. It's simple: she loves Janine and wants to live her life with her.

She has never felt this way for anyone before. There were a couple of boyfriends before Roger, and of course Roger himself. As someone who used to take ages to decide if she liked anyone, and longer still to become romantically involved with them, she is aware that this has all happened very quickly. But she has never been as certain of anything as she is of her feelings for Janine. Her affection grew from the first day they met, in the spring. Looking back, she thinks she was probably in love with her before The Kiss. She feels as if she's been waiting for this girl, for this relationship, all her life. With Janine, she is the best version of herself; she is happy and sexually fulfilled like never before. Finally... *finally!* she understands what all the fuss is about.

She still worries about the age difference. She is almost thirty-three and Janine only twenty. The idea that she is taking advantage of Janine's naïveté in the way Edward did fills her with horror, and actually makes her feel sick. She recognises that the age difference makes her more protective of the young woman than would be the case were they closer in age. On the other hand, although Janine is inexperienced and unschooled with, as Laura has discovered, enormous and surprising gaps in her understanding of the world, she is certainly no child. She is independent, strong-willed and fiercely intelligent, so much so that Laura frequently wonders what she might have achieved had she had a more normal upbringing and the chance to continue in education. As the weeks pass, it becomes clear that they are equals in this relationship despite the difference in years, and Laura's concerns recede.

This evening, a cold but beautiful evening with both the sinking sun and the rising moon in the sky, both households are in Magnolia Cottage. The children are in bed, Luke in his own room and Bobby on Laura's bed. The women sit at the kitchen table. Janine has a pad of graph paper before her and a pen in her hand. Between them lies what Janine calls her file. It is a flattering description for a foot-tall miscellany of receipts, invoices and smudged notes covered with muddy fingerprints.

'Oh dear,' exclaims Laura softly as she sees it.

'Yes,' replies Janine, embarrassed. 'Sorry.'

'No wonder we're struggling.'

'Are we struggling?' asks Janine anxiously.

'We are,' confirms Laura categorically.

The women have combined their day-to-day finances but Laura has realised that, even with the occasional contribution from Ianto, they cannot continue as they have been. Ianto's assistance with the children and his general support have been invaluable but, like Janine, he earns almost nothing. Laura has been funding all of them by dipping into the capital received from the divorce, the money she hoped to use to buy a house.

'I'm so sorry,' says Janine. 'I've got no idea about tax, national insurance or record-keeping. I've never lived alone before, let alone run a business.'

'Well, at least you're a hoarder,' replies Laura with a wry smile.

'I didn't want to throw the wrong thing away, so I kept absolutely everything.'

'So I see.'

Laura starts work. She reads each document and directs Janine to jot figures on her graph paper. Janine picks up the rules very quickly. An hour later they are halfway through the pile and Janine has several different columns of figures.

'So, this is a business expense,' she says, showing Laura a piece of paper, 'but it's a capital item. Three pounds four shillings. So it goes in this column?'

'Exactly. Can you explain why?' asks Laura.

'Because I can't claim it all this year.'

'Very good. Twenty-five per cent of its value every year.' She shows Janine a muddy scrap of paper. 'What was this for?'

Janine looks at it briefly and hands it back. 'One bag of compost, for Mrs Reid's flowerbeds.'

'Who paid for it?'

'I did.'

'Okay. General expense column, nine shillings exactly. On that, I can't see what you've received from Mrs Reid. Is there any documentation?'

'She paid me in cash, in those envelopes every fortnight, and I dated them.'

'But,' says Laura, leafing through them, 'there aren't enough.'

'Yes, I know. She was finding it a bit difficult, so I let her off paying for a while.'

Laura looks up at her. 'How long for?'

Janine shrugs. 'About two months, I think. Maybe three.'

Laura shakes her head. 'And she still sacked you. What a

cow,' she mutters. 'That was very kind of you but, sweetheart, that's no way to run a business.'

'I know. That's why I have you,' replies Janine.

'Hmm,' says Laura doubtfully.

'How do you know all this stuff?' asks Janine, pointing at the documents.

'I like numbers. You know I was a statistician before Luke. And my father's an accountant, so I guess I picked up the tax stuff. It's actually simple once you know the rules.'

'I'd have given anything to go to college and do something like that. I really don't understand why your parents wouldn't be proud of you.'

'Odd, isn't it? But so far as they're concerned, I'm the family dunce.'

She bends her head to the accounts again. They work together silently for a while before Laura sits back, puts down her pen and shakes her head.

'How much do you have left in your building society?' she asks.

'Just under three pounds. And you?'

'We're not talking about me.' Laura prods the table with her forefinger twice in quick succession, to indicate the mess before her. 'Right now I'm asking about the parlous state of your new business.'

'Yes, but how much? Am I broke?'

'Not quite.'

'Are *we* broke?'

'No, it's not as bad as that yet. I've just under twelve hundred pounds left from the divorce.'

'Oh, that's not too bad, is it?'

'It's not much at all if you think about it. Even with just me and Luke, that wouldn't last more than a year, two at best. And now there are five of us.'

'I'm contributing,' says Janine, clearly stung.

Laura puts her hand over Janine's. 'I know you are, but some of the cash you put into the kitty every week belongs to the taxman. If you're self-employed, you have to keep some money back to pay tax on your profits. You should be saving it to pay at the end of the year.'

'But I'd be working for almost nothing!'

'I've not done a tax calculation yet, but very likely.'

Janine is horror-struck. 'But I've been working so hard!'

'Yes, but you've bought loads of equipment too, like the mower.'

Janine sits back in her chair, her face contorted with worry. 'What are we going to do?'

Laura draws a deep breath. 'I don't see we've got a choice. I need to find a full-time job. I've only been looking for part-time, but it's limiting my chances and, frankly' – she points at the documents again – 'it's not sustainable.'

'What about Luke?'

'A part-time nanny maybe?'

'But aren't they expensive? Would it be worth it?'

'I don't know. I'd need to look at the sums.'

'And, anyway, we can't have someone else in the house. It's too risky.'

'Yes, there is that.'

'Then what?'

'Well, you could give up your semi,' offers Laura. 'Other than the garden, we barely use it. Not paying rent would help.'

'What about the veg I grow there?'

'That's only worth a few shillings every week. Less than the rent, certainly.'

Janine shakes her head. 'I don't want to do that unless we have no choice. Firstly, what about Ianto? I know what he says, but he really can't live in the van over winter, so he'll probably leave. And it would mean having other people as neighbours. And then...'

'And then?'

Janine leans forward and takes Laura's hand in hers. She kisses it repeatedly.

'I love you,' she says, 'you know I do. But what if this goes wrong? What if you meet a... nice man, for example, and decide you've had enough of me? Especially if you go out to work, you'll get all sorts of offers. I need my own place, just in case.'

'I am not going to meet a nice man, or woman for that matter,' reassures Laura. 'I love you too. These last few months have been the happiest of my life.'

'But we fell into this so quickly, and I'm frightened you could fall out of it just as quickly. Having Apple Tree gives me security.'

'Okay,' says Laura, 'I understand. Keep it for the present. We'll find another solution.'

'I could look after Luke, when you're not here.'

'And cut down your gardening hours?'

'But if I'm making no profit anyway, what's the point? And once autumn's over there won't be much work to do.'

'But you *will* make a profit. Now you've bought all the tools you need, what you make from now on will be profit. Anyway, you love it, and have an amazing affinity for it.'

Janine pauses. 'Actually, I did wonder...' she says hesitantly '...if I could find the money somehow... well, a car or a small van would make a big difference. If I learned to drive I could look further afield, find clients who aren't in Chapelhill.'

'And not part of the local gossip.'

'Exactly.'

There is a knock on the door and Janine leaps out of her chair.

'That wasn't here,' says Laura. 'It was your door. Wait there.'

Laura goes to the front window and looks out.

'I think it's our landlady,' she says. 'Large woman, say, in her seventies, with white hair under a beret?'

'Can you see a car?'

Laura cranes her neck and looks the other way. 'Yes, a big grey thing, like a Rolls Royce.'

'It's a Bentley. Yes, that's Lady Margaret. What should I do?'

Lady Margaret knocks again on the door of Apple Tree Cottage. Laura moves away from the window.

'There are no lights on next door,' she whispers. 'Maybe she'll assume you're not home and go away.'

That hope is extinguished when a knock comes on Laura's front door.

Laura opens her hands in enquiry. 'What do you want me to do? She can see the lights in here, and my car's outside.'

'Go on then,' says Janine.

Laura straightens her dress and goes to the front door. She opens it.

'Good evening,' says Lady Margaret. 'Sorry to trouble you. You may not remember me, but I'm your landlady, Margaret Wiscombe.'

'Yes, Lady Margaret. Good evening. How may I help you?'

'Well, as I say, I'm sorry to trouble you, but I need to get hold of Nadine urgently. I'm surprised to find she's not in. I'd have expected Bobby to be in bed hours ago. Do you know where I can find her?'

Laura's hesitation is cut short by Janine's voice from behind her.

'I'm here, Lady Margaret.'

'Do you want to come in?' asks Laura.

Lady Margaret turns towards her car, making a gesture, and Laura appreciates for the first time that there is someone with her, sitting in the passenger seat.

'Yes, please.'

Laura stands back to allow the large woman to precede her down the hall and closes the door.

'Ah, you've made this look lovely!' says Lady Margaret, looking around as she enters the lounge.

'Thank you,' replies Laura, following her.

'Would you like to sit down?' asks Janine.

'No, thank you.'

'Can I get you something to drink?' asks Laura.

'No, thank you. Look, Nadine, I've something rather delicate to say... could we go next door perhaps?'

'That's fine, Lady M. You can say whatever you want in front of Laura.'

Lady Margaret looks around again thoughtfully and nods.

'I see. Then, I think I will sit down, if you don't mind. And a glass of water would be welcome.'

'Of course,' says Laura, clearing some space at the table and pulling out a chair for Lady Margaret.

Janine goes to the kitchen and fills a glass of water. She brings it back, places it in front of Lady Margaret and sits opposite her. Laura places a reassuring hand on Janine's shoulder. The old lady takes a sip of water, puts the glass down and regards Janine steadily.

'I'll come straight to the point. I've had an unexpected visit at Windyridge. Two people. The first was a woman calling herself a social worker, a Mary O'Reilly. Do you know her?'

'Yes. She came here, asking questions about Bobby's father.'

'Yes, indeed,' replies Lady Margaret. 'She asked me similar questions. She's a Catholic, I understand, and believes Bobby's in moral danger. The second person, whom I know slightly, is a man called Carter. He married into the Howard family, over at Little Hayfield. He is also a Catholic, some sort of pastoral chairman of the parish, if I understood him correctly. Do you know him?'

'Yes.'

Lady Margaret doesn't respond, evidently waiting for Janine to continue.

'He's... he's been telling people that I... I offered myself to him. For money. But it's not true! He grabbed at me, and I had to fight him off. I'm so sorry you've been involved.'

'These two people requested that I terminate your services and give you notice to leave the cottage. They said that I should not allow myself to be seen supporting a woman of your low moral character and–'

'But–'

Lady Margaret holds up her hand to halt her.

'Hush, child, let me finish. I tried to ascertain their purpose. It seemed an odd alliance. I can't be sure, but I think they wish to persuade... to *force* you to go into that home, Cedars Moral Welfare. If you had no income and no home, you'd have little choice.'

'No!' shouts Janine, trembling. 'I won't give up Bobby!'

She turns her frightened face to Laura.

'It's okay,' says Laura calmly. 'I won't let that happen.'

'No one's asking you to, my dear. And I didn't believe a single word of it.'

Janine looks back to Lady Margaret. 'You didn't?'

'Let us say, you're not the first. There was a nanny a few years back who left overnight, and a housekeeper. Word gets round. Christine seems to have a blind spot about her husband. She probably can't admit to herself or the family that he's just as bad as the one before. Anyway, I'm definitely not going to be dictated to. Your job's still open to you if you want it and of course you may remain in the cottage.'

'Thank you,' says Janine, her voice wobbling.

'Don't upset yourself, dear,' says Lady Margaret. 'Although you do need to be careful with Mr Carter. He's a man who's used to getting his own way, a right little Napoleon, and he doesn't like to be crossed. I'm afraid you've made an influential and vindictive enemy.'

Janine shares a frightened glance with Laura, who grips her hand briefly.

Lady Margaret continues. 'And I believe another of my friends is also your client, isn't that right?'

'Mr Barron,' confirms Janine.

'They've been to see him too. He's a tricky customer, so it's difficult to predict his response, but he has skeletons in his own closet. And he's not a hypocrite.' She stands. 'I'll leave you to your evening, but I thought you should be aware.'

She turns to Laura. 'And how are *you* getting on, my dear? All settled in?'

'Yes, thank you. I'm very happy here.'

'Good.'

Lady Margaret turns in a slow circle, taking in the room. Her gaze halts at a framed drawing above the mantelpiece.

'Good heavens,' she says, 'is that a Frida Kahlo?' She goes over and peers at it closely.

'I wish it were,' says Laura.

'It's very like her work though, isn't it? Where did you get it?'

'My uncle picked it up in New York, just before the war.'

Lady Margaret spends a few further seconds examining it. 'I'd get that looked at, if I were you. You might have a treasure hanging there. Anyway,' she says, turning back towards the younger women, 'I should let you get on with your evening.'

She takes a couple of steps towards the hall.

'You know,' she says, pausing and pointing towards the lounge wall, 'that wall's not stone. It's just studwork, put in to divide the building in two. I wouldn't have any objections if you were to knock it through again.'

'Yes?' says Laura noncommittally.

'It would give you a much bigger house for all four of you. You've got a little boy, as I remember?'

'Yes, Luke,' replies Laura.

'Just a suggestion,' says Lady Margaret.

She looks around the room again and smiles, as if reminded of something.

'Well, I'll bid you goodnight,' she says.

They follow Lady Margaret to the door, and watch as she gets into the Bentley, executes a fast U-turn, waves through the window at them and races off down the hill.

Laura and Janine return to the lounge.

'Do you think she knows?' asks Janine.

Laura nods. 'Yes. We've been careless.'

She points in turn at the pile of nappies in the corner, the changing mat by the window and the half-finished bowl of stewed fruit on the side. 'All that should be next door. And she referred to "all four" of us.'

'Crickey.'

'Have you ever wondered about her and Chivers?' asks Laura.

'Not 'til now.'

'She's a remarkable old lady,' says Laura after a moment's reflection.

Janine nods. 'She's lovely.'

Part Three

Chapter Twenty-Two

LAURA

It's a cold Sunday afternoon in the first week of October, just before dusk. Laura and Janine are wrapped in jumpers and scarves, and have managed to carve out an hour together down by the lake. Luke is with his father and they have left Ianto playing with Bobby in front of the fire.

These are precious moments. Laura started working full-time for Manchester City Council a fortnight earlier, and they see much less of one another. She had to accept work well below her abilities, and the pay isn't great.

Childcare has also been problematic. Ianto, who is still parked, rent-free, in the garden, and who now divides his time between the cottages and the campervan, would help if he could, but his work is unpredictable. With the cooperation of Lady Margaret, Janine has reduced her hours and moved some gardening work to the weekends so she can collect Luke from school on three days of the week. There is much less gardening to do now at Windyridge anyway.

Janine's other client, Mr Barron, was more difficult. He said nothing about being spoken to by Mike Carter, and Janine left that subject well alone, but he was reluctant to allow her to change her hours to the weekend. He eventually agreed to let her start work later on two weekday afternoons and Laura was forced to negotiate different hours with her new employers for those days. Now she leaves home at six o'clock and is at her desk by six forty-five, which enables her to collect Luke from school while Janine tidies Mr Barron's garden.

Both women are tired, and they know these arrangements only offer a temporary solution. As the evenings draw in, Janine won't be able to work after three o'clock or so, and Laura can't possibly get home before then. Janine is planning to get Mr Barron's garden ready for winter so that, by the time the clocks go back, there will be nothing left to do. If he dispenses with her services thereafter, as she fears he might, they'll have to manage somehow until the spring.

They have walked, hand in hand, around the lake twice, talking.

Laura checks her watch. 'Luke's due home soon,' she says. 'Shall we head up?'

'Yes,' replies Janine. 'I'm getting cold, anyway.'

They start back up the steep hill, careful to avoid the sheep and rabbit droppings that stud the field.

The peaceful evening calm is interrupted by the sound of a vehicle turning into The Rise and approaching.

'That must be Roger,' says Laura.

'I'll get on with supper,' says Janine, and she sets off.

Laura diverts to her right and walks parallel to the dry-stone wall towards the top of The Rise. Roger's car is parked outside the building and he is handing a rucksack out of the car to Luke.

'Hello! Had a nice weekend?' she shouts.

'Yes, thank you,' calls Roger.

Laura joins them, bending to give Luke a hug. He runs off towards the house without speaking.

'I saw you coming up the hill,' says Roger. 'From a distance you and your neighbour look very alike, you know. Same height and shape. It's just your colouring that's different. And isn't she wearing that green jumper of yours?'

Laura shrugs nonchalantly. 'Possibly. We use the same clothesline across both gardens so occasionally things get muddled.'

'What was so funny?' asks Roger.

'Funny?'

'I heard you both laughing before I could see you.'

'Oh, I don't know. Something one of us said, I expect.'

'And you were holding hands.'

'Were we?'

'What's going on, Laura?'

'Nothing is going on, Roger. Why all the questions?'

He shrugs.

'Is everything all right with Luke?' she asks, changing the subject.

'As far as I know.'

'When you stopped here on the way to Chatsworth I thought he'd been crying, and just now he went off without saying anything. He's normally so chatty.'

'I didn't notice.'

'But don't you talk to him?' she asks, slightly exasperated. 'It's part of parenting, Roger. If he seems miserable, it's quite a good idea to find out why.'

'He didn't seem miserable to me. We had a perfectly good weekend. We went camping.'

Laura pauses. Nothing can suppress Luke's ebullience for long and on his return from Chatsworth he was his usual bouncy self. But this is the second time.

'Would you mind waiting for a couple of minutes?' she asks.

'What for? I need to get moving.'

'Just a couple of minutes,' she repeats. 'I want a word with him. If there's something bothering him, we might need to tackle it together.'

'It's probably nothing.'

'Then we'll find out and it'll all be fine.'

He sighs theatrically. 'All right then. I can wait a few minutes.'

'Thank you.'

Laura turns and walks into the house. 'Luke?' she calls.

'He's in his room,' says Janine, pulling a face. 'Something's up,' she adds quietly.

Laura nods and climbs the stairs to Luke's bedroom. She knocks on the door and enters. Luke is sitting on his bed idly playing with a toy car. Laura sits next to him.

'Hello?'

'Hello,' he says, his head bowed.

'You're very quiet. Anything you want to talk about?'

Luke doesn't answer but continues to run the toy car backwards and forwards beside him on the bedspread.

'Feeling sad?' asks Laura. Luke nods. 'Would you like to tell me why? It's always better when you can tell someone else.'

'Why is Dad's car full of his clothes?'

'You've been camping, haven't you?'

'But they were there last time as well. And his books, and loads of other things. And he's sad too, but he won't say why.'

'Is he?'

Luke nods. 'Very.'

Laura takes a deep breath. 'Okay. I'll talk to him and see if there's anything I can do. But don't you worry about it, okay? Lots of things make adults sad, it's part of being a grown-up, but it's probably nothing.'

She puts her arm over his shoulders and, pulling him towards her, kisses the top of his head. He smells of little boy and bonfires.

'All right?' He nods reluctantly. 'Why don't you go downstairs? Janine's making something to eat.'

'Can I stay up here for a little while?'

'Of course you can. I'll be back in a minute.'

She leaves the room and returns to Roger. He is leaning against the passenger door of the car, cleaning his fingernails with a penknife. Without speaking, Laura bends to see inside the car, circling the vehicle and looking in each window.

She arrives beside Roger. 'What's going on?'

'Nothing.'

'I don't believe you. This isn't just camping stuff, there's a week's food wrappers in the footwell, and the car smells as if you've been on a stakeout.' She stands in front of him and lifts his chin so he has to look into her eyes. 'Are you living in your car?'

Then something completely unexpected happens to her tall, handsome ex-husband, the competent City solicitor whose confidence had always been his impenetrable armour against the world. A shudder shakes his chest and a tear falls out of each light blue eye. She has never seen him cry before, not even after his father died.

'Oh, Roger!' she exclaims. He turns away, hiding his face from her. 'What on earth is it?'

There was a time when she would have put her arms round him, and she almost does it. Instead, she allows him a few seconds. When he faces her again he has regained his composure, but his face remains contorted.

'You might as well know now. Luke's worked it out, I think.' He pauses. 'I've been sacked.'

'Sacked?' she repeats, shocked.

'And the bank called the loan in. When I couldn't pay it, they repossessed the house and changed the locks.'

'And you're living in your car? Surely you can afford a hotel?'

'No, not 'til they sell the house. And not if I continue paying maintenance. I'm desperately looking for a new job. I didn't want you to know.'

'Oh, you poor thing. I'm so sorry. But don't tell me you've been going to interviews in clothes you've been sleeping in?'

He nods. 'What's happened, Laura? Less than a year ago we were living the life, we had a fabulous house in London, I earned a fortune, and I was someone to be reckoned with. Look at me now.'

Laura doesn't love Roger, at least not in the way she did, but she looks up at his thin face and its expression of puzzled disbelief and her heart goes out to him.

Since the divorce he has surprised her. She doubted that he would actually move north, despite the job offer. The cynical side of her was convinced that the lure of London, where he'd lived all his life; where all his friends and colleagues were; where he could still be a mover and a shaker, would win. But he did move. He gave it all up and relocated two hundred miles to somewhere where he knew no one, to be close to Luke. She'd also been completely sceptical about his willingness to put work aside and actually spend time with his son on his alternate weekends. He would be the new boy in a new job; he'd work every hour possible, burn all the midnight oil there was, to prove himself. And, again, he exceeded her expectations. Until recently Luke used to come bounding home full of the excitement of what he and his dad had been up to that weekend. Finally, now it appears he's been prioritising Luke's maintenance over his own needs.

Laura reminds herself that he betrayed her during the marriage, and more than once. More corrosive in many ways, he constantly let her and Luke down by prioritising his work over them, and he patronised and ignored her. Despite all that, since the divorce he has gone a long way towards proving that he is still, essentially, a decent man.

Why did it take a divorce and all this upheaval for him to be like this?

'Wait there,' she orders. 'Are you listening?'

He nods, and Laura turns and strides back into Magnolia Cottage.

Luke has come downstairs and now sits at the table opposite Bobby in her high chair. Janine is about to serve them tea. Ianto is also in the kitchen, at the far end of the table, disassembling something small and oily. Janine looks up and pauses, a saucepan of macaroni cheese in one hand and a wooden spoon in the other.

'Well?' she asks.

Laura beckons urgently, turns, and goes into the lounge. Janine follows, saucepan and spoon in hand.

'He's homeless,' says Laura quietly. 'He's been living in his car.'

'Crikey.'

'I have a massive favour to ask you.'

'I can guess.'

'He really hasn't anywhere else to go. His father's dead and there's no room at his mother's. Anyway, she's a cow and I wouldn't ask anyone to live with her. So... and I do appreciate how big an ask this is, honestly, I do, but... could we offer him a room, just until he finds another job? Say, one month?'

'Here? In this cottage with you and Luke?'

'Or in Apple Tree. If we moved Bobby's nursery over here, he could use the box room there.'

'And we'd tell him about us?'

'I don't know. Would you prefer me to?'

Janine thinks for a moment. 'I don't know. I don't want him

thinking you're... available, but I'm not sure I would trust him with the knowledge. Would you?'

'Maybe not. So, we won't tell him.'

'But do you want him living here at all?' asks Janine. 'I mean, you divorced him.'

'I know, and obviously it's not ideal, but he's in a crisis. His whole life has come tumbling around his ears, and I do feel sorry for him. And perhaps most important, I don't want Luke seeing his father like this.'

Janine shakes her head slowly, obviously reluctant. 'He'll try to win you back.'

'He won't, and if he does he'll be wasting his time. I've never been as happy as I am now.' She takes Janine's face in her white hands and whispers so Luke can't hear her. 'I'm yours.'

'That won't stop him trying.'

'I give you my solemn promise, my darling, darling girl. The first sign of anything like that, the first inappropriate word or touch, the first joke, the first flirtatious comment, and he'll be out on his ear.'

Janine takes a deep breath. There is a sudden noise behind them and Laura drops her hands quickly. Luke is standing in the lounge doorway. Ianto appears behind him, looking flustered.

'I'm so sorry,' he says over Luke's head, very contrite. 'I was concentrating and didn't see him slipping out. Come on, Luke,' he says, trying to guide the boy back to the kitchen.

Luke resists for a moment, looking from one woman to the other, his face alive with hope. Neither woman speaks until he has disappeared into the kitchen.

'Shit! He obviously heard,' says Laura. 'Well?'

'Do I have a choice? If I say no, I'll be the baddie, especially to Luke.' Janine pauses. 'All right, then,' she says grudgingly. 'I can't say I'm not worried about it, and we'll probably go bankrupt with another mouth to feed, but... okay. One month, not a day more.'

Laura hugs her. 'You are a wonderful, wonderful person!' she says.

Janine pulls a face and returns to the kitchen to resume serving the children.

Laura takes a few deep breaths before following her. Ianto is back at the table, screwdriver in hand. He looks up as she enters.

'Are you okay with this?' Laura asks him.

'Me?' He shrugs. 'It's your house, so I'll fit around you guys. If you're all cool with it, so am I. But... are you sure you've thought this through?'

'Yes.'

He looks across at Janine but she's spooning macaroni cheese into bowls and is looking down. He shrugs again. 'Okay then.'

Laura blows a kiss at the Welshman and hurries back outside. The sun has sunk almost to the horizon and is now a ball of red seen through the silhouetted trees. Laura shades her eyes and runs towards the road.

Roger has got back into the car to shelter from the cold. Laura gets into the passenger seat and closes the door. Roger seems more composed.

'Now, Roger,' says Laura, turning in the seat to face him, 'please listen carefully to me. I have a suggestion to make, but there are strict conditions attached.'

'Okay,' he says, frowning.

'We can offer you a room in Apple Tree. It's for one month only, while you look for a new job. It's on condition that you *do* look for a new job. In that time, you needn't pay any rent, but you must continue with the maintenance payments for Luke. I'm doing this for him, because I don't want him to see his father in this state. And you'll probably be sharing a bathroom with Ianto.'

'The guy who owns that?' he asks, pointing towards the van.

'Yes. And, just to make everything completely clear, you'll be a lodger. Do you understand me?'

'I think so.'

'What I mean is, there'll be no casual touching, no flirtatious or salacious comments, no crossing the line. I know we've been getting on better recently, but I don't want you thinking this is a way back for us. It's not.'

He nods. 'I understand.' He takes her hand. 'Just let me say, thank you. From the bottom of my heart, thank you. I don't deserve your kindness.'

'Probably not.' She extricates her hand. 'That's settled then. Why don't you come in and I'll introduce you? Luke's going to be very excited. And probably confused, so it's up to both of us to make sure that he has no unrealistic expectations. Agreed?'

'Yes, agreed.'

'Come on, then.'

Chapter Twenty-Three

JANINE

Janine pedals slowly up The Rise and turns into the front garden. She sees Laura outside the house, still in her work clothes and with briefcase in hand, peaking through the lit kitchen window of Magnolia Cottage. Something about her posture suggests she is spying on those inside.

Janine dismounts and approaches Laura quietly.

'What is it?' she whispers.

'I'm just watching Roger and Luke.'

Janine follows her line of sight. Father and son are lying on their fronts on the lounge floor, concentrating on an exercise book between them. Both have pencils or crayons in their hands, and Roger is explaining something to Luke.

'I honestly wouldn't have thought it possible, six months ago,' says Laura softly.

Roger has been living with them for almost a month. Janine is aware that, from Laura's perspective, it could not have gone better. The ex-husband can contribute little to the finances of the household, but he immediately volunteered to be responsible for the school run, allowing Laura and Janine to return to more convenient working hours. Without being asked he started mucking in with housework and laundry, and he has gone out of his way to be charming to Janine and Ianto. Even the Welshman expressed surprise, having pictured Roger as a city slicker with an overbearing manner and an excessively high opinion of himself.

Luke's joy at having his father living with them is obvious to everyone. He spent the first fortnight running from one cottage to the other as if it were perfectly normal to have divorced parents living in adjoining, and linked, accommodation, and excitedly dragging Roger across fields and through woodland to show him all his new discoveries.

Only Janine is unhappy, and her unhappiness and the conflict inside her grow with every day.

On one hand, Luke is again living with both his parents, which is obviously wonderful and she would hate to see that end, and Roger is far from an unpleasant housemate. He is easy-going and accommodating. Furthermore, she can see that he is genuinely trying hard to find a new job. Having dropped Luke off at school he spends the whole day at the kitchen table researching and writing applications, making telephone calls and perfecting his CV.

On the other hand, he was only supposed to be staying for a month at most, and all but a couple of days of that have gone. If he's received any offers or interviews, he's not mentioned them. Laura has said nothing about the approaching expiry of the month and seems completely relaxed about the situation. Janine is increasingly worried that Roger's stay will gradually be extended until it is indefinite.

In short, Roger is helpful, good-natured and friendly, not at all what Janine expected, and she doesn't trust him an inch.

She feels Laura's hand grab hers in a quick pulse of affection but, before she can respond, Laura has moved off, leaving Janine stewing in her old, aching loneliness. Once her constant companion, a malignancy experienced high in her chest, it disappeared soon after she moved into the cottage. She couldn't have said exactly when; she simply noted that it was no longer there. She lived alone, but she was no longer lonely, and she attributed it to the baby growing inside her. She was connected at last to another being. But now, despite her bond with Bobby, it is back, and it almost takes her breath away.

I never knew how perilous it is to love someone.

'Come on,' says Laura as she enters the front door, 'we need to get tea on.'

'Yes, coming.'

Janine starts unbuckling Bobby, who is fast asleep on the trailer.

'Hello,' she hears Laura saying cheerfully as she enters the lounge. 'What are you two up to?'

'Maps,' says Luke. 'Dad's showing me how to do a leg... ledge... what is it again?'

'Legend,' replies Roger, ruffling his son's hair. 'Like an old story.' He looks up at Laura. 'How was your day?'

'Busy, but enjoyable. I don't have to go in until a bit later tomorrow,' she replies, hanging up her coat. 'And yours?'

'Six more applications posted, and that interview's been confirmed for the morning. So, quite productive. The potatoes are peeled and in a bowl of water on the drainer,' he says, pointing with his crayon.

The household has eaten, Bobby is asleep in her cot, and Luke's had his bath. Roger suggests there is time for a game of Snakes and Ladders before the boy goes to bed. All agree except Janine, who says she wants to finish her book. She sits on the couch, book in lap, pretending to read and watching the game from the corner of her eye.

Here, right in front of her, is proof that her relationship with Laura is over. Laura, Roger and Luke laugh and tease one another as they play. They are happy, all conflict forgotten, an ideal family, the sort of family for which Janine longed so desperately as a child and for which her heart still aches. The sort of family she and Bobby could never offer. Roger and Laura talk about things she doesn't understand, and share anecdotes of which she was no part. It's as if they never separated. Roger is handsome and funny, and Laura is kind and beautiful. Basically, a perfect match.

The fact that she and Laura still spend most nights together in Laura's bed and, when alone, they are as close as they were before Roger moved in, does nothing to assuage Janine's fear. She's certain that it's only a matter of time before Laura falls for him again, if she hasn't already. Janine is, once again, a lonely child on the outside looking in. And, like a child, she is too frightened to articulate her fears.

After a while she excuses herself, saying she has a headache, and goes to her bed, where she cries silently. She listens to the laughter downstairs and, later, to the members of the household making their way to their respective beds. After Bobby's final feed, and for the first time since Roger's arrival, she does not creep into Laura's bedroom.

The following morning Roger leaves early to go to his interview, dropping Luke at school en route. Janine waits for the sound of his car to fade away. Then, instead of getting Bobby ready to depart, she takes off her jacket again and heads upstairs, putting the child back in her cot with some toys. She has a plan.

She needs reassurance. Further – and she knows that this is juvenile, but she can't help herself – she's going to remind Laura what she'd be missing. Finally, and most importantly, she wants to create the intimacy that might give her the courage to express her greatest fear.

Laura emerges from the shower and goes into her bedroom to find Janine lying on her bed.

'Hello there,' she says. 'Shouldn't you be on your way to work?' Janine doesn't answer but instead reaches under the towel. 'Where's Bobby?' asks Laura.

'Playing in her cot.'

'Have we time for this?'

Janine answers by sitting up and untying the towel. The older woman's skin glows pink. Janine puts her arms around Laura's bottom and pulls her towards her. She kisses Laura's belly, inhaling deeply: damp skin and Imperial Leather soap.

'I missed you last night,' starts Laura, but then Janine's hands and tongue make further speech difficult.

Janine pulls Laura down onto the bed and they make love urgently. They climax quickly, almost simultaneously, and remain clinging to one another as their breathing subsides.

'Wow!' whispers Laura. 'That was... unexpected. What's got into you?'

'Nothing. Why?'

'I don't know. You've been a bit... different... recently.'

'Have I?'

'I think you know you have. A little distant, perhaps.'

'I'm sorry. Was I distant just now?'

Laura laughs, that deep growl of pleasure that Janine loves so much. 'Not at all. I've already told you, what we do... together... is the most powerful thing I've ever experienced. For the first time in my life this feels right. You do all the right things without thinking, like your body's in charge.'

Janine shrugs. 'I'm not like you. I've very little experience, so I just let go.'

'Not like me? Are you saying I'm a pushover?' teases Laura.

'No, no! Sorry, that came out wrong! It's just that you're so... sophisticated, compared to me.'

'I'm not at all. I've slept with only one man apart from Roger, and that was a one-off. I've never actually enjoyed it much. I thought there was something wrong with me. It seemed so... *contrived*. Like they were reading a car manual, you know, press this button, twiddle this knob. The opposite of instinctive.'

'Then why did you marry Roger?'

Laura disengages, plumps up her pillow and leans back.

'Ah, well, there's the question. I loved him, or so I thought. Something didn't feel right, but I couldn't talk about it to anyone and my parents were really keen. And it's what everyone does, isn't it? If you want children, you get married.'

'But this feels right? Really?'

Laura lifts her hand and strokes Janine's hair. 'Oh, yes,' she says softly.

They fall silent, Laura half-sitting with her back to the headboard stroking Janine's hair, and Janine herself further down the bed, her hand caressing Laura's legs. They can hear Bobby playing contentedly in her cot in the adjoining room.

Now is the time. There will never be a better time.

I must tell her.

Janine's heart accelerates as she tries out opening gambits in her head, desperately seeking the words that will explain her fear, but she is *so* frightened. Saying it out loud will make it real.

What if I'm right? What if by saying something I make it come true?

She reminds herself that the last few minutes were gloriously powerful, intimate and comforting. As always with Laura, she was lost in a sea of desire, with Laura there, alongside her. At those moments she feels closer to this woman than she has ever felt to anyone in her life, like they are one person. No, not quite. She struggles for an appropriate metaphor. They are like two dolphins slicing through blue water, leaping in a cascade of drops into the air, perfectly in their element, separate but totally synchronised. Yes, that's what it feels like.

Surely, *surely* that must mean something?

Yes, but what if...

And she has no reason to doubt Laura's expressions of love. The older woman is an open book, almost childlike in her honesty.

But what if...

The seconds tick by. Any moment Laura will get up and hurry on with her day.

What can I say?

Janine ransacks her mind, desperate for an opening, and finds every formulation inadequate. Useless.

Useless. Mother was right. I am useless.

'Was your mother very tactile?' asks Laura.

Janine is so lost in her anxiety spiral that Laura's actual voice is a jolt.

Could she have read my mind?

She sits up, brought down to earth, panic receding.

'No, just the opposite, actually,' she says slowly. 'Mother didn't go in for kisses or cuddles.'

'Never?'

'No. She hated me.'

'Hated you?' says Laura in disbelief.

'Yes,' says Janine, feeling her way as if in a dark and unfamiliar house. 'Have I ever told you about our trip to Lowestoft?'

'No. But I'm really sorry, love, I've got to go. I'm already late.'

'It won't take long.' She turns to face Laura, their faces only inches apart. 'Please.'

Maybe this will explain. Maybe...

Laura looks at the clock on the bedside table and then back at Janine's expression. 'Okay,' she says.

LOWESTOFT

The train slows as it pulls into the station. It judders to a halt with a loud hiss of steam. Lowestoft, reads Janine, remembering the name from the postcard she found in Mother's bedroom. She says nothing.

Mother steps off the train onto the windswept platform leaving Janine to clamber down alone. The steps to the platform are deep and she is frightened. She has never travelled on a train before. She clings tightly to the vertical rail and lowers each foot cautiously.

Mother had not intended to come all the way into Lowestoft but to get off at the stop before. She made Janine memorise it, Oulton Broad, in case she fell asleep. Then, just as they'd been about to step down at that stop, Mother saw someone she recognised. She seemed unable to decide what to do and by the time she stirred, the train had started moving off. She sat Janine down again, muttering under her breath.

Mother is standing a few feet away, hesitating, scanning the platform. She is a solid block of a woman of average height with sturdy calves. She turns her beaky nose to Janine, grabs her hand, and hauls her off towards the ticket office and the exit. In her other hand she grasps the handles of a battered holdall. She hunches her shoulders against the wind off the North Sea.

'What's that smell, Mother?' asks Janine.

'Seaweed. And the cannery.'

'And that noise?'

'What noise?'

Mother looks up. There are dozens of gulls wheeling and diving above them, the grey and white of their wings sharp against the sky. 'Herring gulls.'

They continue towards the exit. Every now and then Janine's arm knocks against something hard in Mother's coat pocket. She knows what it is and dreads Mother reaching for it.

They are the last to leave the platform, and the station building seems deserted. No one is interested in taking their tickets. Janine was permitted to hold them in preparation for handing them in, and she was looking forward to it. She tucks them carefully in her coat pocket, hoping someone will ask for them later.

As they step from the ticket office onto the empty station forecourt Mother halts again, looking to left and right. She bends to speak and Janine smells the alcohol on her breath.

'Now, girl, that man at the station before was a friend of your grandfather's, and I didn't want him to see us. So we now have a long walk. Very long. Do you understand?' Janine nods silently. 'I want you to keep hold of my hand and not dawdle.'

She looks up, apparently considering options.

'Not the front, no,' she mutters, as if discussing the matter with someone. 'Too many hotels where he drinks, and all those layabouts who drink with him. The park and the cemetery, then?' She looks down at Janine, almost as if expecting a reply. 'Plenty of places into which we can duck if necessary. Yes? Come on.'

They walk in silence for fifteen minutes. There are only a few shoppers on the pavements, and all seem to have red noses and chapped cheeks. When two people meet they hug themselves, shuffle from foot to foot to keep warm, and exchange a few short words before scurrying into the warmth of a shop. The wind is blowing directly in Janine's eyes and is making them water. Mother hands her a tissue.

'Wipe your eyes. You look like you're crying. It's always like this.' She points. 'That's the North Sea.'

Now she has started talking, Mother continues. This is unusual, but Janine knows she's nervous. More than once her hand reaches to her coat pocket before moving away again.

'This place hasn't changed at all. Same grey shops, grey streets and grey sky. Time crawls here.'

They pass the stained stone pillars and damp entrance porch of a pub. Mother checks her stride to peer through the bay window into the lounge bar.

'See that chair?' she says, pointing.

Janine stands on tiptoe and follows the line of her mother's finger. She is pointing at some tall stools next to a shiny bar with a brass foot rail.

'There, the end stool,' explains Mother. 'That was his. He spent more time sitting on that stool than anywhere else in the entire world. He'd talk to anyone. All brass and dazzle, he was.'

Janine isn't sure, but something about the way Mother speaks tells her she doesn't mean Grandfather.

Mother turns and casts a sharp glance to the other side of the road. Two middle-aged women stare at them, their heads close together as they whisper. Janine feels her hand yanked, and they continue on their journey, walking faster than before.

Janine is struggling to keep up, having to skip every third or fourth step.

'Come on!' says Mother, 'before it's all round town. That Mrs Pallant's like a town crier, and I don't want him warned.'

They continue walking for half an hour without speaking. Janine is getting tired and the cold air is making her asthma worse. She can feel the wheezing in her chest but she says nothing.

Mother slows again.

'Your granny's in there,' she says, nodding towards tall gates opening onto a drive and what looks like a park. 'I used to go every week.' She looks down at Janine, weighing something up. 'Would you like to see where your grandmother's buried?'

'In the ground?'

'Yes, of course in the ground! Look, do you want to rest for a minute?'

'Yes, please,' answers Janine without hesitation.

'All right then. Come on. Just to say hello.'

They pass the lodge and walk into the cemetery. Mother leads Janine westwards, zigzagging between the graves. Then she stops and points.

'There.'

There are words cut into an upright stone but they are blurred with weathering and moss. Janine leans forward to read them.

'Edith,' supplies Mother. 'Edith Watts. Born 1st February 1872, died 31st March 1929. Only fifty-seven she was, and dead and gone in three days.' She continues, under her breath, her voice brimming over with bitterness. 'Taking all my dreams, and leaving me nothing 'cept five smelly fishermen. And me nowt but a girl.'

'If granny was called Watts, why are we called Taylor?'

'Because I didn't want anything of your grandfather's, so I took granny's maiden name.' Mother pauses again before continuing. 'Didn't even get her silver candlesticks or her Irish table linen, which were mine by rights. Just her bloody name.'

The grave is well-tended, in contrast to most of those around it. Mother picks up a stone and places it at the edge of the marble slab. Janine is about to ask why she did it when she speaks again. 'You're very like her, you know.'

'Granny?'

'Of course your skin colour's foreign but, oh my! Just like her in every other way, your hair and your eyes especially. And sometimes your face... when you're concentrating... it reminds me so much of her, it hurts. I'll show you a portrait when we get home. She was so beautiful as a girl, my grandfather paid a man to have her painted. Come on now,' she says, turning immediately and walking away from the grave.

Janine follows her, trying to count the number of dead people lying here, together, under the gunmetal sky. She imagines them whispering to one another from their damp beds, waiting for the gaps between the passing trains. Being buried must be very lonely, she thinks.

They run across London Road South to avoid the fast-moving traffic and walk into Kendal Road. Janine is tired and begins to slow. Mother stoops and picks her up. She turns right at the end of Kendal Road and continues walking until there are no more houses. There, Mother stops. The sea, huge, flat and grey, stretches before them. To their right, the last building in the street, is a small well-maintained house with a neat front garden. There are few plants, and those that survive are crusted in salt.

'Perfect for a fisherman, isn't it? You can see right out to sea from here. Your grandfather would tell us what the weather was going to do just by stepping into the back yard, smelling the air and watching the clouds. He once walked all the way to the post office to telephone the Meteorological Office and put them right. He was always right.' She laughs bitterly. 'So right, he never knew when he was wrong.'

Mother puts Janine down, smooths her dress and pats her

golden hair into shape. She stands back to examine the result. Janine is chocolate-box pretty.

'You remember what to say?' she asks.

'"How do you do? I'm pleased to meet you, Grandfather Watts".'

'Good.'

Mother's worried eyes flick from Janine to the front door and back again. Janine senses her anxiety and almost unbearable expectation. She knows that something very important is about to happen. Mother's hand reaches again for the bottle in her pocket, but still she resists.

'Be a good girl, and make me proud of you,' she says quietly.

She takes two deep breaths to compose herself, takes Janine's hand tightly in hers, and walks up the path. She knocks on the door.

There is a noise from inside and someone comes towards the door. An old man opens it. There is a newspaper held loosely in his hand. He stares at Mother and then down at Janine. Janine remembers to smile as she puts out her hand.

'How do you do? I'm pleased to meet you, Grandfather Watts,' she says.

The expected hand of her grandfather does not come forward, but she keeps her arm outstretched. The man looks down at Janine for a long time, his brow contorted into a frown. Janine knows then, long before it occurs to Mother, that this trip has been a waste of time. There is not the faintest flicker of affection or warmth in Ernest Watts's eyes; they're the eyes of a cold, unforgiving man. He slowly shakes his head and lifts it to look at Mother. He stares straight at her and then, without uttering a word, closes the door, leaving them standing on the path.

For a long moment, neither of them moves. Then Janine takes Mother's hand and tugs it gently to pull her back down the path, but Mother shakes her off and returns to the front door. She lifts the knocker and knocks hard, waits a second, and knocks again. There is no response. She starts to hammer on the door with both fists, as if she could smash it off its hinges and break into the narrow hallway. Still the door does not open, and Janine can imagine the old man inside shutting his ears to the desperate banging. She takes Mother's hand again but this time she is almost thrown off.

'Get away! I hate you!' cries Mother, and turns back to the door. 'Father!' she calls. 'Please, Father!'

Janine walks back down the path and sits at the end of it. She knows that her grandfather will not come. She knows better than anyone the unyielding obstinacy in the glacier that passes for the Watts soul. She lives with it every day.

She waits for Mother's efforts to break through the hardwood of the door and of her grandfather's heart, to subside. When Mother finally gives up, they retrace their steps to the station in silence. There they sit on the freezing platform, waiting for the next train to take them home, Janine listening to the shrieks of the gulls punctuated by Mother's drinking and sobbing.

'You poor love,' says Laura, stroking Janine's hair gently. 'You poor, poor love.'

But it's not been enough to explain, and now Laura is checking her watch and getting up from the bed and there's no more time.

Chapter Twenty-Four

LAURA

Winter is approaching. The Canada geese pair that made their nest by the lake have departed with their two surviving, and now fully-fledged, goslings. The trees around the lake have shed their last leaves, and it is now possible to see the water clearly from the cottages' bedroom windows. Luke loves to stride around the lake, every step crunching as if he were marching on a bed of crisps, and kicking leaves high into the air. At the foot of the valley, behind the trees, thin grey twists of bonfire smoke rise lazily into the cold blue sky from the gardens of Chapelhill.

It is a brisk but sunny Sunday morning. Roger and Luke have cycled down to Luke's school. Luke has been selected for the Under 10's for the first time, and his father is going to watch the football match and cheer him on.

Roger has now been at Chapel Hill for seven weeks. He has, at last, received a job offer from a solicitors' firm in Stockport. As he told his housemates, the offices are cramped, the work mundane and the pay derisory compared to what he earned in London. On the other hand, the two partners seem genuinely friendly and no one in the firm is expected to be in the office at weekends or after five thirty during the week. Most importantly of all, the hours would allow him to continue being part of Luke's daily life.

'I'm still to make a final decision,' he said, sitting with the others at the dinner table. 'I know what it'll do to my career, long-term, and I need to be really sure I've come to terms with it. But I'm considering it seriously.'

Laura noted a definite improvement in Janine's frame of mind following Roger's announcement, although she gradually became quieter in the days that followed. Laura knows she should probably remind Roger that the agreed month has long-since expired, but she's been putting it off. She doesn't want him to feel as if he's being thrown out, and she does wonder how they are going to cope without him. Most importantly, they need time to discuss it with Luke, who is likely to need help in understanding.

Bobby, who has a cold, has been put back in bed and is sleeping. Ianto is outside in the van. Taking advantage of the cottages being empty, Laura and Janine have returned to Laura's bedroom with a pot of tea. They are in bed, reading. Chapel Hill is quiet and peaceful.

After a while Laura looks up and out of the window. The sunshine has gone and heavy clouds are gathering.

'Damn,' she mutters. 'Looks like it's going to rain. There's still a load of wet washing in the machine.'

Janine also looks up. 'It's already started, look,' she says, as a gust of wind spatters the windowpanes with raindrops. 'Poor Luke.'

Laura returns to her reading, but Janine closes her book and snuggles down into the bed until her shoulders are under the covers. The rain on the windows is very noisy now, but the bedroom is warm and cosy. Within a few minutes Laura hears

Janine's breathing becoming more shallow and regular as she slips into sleep.

Laura is not sure what makes her look up. A noise perhaps at the bedroom door, so light that she didn't consciously hear it over the rain on the glass, or perhaps a creak from one of the old floorboards. In any case, she looks up.

Roger is standing in the half-open doorway. His hair is plastered to his head, and his face is wet. The jumper he was wearing when he cycled down the hill is soaked. He is staring at the bed and the two women in it. Laura sees shock and anger in his expression but, mostly, puzzlement.

'Roger–' starts Laura, but he immediately spins round, walks swiftly along the corridor and clatters downstairs.

She jumps out of bed, waking Janine, who sits up.

'What is it?' she asks, groggily.

Laura is hurriedly pulling a dressing gown over her nightdress. 'Roger.'

'He saw us?' gasps Janine, her hand going to her mouth.

'Yes,' says Laura. 'Stay here. I'll talk to him,' she says, and she follows Roger downstairs.

She half expects him to have stormed out of the house but he is in the lounge, staring out of the front windows towards the lake at the foot of the hill. The usually flat surface is pot-marked with heavy raindrops and the wind is whipping up tiny white-crested waves.

Laura stops just inside the door, twelve feet or so from where Roger stands. He whirls round as he hears her enter.

'Roger–' she starts again.

'I knew it!' he says, his voice low but intense. 'I knew it! I just didn't want to believe it. How long's this been going on? She was obviously more than just your neighbour – I mean you're living together, right? Why else take down the wall between the two cottages? – so it was obvious you were close but… this?'

'We were going to tell you, when–'

'When? When did you think I'd have a right to know you're having an… *affair* with that woman?'

'Actually, you have no right–'

He interrupts again, shouting this time. 'No right?'

'Calm down, Roger. This is my house, and what Janine and I do here–'

'What you do in *front of our son*,' he interjects.

'Nothing has been done in front of Luke, but he's the reason we thought we should wait–'

'"*We*"?' he interrupts, yet again. '"*We*"? You and that… *lesbian*?'

Laura turns on her heel and heads for the door.

'Where are you going?' he demands. 'We need to talk about this!'

She turns back to him. 'I agree. We need to talk about this, calmly and with Luke in mind. But I'm not having this discussion until you act like a grown-up and stop interrupting me. This is my home, and you're my guest. You have absolutely no right to tell me how to live my life. Now, go away and calm down. When you come back we can discuss it.' She pauses and then adds, 'Including when you'll be moving out.'

She continues out into the hallway. Janine, having thrown on some clothes, is halfway down the stairs.

'Come on,' says Laura, turning her round gently. 'Leave him to it.'

They have almost reached the head of the stairs when they hear Roger's angry footsteps on the flagstones and the sound of him wrenching open the front door. Still without a coat he strides into the garden and slams the door behind him.

Laura and Janine watch him through the landing window.

He goes to his car and reaches for the door handle. He stops and his hand falls. He spins round and heads back towards the front door but again changes his mind. He comes to a halt on the garden path, evidently undecided. Then he sees Ianto's campervan, the lights on inside. He wades downhill through the long, wet grass of the orchard and climbs the two steps to the door.

'Good,' says Laura. 'Maybe Ianto can talk some sense into him.'

Chapter Twenty-Five

ROGER

The sounds of a guitar and Ianto's voice reach Roger from inside the campervan. He knocks on the door and the music stops.

'Come in,' calls the Welshman.

Roger opens the door to be met by a warm fug of cannabis smoke. 'Jesus, Ianto, how can you breathe in this?' he complains irritably.

Ianto rises from the banquette and cracks open the window above his head. 'It'll clear in a moment,' he says calmly, sitting again. 'Anyway, it might do you some good. Come in, man. Take a pew.'

He reaches over to the opposite banquette, picks up a towel and throws it at Roger, who catches it. 'It's clean, I promise,' says Ianto. Roger is still on the threshold. 'Well, are you coming in?'

Roger hesitates for a moment longer and then steps up into the van, closing the door behind him. He shuffles into the tiny space, sits heavily on the banquette opposite Ianto, pulls off his saturated jumper and starts rubbing his hair dry. The rain hammers on the campervan roof.

The Welshman reaches across, offering Roger his joint. Roger eyes it sceptically.

'Medicinal,' says Ianto, raising his eyebrows and gesturing towards the house.

'Did you hear that, then?'

'No, too far. But I knew what the girls were likely to be doing with the house quiet. Then you return unexpectedly and storm out minutes later. It doesn't take a genius.'

'So you knew about them, then?'

Ianto keeps his arm outstretched. Roger takes the joint, puts it to his lips and inhales deeply. He is not used to smoking grass. He coughs and his eyes water. Ianto picks up the guitar again and continues playing softly, no longer singing.

'Well, did you?' asks Roger.

'Course I bloody did. Anyone with half an eye could've seen it.'

Roger shakes his head. 'I don't understand it,' he says, calmer. His tone is more perplexed than angry.

Ianto doesn't reply.

Roger offers the joint back but the Welshman shakes his head. Roger sits back to listen and smoke. His head is already starting to swim.

'I don't think I've listened to you properly before,' he says. 'That's pretty good.'

'Thank you. I've busked all round Europe,' replies Ianto, still playing, 'and played a few gigs here and there. But singing's my thing. The guitar's really only for my own accompaniment.'

He continues playing while Roger finishes and stubs out the joint. Ianto seems to take that as his cue. He puts down his guitar.

'Feeling better?' he asks.

'Squiffy,' replies Roger. 'And a little foolish.'

'So, what is it you don't understand, then?' asks Ianto.

Roger raises his arms to the heavens as if the answer were obvious. 'Laura's not a lesbian, for Christ's sake! She was my wife! You think I wouldn't have known?'

Ianto smiles gently. 'But here she is, in a relationship with a woman. It's a fact. And she's happy.'

'That's what I don't understand.'

'Laura's a free spirit. She was always open to love men or women; she just never met the right woman before. You think in labels, man, but she doesn't. She's just a woman in love.'

'In love?' says Roger. 'You think so?'

'So, Janine, a twenty-year-old innocent, seduced your strong-willed, thirty-something, professional ex-wife against her will? Come off it! You're just jealous.'

'No.'

'Yes.'

'No!' insists Roger. He pauses, and then harrumphs. 'All right,' he concedes reluctantly, 'maybe part of it. But–'

'Good. Honesty. And what right have *you* to be jealous? From what I hear you were screwing around.'

'I wasn't screwing around! I got entangled with someone else, yes, but I never stopped loving Laura and we're together now, here, Laura, Luke and me, so...' His protestations falter as he sees Ianto shaking his head.

'You're fooling yourself, man. She wants you to be a good father to Luke, yes, and the two of you have been getting on better than I'd have expected. She might even be your friend one day. But she doesn't love you anymore. Not the way she did, anyway.'

Ianto sits back, still shaking his head, this time to himself.

'Dduw! I knew it was a terrible idea letting you move in! This is partly my fault; I should've said something. Look, Roger, you need to leave. Unless you can really come to terms with it, accept it, you being here will eventually make everyone unhappy, including Luke. The way I see it, those two are in love, crazy in love, and you're like a... a hex, a destructive force, hoping to cut in.'

'I'm not hoping to cut in! I didn't think there was anything to cut *into*!'

'Really?' asks Ianto sceptically. 'You've not watched the two girls together? Listened to the way they speak to one another?'

'Yes, of course, and I suppose I thought they were... you know, close, because of what they've both been through...' Roger hears his own tone and realises that even he doesn't buy it. 'Okay. Yes. I guess I suspected. I just didn't want to believe that I was such a crap husband I've put her off men altogether.'

'That's plain daft,' says Ianto, but not unkindly.

There is silence as Roger sinks into his own swirling thoughts. He wishes he'd not accepted the spliff as he can't think clearly.

'We've been getting on so well,' he says eventually. 'Like at the start. I allowed myself to hope...' he finishes sadly.

Ianto shakes his head. 'Then you were fooling yourself. There's no way back for you.'

'Luke loves having me here,' protests Roger. 'He's not unhappy.'

'Maybe so. But consider this: the longer you're here, the longer he'll cling to the hope that you and Laura will eventually get back together. That's never going to happen. You may not mean it, but you're misleading him, isn't it? It's not fair on the boy. Accept the new reality. Laura's moved on and found someone else. You should do the same. Let me tell you something. My mother's Dutch; it's how I got this hair,' he says, pointing to his white-blond ponytail. 'She and my father were thrown together in Europe, before the war, so it was more circumstance than true love. Years later, back in Wales, my father met someone who he *really* loved. My mother refused him a divorce, but eventually she moved back to Holland. They're still married, and ten years later she's still clinging to the hope that he'll come back to her.'

'So?'

'She's wasted her life, deluding herself. My father's in love with someone else but my mother won't accept it. And until you adjust, you're going to be unhappy like her. You certainly shouldn't be here, looking for the main chance if Laura and Janine fail. She won't come back to you even then. Move on,' he says, picking up the guitar again. 'You dig what I'm saying?'

That produces another long silence from Roger. Finally he stands.

'Well?' asks Ianto.

Roger doesn't answer.

Chapter Twenty-Six

LAURA

The following morning Laura is in the shower when Janine pops her head into the steamy bathroom. She announces that she has to take delivery of some root stock at Windyridge, and she is leaving early. Before Laura can wash the soap off her and cover herself with a towel, the bike and trailer have disappeared. Laura knows the real reason for the early departure; Janine doesn't want to risk seeing Roger.

No one had a comfortable night. After leaving Ianto's campervan, Roger took a coat and drove back to Luke's school. He stood in the rain, watching Luke's team lose their football match. Then he loaded Luke and his bike into the car and left both outside Magnolia Cottage before driving off with barely a word.

He had not shown up again by the time everyone went to bed. Janine slept in her own room in Apple Tree and Laura stayed up late, listening for movement from the box room usually occupied by Roger. She heard nothing. However, when she looked out of the window the following morning, his car was again parked outside, behind hers.

He comes down to the kitchen wearing his suit. Laura is already at the table, eating breakfast.

'Good morning,' says Laura, looking up. 'Where did you get to last night? We were worried about you. Especially Luke.'

He sits at the table. 'I needed time to think. Where is he?'

'Brushing his teeth.'

'Janine gone?'

'Yes.'

'Avoiding me, I suppose.'

Laura doesn't reply to that.

Roger takes a deep breath. 'Okay. Firstly, I need to apologise for yesterday. I was very rude, and not very nice.'

'I agree.'

'It was just a hell of a shock.'

'Okay,' replies Laura guardedly, waiting for what is to follow.

'Secondly, I want to say how grateful I am to you – and Janine – for taking me in. Most people wouldn't have done it. It helped me regain my balance when my life was in freefall.'

'Until yesterday's little outburst, I'd have said you were happy. You certainly looked better. Those rings under your eyes and the hollowed cheeks had gone.'

Roger looks down at the table. 'In some respects, I can't remember ever being this happy.'

'Really?'

He looks up. 'Yes. You've given me a second chance at being a good father. I never knew what it looked like; I thought it just meant being a successful breadwinner.'

'You got that from your father.'

'Who, as we both know, was not much of a role model as a parent. I know now that Luke is the most important thing in my life. I love being involved, hearing about his day, reading with him, all of it. I couldn't bear to lose that.'

'Good to hear. But what about your career? Childcare isn't compatible with being a big shot solicitor. You were never at home.'

'Well, here's the thing. I've decided I don't want to be a big shot solicitor. I'm going to accept the offer from Hardcastles. In fact, I'm going in today.'

'Really? You said you'd be bored out of your mind.'

'I did. And I'm still a little uncertain about it. But, like I said, they seem a nice bunch, and the hours mean I can still see Luke every day. Work isn't everything.'

Laura sits back and studies her ex-husband with a gentle smile.

'What?' he asks.

'Just looking at you afresh. If you really mean that, well... perhaps you *have* changed.'

'I have. At least, I think I have. Despite the evidence of yesterday.'

She leans forward and pats his hand. 'Well done. Better late than never.'

Roger places his hand over Laura's and grips it gently. Her smile fades a little.

'It *is* over, isn't it?' he asks. 'Us, I mean.'

Laura extracts her hand. 'We're divorced, Roger. I'd have thought the answer was obvious.'

'Yes, but... we're getting on so well now. For Luke's sake, wouldn't you like–'

'No,' interrupts Laura firmly. 'I'm in love with someone else. We might be friends, you and I, but that's all. I thought you understood that.'

'I do,' he replies, 'or if I don't yet, I'll learn to.'

He sweeps his flop of dark hair out of his eyes and looks up at her. *He looks very young*, thinks Laura. *That lost boy again.*

'I thought I should ask,' he says, 'one last time. Just in case.'

'Well, you've asked. And the answer's no. I'm in love with Janine. If it were possible, I'd marry her, if she'd have me.'

'So, you're... a... lesbian, then?'

'I don't know what I am, Roger. I just know I love Janine.'

'Do you think you've always been... interested... in women?'

She laughs briefly. 'I guess from your perspective, that's a reasonable question. But I can't tell you. I was interested in *you*, wasn't I? And I married you.'

He pauses and colours slightly. It takes him a few seconds to continue speaking. 'Were you ever... this happy... with me?'

'Oh, Roger, of course I was, at the start!' she replies. It's not the complete truth, but she can't see the point of brutal honesty at this stage; it would only hurt him needlessly. 'But then, well, you know what happened,' she says.

'Yes. Yes.' He pauses. 'You know how sorry I am, don't you? You did nothing wrong, and I just... blew it.'

'Yes, you did. We had something, and you broke it. But I believe you when you say you're sorry.'

He falls silent for a while, but then emphatically shakes himself out of his sadness.

'Right, well, that's all understood.' He stands. 'I shall be moving out.'

'When?'

'I'm going to start looking at rentals today. Hopefully by the end of the week. I want to find somewhere close enough to continue taking Luke to school every day. Or every day that we agree.'

'Okay. I think that's for the best. We need to decide what to say to Luke.'

'I agree–' starts Roger, but at that moment Luke's tread can be heard on the stairs and a second later he bounces into the room in his school uniform, his bag over his shoulder.

Roger stands. 'Ready?' he asks.

'Yes,' says Luke.

'Come on then.'

'Have a nice day,' says Laura to both of them.

Roger ushers Luke out of the house and into his car.

Laura clears up her breakfast things, and also departs.

Chapter Twenty-Seven

JANINE

Lady Margaret was somewhat surprised to see Janine and Bobby arriving at Windyridge before eight o'clock, and insisted that they leave early to compensate. So Janine arrives home not long after lunchtime. No one else is home. Even Ianto's campervan is missing from the garden.

Magnolia Cottage is full of winter sunshine, quiet and peaceful. Janine makes herself a sandwich and a cup of tea and some mashed banana for Bobby. Bobby is less interested in eating it than in making sticky patterns of it on her high chair tray.

'Oh, Bobby,' sighs Janine as she sponges banana gloop from her daughter's face and hair. 'You're going to need a bath.'

There is a knock on the door of Apple Tree Cottage.

Janine's heart jumps. None of them uses that door any longer. She peers out of the front window of Magnolia Cottage. There are two people standing outside the other door, O'Reilly and Michael Carter. She ducks quickly out of sight, but is too late.

'I saw you there, Nadine,' says Carter's voice through the door. 'Don't be silly, now. Open up and let us talk to you.'

Janine doesn't move.

'It's up to you, but if you don't let us in we'll return with officials from the council and the police.'

Then O'Reilly chips in. 'Nadine, my dear, we wish you no harm. I have a duty to make sure your little one is safe and well. We don't want to involve the council or, God forbid, the police. We just need you to open the door so we can talk to you.'

Still Janine doesn't move.

Have they been watching outside, waiting to get me alone?

She feels completely exposed and vulnerable. She wishes with all her heart that Laura or Ianto were there. Even Roger. They would know what to do.

'Last chance, Miss Tyler,' comes Carter's voice.

Janine turns and opens the door to Magnolia Cottage.

'What do you want?' she asks.

'There you are,' says O'Reilly, smiling. 'That's better, isn't it? Are you going to let us in? You still owe me that cup of tea, so you do.'

'What do you want?' she repeats, standing firmly in the doorway.

'As I explained last time, I'm a social worker, and I have a duty to make sure the child is being cared for properly. If I formed the view that she is at risk in any way, I have a duty to report it.'

'My daughter is not at risk. She's perfectly happy.'

'Then you won't mind letting us see for ourselves, will you?' says Carter, moving towards the door.

'What are *you* doing here?' demands Janine, still barring the way.

'I'm the chairman of the Pastoral Council of this Catholic parish, and on the board of Cedars Moral Welfare and–'

'I'm not interested in Cedars Moral Welfare! I've had legal

advice! You have no right to put me under pressure to go there or threaten to take Bobby from me.'

'Oh, you've had legal advice, have you?' scoffs Carter. 'But then I guess a woman in your profession would need lawyers on a regular basis.'

'What do you mean by that?' demands Janine. She whirls on O'Reilly. 'If he's told you I offered myself to him for money, he's a liar! He assaulted me!'

'Now, now, Nadine, let's calm down,' replies the Irishwoman. 'Nothing bad is going to happen here. If you let us in and we can assure ourselves that Bobby is well cared for and safe, that'll be the end of it. We'll be on our way. Now, are you going to be sensible or do we have to come back with the police?'

Janine thinks. 'You can come in, but not him!' She jabs her finger at Carter.

O'Reilly and Carter look at one another for a moment and it seems to Janine that there is some unspoken communication between them.

'Very well,' says O'Reilly. 'I'll come in, and we can leave Mr Carter here on the doorstep. But I want the door left open. You have quite a temper on you, girl, and I'm not happy to be in the house with you on me own.'

'What? What are you talking about? I don't have a temper. You're threatening to take my daughter from me!'

'Well, that's all good then. So I'll come in and Mr Carter will stay here.'

O'Reilly steps into the hall and Janine gives way. She follows the woman's bun as she goes into the kitchen. Bobby has been having a fine time with her mashed banana. Left to herself, her hands, face and hair are now sticky with it. She gives Miss O'Reilly a big smile, her four new teeth gleaming white through the gloop.

'Well, now, how are we, me little darling?' coos O'Reilly, bending down.

'What do you need to know? I'm going to be late for work,' says Janine.

'Yes, the work for which you are paid in cash and make no tax returns, I daresay,' says O'Reilly, not looking round at Janine. 'You know that's a criminal offence, don't you?'

'That's not right,' protests Janine. 'I told you, I've had legal advice. As a new trader I don't have to file any accounts until after the first year.'

'Is that right?' replies O'Reilly, but Janine sees that she's not really listening. She's unfastening Bobby from her high chair.

'What are you doing? Leave her alone!'

'Don't be silly, girl, I have to weigh her and measure her to make sure she's thriving. She's never been seen by the district nurse, has she?'

'Bobby is perfectly healthy. You can see that for yourself. She's already walking and using some words, and her teething's been fine. She's had no illnesses and you can see she's eating well.'

O'Reilly now has Bobby out of the seat and in her arms. 'Yes, she certainly feels a good weight for eleven months. But I'll need to take her to the car where I can weigh her properly.'

'No!' shouts Janine, and she wrenches Bobby from the woman's grasp.

Bobby doesn't like the sudden movement – Janine might have caught her accidentally as she grabbed her – and she opens her mouth wide, scrunches up her eyes and, after a pause to take a full lungful of breath, she lets out a high-pitched wail.

'Now look what you've done,' says O'Reilly. 'I don't think that's good parenting, not at all I don't.'

She is reaching for Bobby again when they hear a man's

voice calling from above them. Janine whirls round to see the front door gaping open onto the hill. Carter is not there.

'Up here!' he calls.

O'Reilly brushes past Janine and runs up the stairs. Janine follows, trying to shush Bobby.

Carter is standing in the open doorway of Laura's bedroom. He points dramatically.

'There's your evidence,' he says to O'Reilly.

O'Reilly steps into the room. Carter has pulled back the bedspread and overturned the pillows. O'Reilly looks at the two nighties, pink and blue, one from under each pillow.

'And there,' says Carter, pointing at the miscellaneous bras and other female clothing on the chairs to either side of the bed. 'They're having an unnatural relationship.' He turns to Janine, a sneer on his face. 'Which explains a lot,' he says.

'So,' says O'Reilly. 'This is your bedroom, which you share with another woman.'

'N-no... that's not... my room is next door,' stammers Janine.

'I've seen enough,' says O'Reilly.

She turns and walks back down the stairs. Carter waits for a moment and then bends his head to spit in Janine's ear: 'Dyke!'

Janine runs after O'Reilly and catches up with her at the front door.

'Where are you going?' she demands.

O'Reilly spins round quickly. Her smile and wheedling voice are gone. Her face is as hard as a hatchet.

'You are a common prostitute and you are living in an immoral relationship with another woman. On top of that you are probably living under a false name because there's no one called Nadine Tyler, which suggests to me you're also guilty of tax evasion and fraud. But that's for the police and the tax authorities. One thing is certain: you are totally unfit to bring up a child, and I will be back with a social worker from the local authority and a police officer to take her to a place of safety.'

She stalks out into the garden without another word. Carter pushes Janine roughly out of his way and follows. As he gets into the car he turns and smiles triumphantly at her.

Janine slams the door shut, her heart pounding in her throat. Nonetheless, after all the anxiety and the tears of apprehension when she feared this outcome, she is now, oddly, icily calm.

'Well, that's that,' she says. 'We're leaving.'

Chapter Twenty-Eight

JANINE

Janine arrives at Stockport station with Bobby on the trailer and absolutely no idea where to go next. She is so frightened of being spotted outside, she buys a platform ticket, seeking camouflage in the shifting crowds of travellers.

She stands on the station concourse in front of the timetable boards, looking through them again and again, praying for inspiration. If she were to travel one stop into Manchester she could go almost anywhere in Britain, but not with only ten pounds in her purse. The fare to London would use up over half of that, and then what? She could even go to Scotland, and surely no one would find her there, but that would leave her with less than three pounds.

If I remain local I'll have money for food and perhaps a room for a couple of nights, but they're more likely to find me. But if I go a long way away, I'll arrive penniless.

Her thoughts go to Laura, working only one short railway hop away from her. She is hugely tempted to take the train for ten minutes into Manchester. She's sure she could find Laura's office to tell her what's happened. But then what? Beg her to take Luke out of school and run away with her? No, that's a wild thought. She couldn't ask it of Laura. Her sweet, funny, sensible and bonkers Laura, who she thought she'd be with forever. Or Luke, for that matter. How could she expect him to leave his home and new school just as he's making friends? And lose his father again? No.

Bobby is becoming impatient and is struggling to get out of the trailer. Janine finds a shop and buys a bottle of milk, filling the child's beaker with it, which keeps her quiet for a short while.

I should have kept some money back for this eventuality.

This is not like the time she was thrown onto the street by Mother. Then she had a building society account full of savings; she had choices. The account is now empty, everything spent.

Who do I know who might help me? Where can I go?

Her mind is a torrent of thoughts and possibilities while, at the same time, a complete blank. She can't even think of anywhere she's visited during the course of her life to which she'd want to return.

And then an idea occurs to her. There is one place she's been and where there may be some succour: Lowestoft. There's no point expecting help from her grandfather – she still remembers those fish-eyes staring from Mother to her and back again without a glimmer of compassion – but didn't Mother have four or five brothers? And one of them might even be Uncle George. His postcard to Mother seemed so kind. Maybe he would help a niece in desperate straits?

Like a drowning woman grasping a piece of flotsam not quite sufficient to support her weight, she clings to the possibility that, just maybe, she might find some kindness in the far easternmost reaches of England.

She goes to the ticket office. The man behind the window has to look up several timetables and it takes a while, causing everyone behind her in the queue to become impatient but, yes, it would be possible, he says. You can get to Lowestoft from here, but the journey is difficult. You have to travel south to Doncaster, then to Stevenage, and then to Cambridge – in other words half across the country in the wrong direction – to pick up the East Suffolk Line service to Ipswich. From Ipswich a single train will take Janine all the way to Lowestoft and, because there is so much freight on the East Suffolk Line, there shouldn't be any difficulty travelling with the trike and trailer.

The journey will cost three pounds six shillings and four pence, and even if everything goes perfectly, it will take over seven hours. The man warns Janine that if any of the trains are delayed, if she misses a connection, she and Bobby may have to have to spend a night on a platform somewhere.

She hands over the money and buys the tickets.

She has twenty minutes before the train departs. She settles Bobby back in the trailer and cycles to the shops where she buys fruit, sliced ham, another bottle of milk and four Scotch eggs. She has enough Terry towelling nappies and changes of clothing for Bobby to last two days, barring unexpected accidents. Then she cycles back to the station, locates the relevant platform, and makes herself known to one of the ticket inspectors. At this time of day she is allowed to ride with the trike and trailer but she will need help getting on and off the train.

Minutes later, she and Bobby are watching the houses and factories of Stockport stream past the window, travelling ever further away from Laura and Luke, on the first leg of their cross-country odyssey. Now she is settled in her seat with nothing to occupy her mind, the enormity of what she has done strikes her with full force. She can no longer prevent the emotional whirlpool of the last few hours from overtaking her, and she weeps for the loss of her lovely home, her job, her friends and, most of all, for her Laura.

Chapter Twenty-Nine

ROGER

Roger and Luke arrive at the cottages shortly before six o'clock. It is dark, and frost is already forming on the more exposed parts of the hill. They are later than expected because they went into Glossop to buy Luke some new gloves.

Roger has spent the day signing his employment contract at Hardcastles, being introduced to the staff and, after leaving them, looking at rental properties. One was a lovely little cottage on the Mellor Estate, recently refurbished and on the market for the first time in years. It's not cheap but, with the new job, he can afford it and it's only a fifteen-minute drive from Chapel Hill. He could move in as early as this weekend. It will be perfect, at least until the Didsbury house is sold and he can think of buying something else, something smaller, for him and Luke.

He looks down the hill for Ianto's campervan, but that too is missing. He notes a car parked towards the top of The Rise but it's showing no lights and its windows are steamed with condensation. A courting couple, he thinks.

He gives a Luke a biscuit and a glass of milk, and sits him at the kitchen table to start his homework while he looks inside the fridge. Cooking is not among his skills but perhaps he can make a start. Another expression of goodwill.

He finds a bowl of marinating chicken and, on the kitchen table, a note from Laura addressed to Janine with instructions for their supper. It requires onions to be browned and vegetables to be added before the chicken. He can manage that, at least. The note ends: *Love you, xx*. The quotidian affection causes Roger a momentary pang of sadness, but he removes his jacket, rolls up his sleeves, and starts chopping vegetables.

They hear the front door open and close just after six.

'Hello!' calls Laura from the hall as she takes off her coat and hat. 'Where are the trike and trailer?' She walks into the kitchen. 'Is Janine late again?'

'We don't know,' replies Luke.

'If you give me a moment to get changed, Roger, I'll take over,' she says, indicating the chopping board.

She goes upstairs, but is only gone for a couple of minutes before they hear her footsteps coming back down.

'What is it?' asks Roger.

Laura doesn't answer but races across the room, throws open one of the kitchen cupboards and takes out the biscuit tin used for household petty cash. She opens it, the metal lid skidding off the surface and clattering onto the flagstones.

'Roger! She's gone!'

'How do you know?'

'Most of her clothes are missing, and her books.'

'Yes, but–'

He stops as Laura shows him a small folded piece of paper she's taken from the biscuit tin. He looks over her shoulder as she opens it.

Sorry. I've borrowed ten pounds from the tin. I

promise I'll post it back to you as soon as I can. I have to go. I love you all.

The handwriting is messy, hurried, but they both recognise it as Janine's. Laura's hand goes to her mouth.

'Something must have happened. Have you spoken to her?' she asks, suddenly suspicious.

'No. She left before me this morning, remember?'

There is a noise in the hall as the front door opens again.

'Janine?' shouts Laura, running from the kitchen. 'Oh, it's you,' she says, seeing Ianto.

'Charming,' he replies, kicking off his boots.

'No, I'm sorry, Ianto, but Janine's gone.'

'Gone?'

'Yes, left.'

'O Dduw!' he exclaims softly. 'Where?'

Ianto has not closed the door behind him and he whirls round at a sound. Two women have arrived on the threshold. One already has her foot inside the hall.

'We need to see Miss Tyler, please,' she says, trying to walk past Ianto.

Roger follows Laura to the door.

'Who are you?' he asks.

'I am Wilhelmina Murray, and I am a senior social worker with Stockport County Borough,' she says. 'And this is Mary O'Reilly, from Cedars Moral Welfare. We have reason to believe that a child known as Roberta Tyler who lives here is at risk of abuse and we are here to take her into the care of the local authority.'

'She's not here,' says Roger.

'We are obliged to come in and check,' says the woman.

Roger looks over their shoulders towards the car he saw earlier. 'That's your car, is it?'

'It's mine,' answers O'Reilly.

'So, you've been watching since before anyone arrived home, haven't you? You know perfectly well there was no one home before my son and I arrived, so you know Miss Tyler and her child are not here.'

That causes a momentary hesitation, and the two women on the doorstep look at one another.

'We have a legal duty to protect that child,' says O'Reilly, her colour rising, 'and we are going to come in to check whether she is here or not.'

'Not without a warrant, you aren't,' says Roger, squaring his shoulders in case they try to push their way in.

'We don't need a warrant.'

'I am a solicitor of the Supreme Court, madam, and I am telling you, you need a warrant if you wish to enter these premises, and a court order permitting removal of a child. Unless either of you is a police officer and suspects, on reasonable grounds, that a felony has occurred.'

'In any case,' adds Laura, 'she's left. She no longer lives here.'

'I spoke to her here only this afternoon,' asserts O'Reilly.

'At which time you again threatened to take Bobby away from her, yes?' says Roger. 'So, now, quite predictably, she's decamped.'

'Where is Miss Tyler?' demands Murray.

'We don't know!' replies Laura, her voice rising. 'We got back to find her gone, you evil-minded, malevolent bitch!'

She aims the last at O'Reilly, who recoils at the attack.

'Now,' says Roger calmly, 'you can either go away and get a warrant if you think you have reasonable grounds, or you can camp outside the house indefinitely for all I care, but I'm closing the door now.'

And he does just that. Murray just manages to get her foot out of the way in time.

There is silence inside the hall as the three adults listen to what's happening on the other side of the door. They hear the two women speaking quietly, and then their footsteps retreat to the road. A few moments later O'Reilly's car starts up, turns round and its lights disappear down the hill. The noise of the car fades away.

'I've got to find her,' says Laura, her eyes wild and shining.

Roger puts a hand on her shoulder. 'Come and sit down. We'll talk it through,' he says gently.

'Was all that right, the law you threw at her?' asks Ianto, looking impressed.

'Well, it's a bloody long time since I did any family law, but I think so. Come on, Laura.'

Ianto taps Roger on the shoulder and speaks with a lowered voice as they move towards the kitchen.

'You don't think there's any chance of the police actually turning up, do you?'

'I doubt it. Why?'

'I just wouldn't want them searching my van, that's all.' He lowers his voice further still. 'It's not actually illegal to grow it but, well...'

'Let's deal with that later, yes?'

'Sure, sure,' says Ianto, nodding repeatedly. 'First things first.'

As Laura and Roger enter the kitchen they find Luke standing there, looking very small and very lost. There are tears in his eyes.

'Have Janine and Bobby left us?' he asks, his voice cracking.

'Oh, darling!' cries Laura, and she runs to her little boy,

kneeling on the stone flags and hugging him to her tightly, her own eyes brimming with tears.

Roger shakes his head in disbelief. For weeks he wondered if circumstances might arise where Laura, Luke and he would be together, alone, in the semi-detached cottages. Now, totally unexpectedly, and after he conceded defeat, it's been presented to him on a plate.

He looks down at his scared and heart-sick ex-wife and son.

I'm being tested, he thinks wryly, shaking his head. He is aware of Ianto staring at him with unusual intensity. Roger bends down and puts his arms around Laura and Luke at the same time.

'I promise you both,' he says earnestly, 'I will do everything I possibly can to help you get them back.'

He lifts his eyes to meet those of Ianto towering above them. The tall Welshman smiles and nods in approval.

Chapter Thirty

JANINE

The guard in the goods van helps Janine lower the trailer onto the platform at Lowestoft. When not going up and down the train to clip tickets, he spent most of the journey from Ipswich with Janine and Bobby in the goods carriage, chatting about his forthcoming retirement and the golden wedding anniversary he and his wife shared earlier that year. Mercifully, Bobby has been so exhausted that she slept for most of the last leg.

It is a little before ten when he waves goodbye, blows his whistle and slides the goods carriage's door shut with a bang. Janine is grateful to him for having made the last part of the journey bearable.

By the time she has attached the trailer to the back of the trike, only a single taxi remains on the dark station forecourt. Janine walks the trike over to him and taps on the window. The driver winds it down and a cloud of hot air and cigarette smoke hits her in the face.

'Yes?'

'Can you point me in the direction of the cemetery, please?'

Janine can't remember how she and Mother got to the cemetery, but she's confident she will recognise the road to take from there to her grandfather's house. She'll know the house; it has remained embedded in her memory since she was a child.

'Which one?'

'There's more than one?'

'There's the main one–' he starts.

'It's somewhere near London Road,' says Janine.

'Right. You know it's not open at this time of night?'

'I know that, thank you, but I still need to know how to get there.'

The driver gives directions and Janine sets off.

Her recollection is that it took hours to walk the distance from the station to the cemetery when she was six or seven, so she is surprised when she reaches it in little more than ten minutes. But then, she reminds herself, she was a skinny little thing with short legs, she was bored and frightened, and she still suffered from the asthma that afflicted her until her early teens.

Outside the cemetery, she pauses, looking around. It takes a moment for her to get her bearings, but then she sees the road on the other side of the main thoroughfare. Yes, this is it, London Road South, the only busy road she and Mother crossed. As soon as she cycles over into Kendal Road and heads towards the sea, she knows she has reached the right place.

The house, when she stops outside, is exactly as she remembers it, although the garden is now paved with concrete slabs. In the parking space created there is a small Austin 1100 vehicle. Its driver's door is slightly open and the interior light is illuminated. Janine dismounts and pulls the trike and trailer onto the slabs behind the car. She checks on Bobby, who is still asleep.

Janine straightens her clothes. Laura's clothes, she reminds herself.

I'll have to post them back to Chapel Hill in due course.

She has rehearsed exactly what she's going to say.

She walks purposefully towards the door, and only then realises that it's open. There is a young woman in the hallway who seems to be wheedling or cajoling someone. As Janine gets closer, she starts to hear the conversation.

'Ernest, please! You can't go out now. It's freezing, and the shops are closed.'

Janine hears a man's voice say something in reply but she doesn't catch the words. There is a whining, self-pitying tone to it.

'Come and sit down,' says the woman, 'and I'll put the television on.'

Janine lifts her hand and knocks gently on the front door so as not to startle those beyond it. The door opens a few more inches and a woman appears in the gap. She wears a blue hat and an overcoat over a nursing uniform.

'Yes?' she says, sounding flustered and surprised to find someone on the doorstep this late.

'Is Ernest Watts at home?'

'Yes,' says the woman. 'Who are you?'

'I'm Janine, his granddaughter–' starts Janine, but she is interrupted.

'Thank heavens,' says the woman. 'I'm already terribly late. Do you think you can persuade him? He was already out the door, and it's taken me twenty minutes to coax him back inside, but he won't take his coat off and he insists he's walking into town.'

'I don't think he'll listen to me,' says Janine uncertainly.

'Let me out, let me out!' says a voice, and the door is pulled open wide.

Janine doesn't recognise her grandfather.

The man she saw as a small child was elderly but tall,

upright and strong. He was smartly dressed, shaved and his hair was styled and plastered to his square skull with Brylcreem. This man looks thirty years older and is no taller than Janine herself. He wears a heavy overcoat which must be at least a size too large for him. His eyes are red-rimmed and watery, his hair is unkempt and he needs a shave. He also, quite obviously, smells like someone who has not bathed in several days.

Janine is well illuminated by the light falling on her from the hallway, but it takes the man a while to focus on her.

'Hello, Grandfather,' says Janine nervously.

'Edith? Thank God! This bloody woman is telling me I can't go into town! Will you tell her, please?'

The district nurse turns to Janine. 'You said your name was Janine,' she challenges.

'It is. Edith's my grandmother. She died years ago.'

'Edith, please!' begs Ernest.

'It's not Edith, Grandfather, it's Janine.'

He peers into her face, breathing heavily, his mouth slack. When he speaks, it is almost under his breath. 'No, no, not Edith... not Edith... but just like her. Just like her.'

He sags suddenly as if his knees have given way, and throws his arms out to brace himself against the walls of the narrow entrance. Janine and the district nurse leap forward to prevent him falling, and they each manage to grab one elbow.

'Come on,' says the nurse, 'let's get him into the lounge.'

'My baby's outside,' says Janine.

'This won't take a second.'

They manoeuvre the ailing man through the first door they encounter. The lounge they have entered smells bad – stale cooking and toilet odours – but there is a large comfortable armchair facing a television.

'Here,' says the nurse, and they lower him into the chair.

'What about his coat?'

'Leave it for the moment. It's always chilly in here. In any case, it's often a battle to get him into bed, so sometimes I let him sleep in the chair.'

'Can he still manage stairs?' asks Janine, surprised.

'Not really, and definitely not alone. He's been on the list for a council flat for nearly five years. I keep telling them, but there's nothing suitable. Most of the people in his condition die while they're waiting.'

'From falling downstairs?' asks Janine.

'Some.'

Janine runs out of the room to the trike and trailer. Bobby is still asleep. She lifts her out of the harness and brings her into the house. The nurse looks into her little face, which is almost completely hidden by her clothes and hat.

'She's a little darling, isn't she?' she comments. 'So, can I leave you with him? He's been fed and changed, and I've emptied the commode. That's what I was doing when I heard him opening the front door. He may not be all there, but he's canny; he waited 'til I was out in the yard.'

Janine hesitates.

'Give me a second,' she says, and she darts out of the lounge and heads up the narrow staircase.

On the first floor is a landing with two rooms opening off either side. She opens each door as she reaches it. The first room is so full of old furniture the door won't open fully. The others are bedrooms, one obviously used by the old man and one with two stripped single beds in it. The last door opens onto a smaller room than the others. There is a single bed under the window with a bedspread on it, a chest of drawers and nothing else. She lifts the corner of the bedspread. No sheets, but a mattress cover.

No bathroom? Oh, yes, the nurse mentioned the yard.

She squints out of the rear window into darkness. There's no moon and little illumination from the house, but Janine can make out a small building in the corner.

Outside privy.

She returns downstairs to the lounge. The district nurse has turned on the television. The sound is off, but Ernest is staring at what looks like ballroom dancing, with men in white tie and tails, and women in big dresses spinning round under spotlights. Janine didn't know you could watch dancing on TV. Ernest's mouth hangs open. It is difficult to know if he is actually watching or the set merely happens to be in his line of sight. The bar heater is now on but the room feels no less chilled.

'All right,' says Janine to the district nurse. 'I can take over from here.'

'Really? That would be so helpful. I still have one visit to do and I'm so late, my husband's going to kill me!'

'When do you come back? I mean, how often does someone visit to care for him?'

'I won't be back for another fortnight, but your aunts come in every day at least once.'

'Which aunts?'

For the first time the nurse hesitates. 'Don't you know?'

'No,' says Janine, thinking quickly. 'I live in Cheshire. I came to visit, but I'm half a day late. The trains were terrible.'

'Oh, I see. Well it's usually Betty or Alice, though I've also met a third lady, married to another of your uncles. I don't know her name. One of them will be in tomorrow I expect.'

'Thank you,' says Janine. 'I can take over from here,' she repeats, anxious to have the nurse depart. 'I'll give them a call as soon as I've settled Grandfather.'

'Thank you.'

The nurse hurries out of the house. Janine leaves Bobby on the couch and goes outside to move the trike. As soon as the Austin has backed off the garden paving, she waves to the nurse and pushes the trike and trailer into the vacant space. She lifts the single holdall and goes inside, locking the door behind her.

Chapter Thirty-One

LAURA

'And you can't think of anywhere?' asks Ianto. 'She never mentioned friends, or family?'

Luke is in bed and the three adults have finished eating. The plates and saucepans are piled on the kitchen counter and a small pile of tiny cigarette butts has formed in the ashtray on the kitchen table in front of Ianto.

Laura thinks. While waiting for a response, Roger stands, goes to the pile of cut logs stacked in the inglenook and throws a new one on the fire. He returns to the table.

Laura shakes her head, giving up.

'No, nowhere. I've told you, she didn't really have any friends. She had a very isolated childhood. The only place I know she had relatives was in Lowestoft, but I don't think she'd go back there.'

'Why not?' asks Roger.

'Because she only had unhappy memories of it. She was dragged there by her mother when she was very small. Her grandfather threw her mother out when *she* got pregnant, and her mother took Janine up there to meet the old man and... I don't know... I suppose, to introduce him to his granddaughter, maybe persuade him to let them come home. He slammed the door on them. Janine still remembers it.'

'And it was just the grandfather, was it?' asks Roger.

Laura casts her mind back to Janine's story about meeting the man for the first and only time.

'No, now I think of it, she mentioned four, or maybe it was five "smelly fishermen". I think her grandmother died young, and Janine's mother had to take over looking after the men in the family. So there might've been uncles. But I don't think Janine ever met them or even knew their names.'

There is silence around the table.

Ianto stands and ambles to the stove. *He moves like a daddy-long-legs,* thinks Laura distractedly, *as if his limbs were disproportionately long and thin for his body.* The Welshman illuminates a gas ring and, holding his long hair back, bends to light another roll-up. He takes a deep drag.

'Is that what you were talking about?' asks Roger, pointing at the cigarette. 'The plants in the campervan?'

'Yes,' replies Ianto. 'Like I said, it's not actually against the law to grow them, but I'd still prefer the police not to come poking around.'

'I'm sure you wouldn't–'

'Can we get back to Janine, please,' interrupts Laura.

Ianto rejoins them at the table. He exhales smoke. 'I don't mind driving over to Lowestoft for a few days, ask a few questions,' he offers.

'There's nothing to suggest she's gone there, and very good reason to think she hasn't,' points out Roger.

'But where else can we look?' says Laura, her voice taut with anxiety. 'It's the only place I can think of. Otherwise she could be anywhere. I think it's worth a try.' She turns to Ianto. 'I'll come with you, and Roger can look after Luke.'

'But what will you do when you get there?' asks Roger. 'It's a big town. You can't go round asking random strangers if they've seen a young woman on a trike with a baby.'

'Do you know the grandfather's name?' asks Ianto.

'Ernest,' replies Laura.

'Surname?' asks Roger.

Laura shakes her head. 'I can't remember. It wasn't Tyler, which she made up, or Taylor, for that matter, which was her mother's maiden name. It was something else.'

'Maybe we could get a Lowestoft telephone directory,' suggests Ianto.

'And go through thousands of names hoping Laura will recognise it?' says Roger. 'Sorry, but that doesn't sound practical to me. And I think we're focusing on the wrong thing. Finding her is impossible enough, but that's not the worst of it.'

'Yes,' agrees Laura, 'it's persuading her to come back.'

She glares accusingly at Roger.

'Are you saying she ran because of me?' he asks. 'I was perfectly nice to her!'

'But you're still here–'

Ianto interrupts. 'Hey now, Laura, finger-pointing's not going to help. And whatever she thought about Roger, she'd never have disappeared without saying goodbye to you. You heard the social worker: they spoke to her this afternoon. *That's* why she ran.'

'Mummy?' comes a tiny voice.

Luke is standing just inside the kitchen doorway, his face contorted with apprehension. He has a book in his hands.

'Not now!' shouts Laura, looking up briefly. Luke's lower lip wobbles and he bursts into tears.

Roger stands immediately and goes to his son, casting an exasperated look at his ex-wife.

'Mummy didn't mean to shout at you,' he says, 'she's just very upset. Come on, I'll tuck you in again.'

'Daddy?'

He offers up the book, a tattered old copy of *Winnie the Pooh*.

'Yes, we can read for a bit.'

'No, it's not that.'

'Sorry?'

'Please don't get cross with me,' says Luke, sobbing.

Roger crouches down next to him. 'No one's cross with you, silly,' he says, hugging him.

Laura rushes over to join them. 'Oh, Luke, I'm so sorry,' she says, full of remorse. 'I didn't mean to shout, and I'm not cross with you, I promise.'

Luke is still crying, but he manages to speak. 'I couldn't sleep. I came down and I was listening outside the door. I didn't mean to.'

'It's okay,' says Laura, stroking his hair. 'Don't worry about it. Everyone's a bit upset.'

'But I heard you wanted to find out Janine's grandfather's name.'

'Yes?' says Roger.

'Look,' says Luke, opening the front cover of the book.

His parents look. The book is a well-thumbed original of the AA Milne classic, dating from 1926. Little graffitied additions, childish drawings of spiders, ladybirds and rabbits, have been made in pencil to the illustrated frontispiece.

'Here,' says Luke, wiping his nose on his pyjama sleeve and pointing to the inside of the cover.

There, right at the top, inked in a childish hand, are the words *Joyce Watts, Form 3C*.

'Janine was reading it to me and Bobby,' explains Luke. 'It was under my pillow when I went to bed tonight. She said it was the only book her mother ever gave her, and it belonged to her mother when *she* was little. So I think that, maybe, that's Janine's mother's name.'

'Watts,' says Laura. 'Ernest Watts,' she says experimentally. 'Yes, Ernest Watts! *That* was the name!' She hugs Luke to her, squashing the breath from him. 'My brilliant, brilliant son!' she says into his hair.

'Well done, Luke,' says Roger.

'Quite a little detective,' comments Ianto approvingly.

'Okay,' says Roger, standing. 'But it's still time for bed. It's very late, and you've school tomorrow.'

'Can I take him up?' asks Laura.

Roger smiles. 'Of course.'

Laura stands, lifting Luke into her arms. 'Come on, Julian Kirrin, let's get you back to bed.'

'Julian Kirrin?' asks Luke as they leave the kitchen.

'We've read *The Famous Five*, haven't we?' asks Laura.

'Oh, yes!'

Laura's voice continues as she carries Luke upstairs. 'Well, he's the oldest boy, very clever at solving mysteries.'

Roger and Ianto remain in the kitchen and begin washing up.

Half an hour later Laura returns.

'Now we've a name,' says Ianto to Roger, 'Do you think it's worth going to Lowestoft? It's the only lead we have.'

'Maybe. I'm supposed to be starting a new job next week, but if you meant it when you said you'd go with Laura, I can manage here with Luke.'

'Yes, please, let's go,' says Laura eagerly to Ianto. She turns to her ex-husband. 'And thank you, Roger. Really... thank you.'

He smiles. 'That's okay. But I think we need to do a little research first.'

Chapter Thirty-Two

JANINE

'Wake up, Goldilocks.'

Janine feels her shoulder being shoved. She is suddenly awake, but instantly confused. Her eyes open onto somewhere she doesn't recognise, a dark room with patterned wallpaper and thick curtains. For a second she can't remember how she came to be here.

'Wake up!' repeats the voice, a woman's. An angry woman's.

Janine lifts her head, and recollection comes flooding back. She sits up in alarm, only to see with a wave of immense relief that Bobby is still asleep next to her on the narrow bed.

'Would you mind telling me what the hell you're doing sleeping in my father-in-law's spare room?'

The owner of the voice strides past the foot of the bed and throws back the curtains.

'What time is it?' asks Janine, her voice croaky.

'Never mind what time it is. What are you doing here?'

Janine swings her legs down and sits on the edge of the bed. She and Bobby are still in the clothes they travelled in. She looks up at the woman interrogating her. She is in her early sixties, with shoulder-length grey hair and a ruddy complexion in what might normally have been a rather chubby, friendly face. Right now, however, the face is anything but friendly.

'I'm Janine Tay – Watts. I'm Mr Watts's granddaughter.'

'Don't give me that! I know all Ernest's grandchildren and, believe me, you're not one of them! I'm calling the police,' she says, and she disappears from the room.

Janine hears her footsteps going down the staircase to the ground floor. She stands. Bobby is stirring but not yet awake. Janine tucks her tightly under the bedspread and then follows the woman.

Downstairs, Ernest Watts is sitting in his armchair with a tray on his lap, eating toast. He is wearing day clothes and the overcoat he slept in is absent. The television is on in front of him, showing the BBC test card. The woman is on the far side of the room, lifting the telephone.

'No! Please don't,' pleads Janine. 'Honestly, I am his granddaughter. I'm Joyce's girl.'

The woman has part-dialled the number but now she hesitates and looks up.

'Joyce?' she says.

Janine turns to the old man. 'Grandfather, tell her!'

'It's no good talking to him. He dun't usually recognise me, and I'm here most every day,' says the woman in a strange accent.

'He told me last night I look exactly like Edith.'

'Well, that's as maybe. It dun't prove nothin'.'

Nonetheless the woman seems to have stopped dialling. She presses down on the receiver and lifts it up again.

'That your baby upstairs?' she asks.

'Yes.'

'Go fetch her, sit in that chair and don't move. All right?'

'All right.'

Janine leaves the room. As she climbs the stairs to the

bedroom, she hears the woman dialling again. Bobby is sitting up waiting for her. She has her hands outstretched, asking for her drink, which is usually the first thing she wants on waking. Janine picks her up and carries her downstairs. She enters the living room to find the woman speaking to someone on the telephone.

'Yes, that's what I said. So, you're coming? Good.'

She hangs up and looks at Janine, still full of suspicion.

'Sit over there,' she commands. 'I need to check that everything's here.'

'You think I'm here to steal from him?'

'I dun't know why you're here or who you are.'

'I'd never do anything like that,' asserts Janine. 'I came because I needed help,' she says, but she sits where directed. 'I have to feed the baby.'

The woman hesitates. 'Well, go on then,' she says eventually.

Janine slips off her coat and starts unbuttoning her dress.

'Now just one minute, young woman! You can't do that 'ere!'

'Why not?'

'In front of Ernest?' says the woman, her eyes wide with outrage.

'He's watching the television, and I'm behind him, but if you're unhappy about it I'll go back upstairs.'

The woman looks to Ernest and then back at Janine, evidently undecided.

'I'm not having you peerking round upstairs,' she says. 'But we don't do that sort of thing in public round here,' she says, pointing at Janine's half-undone dress.

'Do you have children?' asks Janine.

'Didn't I just tell you? Three of his grandchildren are mine,' she replies, nodding towards Ernest.

The old man seems completely oblivious to the conversation and is slowly munching his way through toast and jam while watching the screen in front of him. The test card is unchanging and there is no volume, but it doesn't seem to bother him.

'Well, it's nothing you haven't seen before, is it?' says Janine. 'But she's not had anything since yesterday afternoon.'

The woman considers the situation further. 'All right, but you best have it done before my gaffer arrives. I'm not having some pert young thing exposing her parts to him.'

Her voice softens, and for the first time Janine hears something other than suspicion and anger. 'Like as not give the poor bloke an 'eart attack.'

Janine puts Bobby to the breast, and she suckles hungrily. As soon as she is settled, Janine asks, 'Do you mind telling me your name? I don't know who you are.'

'Huh!' snorts the older woman, as if Janine had some cheek asking *her* identity, but she nonetheless answers. 'I'm Betty Watts, Ernest's daughter-in-law.'

'So you're married to one of Mother's brothers.'

'Mebe.'

'Which one? I know there were four or five, but I don't know their names.'

'If you're Joyce's daughter, how is it you don't know your uncles' names?'

'Mother never talks about them. She doesn't talk about her family or living here at all. I just know this used to be her home.'

The woman lowers herself onto the arm of the couch and studies Janine. 'How do you know that?'

'She brought me here once, when I was little. Grandfather came to the door but he wouldn't speak to us. Mother was very upset.'

There is silence, interrupted only by the gentle noises of the old man chewing and Bobby snuffling as she feeds. The sounds seem to Janine to be connected, as if she were somehow mediating between two toothless generations.

'So,' continues Janine, 'are you married to one of my uncles?'

The woman's expression seems to soften, and her shoulders, previously tense, relax. She nods slightly. 'Hugh, the eldest. Though there's only three now. Poor George, God bless him, passed on three years ago. It's a shame, cos he was closest to Joyce. If you're who you say you are, he'd've loved to see you.'

Janine can't decide if the woman has provisionally accepted her as the person she says she is or is killing time until the arrival of whoever it was she called, but the comment about George encourages her to speak again.

'Was he...' she pauses, reaching for the right words, '...lost at sea?'

It's the expression she's encountered in adventure books and it sounds odd, stupid in her ears. The woman seems unconcerned.

'No, cancer.' Betty Watts's eyes lose focus for a moment. 'Lovely, gentle man. We all miss 'im.' She stands. 'Anyway, I were making tea for Ernest when I realised you were 'ere.' She stands and considers Janine. 'Would you like one while we wait?'

'Please. And if it's okay with you, I need to eat something. I'm starving. I've got some bits and bobs of food left. They were in a holdall. I left it in the kitchen.'

'I found it,' says Mrs Watts sourly, lifting up Janine's bag. 'Went to fill the kittle and tripped over it. Why'd you leave it in the way like that?'

'Sorry. I didn't want to put food into the fridge without asking first.'

'But you were okay using the spare bed.'

Janine ignores the last swipe, which was delivered without real animosity. 'If it's all right with you,' she continues, 'I'd like to give Bobby some rusk too when she's finished with me. I'll need to warm some milk.'

'I'll do that for you. Just stay there.'

She rises, places Janine's holdall by the side of her chair, and returns to the kitchen. Janine digs into the holdall while still feeding Bobby and feels for the paper bag containing the last of her Scotch eggs. She locates it and devours it hungrily in three bites. She can hear Mrs Watts putting a saucepan on the hob. A couple of minutes later there is a noise at the back door and then a man's voice.

'Right now,' says the voice, 'where is she?'

'Wait a second,' says Mrs Watts. 'Are you decent in there?'

Janine lifts Bobby off the breast and the child's mouth detaches with a little *plop!* She starts to complain, still hungry. Janine covers herself up.

'Yes.'

'Go on in,' instructs Mrs Watts.

A tall man enters from the kitchen. Like his wife, he's in his sixties, and Janine sees in him something of her grandfather when he was younger. He stops in the doorway.

'Crumbs,' he exclaims softly. 'She's–'

'I can see what she is,' intervenes Betty swiftly.

'Betty says you're a burglar,' continues the tall man.

'I'm Joyce's daughter. The district nurse let me in last night.'

'Got any proof?'

'Like a birth certificate or something? No.'

'Well, it's an easy thing to say, ent it?' says the man.

'Mother and Grandfather both said I was very like Edith, your mum.'

The man takes a further step into the room and bends to look more closely at Janine. His wife leaves the stove and stands in the doorway to the kitchen, observing.

'Possible, I suppose,' he concludes, standing to his full height again, 'but no more or less than any blonde girl. And your... your skin colour is... different.'

'Yes, Hugh, but remember–'

'Oh, my! Yes, I do remember!'

He bends again to continue his scrutiny. After a couple of seconds he stands and turns to address his wife, shrugging. 'I dunno. I remember Mum in her forties, not as a young woman, like this.'

He faces Janine again.

'Hugh?' says Mrs Watts from behind him.

'Yes, love?'

'There's that photo on your father's nightstand, from their wedding day, dated 1920. What age would your mawther've been then?'

He calculates. 'Twenty-two, I think.'

'Go fetch it.'

The man nods, walks past Janine and goes upstairs. He returns a few moments later and stands in the kitchen doorway with his wife, holding a photograph frame at arm's length, comparing it to Janine.

She watches as the eyes of both of them widen.

'Goodness gracious,' whispers Betty. 'Ent that a caution!'

'I'm fair quackled,' says her husband in a similar tone.

'She's the absolute spit of Edith,' concludes Betty.

'Edith,' says Ernest suddenly in his quavery voice.

Everyone in the room turns to look at him. He is looking back over the arm of his chair, a last morsel of toast held between his fingers. He is nodding and smiling. He gesticulates towards Janine with the toast.

'I said it was,' he says.

Chapter Thirty-Three

LAURA

Roger runs Laura to the station the following morning where they both catch a train to Manchester Piccadilly. Laura is going to work via Manchester Central Library to look for the Lowestoft telephone directory. Roger's destination is Manchester University, specifically the Law School.

They meet again after work and travel back to Chapel Hill together. Laura has the telephone number and address of Ernest Watts; at least, she has the telephone number and address that were current four years earlier, when the most recent directory she could access was compiled.

Back at the cottages, Laura goes straight to the telephone. 'Where's Luke?' she asks, lifting the handset.

'Apple Tree's lounge,' says Roger. 'I saw him through the window.'

'Ianto's not got him watering those damn cannabis plants again, has he? I really wish he'd move them back to the van. Or chuck them altogether.'

'He says it's too cold for them out there now. But no. He's giving Luke a guitar lesson.'

'Good. Would you mind?' she says, asking Roger for some privacy to make the call.

'Not at all. Just a suggestion, but have you planned what you're going to say? You can't just blurt out the nature of your relationship with Janine. What if she hasn't told them? I know she's naïve but, bearing in mind what's happened, it's got to be the *last* thing she'd say, especially to people she's never met before.'

Laura's hand hovers in mid-air as she answers. 'Yes. I'm going to say she's a close friend, she disappeared and we're worried about her.'

'And if they say she's there and perfectly well, you're just going to leave it like that?' probes Roger.

'No. I'm going to ask to speak to her, maybe not right now, but when we can talk without anyone overhearing. I've thought this through, Roger.'

'What if...' he hesitates, and continues more gently, '...what if she's there, but she won't come to the phone?'

'That I don't know. I'll play it by ear. But I need to know she's safe. I've had no sleep for the last two days.'

He approaches and crouches next to her. 'Lastly – and I'm afraid you have to be prepared for this – what if she's not there? If they know nothing about her?'

Laura shrugs and her eyes fill with tears. 'Then I'll just have to get over her, won't I?'

He nods sympathetically. She looks at him, their faces only inches apart.

'Why are you being so nice?' She sniffs. 'You should be crowing.'

'I might've been, a few days ago. But a lot's happened since then. Things haven't worked out how I hoped, but I still want you to be happy.'

She smiles sadly and pats his hand. 'Why weren't you like this before?'

She takes several deep breaths to steady herself, and starts to dial.

Roger stands. 'I'll be with Ianto and Luke when you're finished.'

The kitchen door closes.

Her heartbeat thuds in her throat and her stomach churns. It is Roger's last question that really chills her. What if they've never heard of Janine? She'll have gone altogether, disappeared from Laura's life into some anonymous town or city, probably with a new name. That really would be the end.

Offering a silent, fervent prayer to a God she isn't sure exists, she starts to dial. There is a series of clicks and then a ringing tone. She exhales in relief. At least the line is still in operation; she's been dreading a 'disconnected' tone.

The Lowestoft telephone exchange has an odd, old-fashioned ring tone. She has the sensation that she's dialled a foreign country or a past era.

She waits.

She waits some more.

No one answers. She hangs up and tries again. Half a dozen attempts over the next ten minutes produce the same result.

There is a light knock and Ianto tentatively puts his head round the kitchen door before coming in. Roger follows.

'There's no answer,' she says. 'Perhaps he's dead.'

'Then the line would've been disconnected, wouldn't it?' says Ianto.

'Maybe he's moved then.'

'Let's eat, and try again later,' suggests Roger calmly.

Laura's mood, determined and upbeat during the day while she had something practical to do, plummets. She sits silently while the others produce a meal and lets Roger take Luke to bed. She spends the rest of the evening pacing silently from room to room without purpose, most often coming to rest by the lounge window to gaze down Chapel Hill towards the lake where she and Janine spent so many happy hours. Either Ianto or Roger follows her around and sits with her when she settles for periods, reluctant to leave her alone.

After trying the number unsuccessfully a few more times, Laura takes herself off to bed.

The following day she tries the telephone number again, repeatedly. Still no response.

It is the next afternoon when her call is finally answered.

'Kirkley five-four-seven,' announces a woman's voice.

'Hello, may I speak to Ernest Watts, please?' asks Laura, so surprised to have reached someone that her voice doesn't sound like her own.

'No, that won't be possible. Who's speaking please?'

'My name's Mrs Flint, and I'm trying to locate Mr Watts's granddaughter, Janine. Is she there by any chance?'

'No, I'm sorry,' says the woman.

Laura's heart sinks. 'You've not seen anything of her in the last week, then? She left Cheshire a few days ago and we've not heard from her since.'

'Is that a dark-skinned girl with a baby?'

'Yes!'

'Oh, yes, she's been here.'

Relief washes over Laura like a warm wave.

She's there! She's safe!

'But her aunts took her and the baby to see the Pavilion. Have you been trying this number over the last few days, by any chance?'

'Yes, I have! Why hasn't anyone answered?'

'Well, Mr Watts wouldn't be able to I'm afraid, but he's been saying something about ringing, and we did wonder if that was what he meant.'

'Yes, it was me.'

'Well, I'm from next door. I'm leaving shortly, but I can leave a message if you want.'

Laura is about to ask the woman to have Janine call her when she changes her mind. 'No, that's okay. I'll call again. Thank you.'

She hangs up quickly.

She runs upstairs, shouting for Ianto at the same time. Ianto and Roger follow. They find her in her bedroom, throwing clothes into a bag.

'She's there!' she says. 'I changed my mind and left no message. I want to get there before she can move on somewhere else.'

'Right now?' asks Ianto.

'Would first thing tomorrow morning be okay?'

'Righty-ho,' says the Welshman. 'I'll pop out now, before the garage closes, and fill the old girl up.' He runs back downstairs and out of the front door towards the campervan.

Laura looks up at Roger as she continues to pack. 'What? You think I shouldn't go?'

'No, it's not that. Can you sit down, just for a second? I've been working on an idea that may persuade Janine to return.'

'And?'

'It's only an idea, and I'm not sure it'll work. Give me a minute and I'll explain. It all depends on Ianto.'

Chapter Thirty-Four

JANINE

Janine, wearing her overcoat and hat and ready to depart, opens her grandfather's front door to find a wiry middle-aged man in a cloth cap, smoking a roll-up on the doorstep.

'Arternune,' says the man. He studies her through narrowed eyes. 'Yep, I can see it,' he concludes. 'So you're Joyce's girl, eh?' He has the same strong Suffolk accent as Betty Watts.

'Yes. Uncle Wilf?'

'That's me. Though Wilf will do. Ready to go?'

'Almost. Let me get Bobby.'

She leaves the man at the door and returns to the kitchen. Bobby is playing on the floor with her bricks, the only toy Janine had time to grab in her hurry to depart. The child is wrapped up to go out in the cold but has pulled her hat off again. She doesn't like anything on her head.

Mrs Wilson, the next-door neighbour, is moving around her, tidying up after Ernest's lunch.

'My uncle's here,' says Janine, 'so we're off.'

'Have a nice time, dear,' says the neighbour. 'Don't worry about your granddad. I'll be popping in and out until supper time.'

'Thank you.'

Janine picks up Bobby and her hat and returns to the front door where she collects the changing bag. Wilf holds out his hand, takes the bag, throws his cigarette stub on the path and grinds it out. He heads to the road where a taxi waits, its engine idling. Janine follows him and gets into the rear with Bobby. Wilf climbs into the driver's seat and they pull away. Janine is suddenly concerned that she's expected to pay the fare but Wilf reaches forward and turns off the meter.

'Is this your taxi?' she asks.

'Yes,' replies Wilf shortly.

'Mother told me you were all fishermen,' says Janine.

'We were when she left,' replies the man, 'but that were over twenty years ago, and she's not been in touch since. Fishing's finished. There's been men catching herring of this coast for a thousand years, and in another ten there won't be any of us left. We've all got out of it, 'cept Hugh, who's past retirement anyway, but even he just crews every now and then. So, how is Joyce, then?'

Janine has anticipated this question. 'Up and down, I'd say,' she replies carefully.

Wilf snorts unsympathetically. 'You mean she's still drinking, then?'

Janine is surprised by his response. How do they know about Mother's drinking? Janine always imagined that it had started in Hulme.

'Do you mind if we leave that 'til we arrive?' she says. 'I'm sure Uncle Hugh and the others will ask the same questions.'

'As you like.'

Janine changes the subject. 'You said Uncle Hugh just crews now. What does that mean?'

'He works for other skippers. The *Rosy* were sold. She were the family boat, your grandfather's.'

'What do the others do now, then?' asks Janine.

'Joe, he's ter second eldest, works at Birds Eye. He met Alice, his wife, at the factory.'

'Then there's you and Aunty…' offers Janine.

'Etta.'

'Right, Etta,' she says, trying to commit all the new names to memory. 'Then the youngest, George, is that right? Aunty Betty told me that George died.'

'Yup.'

'Was he a fisherman too?'

Wilf laughs, a short bark.

'What's funny?' asks Janine.

'George being a fisherman. He tried for a coupla years to keep the old man happy. Father thought it'd make him a man, but we all knew it never would. More of an artist, was our Georgie.'

There is something unpleasant in the way Wilf speaks of George. Janine decides not to enquire further. She is not sure she is going to like Uncle Wilf.

They drive on. Bobby chatters on her lap and plays with Janine's hair slide while Janine looks out of the window. They are following the line of the coast and every now and then gaps between buildings reveal wide, flat expanses of grey seas merging with grey skies.

The only time Janine has ever seen the sea was on her last trip to Lowestoft, when she was a child. On that occasion Mother hurried her along so fast there'd been no time to look at the scenery. In any case, she'd been too nervous to pay much attention. But in all the books she has ever read, the sea is blue, or green, a white-flecked living, moving thing; frightening and magnificent. She is disappointed to find that off the coast of Lowestoft it is flat, still and iron grey, like a sheet of dull steel. *Perhaps it's not always like this*, she thinks. Nonetheless, there is nothing green anywhere she looks and she suddenly misses the lush hills of the High Peaks and Cheshire.

Her thoughts return, as they have every few minutes, to Laura. Janine's ache for her is like a boulder compressing her upper chest. Sometimes the weight is so great it's difficult to draw a full breath. Every night, sleeping in her grandfather's spare room, she dreams of her. Every morning she wakes believing herself still to be in the stone cottage on Chapel Hill. Then the foreign smells and sounds of the house overlooking the North Sea creep into her consciousness, stealing anew her happiness, like a cockcrow thief, and she is bereaved afresh. Each day she has to rebuild a fragile composure and fix her eyes rigidly on the future. Maybe now she's out of the picture, Laura and Roger will get back together after all. She's not sure how she feels about that.

Happy for Luke, I guess.

She looks down and starts joggling Bobby up and down gently on her knee, humming as she does so, forcing herself to think of something else.

They have been travelling for no more than fifteen minutes when Wilf slows and turns right, away from the sea, and almost immediately pulls into the drive of a new bungalow. It is a large, sprawling property and three cars are already parked on the drive. As the vehicle comes to a halt, the front door opens and Betty Watts appears. She looks exactly as Janine thinks a fisherman's wife should look; dumpy, practical and caring, with a round, ruddy face that creases into a big smile as she sees Janine getting out of the taxi. Wilf follows with the changing bag.

'Hello, my dear,' says Betty, and she kisses Janine on the cheek. She chucks Bobby under chin. 'And how are you, Bobby?' she says to the child. 'Come and meet everyone.'

She bends her head to Janine's and whispers. 'Don't be

scared. Everyone's excited to meet you, and they're all very nice. Well, mostly.'

Janine is escorted into the house. It is modern and warm, with double-glazed windows and thick carpet, somehow completely different to what she expected. In the books she'd read, fishermen lived right on the beach or harbour, with fishing nets drying outside and odds and ends of fishing equipment hanging from low beams inside. This looks like the normal suburban home of a retired couple, with wide picture windows to front and back and central heating radiators. The lounge, as she enters, smells of baking. There are photos and knick-knacks on every surface, and plump pink cushions on the armchairs and settee.

Four people rise to greet her. Hugh, her eldest uncle, she has met several times now and he winks at her. She smiles shyly at him. Betty extends her hand to the couple who were sitting on the couch.

'You've not met Joe and Alice before. Joe, Alice, this is Janine, Joyce's daughter, and her baby, Bobby.'

Janine estimates that Joe is two or three years younger than Hugh, perhaps in his early sixties. She can see the family resemblance, but Joe is shorter and stockier than Hugh, and his hair lighter. His wife, Alice, is a surprise. She's very striking, a lot younger than the brothers or their womenfolk, in her forties Janine guesses, and she has long dark hair, an olive complexion and black, flashing eyes. She is beautiful. Her skin colour is almost as dark as Janine's own. Janine thinks she must be a gypsy or perhaps a Spanish flamenco dancer. She nods at Janine and smiles.

Betty indicates the remaining person in the room whom Janine has not yet met.

'And this is Etta, Wilf's wife,' she says.

Etta is tall and thin, with prominent high cheekbones and a

strong jaw. She is in her fifties.

'Take a seat, dear,' says Betty, 'and I'll put the kittle on.'

Janine sits in an armchair with Bobby on her knees. She is extremely uncomfortable being the focus of attention. Everyone in the room is staring at her. No one speaks at first, and Janine busies herself taking Bobby's coat off.

'Well, now,' starts Hugh cheerfully, 'what do you make of Lowestoft?'

Janine doesn't look up as she answers. 'I thought the sea would be blue, with big waves. But it's flat and grey.'

The three men laugh.

'It ent always like this,' says Hugh. 'This time of year it's usually much wilder.'

'You've not seen the sea before then?' asks Joe.

'No. Except the time Mother brought me to see Grandfather when I was little.'

'Where you been living then?' asks Wilf.

'In Hulme, Manchester,' replies Janine. 'Until I moved out, eighteen months ago.'

'Moved out?' says Etta, with an odd emphasis on the word 'moved'. 'Aged nineteen, and...?'

She doesn't add the word 'pregnant', but everyone in the room hears it nonetheless.

'Yes,' says Janine, her face colouring. She sees glances passing between the family members.

'Where's the father?' asks Wilf.

'Wilf,' admonishes Hugh, gently. 'We agreed.'

Wilf turns his back to his older brother, faces Janine and is about to speak further when Joe interrupts him.

'Ent you learned nothing?' he snaps. 'Father got on 'is high horse over Joyce, din't 'e? Look how well that turned out!'

Betty enters with a tray loaded with cups, saucers and a huge teapot.

'Now, now, everyone,' she chides, lowering the tray onto a coffee table. 'Janine's our guest, and I, for one, am delighted she and Bobby are here.'

'Yes,' agrees Joe. 'So am I. Tell us, Janine, how is your mother? We haven't heard anything from her since she left.'

'We didn't even know if she was still alive,' adds Alice.

'She's alive,' says Janine. 'Or she was when I was last in touch.'

'How long ago was that?' asks Hugh.

'I spoke to one of the neighbours a few weeks ago. He has the corner shop. She gets her milk and cigarettes from there.'

Bobby is wriggling to get down and Janine puts her on the carpet. She crawls to the coffee table and hauls herself upright.

'How old is she?' asks Alice.

Janine makes eye contact with her and smiles shyly, grateful for the attempt to steer the subject into safer waters.

'Ten and a half months.'

'She's walking young,' says Alice.

She holds out her hands to encourage Bobby to walk to her. Bobby is clinging to the coffee table with one hand, her chubby legs slightly wobbly, clearly pleased with herself.

'Can you walk to Auntie Alice?' coaxes Alice.

Bobby looks to Janine and back to the outstretched hands. She takes a tottering step sideways and promptly sits on her backside.

'She can walk around furniture,' explains Janine, 'but not unsupported yet.'

'It won't be long,' says Betty kindly. 'Now, who wants tea? I've baked a sponge cake too.'

The next few minutes are taken up with filling orders for tea and cake, and no further questions are fired at Janine for a while.

It is Hugh who reopens the cross-examination. 'Janine, do

you think your mother would welcome contact from us?'

'I've been thinking about that,' she replies. 'I don't know. Mother is very... insular.'

'What's that mean, then?' asks Wilf.

'Sorry. She lives her life alone. She almost never goes out and she has no friends. She seems to hate everyone, especially... when...'

'When she drinks?' says Wilf.

Janine turns to the taxi driver. 'Yes. You mentioned that on the way over. How did you know?'

The others share meaningful glances and no one answers for a while.

'Alcohol has done a fair bit of damage to this family,' says Hugh. 'She's not the first.'

'She was your grandfather's favourite,' explains Betty. 'His only daughter and the apple of his eye. Perhaps because she was so like Edith, so fiery and independent. And like her mother, Joyce liked a tipple. Ernest adored her but she drove him mad, especially when she got into her teens. Boys and booze.'

'Did Grandfather throw her out because she was pregnant with me?'

There are more shared glances between her aunts and uncles.

'He never told us,' says Hugh eventually, 'but we assumed as much. She'd been seeing a chap. He had... your... colouring.'

'And after that he wouldn't hear her name spoken in the house,' explains Joe. 'If he knew where she went, he didn't tell any of us.'

Janine nods. 'I hope you'll forgive me for saying this, but I think she felt abandoned, by the whole family,' she says.

There is another embarrassed silence, broken eventually by Betty.

'George did try to find her,' she says. 'They were the two

youngest and very close. He spent months looking.'

'He told me he even hired a private detective,' says Hugh.

Wilf makes a scoffing noise and looks away.

Hugh raises a hand and points at his brother. 'Don't, Wilf. Where's the point, now he's dead?'

Wilf remains silent and stares out of the front window. Janine is on the point of mentioning the postcard which proves that George did in fact find Mother before he died, but thinks better of it. She is not sure why, except that there are obviously undercurrents in this family which she doesn't yet understand.

'Families, eh?' says Alice, lightly. 'Always fighting.'

'You were living in the Peak District, I gather?' asks Joe.

'On the edge, yes, towards Manchester.'

'Are you going back there? I mean, is this a visit or are you thinking of staying?' asks Hugh.

'I don't know,' says Janine, putting down her cup and reaching for Bobby who's about to touch the teapot. 'Now I've met my family, I'd like to stay in touch... if I may.'

'May? Of course you may, darling,' exclaims Betty. 'You've got a whole load of cousins too, and their babies, to meet.'

'But I guess there's someone, isn't there?' says Alice shrewdly. 'Someone special back in the Peak District?'

'There was,' Janine answers, dully, staring at the thick beige carpet by her feet. 'But not anymore.'

'Right,' says Betty firmly. 'That's enough. We want to make Janine welcome, don't we? Not terrify her with questions. We've got twenty-years worth of 'em, and I 'spect she has a few too. We're strangers to her. There'll be plenty of time for us to get to know one another properly.'

'Yes,' says Hugh. 'Where's that photo album, Betty?'

'Ooh, yes!' says Betty, standing. 'I was thinking you might like to see some old photos of your mum when she was a girl, so I dug out the albums. Now, where did I put them?'

'I was looking at them in the kitchen,' replies Etta.

'Thank you,' says Betty, scurrying off and returning with three fat albums of photographs. 'Now, if you two wouldn't mind budging up,' she says, nodding at Joe and Alice, 'I can sit next to Janine, and explain who's who.'

Betty spends the next hour or so giving Janine a crash course in what, to her astonishment, is an enormous extended family. Within a few minutes she has forgotten which child belongs to which uncle and who has which grandchildren. She sees family resemblances throughout the photographs. There is more than one cousin with thick blonde hair like hers, although no one with her dark complexion. It is unsettling to think that all that time, living such a strange life alone with Mother in Hulme, she had dozens of relatives, many of whom looked like her, living here in this small fishing town.

Janine thinks more than once of asking about the man Mother was seeing when she fled Lowestoft. She has no particular desire to incorporate a father she has never known into her life, but she is curious. If that was, indeed, her father. She notes that there are no dark-skinned faces staring out of the photos. Whoever he was, her father must have stood out in such a homogeneously white community. Maybe he was a foreign sailor, passing through, and Mother fell madly in love with him? For a second she allows herself to imagine clandestine meetings, stolen kisses and whispered elopement plans, but she immediately chides herself.

Grow up, Janine Taylor! Life isn't like that. As you have discovered.

Of most interest to her, however, are the photographs of her mother as a child and of her grandmother as a young woman. Even through the grainy black-and-white photographs dating from the early part of the century, she can see the striking resemblance she bears to Edith. Her grandfather is a surprise too. The pictures of him – he is shown in a crowd of other young people on the seafront, posing with his crew at the rail of a fishing boat, looking nervously at the camera in army uniform – reveal a handsome young man with laughing eyes and a ready smile. She finds it difficult to reconcile these photos with the bitter, cruel man she met briefly almost fifteen years ago, or the old man with only half his wits with whom she has been lodging. What losses, what unhappiness, must he have endured to cause such changes? she wonders.

Eventually Bobby starts to become more fractious and less consolable. The aunts have taken it in turns to distract her, but now she only wants to be in her mother's arms.

'I think perhaps we should go back to Grandfather's,' says Janine. 'She needs a feed and her afternoon nap.'

'You can put her down here, if you like,' suggests Betty.

'That's very kind,' replies Janine, 'but I don't think she'll settle. She's only just getting used to Grandfather's. Uncle Wilf, would you mind driving us back?'

'No, that's fine by me,' he answers.

'We're going to see you again, aren't we?' asks Joe.

'I should think so,' replies Janine.

'So, are you planning to stay in Lowestoft?' he asks.

'I don't know yet. Is it all right if I stay at Grandfather's for a couple more days while I think things through? Maybe see if I can find some part-time work?'

Hugh and Betty look at one another and nod.

'I don't see why not,' answers Hugh. 'Mrs Wilson from next door says you've been very helpful, and as a family we all feel happier knowing someone's there with him.'

'I've been terrified he's going to fall down those stairs,' says Betty.

'I might be able to pay some rent...' offers Janine.

'Don't be silly,' says Betty. 'We wouldn't dream of it, would we?'

She addresses the question to Hugh, who shakes his head in agreement, but Janine notes that Wilf doesn't readily agree.

'No,' says Hugh, 'I'm glad you're there. Have you managed to get father to speak to you?'

Janine answers as she kneels and begins re-dressing Bobby for the journey back. 'He's very sweet to me but most of the time I don't think he knows who I am. He calls me Edith sometimes, but more often he looks puzzled when he sees me. But he's never been unpleasant and he seems happy to let me help him on and off his commode.'

'You've been doing that, have you?' says Etta with some surprise. 'You definitely shouldn't be paying rent, then,' she adds, and everyone laughs.

'I agree,' says Joe. 'In that case I don't care if you're Joyce's daughter or not!'

Janine looks up in alarm.

Was that a joke?

'You do believe me, don't you?' she asks, looking anxiously round the other faces. She is met with a chorus of reassurance.

'Of course we do,' says Betty. 'Let me get your coat.'

A few minutes later Janine and Bobby are back in Wilf's taxi. The others crowd around the front door to wave goodbye. Wilf pulls away and heads back to Ernest's house. Janine is lost in thought.

'Well?' asks Wilf after a while, looking at her in his rear-view mirror.

'Sorry?' asks Janine, looking up.

'How was that?' he asks. 'Pleased to meet your family for the first time?'

'Yes,' she says. 'Families are complicated, aren't they?' she adds.

Janine wakes the following morning and takes Bobby downstairs for breakfast. They have moved into the bedroom containing two single beds, for which Janine found bedlinen in one of the chests of drawers. She tried Bobby in the bed opposite hers, but was so worried that she would wriggle out and perhaps fall, they have resumed sleeping together.

It has taken a couple of days, but she has worked out a morning routine that works for her, for Bobby and for her grandfather. She gives Bobby her beaker of milk and lets her play on the lounge floor, which keeps her occupied for ten minutes, fifteen if she is lucky. If Grandfather has slept in the chair she puts the kettle on and, while it is heating up, she has time to get him onto his commode and empty it. First thing in the morning, he usually only needs to pass urine. If they managed to get him upstairs to his bed the night before, she takes him a cup of tea, places it by his bedside, and helps him out of bed so he can use his urine bottle. Once Grandfather has been helped to the table, still in whatever he wore to sleep, she feeds both him and Bobby at the same time. Bobby is now eating three meals a day as well as milk, and both she and her great-grandfather like toast and honey for breakfast, which is convenient. They both like it cut into soldiers, which makes it easier still.

A carer, one of the aunts or a professional, usually arrives mid-morning, and that's when Grandfather has his wash and shave, and his clothes are changed.

Janine is not sure what her grandfather makes of Bobby. He has never asked about her or questioned why a baby is now living in his home, but he seems unconcerned and accepts her presence with equanimity. He addresses Janine as 'girl' ('I need a cardigan, girl' or 'How's the swell, girl?') or, occasionally, as Edith.

Grandfather Watts has finished his breakfast and is dozing in his chair. Bobby is crawling under the table, chasing a ball. Janine is finishing her cup of tea, looking out of the living room window when, through the net curtains, she sees a familiar multi-coloured vehicle pull up outside. Her heart leaps in her chest. She recognises Ianto's campervan instantly. Then she realises that it's not Ianto in the driving seat; it's Laura!

Janine's first impulse, bizarrely, is to hide. She wants desperately to run to Laura and take her in her arms but she knows that if she does, she may not have the strength to leave her again. Then she realises that she can't possibly hide. Her trike and trailer are parked on the rectangle of concrete in the garden. She is frozen, unable to decide what to do.

Laura leads Ianto up the narrow garden path and knocks on the door.

Still Janine doesn't move. Her heart is pounding so hard in her chest, the sound seems to fill her whole being, and her mind is a torrent of questions: how did she find me? Why has she come? I can't go back, surely she must realise that?

Laura knocks again. Ianto leans towards the window and peers in.

'Janine?' he calls, having seen her.

Laura moves from the door and joins Ianto in front of the window. She shades her eyes and also looks in.

'Janine,' she says. 'Janine, oh, darling, please open the door!' she begs.

Janine can see tears coursing down Laura's cheeks, and realises that her own face is wet with tears too.

Laura has both hands pressing against the window frame and brings her face right up to the glass.

'You can come back,' she sobs. 'It's all going to be okay.'

Chapter Thirty-Five

LAURA

A month has passed.

Whenever Laura looks out of a window it's difficult not to believe she is living inside a Christmas card. The fields and walls around the house are covered in a thick blanket of white, and the trees overhanging the brook that winds its way down the valley and surrounding the lake at the bottom have two or three inches of snow on every branch. The temperature outside is only a couple of degrees above freezing, but the sky is a brilliant blue and the sun a low pale yellow orb hovering just above the horizon. There is no wind. The sounds on Chapel Hill, always subtle and Arcadian, seem even more hushed than usual. The scene is absolutely still, almost too perfect to be real.

While it is bitterly cold outside, inside the cottages it is, if anything, too hot. Ianto has built fires in two of the downstairs fireplaces, the dining room and the kitchen, and he has spent the morning shuttling between them every few minutes, poking, clearing ash and adding logs. In retrospect the one in the kitchen was probably unnecessary; the heat from the oven in which an enormous turkey is roasting, and from the hob on which vegetables and sauces are in various stages of preparation, is so fierce that Laura has already stripped off her many layers down to her blouse and a chef's apron.

Luke and Roger are somewhere in the house putting up decorations. For a fortnight Luke has been licking the glued ends of his multi-coloured strips and creating paper chains of pink, yellow, blue, red, green and purple, and they now adorn every available horizontal surface in the cottages, above the fireplaces, atop the curtain rails, and looping up the banisters and along the balustrades on the landings. A Christmas tree, so laden with decorations and tinsel it barely has any visible green, stands in the corner of the lounge, an enormous pile of wrapped presents underneath it. The Light Programme is on the radio, playing gentle Christmas classics, to which no one is listening.

The occupants of the semis are celebrating Christmas, early, for very special reasons.

Laura looks again at the clock and returns to her blackboard, which she screwed to the kitchen wall when this event was planned and after Janine, hesitantly, agreed. She frowns, calculating, rubs out a couple of times with the side of her fist and chalks in adjustments.

Patti, Roger's new girlfriend, pops her head into the kitchen again. This is the first time Roger has brought her to the house, and Laura is still not keen to have the woman there, at least not for this event. She's a nurse, in her late thirties, and seems very pleasant, but she's a stranger, and Laura didn't want to risk Luke becoming confused. However, in the end she acquiesced. She wanted to support Roger's new life, and banning his first post-divorce girlfriend would have sent the wrong message.

'Anything I can do?' asks Patti.

At a loose end, she has been offering assistance every twenty minutes since she arrived with Roger.

'You could prepare the Brussels sprouts, if you like,' says Laura distractedly. 'Or maybe rinse and dry the champagne glasses. I don't think Roger's used them since the divorce and they're pretty dusty. I think they're still in the boot of his car.'

'Sure,' says Patti. 'Brussel sprouts to start.'

Laura gives her a knife and a bag of sprouts, and stations her at the kitchen table.

In truth, Laura would prefer to be left alone. Although this was her idea, she finds herself rather stressed at having to produce such a complex meal for so many people, and in a kitchen half the size of that in St John's Wood. She is fearful that if she allows anyone to take over any part of the job, she will make a mistake as to the intricate timings and it will all be a disaster.

She checks the clock, yet again and only three minutes after she last looked. Lady Margaret and Chivers are due in just under two hours.

'Roger!' she shouts.

'Yes?' comes a reply from somewhere upstairs.

'Have you done the table?' she calls.

'Almost!'

Rendered nervous by the vagueness of the reply, Laura wipes her hands urgently and runs from the kitchen into the dining room. Since the ground floors of the two houses were recombined, although it is an odd shape, the double dining room is enormous. Roger and Ianto have pushed together the tables from both properties and now, covered in tablecloths, they are together easily capable of seating nine people.

It looks very pretty. The cutlery and glasses sparkle, Luke has arranged Christmas crackers at every place setting, and in the centre is the table decoration, a gift from Patti: a wreath of green holly, red berries and baby pinecones, with a vase of winter honeysuckle branches set in its centre.

'Napkins and serving spoons!' Laura shouts upstairs.

'Will do!' calls Roger back.

She returns to the kitchen.

A blast of cold air enters the room as the back door opens. Laura looks up.

Janine enters with Bobby on her back.

'All okay?' asks Laura.

'Yes,' replies Janine, stamping her boots on the step to get off the worst of the snow, and then slipping out of them before closing the back door behind her.

'Here,' she says. She hands Laura a large pudding bowl wrapped in kitchen foil. 'I didn't see Lady M, but Chivers says it's ready and only needs an hour's steaming. If we haven't anything suitable, she can bring a steamer down with her.'

'No, I've worked out a solution,' says Laura.

'She says she'll bring the trifle later. We're to call them if we need anything.'

'Thank you,' says Laura. 'How was the ride?'

'Very cold, but beautiful and bracing. I couldn't have done it on a bicycle, but it was fine on the trike.'

Janine leans forward and kisses Laura on the lips. They are both aware of Patti watching them, but the woman stands and slips out of the room. Laura's eyes close as she gives herself to the kiss. She can almost feel her blood pressure dropping and her pulse slowing in response to Janine's cold lips. Janine slips her arms around Laura's waist and they remain locked together for a few delicious seconds until Bobby starts wriggling and kicking on Janine's back.

'Has she got a problem?' whispers Janine, nodding towards the door.

'Patti? I don't think so, not about you and me anyway. Roger says not. Though it must be a bit weird meeting your new boyfriend's ex-wife and her new girlfriend, for the first time. I think she was just being diplomatic. Anyway, I have something important to ask.'

'Which is?'

'Promise you'll never leave me again.'

Laura has been seeking the same reassurance, repeatedly, ever since Janine returned from Lowestoft. Janine does not seem impatient at being asked so often. She answers solemnly, as she does on each occasion.

'I promise never to leave you again.'

'Good. What's that?' asks Laura, pointing over Janine's shoulder to an envelope in Bobby's hands. The corner has been chewed and is now a bit soggy.

'It was in the post box. Give it to Laura, please, Bobby.'

Laura takes the envelope from the child's hand and gives it to Janine.

Janine opens it, reads for a moment and smiles. 'It's a Christmas card from my family,' she says, her face bright with happiness.

She shows it to Laura. It is a simple card, with Christmas greetings from Lowestoft and a wintry seascape on the front. It bears half a dozen signatures.

'And there's this,' says Janine, taking something else out of the envelope.

It is a black-and-white photograph of her uncles and aunts. It was evidently taken some years ago. They look younger and are all dressed up, as if for a family wedding or other celebration. They are standing in a tight group on a pavement outside a large building, squinting through bright sunshine at the camera. Janine shows it to Laura.

'There are my uncles. Look,' she says pointing at one, 'there's even Uncle George, the one who died and was close to Mother.'

Laura examines the photo. 'Looks like they want to be part of your life, then,' she says.

'Yes, it does. And Mother's. Hugh asked for her address in Hulme, and I gave it to him before we left.'

'You didn't tell me that. How's your mother going to react, after all these years?'

'I've no idea. But all the brothers are anxious to re-establish contact with her.'

'I'm so pleased for you. It must be amazing, to discover a huge family you've known nothing about.'

'It is,' says Janine, but she looks troubled. 'Although I'll have to tell them about you. About us.'

'Yes, I suppose you will. But let's tackle that after Christmas, eh?'

Janine thinks for a moment and then nods. 'Yes. I don't want anything to spoil this.'

She slips out of the harness carrying Bobby and lifts the child out. 'Okay,' she says brightly. 'What needs to be done?'

Laura returns to the stove. 'The boys haven't completed laying the table, and the red wine needs opening so it can breathe. You could also check the champagne's not freezing. The fridge is overflowing so I left it outside in the snow. Everything else is under control, I think. After that... why don't you get changed?'

Janine puts Bobby down and keeps her eyes on her as she toddles off towards the lounge.

'Incoming!' she shouts, and Ianto appears in the lounge doorway to take Bobby's hand. She addresses Laura. 'Are you planning on wearing the green velvet with the little red pockets?'

'No. What I'm wearing is laid out on our bed.'

'Do you mind if I do?'

'Of course not. I washed and ironed it for you. I know other people probably think it's weird, but it makes me happy to see you in my clothes. It's comforting,' she leans towards Janine to whisper, 'and sexy.'

'Thank you.'

Janine turns to leave the kitchen but Laura calls her back.

'One more thing,' she says, beckoning.

Janine turns and presents herself in front of Laura again. Laura places a kiss on Janine's cool lips.

'Happy birthday, girlfriend,' she says.

'Thank you.'

'You make me very happy.'

'Likewise.'

Luke is looking out of his bedroom window when the guests arrive. Since the first snows, the local farmers have been bringing additional hay and supplements for their sheep. He and Bobby enjoy watching from upstairs as the sheep crowd noisily around the farmers, jostling and pushing to get at the food.

'They're here!' he shouts.

Below him the grey Bentley is slowing to a halt at the top of The Rise.

Lady Margaret and her companion get out and each opens a rear door of the vehicle as they collect items from the back seat. The two old ladies turn round with arms full of wrapped gifts, flowers and other items.

Laura is still getting changed. 'Can someone let them in, please?' she shouts back.

'On my way!' calls Janine.

JANINE

Janine goes to the door of Magnolia Cottage, takes a deep breath and fixes a smile to her face. She opens the door. Lady Margaret and Chivers are standing between the two front doors.

'Hello, Lady M. Hello, Chivers. Please come in,' says Janine.

'I'm never sure which one to knock,' says Lady Margaret. She bends forward and gives Janine a kiss on the cheek. 'Many happy returns, my dear,' she says enthusiastically. 'Twenty-one today! And Happy Christmas!'

Luke has run downstairs and is now loitering halfway up the hallway, watching on and hopping from foot to foot, too shy to approach and too excited to keep still.

'Merry Christmas, young man,' says Lady Margaret, entering and stamping her feet. 'Would you be kind enough to take these from me and put them somewhere safe?'

She bends and loads Luke's arms with presents and, having done that, steams off to the end of the hall and into the lounge like an ancient battleship, taking up the entire width of the passageway as she does so.

Janine closes the door behind Chivers, and offers to take her coat. There follows some juggling while Chivers extricates herself from her sleeves while still holding a cut glass bowl containing trifle. She is wearing what looks like a Victorian ball gown with puffy sleeves and thick folds of red velvet.

'Would you care to follow Lady Margaret into the front lounge?' says Janine.

She hears her stilted Jane Austen delivery, and flushes with embarrassment. She has tried not to show it to Laura, who so wanted to make a special celebration in her honour, but she has been extremely anxious about this event. Despite working for Lady Margaret for over a year, she is still in awe of her and incapable of making small talk. What on earth would she say, in a social setting, to the lady of the manor, her landlady and her employer? She can hardly talk gardening all afternoon. And what would Lady Margaret make of their unusual living arrangements, which included her partner's ex-husband and a mostly stoned Welsh hippy? Above all, the idea of a party at which she would be the centre of attention, absolutely terrified her.

At that moment Laura runs down the stairs, still fastening buttons, and smiles at Janine reassuringly.

'Hello,' she says to Chivers, offering her hand confidently and smoothing Janine's awkwardness. 'I'm Laura Flint. You know, I don't think I've ever been told your first name,' she says brightly. 'Do you have one and, if so, would you mind if we used it? I don't think we can introduce you to everyone as "Chivers", can we?'

The old lady, as thin as a reed, smiles briefly. 'I do have a first name, and it's Susanne. I don't mind if you use it.'

Laura winks at Janine behind Chivers's back. They have been wondering how to keep straight faces when addressing the companion throughout the meal, as if she was a butler or waiter. 'Pass the bread sauce, Chivers,' has become a private joke between them which sets them giggling every time.

They follow their two guests into the lounge where they find Roger making further introductions. Ianto is shaking hands with Lady Margaret who is also in party dress, her diamond necklace and matching drop earrings glittering in the light. In honour of the occasion the Welshman is wearing his best T-shirt, least worn jeans and a multi-coloured waistcoat, and his hair is tied in a neat ponytail. Lady Margaret turns as Laura enters the room.

'Ah, our hostess!' she says. 'This is for you.' She hands Laura a large bouquet of flowers. 'Thank you so much for inviting us. We're honoured and pleased you felt able to do so.'

'It's my pleasure, Lady Margaret. I know how much you mean to Janine. We wouldn't think of celebrating her birthday without you.'

Lady Margaret looks around the room. 'I see you followed my advice to take the wall down.'

'Yes,' replies Laura. 'It's made all the difference. And if you can smell fresh paint, I'm afraid that's because the redecorations were only finished yesterday.' She looks pointedly at Ianto, who ignores her.

'It's charming,' says Lady Margaret. 'Very different to when I spent time here as a girl, but the house still has the same lovely atmosphere.'

'You spent time here as a girl?' asks Roger.

'Oh, yes.'

'I remember you saying you had friends who lived here,' says Janine. 'The day you showed me round the property.'

'The family of farmworkers whose home this was had a daughter of about my age. We were great chums,' says Lady Margaret.

'Let me get you some drinks,' says Roger.

'Please take a seat, ladies, but if you'll excuse me, I have things to attend to in the kitchen,' says Laura.

Drinks consumed and replenished, and birthday presents opened by Janine, the nine of them take their places at the table. Luke has written each guest's name on a folded card, with a crayoned holly leaf in each corner. Crackers are pulled, paper hats donned and daft jokes recited to groans and laughter. Laura brings in the turkey to general applause, and Janine and Patti follow with an apparently endless stream of other dishes, gravy boats and condiments.

As Laura carves, Roger explains to Lady Margaret and Chivers why they are celebrating Christmas two days before the official date. It was Laura's wish to combine Janine's twenty-first birthday with an early Christmas dinner because Roger and Luke will not be present on Christmas Day; they have been invited to his mother's for Christmas lunch. Ianto will also be absent as he is returning to Wales to stay with his family for a fortnight.

'So you and Janine will have the place to yourselves,' concludes Lady Margaret.

'Yes,' confirms Laura. 'And Bobby, of course.'

Bobby bangs her spoon like a gavel, twice, on the table, in apparent endorsement of the plan and everyone laughs.

Janine watches the merriment around the table as if from a distance. Chivers has remained sphinx-like and has said next to nothing but Lady Margaret is more than making up for it, slipping into easy conversation in every hiatus and drawing everyone in. Even Ianto, whose politics, born in the steel mill towns of south Wales, are inimical to the concept of aristocracy, seems to like the old lady. Roger is opening a third bottle of wine, Laura is serving second rounds of turkey and everyone is bickering good-naturedly over the last roast potatoes.

It feels unreal, almost dreamlike. Janine's childhood books were full of happy Christmas celebrations – she loved Dickens's in particular – but they were fiction, a fantasy. She has never been to one and never imagined she would. Nor has she ever had a birthday party held in her honour. She looks round the table from one happy animated face to another and realises, with disbelief, that everyone here (except perhaps Patti, who looks slightly terrified) cherishes her. At that moment she realises that she is happier than at any time she can remember.

This, then, is what it's like to have a family.

LAURA

As they start clearing away some of the plates to make room on the table for dessert, Lady Margaret quietly excuses herself and heads towards the stairs. The laughter and conversation continue for some time but after a while Laura realises that the old lady hasn't returned. She leaves the table and goes upstairs.

She finds Lady Margaret sitting on the bed she and Janine now share. Her hand is absent-mindedly stroking the bedspread next to her and she is so lost in thought she doesn't realise that Laura is watching from the doorway. She looks up and starts.

'Oh, I'm so sorry, my dear, please forgive me!' says Lady Margaret, starting to rise.

'No, not at all,' reassures Laura.

Laura sits next to her on the bed. She notes that Lady Margaret has a handkerchief in her hand and her nose is red.

'Are you all right?' asks Laura.

'Yes, everything's fine. I'm so sorry. I passed your doorway and... the memories called me in. I wasn't really aware of sitting down. On your bed, too; very rude of me.'

'It's perfectly okay.'

'I know it's silly,' says the old lady, 'and I know it's not actually the same bed, but this room used to be that of my friend, Carys.'

'Were you very close?' asks Laura.

Lady Margaret looks up and meets Laura's eyes. 'As close as you and Janine are now,' she says softly, watching for Laura's reaction.

Laura's eyes widen slightly. 'Ah. I see. And you lost her?'

Lady Margaret nods and her chest heaves with emotion. She looks at first as if she doesn't trust her voice to speak, and it takes her a moment to compose herself.

'We were in the Women's Land Army during the Great War,' she explains. 'We went together, to the Black Country, and had a fine time, working with those wonderful women. All sorts of women and girls, drawn from every corner of the country and every background, all mucking in together for a common cause. It was magnificent, being liberated from... well, from everything. You know, all the usual constraints imposed by men? But then there was an accident... involving a tractor.'

Laura puts her hand over that of Lady Margaret's and grips it. 'I'm so sorry.'

Lady Margaret sniffs and, removing her hand, blows her nose. 'Long time ago,' she says. 'But the house, this room, the perfume I smelled as I passed the door... suddenly it all came back to me. It took me by surprise.'

She falls silent and then, quietly, as if musing to herself, she adds: 'I think... to have experienced a Great Love like that, even once in one's life... well, it's a sort of privilege. It doesn't happen for everyone, does it?'

'No, I don't think it does. Did you never find anyone else?'

'Oh, yes. Susanne and I will have our thirtieth anniversary this year. Not the same sort of thing, but precious too, in its own way. We're best of friends. Ours is like an old, old marriage. We've rubbed the sharp corners off each other and we now fit together like... like dandelions and daydreams.'

She sits up straight, dabs her eyes again and tucks the handkerchief into a sleeve. 'Thank you, my dear,' she says in a more normal voice. 'Sorry I've been so soppy.'

'You haven't been soppy. I understand. I thought for a while that I'd lost Janine.'

'Yes, but she's back now, and I haven't seen her as happy as this. I think you're good together.'

'I hope so. Time will tell. Shall we rejoin the others?'

'I'll be down in a moment, if that's all right?'

'Of course. Take your time.'

Laura returns to the dinner table. Ianto is in the middle of handing round a platter of his "special" mince pies. She looks at him sternly.

'Ianto, please reassure me that–' she starts.

'Don't be daft,' he says, all innocence, but he nonetheless skips Luke while offering the plate.

'Ianto–' tries Roger.

Ianto lowers his head to speak in Roger's ear. 'I give you my absolute word, it's very, *very* mild,' he says in his sing-song cadence. 'I've been scrupulously careful; less effect than a single glass of that claret,' he says, pointing at an empty bottle. 'But I promise you, you won't be disappointed.'

Lady Margaret rejoins the group, apparently as cheerful as when she left, and it is agreed around the table that it would be a good idea to wait a while before dessert.

JANINE

And so, onto the Christmas presents.

Janine's parcels are all squashy, and after the first she guesses what the others contain. By the time she has opened five parcels she has several new outfits, including a dress, a beautiful lilac cardigan with tiny daisy-shaped buttons, a leather belt and a pair of shorts for the summer. She has also, coincidentally, received clothing from Lady Margaret and Chivers: a pair of soft leather gardening gauntlets.

'They'll be perfect for working on the hawthorn bushes and in the new rose garden. Thank you. And as for the clothes, they're perfect,' she says, standing, and going round the table kissing each of the other household members in turn.

'I'm due for a rise in January,' says Laura, 'so there'll be more where they've come from.'

Out of the corner of her eye, Janine sees Luke poking his mother repeatedly, almost beside himself with excitement.

'Yes, okay, okay,' says Laura. She stands and looks at Roger, who nods and winks. 'Please excuse us for a moment, everyone,' she says. 'We have something that needs to be prepared. Janine, please will you join Luke and me outside at the front of the house in fifteen minutes' time?'

'What about the rest of us?' asks Ianto.

'Well, you're all welcome, but Janine's attendance is compulsory,' replies Laura, ushering Luke out of the room ahead of her. They hear mother and son whispering and putting on coats, and then the front door opens and closes.

Fifteen minutes later everyone else dons boots, overcoats, scarves and hats and follows Janine out of the front door.

The sky is darkening into a deep sapphire. The sun has just set and the moon is a perfect crescent. It is very cold.

By the side of the dry-stone wall in front of the Bentley and Laura's Triumph there is now another vehicle, a shiny blue Austin 35 van. Luke sits in the passenger seat beaming through the windscreen and Laura is standing next to the driver's door, holding high a set of dangling keys.

Janine looks at her, frowning, uncomprehending.

'It's for you,' explains Laura. 'My present for your twenty-first birthday.'

Janine remains where she is. 'It's mine?' she asks, doubtfully.

'Read the sign,' instructs Roger, indicating the side of the van.

'"Taylor and Co. Gardeners & Landscape Architects",' reads Janine out loud. 'I don't understand.'

Ianto holds out his hands for Bobby. Janine gives the child to him and walks uncertainly towards Laura.

'May I present you with the keys to your new works vehicle,' says Laura. 'I would like to invest in your business, if you'll let me. I've seen what you can do, and I think you're a brilliant gardener and designer. And possibly the world's worst record-keeper.'

Everyone laughs.

'True,' confesses Janine.

'You need to expand geographically, and this' – she points at the van – 'will permit you. And I think Roger has something else for you.'

Roger reaches into his pocket and presents Janine with an envelope. 'Ten driving lessons, pre-paid,' he says.

'But I only have two clients, and I don't need a van for them,' points out Janine.

'You said it yourself: you need to expand. And I'm sure if Lady Margaret were to go through her address book, she'd find several of her acquaintances desperate to secure the services of someone as talented as you,' says Laura.

She turns to Lady Margaret who, she notes with surprise, is holding Chivers's hand.

'I'm certain of it,' confirms Lady Margaret.

Janine runs to Laura and throws her arms round her. 'Thank you!' she whispers into Laura's hair. 'It's wonderful!'

'Hey!' shouts Luke as a snowball hits him in the back. He whirls round to find Roger already arming himself again.

'Traitor!' yells Luke.

Patti immediately retaliates on Luke's behalf, hitting Roger on the shoulder with her own snowball.

Open warfare ensues.

LAURA

After a couple of minutes of battle, Laura checks that Bobby is safe – she is now in Chivers's arms, trying to feed the old woman a handful of snow – and returns to the cottage to inspect the Christmas pudding and to make a start on the washing up.

Back in the kitchen she starts running the water, smiling at the shrieks and laughter from the front of the house, Luke's shrill voice to the fore. She hums a Christmas carol, feeling happy and warmed by the good food, the plentiful wine and the success of the party.

She has been working for a few minutes when, within the hubbub from outside, she detects the sound of a motor vehicle. She initially assumes it's Janine's new van being moved out of the line of fire, but after a little while she becomes aware that the excited shouting and squeals have stopped. Then she hears Luke.

'Mum! Mum!'

His voice sounds strange, strained and frightened. She grabs a dish towel and returns hurriedly to the front door.

The sound she heard was not made by the pretty blue van, but two other vehicles pulling up beside the Bentley. The first she recognises as belonging to Mary O'Reilly; the second is a police car. O'Reilly and Michael Carter descend from the first and a tall policeman in uniform, carrying his helmet, emerges from the second. He is accompanied by Wilhelmina Murray, the social worker from Stockport Borough Council.

The snowball fighters are still, frozen in attitudes of combat.

The four interlopers come to a halt just outside the wall. O'Reilly is the first to speak.

'So, it's true,' she says, addressing Janine, a look of triumph on her narrow features. 'You've returned. In that case, Mrs Murray here has authority to remove Roberta Tyler from your custody immediately, on the grounds that her physical and moral well-being are threatened. PC Miller is present to make sure you comply.'

Roger drops the snowball in his hand. 'On what grounds?'

'On the grounds that the child was born out of wedlock and her mother constitutes a physical and moral danger to her. That young woman is living in a sinful and... and... *depraved* relationship with *her*,' replies O'Reilly, almost spitting the words, and jabbing her gloved forefinger in the direction of Laura who is standing in the doorway.

'What do you mean by sinful and depraved?' demands Roger.

'You know as well as I do,' says O'Reilly. 'They're lesbians!' Even in the cold, her pinched face flushes as she says the word. There is something faintly maniacal about her blazing eyes and hate-filled expression.

'Are you mad?' asks Roger. '*That* woman,' he points to Janine, 'you're saying that *that* woman is a lesbian?'

'That is exactly what we're saying,' replies Carter. 'Now are you going to hand over the child peacefully or does PC Miller have to arrest you?'

'I don't know what you've been told, constable,' says Roger, 'but that woman is no lesbian. She's my wife.'

O'Reilly laughs. 'That is a ludicrous suggestion, and you know it.'

'I'll prove it to you,' says Roger. 'Wait there.' He strides towards the house.

'On my dressing table,' says Laura quietly as he goes past.

He emerges a few moments later. In the time he has been gone, the four officials have come through the gate and the police officer and Mrs Murray are crowding Janine, who holds Bobby tightly in her grip, her back to them.

Roger runs back through the snow. 'Here,' he says, and thrusts a document towards the policeman.

The officer takes it and reads, Mrs Murray looking over his shoulder. He turns to O'Reilly. 'It's a certificate of marriage, issued out of Stockport Registry, three weeks ago,' he says.

O'Reilly snatches it from his grasp. Roger watches her eyes travel across the document, widening in disbelief.

'Janine Taylor, spinster of this parish, landscape gardener. See?' says Roger. 'And yours truly, Roger Adam Flint, previous marriage dissolved, solicitor.'

He turns to the police officer. 'You can see that it's the original document, signed by the Superintendent Registrar.' Roger puts his arm around Janine's shoulders.

'This document is in someone else's name!' crows O'Reilly triumphantly. She points at Janine. 'That woman is Nadine Tyler, or at least that's what she told the hospital.'

Roger turns to Laura.

'In the same folder,' she says.

'Here,' says Roger, locating a second document. 'She changed her name by deed poll to Janine Taylor.' He thrusts it into the policeman's hands. 'Exactly what evidence do you have that my wife is engaging in an immoral relationship?' he demands of O'Reilly.

'We saw the bedroom they share!' replies Carter, hotly. 'There was women's underclothing on both sides of the bed!'

'The bedroom, inside this house?' asks Lady Margaret, approaching.

'That one,' Carter answers, pointing at the green door of Apple Tree Cottage.

'PC Miller,' says Lady Margaret, 'I am Lady Margaret Wiscombe.'

'Yes, I know who you are, m'lady.'

'That property belongs to me, and I have certainly never given these people permission to enter it. I would like you to arrest them on grounds of unlawful trespass.'

PC Miller now looks extremely uncomfortable.

Roger presses home his advantage. 'And even were the court to admit such unlawfully obtained evidence, officer, are they really telling us they formed their conclusion as to immorality by.... *the whereabouts of women's clothing*?' Roger laughs. 'It's absurd.'

O'Reilly and Carter look at one another.

'Give me a moment,' says PC Miller, and inclining his head to indicate that Mrs Murray should follow him, he walks a few feet away onto virgin snow. There is a brief, quiet discussion, and they return to the group. The policeman takes the marriage certificate from O'Reilly and hands the two documents back to Roger.

'I'm sorry,' says PC Miller, turning to O'Reilly, 'but I've seen no evidence sufficient to warrant taking that child away. Mrs Murray agrees with me.'

'But the child is illegitimate–' starts O'Reilly.

'No, she isn't,' intervenes Laura. 'Not in canon law, which I assume you are relying on. That child has been legitimised by Mr Flint's marriage to Mrs Flint, formerly Miss Tyler. Go away and check. Even your own church wouldn't support the position you're taking.'

'That, officer, is a correct statement of the law,' says Roger.

O'Reilly's eyes bulge. 'You have to do something!' she

demands of the police officer. 'That child is in great moral danger!'

'I'm sorry,' says the policeman, putting his helmet back on, 'but I don't have authority to determine such a dispute, and I'm not getting involved in it. If and when you obtain a court order for removal of that child, that'd be a different matter. But I don't recommend you rely on evidence obtained by entering this property without permission. Now, I'm not going to arrest you, but nor am I going to facilitate the child's removal. I'm going home, where I should have been an hour ago.'

The policeman plods through the snow back to his car, watched by everyone else. After a moment, Mrs Murray follows him and gets into the passenger seat.

'You are, once again, trespassing here,' says Laura, pointing to the position inside the wall where O'Reilly and Carter remain. 'If you don't leave immediately, I'm entitled to use reasonable force to remove you. Ianto?'

'Right here,' says Ianto, standing just behind her.

'Roger?'

'And me,' adds Roger, squaring up next to Ianto.

'So, Miss O'Reilly,' continues Laura, 'I suggest take your archaic attitudes and your meddlesome red nose away, and let us get on with our party.'

O'Reilly looks like a kettle about to blow its lid. She gesticulates and opens her mouth to speak. Carter's hand lands on her arm.

'Let's go,' he says quietly.

O'Reilly shifts her malevolent gaze from Laura to Janine, and then to the two men. Her chest heaves and her mouth moves, but no sound emerges. Then she turns and stomps back to her car, Carter following in her wake.

'This is not a battle you can win, Miss O'Reilly,' calls Laura after her.

They watch as the two cars turn round and disappear down Chapel Hill.

'Shall we go in?' says Laura. 'The Christmas pudding is ready, and the kettle's boiled.' She heads inside.

ROGER

'That young woman is magnificent,' says Lady Margaret to Roger, nodding after Laura.

'She is, rather,' replies Roger wistfully.

'And you really married Janine?' asks Chivers.

Roger nods. 'It was the only way we could think of protecting her and Bobby and persuading her to come back. The original plan was for Ianto to do it.'

'Wouldn't he agree?'

'Oh, yes, he agreed,' replies Roger. 'But it turns out he has a wife in Holland, and I'm not sure she'd have approved.'

'But what about your lady friend, Patti?'

'It doesn't really involve her. We've not been seeing one another for long, and it's not serious yet. If, eventually, I wished to marry again – Patti for example – a divorce wouldn't be difficult, and it wouldn't affect Bobby's status so far as the church is concerned. Once legitimised, always legitimate. In the end it's just a piece of paper, but it ensures Laura and Janine can be together.'

'And it's all legal, is it?' asks Lady Margaret.

Roger grins. 'Almost completely.'

Lady Margaret smiles. 'You're a bit of a dark horse, Mr Flint,' she says, re-evaluating him. 'Very few men – an ex-husband at that – would have done what you have to enable those two women to be together.'

'I can't take all the credit. Your intervention with that policeman was rather helpful too,' he says.

Lady Margaret looks back at the house and the other guests, giggling as they jostle to take off wellington boots and return to the warm.

'It's all pretty irregular, isn't it?' comments Lady Margaret. 'A household made up of your ex- and current wives, the last two of whom are, to all intents and purposes, married to each other. Not to mention two children and a random Welshman.'

'Unusual, yes, I'd agree. But, oddly, somehow it works.'

'I've never been one to concern myself with how others live their lives,' muses Lady Margaret. 'But your little... commune... is really rather remarkable. It reminds one of the Bloomsbury Set, you know, Virginia Woolf and her bohemian friends? I hope you'll let me visit from time to time. I think it'll be fun.'

'I don't live here any longer, so it's not for me to say. But I'm certain you'll always be welcome,' says Roger. He turns to Chivers. 'As will you, Susanne.'

To Roger's complete astonishment, Susanne Chivers leans forward and kisses him once on each cheek.

'Well played, sir,' she says, her beady black eyes shining. 'Well played.'

'Shall we go back in?' asks Roger, offering Lady Margaret his arm. 'It's getting quite cold.'

They move slowly towards the building, Lady Margaret taking great care not to slip in the snow, which is now covered by a crisp crust of ice. Warm golden light spills from the windows and door into a gathering indigo dusk.

As they near the building they hear Laura singing 'Good King Wenceslas'. Her voice is joined by Patti's and then, unmistakably, by Ianto's.

'My goodness, that chap can sing, can't he?' comments Lady Margaret.

'He certainly can.'

'You know, half an hour ago I didn't think I could eat another morsel,' comments Lady Margaret, 'but I'm oddly peckish, and I quite fancy a portion of Christmas pudding after all.'

'I hope you won't be offended, Margaret,' says Chivers, giggling for no apparent reason, 'but I think I'll have another of those wonderful mince pies. I feel like I'm floating a couple of inches off the snow. Do you think Ianto would give me the recipe?'

It is the longest sentence she has uttered since arriving.

Roger laughs. 'Probably,' he says.

Janine is waiting for them on the threshold.

'Well,' says Lady Margaret, as they arrive back at the semi-detached cottages. 'I don't think we could have asked for a better ending.'

Laura arrives, her arms encircling Janine's waist from behind.

'You mean a better beginning, Lady M,' she says. 'This is our beginning. Come and have some Christmas pudding.'

THE END

Acknowledgements

My thanks go to the team at Bloodhound Books for their faith in this book, and to Nicky Lovick and Madeline Cotter, my agents at WGM Atlantic Talent and Literary Group, who have continued to champion my writing despite little or no reward until now. Thanks also to Stevie Garrett, Debbie Jacobs and Neil Cameron for their comments on the text and, as always, to Elaine for her patience, encouragement and all else.

A note from the publisher

Thank you for reading this book. If you enjoyed it please do consider leaving a review on Amazon to help others find it too.

We hate typos. All of our books have been rigorously edited and proofread, but sometimes mistakes do slip through. If you have spotted a typo, please do let us know and we can get it amended within hours.

info@bloodhoundbooks.com

Printed in Great Britain
by Amazon